ONWARD, LIBERTYCON!

Edited by
CHRISTOPHER WOODS
Edited by
T.K.F. WEISSKOPF

WOODS PUBLISHING

CONTENTS

INTRODUCTION

BY CHRISTOPHER WOODS

I guess we should mention how this anthology came about. After Toni and I finished with *Give Me LibertyCon* (Baen) we figured it would be fun to do one every five years or so in the future. Apparently, David Weber had other ideas.

My wife and I attended Brandy Bolgeo and Clint Hendren's wedding and sat at the reception with David and Sharon. David caught Brandy walking by and told her he would love to do a story about her and Clint for a wedding present. She was quite happy to accept.

"I just need somewhere to put it… Oh! I know where that will go, the new LibertyCon anthology!"

I looked at him and said we didn't actually have one planned and he decided he needed to remedy that quite promptly. Soon he and Toni were plotting, and they called me over to discuss what needed to be done.

Now we have a wonderful lineup of great authors for a second charity anthology, *Onward, LibertyCon!* With authors like Eric Flint, Kevin J. Anderson, D.J. Butler, and David Weber how can we go wrong? Many of the authors who joined me for my Fallen World series also joined us and we have a nice group of entertaining stories written for a good cause. As some of you already know, we attempted to

Tuckerize every member of the LibertyCon staff in the first anthology. We didn't have quite as lofty a set of goals for this one but there will be some familiar names scattered throughout these stories.

Like *Give Me LibertyCon* this anthology is intended to be a fundraiser for LibertyCon (a 501c3 corporation) and the Baen Books Timothy Bolgeo Memorial Scholarship (administered by the Interstellar Research Group, a 501c3 corporation). All profits from the volume will go to those entities.

I hope you enjoy reading about our various worlds as much as we enjoyed writing them.

—Christopher Woods

FOREWORD: "HOLE IN THE WALL" BY KEVIN J ANDERSON

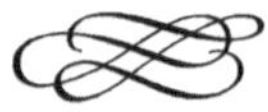

BY T.K.F. WEISSKOPF

I love this story by Kevin J. Anderson. He and his wife, Rebecca Moesta, are some of my favorite people in our community. Kevin writes widely in our field: he's known for his work in the Star Wars universe, for his sequels to *Dune* and work on the recent *Dune* movie, and of course many of his own series that encompass so many subgenres of fantasy and science fiction. But this one is a little gem of hard SF, part of his "Seven Suns" space-opera universe—and just the sort of story LibertyCon founder "Uncle Timmy" would have loved.

HOLE IN THE WALL

BY KEVIN J. ANDERSON

It wasn't that Elias Sandoval hated people; he just didn't understand them, didn't comprehend the confusing niceties of social interaction, didn't know what to say or do. So, he felt he was better left alone.

Even though he was fifty years old, he had little practice with people—intentionally so. He preferred his own company, millions of miles from the nearest neighbor, far out in an asteroid belt. And based on his previous interactions, he knew that most people preferred for him to keep his own company, too.

The best possible solution for everybody was for him to live by himself inside his own private uncharted asteroid on the far fringes of the Portnoy Belt. He could be alone with his own thoughts, entertain himself, and contemplate big ideas.

He named the asteroid Serendipity, and it truly was the perfect home for him. His brothers and cousins had helped provide the resources and equipment for him to turn the asteroid's cracks, caverns, and tunnels into a cozy domicile. Elias had done all the work himself.

The tumbling rock was in an erratic orbit, not part of the overall asteroid belt, just traveling with the traffic for the time being. In composition, Serendipity was stone mixed with ices, but in some previous passage close to Portnoy's sun, the ice and gases had boiled out, leaving the asteroid honeycombed with a warren of voids and habitable passageways.

And something else.

The walls and ceilings, the cracks and crannies sparkled with wonder unlike anything he had ever seen—and Elias had seen some of the most spectacular beauty the Spiral Arm had to offer.

Through a strange combination of mineral deposits, energy, and—as the asteroid's name suggested—sheer serendipity, every interior rock surface was studded with branched snowflake crystals, translucent white growths of angled prisms, more precious than diamonds, because diamonds were found on many worlds. As far as Elias could tell, these Serendipity crystals had been found nowhere else, not in the most isolated or rigorous Roamer settlement, not in any of the Terran Hanseatic League colonies, nor even in the alien Ildiran Empire. Serendipity crystals were delicate, fragile, and extremely valuable. And only Elias knew where to find them.

Every day, he strolled along the crystal-encrusted passages. In the five years Serendipity had been his private sanctuary, Elias had explored the winding passages, but there was always mystery and always wonder. Though the asteroid was only ten kilometers on its long axis, he estimated there were hundreds of kilometers of cracks, tunnels, and fissures to explore, at his leisure, and he intended to spend the rest of his life doing it.

Now he walked along with his bright handlight extended in front of him, and the crystal facets reflected and flared, ricocheting the light in all directions. The ice-mineral crystals branched out in thin fingers like spiderwebs of diamond, which signified that the asteroid must be remarkably stable. A good place to make a home.

Elias hummed to himself, not caring whether or not he could carry a tune because he had a highly uncritical audience. He followed the bright crystals, tracing them deep into the asteroid's interior, where the main crystals were stubbier, smaller. He reached a section of newborn crystals, which had grown in only the past few months. Elias knew this because he had watched it happen.

He had found the proteus spark that created the Serendipity crystals. Seeing that moving flicker always gave him a chill, and each day he traced its movement. Part of him—the long-suppressed social human part—wanted to share this marvel with someone, but Elias knew he had to keep it to himself.

At the end of the tunnel the crystal growths petered out, leaving the rock walls bare. The spark hadn't completed its work here yet, nevertheless the proteus had covered more than a foot in the past day.

The essential spark was like a bright, throbbing ember no larger than his thumbnail, as if someone had plucked one of the brightest stars in the universe and simply hidden it away in a dark corner. The proteus was alive somehow, a glow that fed on the minerals or drew latent energy from the rock. It burned along the tunnels like a spark traveling the length of a fuse.

Elias had tried to do research in his databases but had found nothing like this phenomenon. As a child of the Roamer clans, he was a crack engineer and problem solver. He knew how to fix things, how to make machinery work under impossible situations, but he was no theoretician.

He didn't dare bring the enigma to any of the Roamer clans at Rendezvous, or even to his own brothers and cousins, because one curious person would ask too many questions. Then there would be other questions, other consultations, and Elias Sandoval would lose his privacy. Serendipity would be overrun.

He could live with not knowing all the answers.

The proteus spark crept along the passage like a solitary luminescent snail, leaving newborn crystals behind. Considering the extent of the marvelous growths, Elias imagined this had been occurring for centuries, if not millennia.

The new crystals were only nubs, but they carried that protean sparkle. The larger growths along the main passageways were milky and beautiful, but they were just artifacts, fossils. The new crystals were still alive, and the parent glow would continue its aimless wandering down one passage or another...

Although he didn't need human company or conversation, he did require air, water, food, spare parts. Serendipity was not, and would never be, self-sufficient, and twice a year he needed to make a journey beyond the Portnoy Asteroid Belt and off to the distant Roamer complex. Out in the wider Terran Hanseatic League, the nomadic independent spacefarers were often frowned upon or viewed with suspicion. But Rendezvous was different. It was a place where all clan members could feel at home.

Though he didn't like to leave his sanctuary, Elias knew he had to go, despite his unease. He'd been keeping a list for months, and some of his reservoirs were getting critically low. He couldn't put it off any longer. He could buy everything he needed. Money was never an issue.

Elias spent the next day with a rock hammer in the outer tunnels, chipping away specimen after specimen of the Serendipity crystals and packing them in a cargo container. He had a contact at Rendezvous who would sell them, for a substantial cut.

He packed what he needed, suited up, and boarded his battered private ship, checked the fuel levels, and left his private asteroid, confident that no one could ever find it.

THE ROAMER CENTRAL COMPLEX OF RENDEZVOUS WAS A TRUE wonder. Innumerable asteroids of varying sizes, some even smaller than Serendipity, had been rounded up and maneuvered into a cluster, hollowed out for habitation, and linked together with structural girders and connecting tubes. It was a remarkable waystation, a handful of rocks wired together and orbiting a dim red sun called Meyer. It was an unlikely place for a government and trading center, but the Roamers made do. They always did.

As human colonization spread into the Spiral Arm, the scattered clans had learned to be tough and resourceful. Their critics compared them to cockroaches, but the Roamers took pride in filling any available niche. The Terran Hanseatic League, or Hansa, had no idea where to find the clans to tax them or include them in a census.

After crossing interstellar space, Elias brought his ship toward

Rendezvous while transmitting his ID codes, although any Roamer observer seeing the motley configuration would know he was a Roamer. Clan Sandoval dismantled and repurposed components for their numerous vessels, and Elias's father had given him this ship as a gift when the young man wanted to go out on his own—not to be a black sheep, but to be independent. His spacecraft might not look pretty, but its engines, hull, and electronics were superb and reliable.

After he docked and passed through the transit points into the asteroid hub, he was swallowed up in a bustle of conversation, noises, smells, and deafening colors. Every day inside Serendipity, Elias would hear nothing more than a whisper, but the exuberant bazaar of Rendezvous drowned him in sensory overload. He winced and stood a moment, like a man facing a fierce headwind, but forced himself forward. He guided the heavy cargo box of Serendipity crystals with its antigrav handle.

Families moved together, wearing jumpsuits with clan insignia embroidered on their breasts. Someone clapped him on the shoulder and laughed with a loud welcome, then strode on. Elias was sure he had never met the man before, although his old drab garments still bore the Sandoval clan insignia. Maybe that was enough.

He walked past food vendors who prepared heavily spiced noodles and mushrooms, strips of charred vat meat, and fresh fruits out of greenhouse domes. It was far more expensive for Roamers to produce their own food inside enclosed habitats, but the clans refused to be dependent on the moods of the Hansa.

Elias indulged himself and bought a cluster of grapes and two ripe oranges. He took the fruit to an out-of-the-way alcove, where he ate one of the juicy oranges, licking every last drop of sticky liquid from his fingertips. He saved the grapes for later, admitting to himself that Rendezvous did have certain advantages, so long as he visited only infrequently. With this trip, he would load his ship with packaged food, fresh produce, meat, and tank-cultured seafood.

"Quality of life," he muttered to himself.

Down one corridor, a makeshift band played raucous music and a crowd sang along, although they didn't seem to know the words. Elias pulled his cargo case toward the trading chambers, where he would meet with Skalec the Scar.

Skalec was a loquacious and congenial vendor with a burn scar on his left cheek; he had adopted the name because he wanted to sound fearsome, but he fooled no one. When Elias entered with the cargo case, Skalec's eyes lit up. "By the Guiding Star, I sold out three weeks ago, Sandoval! Been waiting for you."

"Would have put it off longer, if I could."

Skalec muscled forward and cleared a table with a sweep of his forearm. "Let's see what you have."

Elias set down his case, switched off the antigrav handle, and the heavy load settled with a groan. Skalec opened the case and reached inside, marveling at the delicate gleaming crystals. "They're in such high demand, I'll take as many as you want to bring."

Elias raised his eyebrows. "That means I can charge you more."

The trader's waxy scar rippled as he scowled. "If I have to. An additional ten percent."

Elias smiled. "That'll do. I'm not much for haggling. Let's just get this over with."

Skalec shook his head and reverently unloaded the crystals, removing the shards one at a time and placing them on a soft, dark fabric. At the shop doorway, customers were already looking in, curious.

Skalec paid him. "Come back sooner next time. And bring two cases."

"I don't need the money," Elias said. "Just want to buy supplies."

The trader scratched his scar. "You make no sense to me, Elias Sandoval."

"A lot of things don't make sense to me either."

Skalec the Scar hesitated and then added another bonus. "Maybe you'll think about an increased shipment next time."

"I'll think about it," Elias said, "but it likely won't happen."

He bought all the supplies he could think of, and even used the bonus for a few luxury items that tempted him, as well as a full tank of ekti for his stardrive. Soon enough, the people, crowds, smells, and noises were just too much. Serendipity called to him.

With the cargo loaded, he sealed the ship, detached from the docking zone, and flew away from the Rendezvous cluster. He just wanted to get home to solitude, where he could wash away the *closeness* and the conversation.

He flew away from the asteroids on a random vector into empty space. Once he got far enough away, he recalibrated his course, input the coordinates to the obscure Portnoy System, and made his way to one particular speck of rock drifting among the scattered asteroids in the belt.

When he arrived back at Serendipity, Elias was astonished to find two large ships already there, landed on the cratered surface of his home.

THE SIGHT OF THE UNFAMILIAR SHIPS WAS SO INCONGRUOUS THAT ELIAS didn't know how to react. The strangers had landed side by side between the asteroid's two largest craters, which he'd named Martha and Beatrice after a pair of large-boned aunts he remembered from clan gatherings. The vessels were sleek, new models, too large to be scout vessels, not of military design, nor were they cargo ships.

As he entered his final approach, he ran the scans again, increased magnification. Each ship bore the insignia of the Terran Hanseatic League.

Before Elias could figure out what to do, they spotted him and opened the line of communication.

"Unidentified ship, please respond." It was a woman's voice, stern as a schoolteacher.

"Unidentified?" Elias replied. "Who the hell are *you?* You're trespassing!" He did not alter his course. He was going home, and he couldn't think of anywhere else to turn. Just seeing these other ships made him feel violated.

None of the other asteroids in the Portnoy Belt were close enough to be more than bright lights in the sky, nearly indistinguishable from stars. His asteroid was all alone, and so was he.

Until now.

As his ship cruised closer, he could see three exosuited figures walking with fluid, low gravity grace across the dusty surface. No one besides him had ever set foot on Serendipity, as far as he knew, and now these strangers were leaving footprints over the pristine ground.

The comm screen flickered and a woman's face appeared. She had short, dark brown hair that looked as if she cut it herself, and her skin had a dusky cast. "Excuse me? What is your name and how is this your rock?"

"You first." Elias realized he sounded gruff and threatening. He felt out of his league when it came time to make use of diplomatic skills. "I'm Elias Sandoval of Clan Sandoval, and I've lived here for years. Serendipity is my property by right of possession. My ship is heavily armed—consider yourself warned."

"No need for your aggressive posture, Mr. Sandoval," said the captain. "I am Mariah Oko of the Hansa's Portnoy threat assessment expedition."

A round-faced man with grizzled whiskers leaned into view. "We're the nudge-and-budge clean-up crew, and we're here to move your rock out of the way so we can protect the colonists on Portnoy's World."

"I don't care about Portnoy's World," Elias said. The only Terra-compatible planet in the system was far away and he had never bothered to go there. "What does that have to do with me?"

"Nothing to do with you, Mr. Sandoval," said Oko. "We had no idea you were here, but this asteroid popped up on our potential hazard list. We have to take care of it."

"You leave my home alone. I'm warning you. I've got weapons."

"No, he doesn't," sneered the man with the unshaven jowls.

"We can see your wreck of a ship, sir." Oko sounded as if she had strapped on plate armor of patience. "I don't doubt that Roamer vessels have defenses, but you don't want to get into a shooting war with us. We're just here doing our job."

"And I'm just trying to go home," Elias said. "If you'd bothered to run a scan as you approached, you would have found my hangar dock, my air, fuel, and water silos, and the access hatch to the interior. Prior habitation clearly established, per Hansa law. You have no claim here."

His thoughts raced and he wondered if somehow these people, these pirates from the Terran Hanseatic League, had learned about his Serendipity crystals. He was sure they would exploit them all, strip the tunnels bare, and rob him blind.

Mariah Oko struggled to keep her anger in check. "We did not know anyone had claimed this uncatalogued asteroid. We apologize for any inconvenience, but we have work to do. Perhaps if you land and meet us in our main ship, we can discuss this."

"You're not coming inside my asteroid," said Elias.

"Didn't ask to," said the gruff man, but Captain Oko shushed him.

"Please come aboard my ship, Mr. Sandoval. According to Hansa records, this is an unclaimed asteroid." Her eyes met his on the screen. "But we will listen to your claim and try to minimize the inconvenience."

The encounter had already been a tremendous inconvenience, and the very idea rattled him to his core. Elias struggled to find words as he realized he had never filed paperwork with the Hansa, because that would have flagged Serendipity so anyone could find him—which entirely defeated the purpose. After dealing with the noise, crowds, and smells at Rendezvous, he just wanted to hole up and be by himself, to regain his own peace and calm.

Now, though, he felt shattered. Elias did not like to do business face-to-face, but now he realized it might be necessary. The sooner he could get these intruders off Serendipity, the better.

"All right. I'll land my ship next to yours and come over."

"We guarantee your safety, sir," Oko said. "This is just a discussion. We will explain our presence here, and once you understand, you'll agree with the necessity."

"Even if I agree with the necessity, you still have to leave."

The other captain pressed her lips together. "We will leave as soon as we're finished."

"I'm coming armed," he said, bristling but terrified. He thought he had a weapon somewhere, although it hadn't been used, or even touched, in as long as he could remember.

"Bring all the weapons you want. We're not worried," said the gruff man, grinning. "We've got nukes."

When Elias had constructed his home on Serendipity, he hadn't bothered to consider camouflage or security. His greatest defense was obscurity.

But somehow these Hansa scouts and engineers had found him— or, more accurately, found this asteroid. He was surprised the Hansa ships hadn't spotted his fueling depot or the main docking entrance into the tunnels, but Captain Oko and her team had not even looked. They had just come in uninvited, ready to do whatever they wanted. Elias felt intimidated, but he was also pissed off.

After he landed on the near edge of Martha crater, he placed a multitool in his exosuit pocket, the closest thing to a weapon he could actually find; he hoped the bulge would look threatening enough.

Emerging from his ship, he stared across the stark landscape, felt the midnight vault of stars above. The two modern Hansa craft made his own ship look like a junk heap by comparison. No wonder they hadn't believed his empty threat of possessing superior weapons.

Nukes? By the Guiding Star, why would they bring nukes out to his little asteroid?

Five exosuited Hansa workers now swarmed across the surface, taking measurements, drilling cores, running seismic scans. Offended, Elias activated his comm. "Stop what you're doing! You have no right to be here." None of them answered, or even looked up. "Why don't you respond? Take that equipment back to your ships." Maybe they worked on a different comm frequency. He felt completely impotent.

Mariah Oko's voice came over his earphones. "Mr. Sandoval, they need to complete their stability survey and find proper anchor points.

Please come into my lead ship so we can debrief you on the situation. You'll understand as soon as you see our projections."

"What if I don't want to see your projections?" Elias said. "I want you to go. Stop messing with my asteroid."

The larger of the Hansa ships had an open exterior airlock, and he trudged toward it, stewing. If they had performed density surveys and structural mapping, they would have found the numerous fissures and passages that honeycombed the tumbling rock. Did they intend to drill mining shafts, rip open Serendipity's crust so they could strip mine the delicate crystals? They had no right!

When he entered Oko's airlock, he imagined he was walking into the mouth of a shark and trusting the jaws not to chomp down. He sealed the exterior door, waited for the pressure to cycle, and then entered. He stood stiff, his arms at his sides as if ready for a barroom brawl. He didn't like this. Not at all.

Captain Oko came to greet him, straight-backed and formal. She wore an engineer's jumpsuit with the Hansa logo on the breast—printed, not meticulously embroidered like a Roamer clan would do. The rumpled-looking, round-faced man joined her. Despite his pudgy face, he had a surprisingly thin body, probably from a life spent in low gravity. Oko shook Elias's hand and introduced her companion as Terris. In response, Terris pushed out his lower lip as if to emphasize his frown.

Elias did not feel like being warm and fuzzy. He spoke first. "I don't understand what you're doing here, Captain Oko. Why have Hansa ships landed on my asteroid?"

He understood the basic legal principles of habitation and right of salvage—every Roamer did—but he couldn't quote specific chapter and verse. He also knew that the Terran Hanseatic League under the administration of the hardline Chairman Basil Wenceslas often broke treaties and rules whenever it was convenient for them.

Oko had mastered a little more patience. "As I said, sir, we had no inkling that this rock was inhabited." She gestured toward a small conference chamber adjacent to the galley. "Have a seat so I can show you our projections. Would you like something to drink? I have fresh ground klee from Theroc, even a new shipment of Earth coffee, dark roast."

Elias paused. "Earth coffee?"

Roamers had many beverages, some quite distinctive, including alternatives to coffee grown on Earth, but he'd only tasted the real stuff before. Seeing his reaction, Oko smiled. "Coffee it is, then. Terris, go dispense us each a cup."

The other man scowled. "I don't make coffee."

"Read the fine print in your contract," she snapped. "The last clause says, 'other duties as assigned.' I'm assigning you this other duty while Mr. Sandoval and I get to know each other."

Terris went into the galley where he made altogether too much noise while brewing coffee.

Elias warily took a seat at the oval table, rested his elbows on the smooth surface, and looked at the captain. He let the silence stretch until Oko activated the tabletop, turning it into a projection screen. "This particular asteroid—1013X1—"

Elias interrupted her. "Serendipity."

Oko continued as if she hadn't heard. "—is currently traveling with the overall Portnoy Belt, but it's what we call a cuckoo, like an egg laid in another bird's nest. It doesn't belong with the rest of these rocks, but rather came from outside the system. It's on a highly elliptical trajectory, just about to pass aphelion, and before long it'll hook around and start its steep plunge toward the inner system."

The table screen displayed a map of the Portnoy System. The myriad asteroid orbits in the belt looked like a swarm of gnats, but one elongated ellipse, highlighted in red, clearly didn't belong with the others. Serendipity.

"I've lived here for years and I've never had any trouble," Elias said, defensive. He realized, though, that all the cracks and voids inside his asteroid had been left by sublimating ices and gases during previous close passages of the sun.

"My team tracks the asteroids in the Portnoy Belt. Most of them cause no trouble, but every once in a while there's an outlier like

1013X1. Umm, I mean Serendipity." She paused. "We call it a runaway."

Terris delivered the cups of coffee, his expression as bitter as the brew. Elias took a sip, too upset to enjoy the rich taste. "What does that matter?" he asked. "I'm not driving the rock. I just live here."

Captain Oko zoomed in, highlighted another orbit closer to the sun, a terrestrial planet. The image showed an atmosphere streaked with white clouds over blue oceans and brown and green continents.

"This is Portnoy, a well-established Hansa colony, been there almost thirty years, population two hundred thousand." She overlaid the projected orbits, and the steep elliptical line of Serendipity's path intersected Portnoy's orbit. "We've run the projections again and again. When this asteroid heads into the inner system, there's a sixty percent chance it will strike Portnoy."

Terris said, "An impact like that would wipe out all life on the planet."

Elias stared at the diagram, feeling cold inside. "Sixty percent chance... When?"

"About twenty-seven years from now."

He blew out a sigh of relief. "Then you have plenty of time to evacuate the colonists. There's no emergency."

Oko scratched her short, dark hair and frowned at him in surprise. Terris's mouth dropped open in disbelief. "Evacuate the colonists? That's a beautiful, viable world. Think of all the people, their families! And in another quarter century years, the population could more than double."

"Not my problem," Elias said. "Plenty of time for you to figure something out."

"You're missing the point, Mr. Sandoval," Oko said in a crisp voice. "The easiest solution is to alter the orbit of 1013X1 so there is no imminent impact, period. That's why we're here."

"Hence the nukes," said Terris, grinning.

Elias's thoughts were deafened by his anger. "You're not detonating atomic warheads on my asteroid." He thought of the delicate crystals, the fragile snowflakes lining the tunnels and fissures. The shock wave would wreck them all.

Oko shook her head with exaggerated sadness. "I'm afraid there's really no choice. The farther away we make our nudge, the more reliable will be the result. Way out here, it'll take a much lower yield to alter the asteroid's trajectory into a safe orbit."

Elias felt nauseated. "You said there's only a sixty percent chance. That's practically like flipping a coin—I'd want to know for sure before you start blowing up my home."

"Sixty percent. It's a very prominent celestial threat, sir," said Oko.

"I'll take that chance," he said.

But Terris made a raspberry sound. "It's not your choice to make, mister. The Hansa won't risk hundreds of thousands of colonists because some old fart won't move to a different rock. If there was even a one percent chance, we'd still take action."

Elias lurched to his feet and knocked his coffee off the table, spilling it onto the deck. "I don't believe your orbital calculations."

The captain remained seated despite his outburst. She folded her hands together, pushing them through the floating diagram above the tabletop. "The orbital calculations don't care whether or not you believe in them, Mr. Sandoval. The science exists, regardless of your opinion."

She projected a picture of Serendipity with specific red zones marked on its pockmarked surface. "We can deploy low-yield warheads here and here. The energy from those detonations will give the rock a gentle push. However, Serendipity is so riddled with voids and lower-density ices that precise calculations are difficult. We can't take any chances with so many lives at stake."

Elias remained fixated on his original argument. "But you can't just come in here and do this. You have no right! The Roamer clans are independent." He lifted his chin. "The Hansa always walks all over us."

"This has nothing to do with Roamers or the Terran Hanseatic League," Oko said. "It's about gravity and orbits. It's about saving all those people."

"What about my needs? Serendipity is my home and you're trespassing. I don't grant you permission."

Terris muttered, "Told you he'd be trouble."

"You can't just come here and do what you want," Elias said. "I have my rights."

"Society has a greater right, Mr. Sandoval. Your freedom cannot come at the cost of all those colonists. We have to come down on the side of the greater good."

"It's not *my* greater good," Elias said. "What happened to *my* liberty?"

"Oh, get your head out of your ass," Terris growled. "Your liberty does not erase your obligations to the rest of human society. If you recklessly endanger the lives of others, then you forfeit your right to liberty. Selfish prick."

Elias's nostrils flared as he drew in a deep breath wondering if this was going to come to blows.

Oko's eyes widened. "Terris, no—not yet!"

Sensing danger, Elias saw that the other man had pulled out a stunner. "Don't you—"

A wave of blue light smothered his thoughts and consciousness.

WHEN HE CLAWED HIMSELF BACK TO AWARENESS ELIAS FELT SWEATY and bedraggled, worse than the hangover he'd once suffered after being duped into buying a bottle of high-proof algae-based moonshine. His lips were swollen and his tongue was thick as he tried to speak. "What the—?"

When he lifted his hand, it came to an abrupt stop. A plastic restraint clipped his wrist to the side of a chair. "By the Guiding Star..." He looked around, but the world was still swimming.

Terris was there smiling at him. "Welll, good morning, sleepyhead. Don't expect me to cook you breakfast."

"Leave him be," Captain Oko snapped. "We're putting him through enough as it is."

"His own damn fault."

"No, it's not his fault," said Oko. "He picked the wrong rock to squat on—that's not a crime. But you know what the old philosopher said…" She put her hands on her narrow hips and looked directly at Elias. "The needs of the many outweigh the needs of the few. Or the one."

"Must sound like a good justification to you," Elias said. "Throughout history, powerful people make up excuses and emergencies so they can take whatever they damn well want. Eminent domain! My asteroid's in the way. Just nuke it so it's no longer your problem. Sorry for the inconvenience." He felt nauseated.

"Inconvenience!" Terris was exasperated. "It's a whole colony planet, a complete ecosystem, cities full of settlers!"

Interrupted, the captain touched the comm at her ear and acknowledged. She turned to them. "All set. The engineers have anchored and installed two warheads at the appropriate places. They surveyed weak zones and potential fracture points in the asteroid. Serendipity is like a cracked egg, there's no telling whether or not it'll hold together. We're doing our best, Mr. Sandoval. Honest."

"And then what?" Elias said, yanking the restraint again. "You're just going to hold me prisoner, force me to watch?"

Terris snorted. "You can look away if you want."

Oko shot her partner an annoyed glance. "Because of the potential hazards, you will not be allowed to stay during the blast. We have to remove you to a safe distance, but you should be able to return here soon after the detonations. Salvage what you can—if that's what you'd like to do."

Elias felt deep anguish. Even if Serendipity didn't break apart, the warhead explosions would be like swinging a bag of light bulbs mixed with rocks. The infinitely fragile crystals would be destroyed. "You'll wreck everything. I refuse. I'm staying here. This is my home." He swallowed. "I'll take my chances."

"Sorry, can't allow you to do that," she said.

"You have no authority over me! You can't force me to—"

Her extra patience had finally run out. "It is your right to be stubborn and stupid, Mr. Sandoval, but I will not have your blood on my hands. My crew are good people and they've done their work like true professionals. The warheads will go off as scheduled. We will alter the course of asteroid 1013X1 and guarantee the future of the Portnoy colonists."

"But this is my home," he pleaded again. "Let me at least grab a few things." Hope swelled within him. "Give me an hour, maybe two. Just a few personal items, things I can't replace."

Oko looked sympathetic, but Terris rolled his eyes. "Captain, he's just going to barricade himself inside and then we'll have a standoff situation, probably end up leaving him behind anyway."

Oko turned a hard gaze toward Elias. "Is that what you're going to do, Mr. Sandoval?"

The thought had not actually occurred to him. "No."

"Or what if he takes his ship and does a kamikaze run on the site. It's not a good idea, Captain," Terris insisted.

"That's not what I intend," Elias said in a low voice.

The captain considered for a long moment and nodded. "You can have one hour, Mr. Sandoval. Pack up whatever you can take with you, but Terris is right—I'll keep you away from the controls of your ship until the warheads have successfully detonated. You'll ride here with me and my engineers. Terris can fly your craft to a safe distance. We will return it to you as soon as you're allowed back in the vicinity."

"I don't want him flying my ship," Elias said.

"You don't want us to blow up the warheads either, but today isn't your day." Her reservoir of patience had completely run dry. "Go get what you need, sir. One hour."

AFTER ELIAS CYCLED THROUGH THE AIRLOCK OF HIS FRONT ENTRANCE, he removed his helmet to inhale the dusty, metallic scent of his tunnels, his home. He felt impossibly weary and helpless. Yes, he could just seal the door and bury himself, become an indignant martyr when the collapsing walls buried him in a rain of diamondlike crystals.

Or maybe he would survive after all. He wondered if he had better than a 60 percent chance.

With trembling knees, feeling as if every moment was a held breath, he walked down corridors filled with treasures no one would ever know. He was surrounded by a blizzard of prisms, wondrous icicles of petrified light. With his rock hammer, he had time to collect only the best of them.

Elias Sandoval got to work.

EVEN WITH THE ANTIGRAV HANDLE, THE LARGE CASE HAD PLENTY OF mass and momentum, and Elias wrestled it carefully out of his exit hatch and across the asteroid's loose surface. He made his way to the main Hansa ship, where one of the exosuited surveyors helped him carry it onboard.

She grunted with the unwieldy mass. "Prized possessions? What are you taking with you? A neutron star or something?"

His heart felt heavier than the load. "Just some things I need—things I refuse to let your atomic blast destroy."

"Sorry," the surveyor said in a cowed voice. "There must be a thousand asteroids in the Portnoy Belt. Just damn bad luck you picked this one."

When they were aboard with the hatch sealed, Elias made his way to the pilot deck. Captain Oko gave him a quick glance, then turned back to her preparations.

"Countdown's started, Captain," said one of the engineers.

The words filled Elias with both anger and despair. "There's no stopping it."

"Correct," the Captain agreed. "But with any luck, the blast won't damage your asteroid—just bump it out of the way. Look at those craters. Serendipity has shrugged off impacts before. You can go back home, do a little housecleaning, and everything will be back to normal before you know it."

He still felt violated. He had never meant to get into a dispute, had done nothing that should have put him in the center of such turmoil. Elias wasn't responsible for the colonists on Portnoy, didn't want to think about them. But no one had asked for his opinion.

Intellectually, he could understand the obvious choice. He was just one old man who wanted to be left alone, but he had settled on a cannonball that was hurtling toward an inhabited world. Even if he somehow drove off the Hansa engineers, he still would have had to leave Serendipity in twenty-seven years or so... or he could have gambled on the 40 percent chance that there would be no impact at all.

He didn't feel particularly lucky, though.

Adding to the insult, he watched his own ship launch from the pockmarked surface, guided by Terris. The man transmitted in a gruff voice from the piloting deck, "What a piece of junk! I hope I don't have a hull breach."

Elias retorted under his breath, "Just don't leave any disease on my pilot controls."

The two Hansa ships detached from their anchors and drifted away from Serendipity. Before long, they retreated far enough away that the asteroid looked like an oblong potato drifting in space.

"We're at minimum safe distance, Captain," said one of the engineers.

Oko nodded, staring out the windowport. "They're low-yield devices. This is good enough so we can watch."

Elias didn't particularly want to watch, but he could not tear his eyes away as the countdown dwindled to zero.

Twin flares of intense white light blossomed from the long axis of Serendipity and the polarization film darkened the view. He winced, feeling physical pain as he imagined the sledgehammer blow to the crystal-encrusted labyrinth. He feared the entire fragile asteroid, with so many fractures, tunnels, and voids, would just break apart into rubble.

But when the glare died down, he heard Captain Oko sigh. "You're in luck, Mr. Sandoval. Your home looks intact." She added a relieved chuckle. "I was afraid we'd see a bunch of drifting gravel." She wiped an imagined wrinkle from her jacket. "We'll transfer you back to your ship. You can go home, and we'll never bother you again."

His eyes burned, and his vision was blurry. He could not find an appropriate answer for her. Instead, he kept staring at the rolling rock in space where the glow from the unleashed energy had dimmed to faint embers.

The two detonation spots would leave craters larger than Martha and Beatrice, permanent scars. But he was more worried about the scars and damage done internally.

"Just let me go home," he said.

HE FELT EXHAUSTED, ABUSED, AND WRUNG OUT BY THE TIME HE entered through the main hangar dock. After watching the two Hansa ships depart, paying no more attention to a pathetic old Roamer, he had limped back to Serendipity. Captain Oko and her survey engineers hadn't bothered to look inside his asteroid.

The captain probably thought she had saved the world and done a good thing. The others had simply done their jobs. The Portnoy colonists would certainly applaud them, breathe a sigh of relief that the decades-distant problem was solved. They would never think about Elias Sandoval or his private asteroid again.

At least that was his hope.

His ship was still loaded with the supplies he had purchased at Rendezvous, even the fresh fruit in the supply bins. It seemed like years in the past. After leaving the Roamer complex, he had intended to go home and just live quiet and undisturbed.

If there was anything left for him there.

Moving with great trepidation, he entered his tunnels, his sanctuary. He thought of the cathedral of crystals, the shimmering snowflake growths in every cranny, starbeams captured in human tears.

The inside of Serendipity looked like a smashed hall of mirrors. The shock wave from the nuclear blasts had wrenched corridor after corridor, shattering the ethereal growths. The floor was littered with cracked prisms, broken spikes, sharp fragments. Detached crystals were piled knee deep, and he groaned to think of the months—years—of work it would take for him just to clear the debris.

He got the generator working and activated the heaters, life support, and oxygen generators. After a few hours the interior pressure had built up enough that he could remove his exosuit.

Weeping, he looked at the overwhelming wreckage and struggled to grasp hope rather than wallow in the loss. After clearing the rubble, he could sell even the broken Serendipity crystals for a fortune, enough to buy his own small planet, if he wanted.

But what he wanted was solitude, a place like Serendipity. And so he had to do it all himself. He could get the resources he needed. He had created this home in the first place, and he could do it again. After all, he had salvaged the most important, the rarest ingredient.

Finally, he opened his heavy, sealed cargo container, raised the lid, and looked inside, smiling with wonder.

In the one hour Captain Oko had given him, he'd excavated the one tiny proteus spark, carving out the rock around it, like digging out a shrub to be transplanted. Carefully preserved, the glowing blip looked like an ember nested in the glittering, sharp prongs of new crystals that had grown in only the past few hours. The spark was still alive—if it was actually alive at all.

Elias would place this rock at the end of an empty tunnel and let the proteus ember keep burning, keep laying down its trail of diamond growths, and he would be here to shepherd it along. Soon enough, the glitter would return.

ABOUT KEVIN J. ANDERSON

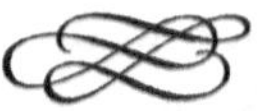

Kevin J. Anderson has published more than 175 books, 58 of which have been national or international bestsellers. He has written numerous novels in the Star Wars, X-Files, and Dune universes, as well as a unique steampunk fantasy trilogy, beginning with *Clockwork Angels*, written with legendary rock drummer Neil Peart. His original works include the Saga of Seven Suns series, the Wake the Dragon and Terra Incognita fantasy trilogies, the Saga of Shadows trilogy, and his humorous horror series featuring Dan Shamble, Zombie P.I. He has edited numerous anthologies, written comics and games, and the lyrics to two rock CDs. Anderson is the director of the graduate program in Publishing at Western Colorado University. Anderson and his wife Rebecca Moesta are the publishers of WordFire Press. His most recent novels are *Clockwork Destiny, Gods and Dragons, Dune: The Lady of Caladan* (with Brian Herbert), and *Slushpile Memories: How NOT to Get Rejected*.

FOREWORD: "THE GRAMMARIAN: A JOE'S WORLD STORY" BY ERIC FLINT

BY T.K.F. WEISSKOPF

This story hearkens back to the very beginning of Eric Flint's career as a writer, predating even his first novel published Baen Books (and found by me!), *Mother of Demons*. It's part of a fantasy series that's been part of Eric's life for decades—and the first published work in this series was a winner of the Writers of the Future contest. Chris was over the moon that we got to publish the latest installment in this anthology, and so was I. In it, Eric lets fly with all the writing flourishes due his philosophical strangler "hero."

THE GRAMMARIAN

A JOE'S WORLD STORY BY ERIC FLINT

From what is short but already bitter experience I have come to recognize which Callings—yes, that's what they call the damn things—will be the most pernicious. What do I mean by pernicious? Start with "perilous beyond all reason," continue with "wounds guaranteed," and finish with "pays worse than you can imagine."

The tip-off is the messenger who delivers the Calling. The more gaunt, emaciated, bedraggled, and with the greatest expression of despair leavened with the tiniest, itsy-bitsy spark of hope in their visage… the worse it's going to be.

Alas, the waif who showed up at our door just after dawn on a dreary autumn day in New Sfinctr made my blood turn to ice in less than a second. *Oh, no—*

Jenny and Angela pushed me aside and shepherded the girl—I think she was a girl; hard to tell when their misery is measured in orders of magnitude—into the foyer.

"You poor dear!" exclaimed Angela. "Would you like some hot tea?"

Without waiting for an answer, Jenny hurried toward the kitchen. "I'll get the kettle going."

"Here, sit on this couch," said Angela. "It's the most comfortable one we have."

Indeed, it was—which was why I'd just sprawled onto it not three seconds before the knock came on the door. So much for my nap after being awakened too early… Well, not exactly that, as frisky as Jenny and Angela's mood had been that morning. But I was tired, I surely was.

By now, there'd been enough commotion to draw the attention of the dwelling's other inhabitants. Greyboar came lumbering down the stairs, yawning and rubbing his face with a hand roughly the size of a dinner plate, except for being a lot thicker. The now-Hero, Excelsior had in his earlier (and way, way, way more lucrative) life been the world's champion professional strangler.

Did he look like it? Does a tiger shark look like an apex predator?

Lucky for them, tiger sharks aren't encumbered by idiot social conventions the way humans are. Greyboar and I had been forced to give up our former contented life as a chokester and his manager and become a Hero and Sidekick. Hero, thanks to his maniac sister's romantic entanglement with a lunatic artist. Rescuing the sod had required us to penetrate to the very depths of the underworld, which we couldn't do without swearing to give up our wicked ways and devote the rest of our miserable lives to righting wrongs and rescuing maidens and other such foolishness.

Speaking of maniac romantic entanglements, Greyboar's own made her appearance right then. First, at the stop of the stairs looking down in her indescribably weird way of examining reality; then—don't ask me how she did it; nobody can figure it out—she was standing on the floor of the foyer making her own way through the sitting room to the kitchen.

"I want mint, ginger, and chamomile!" she called out. "It's good for pregnant women."

With any other woman, you'd assume that meant she was pregnant herself. But with Schrödinger's Cat…

Maybe. Pretty much everything about her is maybe. She might just have decided that if she drank herbal tea made of mint, ginger, and chamomile that it would help some other woman who was actually pregnant.

The scariest thing about that is that it just might be true. I'm convinced the Cat does not live on the same plane of existence the rest of us do.

A loud creaking and groaning from heavily stressed wood and fabric accompanied Greyboar sitting down on his favorite armchair. "Do I take it we have a customer?" he asked.

"Don't call them that!" I barked, perhaps a bit shrilly. "The term 'customer' refers to someone who *pays* for something." I scowled at the girl hunched on the couch next to Angela, being comforted. "Does that urchin look like she has two pennies to rub together? Ha!"

Angela bestowed a scowl upon me. "Greyboar, remind me why Jenny and I are in love with this pitiful excuse for a person."

The Hero, Excelsior let that question slide. It was clearly rhetorical, anyway. The reasons my two ladies adored me were multitudinous if perhaps a bit indistinct.

"I'm just expressing a reasonable complaint at the gross injustice of our position in life," I said. "If it weren't for the money you and Jenny bring in from your seamstress business, we'd all have starved to death by now."

Jenny and the Cat came back into the living room, bearing cups for everyone. I accepted mine in silence. At that time of day, I'd have preferred ale, but that was true pretty much any time of day. Given the grim reality that was about to be unfolded before us, drinking a concoction of herbs I wouldn't normally touch might brace me a little.

As usual, it took the messenger—who was the plaintiff also, of course—quite a while to tell her tale. First, because she was maybe ten years old and not experienced in swift and succinct explication. Second, because Jenny and Angela kept interrupting her with exclamations along the lines of *you poor thing!* and *how horrible that*

must have been for you! And third, because the tale itself was murky and full of inexplicable menace.

Naturally. "Inexplicable menace" is present in at least three-fourths of the Callings that Greyboar and I get saddled with.

The gist of the tale was as follows: An inexplicable and unseen menace—well, it might have been seen by its victims but none had lived to describe the thing, being, or phenomenon—was ravaging a town somewhere out there, where no sophisticates like ourselves would waste our time exploring the non-wonders of rural bumpkinhood.

Naturally. The Callings that a Hero, Excelsior and his sidekick get afflicted with are never to be found in urban palaces where the work might be lightened by fine pastries and liquors. No, no, no. Those are the sort of venues Greyboar and I used to work in quite regularly in our former life as a professional gripster and his manager. Nowadays, our working environs start with muddy streets covered with animal manure and go downhill from there.

The nature of the ravaging was unclear. The corpses the Inexplicable Menace left in its wake bore no physical wounds or injuries. The cause of death was mysterious. What the deceased all had in common was a gaunt and emaciated physique coupled with an expression of utter and disconsolate despair on their faces.

The remains could be found anywhere but seemed to be concentrated in and around the town's cathedral.

Naturally. Leave it to the Old Geister to draw toward Him whatever Inexplicable Menaces might be lurking about. Why not? Being the Supreme Creator, He's the biggest inexplicable menace there is.

So, there it was. Our Calling. Sally forth to… whatever the town's name was, I can't remember. (Hutburg? Dumpville? Whatever.) Uncover and identify the inexplicable menace. Make it easily explicable because we make it deceased, defunct, demolished, or, at the very least, disappeared.

"Doesn't seem like too much of a challenge," opined Greyboar, cracking his knuckles.

I hate it when he does that. Our budget's stressed badly enough as it is, without adding the cost of home repairs due to excessive vibrations.

~

WE SET OUT THE NEXT DAY. TRANSPORTATION WASN'T A PROBLEM. That was one of the few bright spots in our new, impoverished condition. We still owned the huge coach we'd purchased before we were brought down by penury, that we'd used to smuggle Hrundig and the Frissault women out of New Sfinctr a while back. (Don't ask. You really want to hear the tale of how an Alsask barbarian and his upper-class lady and her children got into trouble—never mind. It's too ridiculous to be believed.)

Anyway, we still had the coach and Oscar and his boys were still willing to serve as our teamsters. Without pay, mind you. Oscar said the notoriety—no, Lord help us, they call it "fame" now that Greyboar's an official Hero—brings them more than enough business to make the occasional freebie jaunt worth it to them.

One of the few other benefits of our new status was that the guards at the gates never hassled us any longer. (Not that they'd hassled us much in the old days. Greyboar demonstrating his thumbspread had usually been enough by itself to quell incipient officiousness.)

So, off we went, down one of the roads leading almost due east of New Sfinctr. That was mostly farm country out there—so I heard, anyway—until you reached the southern stretch of Joe's Mountains. According to the waif, her town was nestled in the foothills of the mountains. It'd take us at least a day and a half to get there.

Oh, and it turned out the town's name was Sylvan Springs.

Once we got clear of New Sfinctr's none too salubrious outskirts and reached the countryside proper, Angela and Jenny started ooh-ing and ah-ing over the landscape. But even their indefatigable enthusiasm for all things ran dry soon enough. Acre after acre, mile after mile, of cropland. I believe most of it was wheat. I'm not sure. My skills at discerning different grains start with flour, and don't improve much thereafter. Refined flour, whole wheat flour—I believe cake has its own type as well—and then you get into the really obscure stuff like semolina and durum. There's even something called couscous, but I don't know what it is because I've never asked. I'm afraid I might have eaten it at one time or another. If I did, I don't want to know.

Eventually, toward sundown of our first day of travel, the waif emerged from her semi-comatose state and started talking a bit. Her name was Patty, she was nine and a half years old, and… she ran dry about then. Angela and Jenny tried to get her to talk about her family but that just made the girl shrivel up again.

We spent the night at a rural roadside inn. The less said about it the better. At least the bedbugs were within my weight range.

We reached the town of Sylvan Springs early in the afternoon. I'm not sure what a sylvan is, but I don't think I spotted any. And for sure and certain there were no springs.

We didn't spend much time examining the surroundings, though. At the edge of town, we disembarked from the coach. Oscar and Patty remained there while the rest of us proceeded into the town itself.

Soon, a great sense of foreboding came down upon us, which got heavier and heavier as we neared the spires of the cathedral. It was a weird sort of foreboding. Not so much full of menace as full of something between hopelessness and self-loathing.

You are inadequate, deficient, faulty, incapable, stunted.
You always will be.
There is no joy, no triumph, no cheer, no bliss, no satisfaction.
And never will be.

Around then—still two blocks from the cathedral—we all began stumbling; and, before long, started falling to our knees. Soft moans escaped from our lips.

Well, all except those of Schrödinger's Cat. She started jittering all over the place. Aimlessly, so far as I could tell. Then, after maybe half a minute of this, she jittered over to Greyboar—he'd managed to get back on his feet again—and said, "We need to get out of here. This is nothing we can handle on our own."

There is only failure, fault, loss, contempt, dismissal, decline, defeat.

Stretching to eternity. Such is your existence. Such is your destiny.

"Move!" she shouted. "Move *now*."

I got up, reached over, and helped Jenny and Angela to their feet. I began to guide them toward the coach—using the term "guide" pretty loosely. Our progress was more or less three steps forward, two steps back, five steps—no, stumbles—to the side.

I heard Greyboar bellowing and looked back. It seemed the numbskull still wanted to fight whatever hideous thing was lurking in that cathedral, but the Cat was driving him back by the crude expedient of smacking him on the head, shoulders, belly, you name the body part, using the blades of her lajatang for the purpose.

Thankfully, she was smiting him with the flat of the blades. I'd seen her use that weapon the way it was intended to be used. It made me think of a two-legged shredder.

If it had been anyone else doing that, Greyboar would have already broken multiple bones in their body. But this was his true love, after all —and besides, all she was doing was trying to save the cretin from his own cretinhood.

By now, the girls and I had gotten far enough away from the cathedral that I could feel the horror's grip loosening on us. So, I gave them a little final push and turned back to help the Cat.

Immediately, I was driven to my knees.

You are a pitiful specimen of incompetence and ineptitude, doomed to mediocrity in all things. Your life is and will forever be a dreary miasma. You will long—in vain—to achieve fourth-rate status in any trade or profession you choose to follow. You will long—in vain—for any satisfaction in your personal life. Joy, happiness, exhilaration, even simple contentment: abandon any hope for them now. They are and will forever be beyond your reach.

I managed to struggle upright—barely. By then, thankfully, the Cat had driven Greyboar far enough away from the cathedral that he was able to shuffle along on his own. I'd done my duty as a Hero, Sidekick well enough, I figured. I turned back toward the coach.

Once all of us were in the coach, Oscar set off down the road, moving as fast as the vehicle allowed—which was pretty damn fast.

We'd bought that coach back in our salad days as successful entrepreneurs.

～

FIVE MILES OR SO DOWN THE ROAD, GREYBOAR ORDERED OSCAR TO stop the coach.

"What do we do now?" he demanded. "My professional ethics as a Hero, Excelsior don't allow me to just up and quit on a Calling. Come hell or high water—do or die—I've got to keep at it."

So did I, according to the rules of the Heroes Guild, although I didn't see any need to say it out loud.

"You can't take that thing—whatever it is—just with your thumbs, Greyboar!" protested Jenny. "There's magic involved here."

"Which means we need a sorcerer," said Angela.

Oh, no. I could see it coming…

"Lucky for us, we know the best sorcerer in the whole world!" said Jenny.

"Except for maybe God's Own Tooth." Greyboar turned to me. "What do you say, Ignace? And where is Zulkeh these days, anyway?"

Zulkeh of Goimr, physician. The world's most puissant sorcerer… yeah, maybe. The world's most insufferable egotistical windbag, for a certainty.

I sighed. "He's in Murraine, I heard. Doing some sort of investigation that won't mean anything to anyone except himself."

"What a piece of luck!" exclaimed Jenny. "Murraine's not far from here."

Yeah, piece of luck. A day's ride, by coach. One short, little twenty-four day before being afflicted—

"Okay," I said. Windbaggery couldn't actually kill you, after all, even though it could make you wish you were dead.

～

"RIDICULOUS," PRONOUNCED THE WIZARD. "ABSURD. I AM SUPPOSED

to abandon my imperative studies in order to assist you in dealing with some pastoral nuisance? You have taken leave of your senses!"

His glowering gaze swept across all of us. "Each and every one of you. Mad as the proverbial hatter."

I wasn't paying much attention to him, though. I knew from experience that before Zulkeh would agree to do something, you'd have to listen to his long perorations on eighteen subjects under the sun, precious few of which had much to do with the subject at hand. The wizard was the sort of pedant who, if you took him out to dinner at a restaurant, would spend the first half hour giving you the history of the term "restaurant," most of which would focus on its inadequacy compared to the term he preferred, which he'd uncovered while investigating an obscure dialect of a long-dead language whose script only he could read.

Then he'd complain about the menu, explaining that a properly organized one would present the foods not in the order in which they'd be eaten—appetizer; salad; soup; main course; dessert—but according to which food group they belonged to—grains; meats; vegetables; dairy products—except that the commonly accepted food groups were grossly erroneous because they were based on the shallow thinking of such clods as farmers, grocers, butchers, and other proletarians, instead of the ontological principles enunciated by the great ancient culinary scholar Julia Sfondrati-Piccolomini.

About midway through Zulkeh's rant on the effrontery involved in disturbing a great mage in mid-scrutiny of whatever silly damn thing he was studying, Shelyid hustled into the salon bearing a huge tray laden with various snacks and beverages. The dwarf was the sorcerer's apprentice, valet; servant; porter; aide; caretaker—you name it, and if it involved practical matters and manual labor, Shelyid was the one who'd be handling it. He was a pretty nice kid, too.

"Here, everybody," he said. "You'll need this to keep up your strength while the professor expounds."

Professor was the appellation Shelyid used to refer to Zulkeh. The wizard himself would have much preferred "master," but Shelyid had a labor contract that spelled out just about everything concerning his rights and responsibilities. The notorious malcontents Les Six had negotiated it for him, and the first thing they'd done was get rid of that "master" business. Prior to their intervention, Shelyid's position in life had been indistinguishable from "galley slave."

"I see you've come up in the world," I said, after he set the tray down on a coffee table that was about the size of a small atoll. I waved my hand, indicated the salon we were currently situated in, which had taken a while to get to from the ornate front door of the wizard's domicile. "The last place you guys were living in—"

"Don't speak of it!" said Shelyid, raising his hand. "The memory is still painful. I had to keep the place clean, remember?"

He looked around the room, beaming. "We're just renting, but even after we return to New Sfinctr we'll be able to get a much better place than that overgrown shack we had on the docks. I found us a new revenue source that's a lot more reliable—more remunerative, too— than the professor's slapdash... well, you can hardly call it 'finances.' Be like calling an alley cat a majestic king of the jungle because it's got some stripes."

I would have pursued the matter right then and there—finances being recognized by all sane men as the true harmony of the spheres— but Zulkeh chose that moment to bring his temper tantrum to its peak.

"No! Under no circumstances! I shall not! Is my earth-shaking research project to be brought low by a mere village pest? I think not, sirrahs! I think not!"

"'Scuse me," muttered Shelyid. He advanced upon the windbag. "Hold on a moment, Professor. Judging from all past experience, you're bound to need a favor from Greyboar fairly soon. 'Favor' being a euphemism for a cartilage and bone crushing squeeze or two. Or three. Or it could easily be four. That being the case, doesn't it make sense to store up a favor of your own? Otherwise—you know how much you hate doing it—you'll be driven to plead, implore, and beseech when you need Greyboar's help. Your enemies and rivals will call you a beggar."

The wizard glared down at him, his ridiculous conical hat quivering with outrage. "I have no rivals, impudent gnome! Enemies, yes. Untold numbers of them. Envious and resentful inferiors, the lot! Rivals, no."

"As you say, Professor. I'll see to the preparation of your bag for the trip. Do you wish to bring the usual? That is to say, everything?"

The windbag's glare turned into a scowl. Shelyid had boxed him in and he knew it. He *would* need to ask Greyboar for a favor, soon enough—and the great Zulkeh of Goimr, physician, probably hated being thought a beggar more than he hated most anything else. And he hated as many things as there are stars in the skies, it seemed like.

"Of course, I need everything. See to it, loyal minion."

In days gone by, Zulkeh would have called the dwarf his loyal but stupid apprentice, but that too was now forbidden in the labor contract.

I'd been through this experience before, more than once, so I sprawled in comfort on the most comfortable looking divan in the room. We'd be a while.

For the next several hours, Shelyid scurried about packing the wizard's paraphernalia into the monstrous sack that Zulkeh considered his travel bag. That paraphernalia consisted of a multitude of scrolls heaped untidily upon work benches and shelves, the stone figurines and clay tablets scattered about the floor, the thick leather-bound tomes of great weight stacked precariously hither and yon, the vials, beakers, jars, jugs, amulets, talismans, vessels, bowls, ladles, retorts, pincers, tweezers, pins, the bound bundles of sandalwood, ebony and dwarf pine, the bags and sacks of incense, herbs, mushrooms, dried grue of animal parts, the bottles of every shape and description filled with liquids of multitudinous variety of color, content and viscosity, the charms, the curios, the relics, the urns of meteor dust, the cartons of saints' bones and the coffers of criminals' skulls, and all the other artifacts of stupendous thaumaturgic potency crammed into every nook and cranny of every niche, room, closet, and hallway, not excluding the heavy iron engines in the lower vaults.

By the time he was done, sundown had arrived. None of us— especially Oscar and the boys—wanted to travel at night in a coach as heavily laden as this one would be. So Zulkeh began expounding on the pleasures and health benefits of sleeping outside. Thankfully,

Shelyid bypassed all that nonsense by pointing out that their new lodgings had plenty of rooms available for all.

Well, excepting Oscar and the boys. But they were quite accustomed to sleeping in the coach.

"Can't remember the last time—or the first time, for that matter—that I paid a grasping and greedy innkeeper for a place to sleep," said Oscar. He eyed Shelyid. "And we usually steal our food."

"Won't need to do that here!" the dwarf said cheerily. "I'll bring you something shortly. Just don't mention it to the professor."

Like I said, a nice kid.

THE FOLLOWING DAY, WE SET OUT FOR SYLVAN SPRINGS—WHICH ALL of us except Patty were now calling Suffering Shanties. Patty didn't call her wretched town anything on account of she didn't utter more than a handful of sentences a day, and then only in whispers to Jenny and Angela.

We made good progress, given the wretched state of the so-called roads, but by the time evening arrived we were still some distance from the town of misery. In any event, no one—not even the wizard, who was prone to excessive self-esteem—wanted to come to grips with whatever horror lurked in the cathedral after nightfall.

So, we found a tavern. Using the term generously. To my delight and relief, however, Shelyid rummaged through the wizard's sack and came out with an old cantrip titled *Bugs, begone!* Once Zulkeh intoned it, all manner of creatures with excessive legs promptly fled the premises. So, we even managed to get a decent night's sleep.

Well. Not me. Angela and Jenny were in a frisky mood again. But, manfully, I did not complain.

WE WERE OFF AGAIN THE NEXT MORNING. "BRIGHT AND EARLY," AS

the idiot old saw would have it, ignoring the obvious truth that "early" and "bright" is a ridiculous combination of words.

Oscar brought the coach to a stop right about the same spot he'd done in our first visit. Patty stayed with the boys in the coach. The rest of us sallied forth.

It might be more apt to say that all of us except Shelyid sallied forth. Burdened by that enormous sack, his progress was more in the way of a staggering lurch. How someone his size even managed to hoist the thing onto his back was a mystery. He was incredibly strong.

Right about the same distance from the cathedral as had been the case on our previous visit, the sense of foreboding made itself felt again. Zulkeh immediately ordered a halt.

"Before all else, I need to determine the nature of this menace," he said. "Shelyid, fetch me the *Encyclopedia of Perils, Hazards, Jeopardies and Maledictions*."

The dwarf plunged into the sack and emerged a couple of minutes later with a thick leather tome. After handing it to the wizard, Zulkeh spent some time flipping through the pages.

At length, he seemed satisfied. "I believe we are confronted with one of three vexations. Normally, I would be inclined to think we faced either a wightwoe or a mispecter. Either of which"—he waved his hand dismissively—"would be child's play for a sorcerer of my caliber. But as a rule, those pathetic vermin of the chthonian persuasion avoid cathedrals, churches, temples—anything resting on sanctified soil. So…"

He stroked his long beard. "I fear we may be facing a far more malevolent power."

"How do we find out?' asked Greyboar.

"Pah! 'Tis simple enough. Joyce Laebmauntsforscynneweëld's 'Finnegan's Wake Up' will rouse the monster, if it's what I think it is."

"Just give me a minute!" said Shelyid, diving back into the sack. In less time than that, he reemerged with a slim volume in his hand along with a jewel box and what looked like a small religious icon. "I brought the Molly and the portrait as well."

"I shan't need the portrait. The Molly may come in handy." Zulkeh reached out and took the jewel box. Then, striding forth a few steps, opened the box and cast from it what looked like tiny diamonds. As soon as the jewels—if that's what they were—struck the ground they began chanting the following verse:

riverrun, past Eve and Adam's, from swerve of shore to bend of bay, brings us by a commodius vicus of recirculation

a way a lone a last a loved a long the

riverrun, past Eve and Adam's, from swerve of shore to bend of bay, brings us by a commodius vicus of recirculation

a way a lone a last—

A tremendous hissing sound emerged from the cathedral. That was followed by a clattering of what sounded like the boots of an army. A moment later, the cathedral doors burst open, and a hideous creature emerged into the daylight.

What did it look like? Well, imagine a centaur (of sorts) the size of a gigantic centipede, from whose forward portion emerged a torso that looked more like a skeleton than something formed of flesh. Perhaps worst of all was the head, which looked surprisingly human—but whose facial expression was the quintessence of contempt, derision, and disapproval.

The monster bellowed the following:

DIAGRAM A

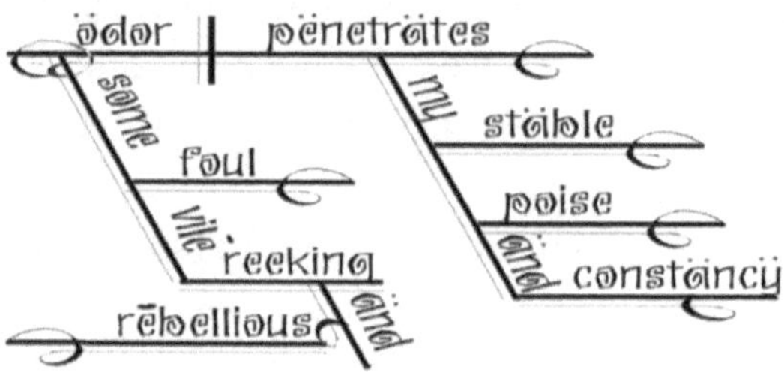

I was driven to my knees by the sheer force of the monster's disapproval. So were all the others except Zulkeh and Shelyid. The wizard might have stepped back a pace or two; the dwarf didn't seem to budge at all—allowing for the tight clasp he had on the fabric of the sorcerer's sack.

"Oh, would you!" cried out Zulkeh. "Well, then—take this, you vile caitiff!"

The sorcerer capered forward and began what looked for all the world like one of those energetic heathen dances favored by primitive barbarian tribes. With each step, he called out the following words:

"swoop (shrill collective myth) into thy grave

"merely to toil the scale to shrillerness

"per every madge and mabel dick and dave"

Again, the monster issued a great hiss. But it also seemed to stagger to one side, as if its ugly hairy legs had lost their footing.

"Haha!" yelped Zulkeh, his tone triumphant. "Can't stand up to the poetic chaos, can you?"

He turned back toward Shelyid. "As I suspected—it's a Grammarian. Horrid things. They wreak havoc among children, especially. Strip the poor tykes of all joy, all spontaneity, all carefree welcome of the world. Shackle them in shrouds of inadequacy, webs of hopelessness, and chains of glum foreknowledge of an empty life to come. But—!"

He capered a few more steps in his dance. "The verses of e.e. sfondrati-piccolomini always drive them mad. Ha!"

In the distance, the Grammarian appeared to have recovered its poise. Some of it, at least. It scurried forward on its multitude of legs, and now screeched:

DIAGRAM B

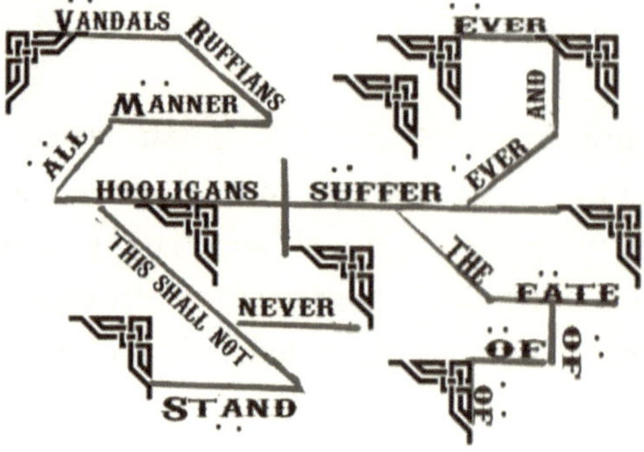

My spirits immediately rose. It was obvious, even to a nonpareil non-wizard like me, that the Grammarian was badly wounded.

"Shelyid! The Molly!"

The dwarf handed Zulkeh the slim volume. Zulkeh immediately flipped it open and chose—completely at random, so far as I could tell —to read the following passage. Very, very loudly.

"or shall I wear a red yes and how he kissed me under the Moorish wall and I thought well as well him as another and then I asked him with my eyes to ask again yes and then he asked me would I yes to say yes"

The Grammarian howled, then suddenly collapsed, its dozens of legs flopping around with seemingly no rhythm or coordination at all. A moment later, it shrieked:

DIAGRAM C

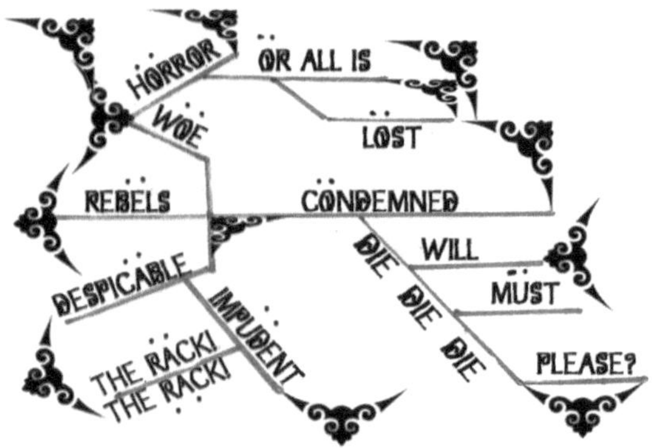

"He's done for, Professor!" said Shelyid gleefully. "Drive home the coup de grâce! What'll it be? Faulkner Laebmauntsforscynneweëld's

The Sound and the Fuzzy? Woolf Sfondrati-Piccolomini's *Mrs. Thataway*?"

"No. For this wretched Grammarian, nothing will do except verses from the Carroller."

"I'll fetch them right off!" The dwarf started climbing back into the sack.

"Bah! Desist, my loyal but needlessly energetic apprentice. I had the Carroller's wisdom memorized by the time I was seven."

I was amazed to see the wizard then do a perfect pirouette. Once, twice, thrice. Following which he chanted:

"The Jabberwock, with eyes of flame,

"Came whiffling through the tulgey wood,

"And burbled as it came!"

The Grammarian tried to retreat back into the cathedral, dragging itself with flailing limbs. To no avail. Before it got barely started it began convulsing, following which a piteous wail came forth.

Diagram D

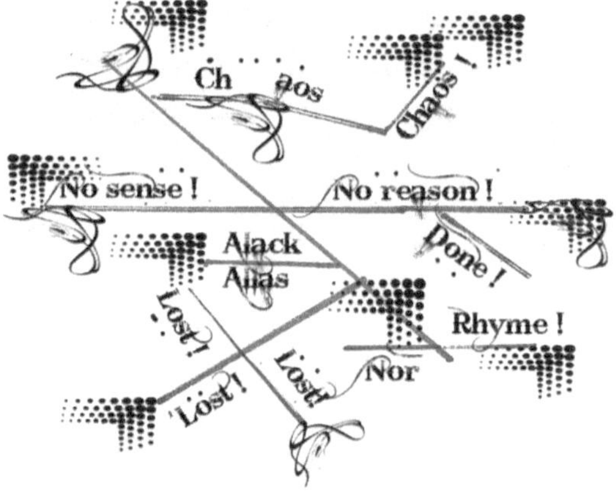

Greyboar saw his chance and rushed forward. A moment later he was throttling the monster.

"A waste of effort!" shouted Zulkeh. "'Tis impossible to silence a Grammarian outright! Go for the skull! It's quite fragile!"

The strangler's—sorry, Hero's—great hands shifted to the withered skull.

Crack. Crack. Crunch. Just a cloud of dust remained.

"'Tis due to the horror's obsessions," Zulkeh explained. "Such traits invariably lead to brittle craniums."

I refrained from comments about pots calling kettles black.

"Don't touch me until you've scrubbed your hands!" the Cat hollered.

Within less than a minute, a few people began making their appearance in the square before the cathedral, emerging from whatever hiding places they'd managed to find. They moved slowly and were all gaunt to the point of being emaciated. They gathered some distance from the Grammarian's carcass, still with no expressions on their faces beyond despair.

By then, Oscar had brought up the coach and Patty emerged from it. Her gaze was fixed upon the dead monster.

Jenny and Angela went over to her. "Do you want to look for your family?" they asked.

The little girl shook her head. "They're all gone. Forever gone."

A great dread seized my heart.

Sure enough—

"You poor thing!" exclaimed Angela.

"But don't worry," said Jenny. "We'll take you in."

Marvelous. Another mouth to feed. With what?

But I didn't think to argue the matter. I'd lose the quarrel. Not even Greyboar would side with me, and the Cat... I shuddered to think what that madwoman might do.

"All right," I said. "Let's be off." *Before my kind but impractical ladies offer shelter to anyone else in this miserable rustic ruin.*

"Not just yet, Ignace!" That from Shelyid, who was climbing out of the sack again. This time, to my surprise, holding an easel, a small canvas, and what looked like a cup full of pencils.

The dwarf pointed at the Grammarian's remains. "You make a lot more money if you accompany your tale of adventure with a few drawings. Mine aren't that good, but the audience isn't really so fussy."

"What are you talking about?"

"I told you. I found a new and much better source of income. They're called Champeon accounts. You set them up—costs nothing—with an amulet from the Wizard Wide Weft."

"I never heard of it."

Shelyid gave me a sideways look. "Meaning no offense, Ignace, but you're not exactly knowledgeable when it comes to modern advancements."

"Modern advancements!" I jeered. "What? Have they come up with something better than ale?"

"I rest my case." Shelyid started toward the Grammarian's remains. So far, only a single rat had approached them—and it fled before it got within two yards.

Before the dwarf took three steps, though, Patty spoke up.

"I like to draw," she said. It was the only thing she'd said in the time I'd known her that seemed to have any spirit to it.

Shelyid turned and looked at her. "Well, come with me, then. Let's see what you can do."

FOR THE NEXT HOUR, SHELYID AND PATTY TOOK TURNS AT THE EASEL, each doing their own pencil portrait of the expired fiend. When they were done, everyone in our party gathered around to examine the results.

The opinion was unanimous. "Patty's a lot better than you are, Shelyid."

"Sure is!" he said cheerfully.

He then turned to me. "Since you're going to be taking care of her anyway, you ought to make her a partner in your new Champeon business."

I scowled "What—"

"That's a great idea!" exclaimed Jenny.

"Yes, it is," chimed in Angela. She started wagging her finger under my nose. "And don't whine, Ignace! I've been talking to Shelyid about how these Champeon things work. All you have to do is tell tall tales about the exploits of Greyboar and his friends and post them along with Patty's drawings. He says as long as you can lie well enough, the contributions will come flowing in."

"And if there's one thing you're a champion of," said Jenny, "it's lying."

Angela smacked her shoulder. "Be nice! When it's professional lying they call it mendacity."

I was tempted to protest. But…

I do have a natural talent for embellishing and improving upon drab and humdrum data. Tedious stuff, facts.

I studied the girl's drawing again. She really was pretty damn good. Maybe…

"Let's be off!" commanded the Cat. "I want to be home before Ignace starts thinking too heavily, or we'll get a broken axle."

No more than two months later things were looking up! To my surprise—okay, I'll admit it, I'm not all-seeing when it comes to money—Shelyid turned out to be right. As soon as I set up our Champeon account, money started flowing in. Not as much as we used to make throttling people, but you can't expect miracles. Our income was still much better and more stable than it had been.

I credit myself with the nifty byline:

The Great Greyboar

Still Has Thumbs, and Now a Hero!

(Excelsior)

The only fly in the ointment was that Jenny and Angela insisted on becoming Patty's managers.

"What for?" I demanded. "I was planning to do that myself. I'm the experienced manager here, aren't I?"

Both of my ladies gave me the beady eye.

"In other words, you'll negotiate with yourself over how much of a percentage Patty gets," said Angela.

"Well…"

"What part of the phrase 'conflict of interest' are you having the most trouble with, Ignace?" Those uncharitable words came from Jenny.

"Fat chance," they now said in unison.

Angela: "We will serve as the little girl's agents."

Jenny: "Who knows the tricks and deceits of the management involved better than we do?"

"I'm hurt! Cut to the quick!"

Jenny yanked up my shirt and started inspecting me. "You see any bleeding wounds, Angela?"

"Not a one."

Then they insisted that Patty had to get one-third of the proceeds!

"Ridiculous!" I said. "She's just a paid contractor."

"A, she's not paid," said Jenny.

"B, her drawings are better than your prose," said Angela.

"C, they're way more accurate, too."

I stumped around for a bit, scowling my best scowl. "Then at least she has to start paying rent!"

"*What?*" exclaimed Jenny. "The girl's not even ten years old and you want to start charging her *rent*?"

"Her percentage just went up to thirty-five percent," hissed Angela.

I opened my mouth to advance the cause of reason.

"And if you keep arguing" said Jenny, "we'll put you on an affection diet."

"Starvation diet," clarified Angela.

My mouth closed. Dammit, that was cheating. But I knew they were serious about it.

And…

Push comes to shove, even for me, affection outranks lucre.

Well, theirs does, anyway.

ABOUT ERIC FLINT

*E*ric Flint is the co-author of three *New York Times* best sellers in his Ring of Fire alternate history series. His first novel for Baen, *Mother of Demons*, was picked by *Science Fiction Chronicle* as a best novel of the year. His *1632*, which launched the Ring of Fire series, won widespread critical praise, from *Publishers Weekly*, which called him an SF author of particular note, one who can entertain and edify in equal, and major, measure. A longtime labor union activist with a Master's Degree in history, he currently resides in northwest Indiana with his wife Lucille.

FOREWORD: "THREAD-SAFE" BY GRAY RINEHART

BY CHRISTOPHER WOODS

I like Gray and met him at LibertyCon a few years ago. He's the Slushmaster General at Baen Books and an all-around nice guy. "Thread-safe" could have taken place in a LibertyCon not so far into the future with a foray into the field of artificial intelligence that's not so hard to see happening today. I enjoyed this one and hope you do as well.

THREAD-SAFE

BY GRAY RINEHART

"First time?" the man asked as he looked at Gregor's ID. He was taller than Gregor by a good six inches and had salt-and-pepper hair, wire-framed glasses, and a wide, happy smile.

Gregor smiled back. "Is it obvious?"

He nodded. "We don't get many first timers anymore. So many people register as soon as we open up. We get used to recognizing people." He held out a hand, which Gregor shook. "I'm Rich Groller." Rich's handshake radiated genuine friendly pleasure, same as his smile.

"Gregor Behringer."

"So you are!" Rich handed back Gregor's ID and started flipping through a box. He asked, "Do you go to many conventions, Gregor?"

Gregor chuckled. "This will literally be my first."

"Good for you for starting with the best! Are you new to fandom?"

"Well," he said, trying to pick his words so as not to offend, "I suppose everyone's a fan of something, right?"

Rich pulled out a badge and said, "I guess you could say that. So, what are you a fan of, then?"

He handed over the badge, and Gregor smiled at the stylized image of a rampaging B9-style robot on it, underneath which his name was emblazoned.

"Not what, but who," Gregor said, and inwardly cringed at how pedantic he must sound. He pointed at the robot image. "I've followed Lu—that is, Dr. Bradley's research for some time." Her married name felt wrong coming out of his mouth.

Rich handed Gregor a lanyard and a little ribbon that said First-Timer. "Put that on your badge, so people know to welcome you." Then he gestured. "And step over this way. I may have a special treat for you."

"O-kay." Gregor moved to the end of the registration table and affixed the ribbon to the badge. He avoided covering up the QR codes for the convention schedule and local information and the sticker that said Banquet.

"Who do we have here?" said a friendly female voice.

Gregor looked up at a small woman who, like Rich, wore a polo shirt with Staff over the heart. Her hair was only a little darker than Rich's, done up in a bun with what looked like chopsticks poking out of it. Her eyes were bright, and her smile was as infectious as Rich's.

Rich said, "This is Gregor. Gregor, this is my wife, Tish."

Gregor bowed a little and tipped his hat. "Pleased to meet you."

Rich put one hand on Tish's shoulder. They looked very comfortable together. He said, "You mentioned that Brandy needed help about now? I think Gregor should volunteer."

Tish's eyes widened. "Oh, really?"

Gregor almost asked the same thing, but Rich just grinned and tapped the side of his nose. "Trust me."

Tish came around the table, deftly put her hand in the crook of Gregor's elbow, and started walking.

Gregor let himself be pulled along, grinning a bit stupidly. "Brandy?"

"She-Who-Must-Be-Obeyed," Tish said in a low voice, nodding as if she were initiating Gregor in a conspiracy. "LibertyCon's Supreme Empress," she continued. "Her father started it all, and she took over as chairperson when he stepped down. I can't believe that's been almost a decade ago."

Gregor said, "She-Who-Must-Be-Obeyed?"

Tish looked at him over her glasses. "And don't you forget it." Then she laughed and led him to a set of double doors. They showed their badges and Tish pulled him into the Dealers' Room.

The soft murmur of the hallway conversations gave way to an insistent buzz in the ballroom-turned-marketplace. Towering racks held T-shirts and assorted other clothing, portable shelves were stuffed with books and games and souvenirs, and orderly rows of tables overflowed with merchandise. Tish pulled Gregor past the vendors, most of whom were putting finishing touches on their displays, to a table along the back wall.

Here Lucinda would display her robots. At the moment, the setup was rather meager, though. Except for the four black plastic cases stacked on luggage carts behind the table, it looked like a grad school poster session... and he recognized one of the posters straightaway.

Tish leaned in with him. "'A Naturalistic Model of Machine Learning,'" she read, then pointed at Gregor's name under the title. "You helped with this?"

Gregor mixed a grin with a shrug. He liked that Lucinda hadn't written him entirely out of her research, but he had never liked her terminology. It seemed contradictory, but he hadn't come up with anything better.

"Did Rich know about this?"

"I don't see how he could," Gregor said. "He just asked me what I was a fan of."

"A lucky guess, then. Still, he'll crow about it for weeks!" Tish looked behind them. "Here comes someone you'll recognize, I'd guess."

Gregor turned. Dr. Lucinda Bradley was walking down the aisle next to a petite, very pretty, dark-haired lady. They were trailed by two men, both also dark-haired, one a good deal taller than the other.

Medium height with dirty blonde hair, Lucinda was, to Gregor's eye, stunning. She was wearing what might have been a costume of some sort: loose green calf-length pants, white shirt, and a vest... no, a corset... that accentuated her already substantial curves. Gregor felt petty, insignificant, even insubstantial in comparison, in his off-brand jeans and AutoDyn company polo shirt.

Gregor struggled not to stare at Lucinda as the shorter lady introduced her to Tish. Then she said, "And this is…"

"Gregor," Lucinda said in a flat, almost bored, tone that broke the spell.

Gregor tipped his hat to her—"Doctor," he said, in deference to the others more than Lucinda—and then to the pretty dark-haired lady. "As she said, I am Gregor."

"Brandy," the lady said. She turned as if to introduce him to the gentlemen with them, then looked back and asked, "Dr. Bradley, were you expecting your friend to be here?"

Lucinda barked out a quick laugh. "Not at all."

Gregor bowed. "Yet here I am, at your service."

"Oh, stop it, Gregor! Don't feign interest—"

Gregor stepped back and raised his hands. He resisted the urge to tell her his interest had never been feigned. "I really only came to observe"—*and to see if you're still building on my work*—"but my new friends told me that 'she-who-must-be-obeyed' required assistance." He faced Brandy fully. "I presume it is you who must be obeyed?"

Brandy smiled but shot a look of mixed exasperation and amusement at Tish. "That's what they say. Feel like helping us move a couple of transit cases?"

"I have been accused of having a strong back and a weak mind," Gregor said.

Lucinda said softly, but loud enough for everyone to hear, "That sounds about right."

They only moved two of the transit cases, so Gregor doubted they really needed his assistance at all. Even though they were on luggage carts, they were heavy and awkward: over a yard square each, and one nearly that tall. The men with Brandy pushed the carts—one of them Brandy introduced as Clint and the other as "minion." Through a service corridor, they entered the back of a ballroom where Gregor helped offload and open the cases.

"Things are going well in the robotics lab, I see," Gregor said.

When he and Lucinda had been grad students together, they had attached their first mechanical nerve bundles to vacuuming robots and watched them learn to avoid obstacles that would hurt them. In the larger of the two cases, though, surrounded by foam padding, sat a midsized version of the robotic dogs the military and some airports used for security patrols. A little over half the size of a great dane, Lucinda's robot was covered in slightly translucent amber skin that appeared to be thicker than Gregor's forearm. The robot's frame and limbs looked fairly standard, but the skin gave it bulk. Aside from black-and-white patches on its shoulders and hips, it looked something like a headless golden retriever.

Gregor reached out—

"Don't touch," Lucinda said. To his quizzical expression, she said, "It's some new type of ballistic gel"—as if it should have been obvious—"or so they told me. Stiffer, I guess, so it stays in place, but expensive. So don't mess it up."

"So, things really *are* going well in the robotics lab."

Gregor tapped the side of the transit case. The outer layer did indeed wobble a bit. Looking closer, the skin was strung with a fine wire net, with openings smaller than his pinky and what looked like tiny bulbs of solder where some of the wires overlapped.

"Sensors?" Gregor asked. "What kind?"

Lucinda shook her head. "Sorry, that's proprietary."

Gregor didn't think she was *that* sorry.

Lucinda swiped a couple of times at an app on her phone and the robot stood up. "Good boy, Snoopy," she said. It flexed its limbs this way and that, and Gregor half-expected it to stretch into a "downward dog" pose like any awakening canine.

"Wake-up call?" Gregor asked. "You don't let them wake up when there's enough light?" If she powered each robot all the way down in its crate, when it was turned on it might be as if it was being born for the first time.

She scowled at him. "We had this discussion years ago. It wouldn't be nice, to leave them awake in the dark."

"I didn't realize you were trying to be nice to them. Especially not with the 'demonstration' I heard about." *Ballistic gel…*

Lucinda frowned. "If you're going to help, then help. Kindly shut up and pull a power supply to feed the mutt."

Clint and the other fellow—whose first name Gregor learned was Jonny—had already moved the second crate off its cart and opened it to reveal four portable power supplies, each a little larger than a car battery. Now Gregor frowned. The robot's case had been big enough that she could've packed it *with* a power supply, kept its processors on at a low level as he had suggested when they were in school together.

Might eventually figure out dreaming, he thought.

After all, what complex creature achieved sentience, let alone sapience, without dreaming? They had wondered how important it was to a newborn baby that it sleep and wake and sleep in certain proportions, that its brain be given a chance, in unconsciousness, to assimilate whatever it had perceived while awake, and whether such cycles might be equally important in the development of a "newborn" artificial intelligence, even if the cycles were greatly accelerated. A newborn baby learned constantly while awake, every experience releasing chemical cascades in its brain. Gregor imagined that set up a feedback mechanism that encouraged a newborn to stay awake as long as possible until, clearly tired, it fought going to sleep with yawns and cries—but then sleep allowed those chemicals to… dissipate? reabsorb? Gregor wasn't quite sure, but they'd never figured out how to stimulate a robot's simplistic brain to remain awake and then to have a productive unconscious period of reordering the machine's thoughts. That was one reason he never liked calling their approach "naturalistic."

Gregor sighed as he carried the power supply around to the front of the temporary stage. They'd had the "electric sheep" discussion —*argument*—too many times before. He tried to remember who'd written that old story about androids dreaming. He couldn't think of it. Tish or one of the others would probably know…

Snoopy the robot bounded up the steps and loped alongside Lucinda. She gestured for Gregor to put the power supply down and watched as he plugged it in to a drop cord Jonny and Clint had run just behind the framing of the low stage. Without any apparent command, the robot turned around next to the power supply, backed up to it, and sat atop it to engage the contacts.

"Things *are* going well in the lab," Gregor said. He leaned against the front of the stage to get a better look at the machine. "So how much of the baby robots' experiences went into this one's matrices?"

Lucinda looked down with disdain. "Not enough for you to get authorial credit on the next article. They're not *tabula rasa*, though."

Gregor shrugged off the jibe. "Just wondered if they might recognize me from the lab."

"No, the sensor suites are different."

"Even the optics?"

Lucinda sighed. "Their pattern recognition is good, but we didn't install facial recognition." She gestured to the mostly empty chairs in front of the stage. "Is that it, then, or do you want a private show?"

Gregor tipped his head right and left, as if he was seriously considering her facetious offer. Then, just to push Lucinda's buttons, he reached up and stroked the robot's gelatinous hide. The wires were rough against his palm, and the gel's friction surprised him. His hand stuck, and the skin pulled and wobbled as he disengaged from it. He patted it gently.

"Must you?" Lucinda asked.

Gregor chuckled. He walked his fingers up the robot's body. Other than the give of the outer layer, the machine stood stiff as stone.

"Afraid I'm going to spoil your pet?"

"You haven't changed a bit."

You have, he thought but didn't say.

GREGOR WALKED INTO THE BIG BALLROOM A FEW MINUTES BEFORE Opening Ceremonies. A few people milled in the aisles looking for seats, but nearly all the chairs were already occupied.

Snoopy still sat on its power supply on the right side of the stage.

How boring, Gregor thought, and chuckled at the way he anthropomorphized the machines.

Just behind the robot was a lectern; center stage was a long table draped with red, white, and blue bunting; and to the left was a man-sized replica of the Statue of Liberty—*Liberty Enlightening the World,* if Gregor remembered correctly.

Gregor turned right, to go along the back wall and around the side to find a seat, but someone grabbed his left arm. He started, then smiled to see Tish Groller.

"I was looking for you," she said. "Rich saved us a couple of seats."

The seats turned out to be on the third row, just off the central aisle. Gregor had an excellent view as an older gentleman with a top hat and cane welcomed the attendees, declared that LibertyCon was officially in session, and introduced Brandy, who said a few words. Then the MC introduced… almost everyone in the room.

Gregor must have looked a bit overwhelmed as the man read off dozens and dozens of names, because Rich nudged him and said, "It's like a big family reunion."

Finally, each of the guests of honor were introduced and said a few words: an author Gregor was vaguely familiar with, though Gregor didn't read much fiction; the artist responsible for the image on the badges; a special guest who received a huge round of applause; and Lucinda, the STEM guest.

Who introduced Gregor, in a roundabout way.

Instead of just saying how glad she was to be there, Lucinda played her fingers across her phone and made her robotic puppet dance—almost literally. Annoyance gnawed at Gregor as the robot moved across the stage, hurdled the table, and jumped down, sprinted to the rear of the ballroom and back again. Gregor couldn't see how that had anything to do with machine learning. He started seething.

"Of course," Lucinda said then, "we don't make any advancements without the occasional disagreement, without sometimes putting forth alternate theories that need to be investigated and even arguing over what our results mean. So, if you want to talk to someone with differing opinions, look for my old colleague Gregor Behringer, who arranged to be with us this weekend. Gregor, where are you?"

Rich elbowed him. "That's your cue, I think."

"Stand up, Gregor," Lucinda said. "Let the people see you."

He hesitated, but before Rich could elbow him again, he stood and waved at Lucinda, his hat in his hand. A few people, perhaps a dozen out of the hundreds in the room, applauded.

As Gregor sat, Lucinda tapped an icon on her phone and the robot sauntered to the power supply and sat back down. "Gregor originated the power conditioning setup we use," she said. "But I don't think he much approves of what we'll be doing this weekend to demonstrate that these robots learn through experience and pass on what they've learned to one another."

She turned toward the audience and smiled a wicked smile. "Tell me, if you don't mind: If we were to conduct the shooting demonstration right here, right now, how many of you are equipped?"

One person in the back whooped, then others echoed the call. Gregor looked around and was surprised to see dozens of hands in the air, and many more people looking as if they were fighting the urge to raise theirs as well.

"I think," Lucinda said, "Sunday afternoon will be *very* interesting."

Even though Gregor thought Lucinda was a fine choice to be on the panel of "mad scientists" Friday night after the Opening Ceremonies, he was more interested in her solo talk Saturday morning. So, it seemed, were a great many others: He had to take a seat near the back of the small meeting room.

Most of Lucinda's presentation, he had heard before—hell, a lot of it he had written in his own Masters thesis—so he didn't learn much. In fact, he was surprised she hadn't made a lot of progress even though her robot subjects—like the one on display at the front of the room, with red patches instead of black-and-white—were more sophisticated than when they had shared the lab. It still burned him that he would have expanded their research into his own doctoral program except that their advisor, Professor Aloysius Bradley, had given Gregor's research grant to Lucinda, back when her last name was still Montrose.

The conventioneers took it all in attentively. Gregor wished Lucinda would emphasize differences more than similarities—that robotic subsystems weren't fully analogous to organic structures, for instance, since their hardware was unalive, while every cell in an organism worked to survive as long as it could. *He*, at least, had never figured out how to give the power components their own "will to live," but *her* focus had been trying to compensate for—or get around—the fact that no machine was built with instincts while every living thing seemed to have them.

Gregor's first contribution had been to suggest that instinct itself might be rooted in the simple fact that living things sought pleasure and avoided pain, or if they seemed to lack those sensory nuances, sought *life* and avoided death. Lucinda had made it her mission to find out whether machine intelligence might develop something like a survival instinct through pleasure/pain learning opportunities, rather than just programming in responses. The two of them had made a good team: He built the "pleasure gate" logic for the robot power supply that responded to a sweet spot of voltage and current such that the robot sensed the best charging response as "pleasurable," and Lucinda set up the programming for ultracomplex matrices of potential responses, with what amounted to fillable spaces for the robots' learned experiences.

She had mentioned his work the night before, and about midway through her talk she alluded to it again. "You wouldn't want your cell phone to start whining like a child when it fell below fifty percent on the battery," she said, "or to start wailing when it fell below twenty percent, or whatever. Sure, it alerts you that it needs to be plugged in, but it doesn't *experience* the loss of power. Lacking viscera, it's hard to feel anything in a visceral way. So, we had to figure out how to give the robot those—for lack of a better word—*feelings* of hunger and satiation."

They had started small, hoping to demonstrate something like an evolutionary path to machine intelligence, and were working with fox-sized machines by the time Professor Bradley had pushed Gregor out. Lucinda had gone on, literally, to bigger and better robots to explore their sensory experiences and had begun letting the robots access one another's... she said "memories," but he knew that wasn't quite it... so each would learn faster.

Gregor smiled as she described what was obviously a version of his "power gate" fed by the "proprietary" sensors on top of these robots' gel padding. Was that really why she hadn't wanted him to touch the machine? Because a soft touch might be pleasurable? Would the robot like it too much, such that it might skew her results? Or had she dropped the "seek pleasure" part of their research and gone fully in the direction of "avoid pain"? Because she clearly intended to teach her robots in a most painful way.

A hand went up in the second row. "Dr. Bradley?" said a slim man with a wild shock of hair and beard, wearing a garish red, white, and blue outfit. "You mentioned that each robot updates its database using inputs from the others. Could you run them through different, simultaneous scenarios, and have them all update at once as they go along?"

Lucinda put her fingers in front of her mouth for a moment as she considered the question. "We've had some trouble with that," she said. "Without being able to make true synaptic connections, we built fillable matrices that are extensible and multidimensional. And we gave each robot its own, rather than have them share a common experience matrix on a server. You might say that we limited their telepathy.

"If they shared a common matrix, then if two of them tried to write to the same cell at the same time there might be contention. We'd have to make sure all the operations were thread-safe. But since each of them has a unique matrix, when one uploads how it's filled in its cells, the one that downloads it will have to store that information in *other* cells. It can't rewrite its own cells, or it would effectively forget what it's learned.

"As a result, the shared experience takes a different shape, so to speak. It's more a replication problem, but the issue of thread safety still applies. Though, as I said, we've had problems."

"What kind of problems?" the fellow asked.

"Sometimes they do things we don't expect. Basically, the robots get confused," Lucinda said, which elicited a few laughs. "But that's something that happens to the best of us!"

When the polite laughter died down, Lucinda invited everyone who wanted to take part in a short demonstration to join her in the main ballroom. Before heading over, Gregor tamped down his disapproval and went to congratulate her. He hung back while she chatted with a couple of people, and found himself next to her robot sitting obediently on its charger.

Gregor knelt and came almost eye-to-facepiece—if "facepiece" was right for the spot where the robot's neck should have protruded— with the machine. He smiled and patted the robot's shoulder.

The robot trembled under his palm: a fast vibration, gone almost as soon as it began.

He pondered that and ran his fingers along the robot's front leg. "Who's a good boy?" he asked, but not too loudly.

"Why is it," Lucinda said behind him, "that everyone else can read the 'Please Don't Touch' sign except you?"

Sure enough, on the table end a paperboard tent read *This is Clifford. Please do not disturb him.*

Gregor almost reached up to scratch between Clifford's shoulders, but instead just patted it a couple more times. "I'm a rebel."

"You're a jerk."

His left knee creaked as he stood. "That's what I love about you, Luce. You're always so kind."

LUCINDA'S INDOOR DEMONSTRATION, THANKFULLY, INVOLVED NO shooting. Gregor thought some of the attendees looked disappointed to learn that.

Most of the chairs had been stacked against the wall of the ballroom, leaving seven rows of seven chairs, widely spaced in each direction, in the center. Lucinda transferred an application from her phone to each volunteer and asked them to select a seat. Gregor, more interested in observing, leaned back against the stage.

"On the floor by your chair," Lucinda said, "you'll see an arrow pointing to another chair—maybe to the side, maybe in front or in back. In order to confuse our robot subject, we're going to play a little Musical Chairs and once you've stopped and sat down, I'll activate the app you just installed. Don't worry—we're not going to take away any chairs so you can't get 'out'!

"Once you've all acknowledged the signal, Clifford here"—she gestured to the robot which had entered the room with her—"will walk among you. The program will select one of you to be the target and one or more of you to be obstacles that he'll need to avoid."

Gregor wondered what Lucinda had rigged for feedback as the music—not canned music, but a guitar player—began. It wouldn't be the direct feedback the robots got from their power stations...

The music stopped, the participants sat, and a moment later Clifford stood and ambled toward one corner of the square of chairs. The robot walked between two rows as if it were entering a maze, which brought back memories of the smaller robots Gregor had put through mazes in the lab. Had Lucinda let those robots' experience matrices transfer to these—

Clifford jumped backward as if it had been shocked.

Gregor sat up a little straighter. He didn't have a direct viewing angle but was afraid to move for fear of missing something if he looked away.

Clifford stepped one foot forward, then pulled back and into itself the way a scolded dog would.

It reached out at an angle, toward the attendee at its two o'clock. The man in the chair shrank back a little. Clifford put its foot down, right next to his chair, without reacting.

Clifford turned toward the attendee at its ten o'clock, reached ahead—

—and pulled back instantly.

The woman in that chair looked offended.

Clifford inched around the obviously disturbing input and continued. Gregor puzzled over the feedback. Was it something Lucinda had programmed in? How did that fit with her "naturalistic" approach?

Clifford turned at the end of that row and proceeded down the back of the square, then turned toward the front—

—and jumped back at another "obstacle." Gregor had a better view this time as Clifford tested its surroundings and maneuvered around that person: the tall fellow in the patriotic garb. A few steps farther along, the robot came to a full stop in front of a woman wearing an all-black military-style uniform festooned with ribbons. She held up her phone, said, "That's me!" and the participants and onlookers applauded, Gregor included.

Clifford exited the faux maze and the guitarist started playing. While the participants moved to different spots in the maze, Clifford stood between Gregor and the chair square.

"Good boy, Clifford," Gregor said, unsure what had come over him. "What do you see?" he asked aloud, wondering what kind of recognition algorithms Lucinda had loaded… or if she had given this set of machines a chance to "learn" what their cameras showed them.

He felt far outside that world now, and jealous.

The music stopped, and after a moment Clifford again entered the square. This time it angled toward the black-clad woman who had held the prize the first time, and Gregor nodded in admiration. Pattern recognition took lots of calculations, even though it couldn't really be categorized as "thinking," and sometimes machines got fixated on patterns to the point they seemed to be obsessed, but Clifford's pattern recognition was impressive—

—the robot jumped back faster and more powerfully than before.

It encountered two more obstacles before finding the prize, and Gregor wondered if Lucinda had somehow dialed up the intensity of the robot's responses. He wasn't sure why, except that at times she did have a flair for the dramatic.

Once more the music played, and the participants rearranged themselves before Lucinda activated her application.

Clifford moved—

—and the way it jerked back Gregor imagined it would have yelped had it been a real dog. Some of the participants and onlookers gasped, and someone to Gregor's left said, "Whoa!"

Gregor said, "Great glory, Luce, what are you doing?" but Lucinda was too far away to hear him—which was probably good.

Clifford moved parallel along the front line of chairs, right to left, toward Gregor, moved forward again, and jumped back as violently. It stepped left twice more, its motors humming and feet landing with pronounced thuds and tried again—

only to jump back nearly to the stage.

"Careful, Clifford," Gregor said. He was close enough to see the robot's skin jiggle when it landed. "There's a good boy."

With mincing little movements of its limbs, the robot turned to face Gregor.

Another onlooker to Gregor's left said, "What's it doing?"

I wish I knew, Gregor thought.

Clifford stepped forward tentatively—

—then leapt and leaned against Gregor's leg.

Oh, crap, he thought.

And then he looked at the crowd.

Forty-nine people in chairs, a few dozen more sitting or standing on the periphery... and one extremely angry roboticist who, after swiping and tapping on her phone, began moving his way.

Lucinda radiated tension. Each step fell with deliberate precision, her long burgundy dress moving around her as if she were trudging through blood, the bangles she was wearing jingling as if they were bells tolling for him. She raised her phone like a hammer and her words fell slowly like blows.

"What in the *hell* did you do?"

Gregor held his hands up in surrender. "You said they sometimes do things you don't expect! I just said it was a good boy."

A few people laughed. Lucinda slowed, stopped, turned toward the now-silent crowd and then back to Gregor. She tried again to control the robot with her phone, but it would not budge. So, she dropped her phone into a leather pouch and harangued Gregor for the last ten minutes of the session. The audience seemed to find *that* quite amusing.

Gregor was thankful when the hotel staff came in to reset the room.

GREGOR SAT IN THE BALLROOM AN EXTRA HALF HOUR WHILE LUCINDA finally got the robot moving. She didn't tell him how she did it, of course, but it had looked a lot more like programming than it did teaching or learning. He kept his mouth shut instead of pointing that out, and when she headed back to the Dealers' Room he went to the hotel lobby. He sat near the front windows, oscillating between naked embarrassment at having interfered with Lucinda's demonstration and —being honest with himself—a bit of unholy glee at being able to do so pretty much without trying.

Was that why he had come? To sabotage her work? Was he really that petty? He didn't like to think so, but the evidence was not in his favor.

He still supported her work in general. How could he not, since a lot of it had been his work, too? The only thing he really objected to was the "live-fire" demonstration she was planning for Sunday. But if she asked him not to go, Gregor would do what she wanted. That was his way: If he thought it would make her happy, he would agree to almost anything.

That's why he'd backed off when Lucinda's interest in their advisor became more than academic. It had seemed simple at the time, straightforward, and he had solved it like an equation. Love isn't just a feeling, an urge. It's a choice. And the hell of it was, sometimes you have the feeling, you have the urge, but the other person doesn't, so you make the choice not to love—or to love in a different way. That's what Gregor had done, or tried to do, but it had been agonizing, and it plagued him.

He hated the fact that, as poor as his memory could be sometimes, he clung to some things with a bulldog's tenacity. More unfortunate was that he was almost masochistic in the things he called to mind— the time Lucinda said they could only be colleagues and friends; the time he found Professor Bradley's love letters to her; the staff picnic where she flirted with the man while trying hard to appear not to—as if by putting himself through the pain again and again Gregor might somehow atone for his own sins and failures.

Gregor sighed. He was always such a fool when it came to Lucy.

"You coming?"

Gregor looked up. Rich Groller continued, "To the banquet?"

Gregor shrugged. "I'm not that hungry."

"After this morning, I'm not surprised."

"You heard?"

Rich laughed. "It's not that big a convention. *Everybody's* heard by now."

"Probably a good reason for me to stay clear."

"Not at all. I don't know what you did, but best thing to do is own it and move forward. Come on, come on."

Gregor acquiesced. And even thought he had to endure some ribbing from his tablemates, it was more enjoyable than he expected. The barbeque, at least, was excellent.

As lunch concluded, each of the guests of honor was given a few minutes to speak. To introduce them the MC had stitched together movie and television clips related, even if tangentially, to their work. Lucinda's introduction consisted of a montage of science fiction robots, moving as if dancing to "Mr. Roboto."

Her talk was more serious: Despite the Renaissance Fair dress she wore, Lucinda was all business when it came to her work. Gregor tried to pay attention to her words, but his mind wandered from time to time.

"What do animals have that robots don't?" she asked. "Not in terms of flesh and blood, but in terms of their minds, their actions, and reactions?

"Instinct. Specifically, the survival instinct. No matter how much memory and programming we cram into one of these"—she held up her phone—"or one of those"—she pointed at another of her robots, sitting dutifully on its charging station at the far end of the head table —"a newly built *machine* won't exhibit anything like instinctual behavior.

"We asked ourselves whether instinctual behavior is 'programmed' in, as part of DNA or RNA or something else, or *learned* through an organism's immediate, reflexive response to the environment. Birth itself is a process that introduces pain and/or struggle, followed by some amount of nurturing. Pain and pleasure are juxtaposed from the beginning. For higher animals the gestation period itself is pleasurable once the fetus is sensate: whether the warmth of a mother hen incubating her chicks or the warm suspension of a mammal in utero, with the resonance of a beating heart always in the background. So, pleasure followed by pain followed by pleasure of suckling and comfort—the contrast couldn't be more drastic, and the results never fail to obtain unless the baby has some defect in its nervous system that renders it insensate.

"Except..." and Gregor had to admit that Lucinda played the dramatic pause rather well, "what about lower animals, plants, single-celled organisms? Don't they, too, have a survival instinct? Intelligence certainly doesn't correlate directly with the drive to survive. Nonintelligent creatures, all living things, possess that drive innately because they're alive. They're driven to do what's necessary to stay alive. Even our individual cells do what they need to do to survive as long as they can. Why do we assume that a machine, and in particular a machine that developed or possessed intelligence, would have that same will? Or, since it's not precisely a question of will, that it would have that same instinct?"

Lucinda took the microphone in hand and walked to the end of the table. She stood behind the robot, which had light grey patches on its shoulders and hips. "So, we asked ourselves, what about approaching the development of intelligence from a more basic level? That is, rather than trying to build an artificial brain from the top down, so to speak, what about trying to emulate or recreate the *evolution* of intelligence from the bottom up? What about starting with the 'lizard brain,' the primitive brain, rather than trying to replicate higher brain function? And why not work on self-preservation, on the survival instinct, as we did so?"

She gestured and a montage of video clips played of the robotics lab—and there was Gregor himself, smiling and holding up one of their first squirrel-sized robots in front of the maze they used to run them through. He found himself sliding down in his seat, especially when the robot flinched away from one of the wrong paths. Yes, the prize awaited it at the end—the first "pleasure gate" charging circuit he had built—but Lucinda had never thought the prize enough… motivation.

The video ended with a shot of one of the larger robots, like the one Lucinda was standing behind, and what she said next surprised Gregor.

"But what if we're wrong?"

He set down his glass of tea and sat up a little straighter. If she was considering *that*, then she *had* changed.…

"We could be wrong in any number of ways, and it wouldn't be a tragedy if we were. It's science, and we can learn as much from failure as from success. At least, I hope so, given that this morning's event didn't go quite as planned." She stared hard at Gregor, but a light murmur of laughter wound through the audience.

"Yes… what if we're wrong? What if a robot can't develop a survival instinct? After all, that instinct manifests much the same in humans as it does in dogs or rats or paramecia, and it's a function of being *alive*—something Astro here"—she waved at the robot, then walked back to the lectern—"is most definitely not. *We* are perhaps more *aware* of the instinct, or the impulse, by virtue of being intelligent, but intelligence doesn't *give* us the instinct. What if we're wrong, and the survival instinct is deeper than simply avoiding pain or death? What if it's something… transcendent?

"But beyond instinct, what about higher motivation? What if an artificial brain can never truly develop internal motivation? We haven't built in the equivalent of dopamine producers and receptors for feedback and general pleasure regulation, and isn't intrinsic motivation essentially seeking after what gives pleasure and fulfillment? It's different from simply being a guide to avoiding pain.

"What if we're wrong about robots, artificial minds, being able to grow in these ways? What if we find that—at least in their cases—it's all programming? Not artificial intelligence, really, not artificial knowledge leading to artificial wisdom, but just... code written by us?

"For one thing, it means that we have to learn to write much better code." She paused a second for a light patter of laughter. "But even if we do, we're left with a troubling question. Does that mean *all* instincts, and maybe *all* higher motivations, are 'programmed' in?

"I don't know about you," Lucinda concluded, "but that gives me pause. Or maybe I'm just programmed to pause there, and to stop here."

The audience applauded, perhaps less enthusiastically than they had the artist guest whose speech had lasted only a minute. Then Brandy gave Lucinda a beautiful hand-carved plaque, and said, "Thank you, Doctor Bradley, and may I say that I hope you're right, not wrong. I hope you go beyond instinct, beyond motivation, and help artificial minds develop something like empathy. Because I, for one, would like our robot overlords to have a little empathy."

As the banquet concluded, thoughts rattled inside Gregor's head like old bolts in a coffee can. Whether they'd been wrong to boil desire down to a coin flip between avoiding pain or experiencing pleasure, and how those two things had played their parts in how he'd structured his own life. Sensitization, the point where impulses no longer produce the same result, and whether an artificial nervous system would ever be subject to such. If an artificial intelligence had the wherewithal to avoid pain and seek pleasure, what would stop it from becoming completely hedonistic, or devoting its entire being to self-gratification?

The banquet broke up, and Gregor meandered toward the exit. To get there, he had to pass the head table. Astro still sat on the end of it, and he noticed that someone had braced the table to support the machine's weight. *Sensible*—the table wasn't made for robots. But what was? Not for the first time Gregor wondered how much Lucinda had tinkered with the circuitry architecture they had originally developed. When it came to the pleasure-and-pain approach that she called "naturalistic," she had always thought he gave too much credence to the carrot and he thought she overemphasized the stick....

Gregor was careful not to get too close, but he couldn't help but smile at the robot. He chuckled and wondered how the robots would do with old games like hide-and-seek, or warmer-colder.

"Or fetch," he said. "Would you like a game of fetch?" He shook his head and walked away.

The robot's motors whirred.

Gregor looked back.

Astro shifted a little, back on its haunches. Gregor watched, but it didn't move again.

~

A RUNNEL OF SWEAT TICKLED ITS WAY DOWN GREGOR'S BACK. THE Tennessee sunshine and the mid-July humidity had pummeled him as he stepped out of his rental car, and the walk down the dirt path only made it worse. He wondered why anyone would deliberately live in a place like this.

The shooting range didn't look like much: a small field that might once have been pasture, with a half dozen lonely target supports set up in front of a grass-topped berm at the far end. Behind the berm, longleaf pines swayed in a slight cross-breeze. Gregor sniffed, but couldn't catch any pine scent, even from the trees lining the side of the range right up to the split-rail fence he was leaning against. He frowned. He loved a piney smell, whether of a natural Christmas tree or sawdust from a freshly cut piece of lumber. Once the shooting started, he wouldn't be able to smell anything other than burned powder and hot brass.

He was surprised at the turnout. Dozens of people milled around two ramshackle sheds at the near end of the range. The closer one was long and low, subdivided such that Gregor guessed it had once been a stable. Where there might once have been horses, marksmen—and markswomen, Gregor supposed—were unpacking and checking their weapons.

The crowd chatted amiably, seemingly unfazed by the heat and humidity. Did they all think they would get to shoot a robot today? Surely not.

"You made it!" said a familiar voice, and Gregor turned to see Rich and Tish Groller.

"Does the shooting always attract so many people?" he asked.

Rich laughed. "This is a record crowd, I'd say—a lot more than came out Thursday, that's for sure! Not here: I'm not sure how they found *this* place, but it was the only range that would allow the special demo."

"You mean the 'live' robotic targets?"

"That's what I mean. But how about you? Are you shooting?"

"I hadn't planned to."

Rich shrugged. "If you want to, I'm sure someone would let you squeeze off a few rounds. Two things before that, though. First"—he fished a small package out of his pocket and passed it to Gregor —"here are some earplugs. Go ahead and put them in now, they're going to open the range any minute." While Gregor manipulated the foam cylinders, Rich continued, "Second, be sure to ask how much they want for ammunition. Nobody here's going to stiff you, but the stuff's Almighty precious!"

Rich's laughter seemed very distant due to the earplugs, and as they set out together Rich and Tish both donned blue plastic earmuffs. Momentarily, a bullhorn crackled and informed the shooters on the line that the range was clear.

Even with the warning, Gregor flinched at the first shot: a light pop from the stables, probably a pistol, followed in quick succession by another, then joined by similar sounds of varying pitches. Gregor felt as if the temperature jumped a few degrees; he rubbed his hands on his jeans as if to dry them. He was glad Rich had given him earplugs.

They walked behind the stables and toward the second shed. It was short and squat, basically a roof held up by four stout poles. Behind it sat a white cargo van, its doors open and Lucinda's transit cases on the ground.

"Cease fire! Cease fire!" The bullhorn voice started issuing instructions for safing the range, which Gregor mostly tuned out as he realized that only two of Lucinda's robots—Astro and Snoopy—were sitting by the shed. Lucinda stood near them, wearing slim-fitting jeans and a black T-shirt emblazoned with two twenty-sided dice. The T-shirt fit her very well....

"Luce," Gregor said as they approached. He tipped his hat as he pulled his gaze up to her face.

She stepped between him and the two robots. "You haven't been messing with them, have you? Snoopy and Astro?"

"I won't even get close to them."

"Good. The other one's still popping error messages, so it may not even be useful today."

Gregor couldn't bring himself to express any regret over that, so he stayed quiet.

"Nothing to say for yourself? Typical." Lucinda walked the long way around the shed as new volleys of gunfire erupted from the stables.

Gregor found Clifford sitting next to the stack of transit cases. The robot made no move as he approached.

"Have you learned your lesson, Clifford?" Gregor squatted in front of the machine. A single indicator showed that the robot was powered up, though it was just sitting on the ground rather than a power station. "You're still a good boy, Clifford—I'm the one who messed up." Gregor reached out but pulled his hand back. "If it were up to me, I'd say that yesterday you figured out pretty well how to avoid pain... which was kind of the whole point, wasn't it? Of course, none of this is exactly controlled experimentation. It's just demonstrating..." Gregor sat all the way down. His legs were tightening up. "What, exactly? Stimulus-response, I guess. If you came in a pigeon-shaped chassis, Luce would make B.F. Skinner proud... or set him spinning in his grave. I'm not sure which.

"But the point was that she set you a task yesterday, which she expected you to accomplish, but you just quit. The test got too painful, and somewhere in there," Gregor tapped Clifford's shoulder, "you calculated that leaning against me—or maybe not me, maybe I was just a convenient reference point—was the best option."

Gregor paused and noticed the shooting range had gone almost preternaturally quiet.

"I'm going to see what's going on. You be a good boy now, okay? Make momma Lucinda proud."

$\sim$

GREGOR SIDLED UP NEXT TO RICH AND TISH. "WHAT'S GOING ON?" HE whispered.

"We wondered where you went," Tish said.

Rich pointed. "While the range is safe, they're putting out the target for the robots—one of the power supplies."

Gregor didn't recognize the people out in the field, but supposed they were more of She-Who-Must-Be-Obeyed's minions. They were about halfway between the shed and the berm at the far end, unloading sandbags from a utility vehicle and stacking them around one of the power stations to protect it from an errant shot or a ricochet.

Offering them a carrot this time, Gregor thought. *More than yesterday, anyway.*

As the team trundled back over the uneven ground, Lucinda prevailed upon Brandy to draw a number from a hat—literally, a top hat to which someone had affixed a pair of goggles. Brandy verified the shooter who came forward—a rather fetching young lady wearing what looked like safari clothes—had the same badge number as what she'd called. While the lady readied herself at the front of the shed, Lucinda had Brandy flip a coin.

"Heads," said She-Who-Must-Be-Obeyed.

"That's Astro," Lucinda said, and tapped her phone screen.

Gregor couldn't help but smile as the grey-tagged robot bounded away, much like an oversized puppy anticipating a treat. It veered left, then right, either avoiding terrain features or triangulating on the power station's Wi-Fi signal. Gregor couldn't tell.

It stopped cold, about thirty meters away, when the first bullet struck. Gregor winced.

The bullet hit just ahead of Astro's left rear leg. Gregor wished he knew more about ballistic gel and how far a round would penetrate at that distance. Could it have hit something vital?

The robot stood still for a few seconds, then tentatively moved its left hind leg through its full range of motion. Gregor snuck a look at Lucinda to see if she was entering commands on her phone, but she had her arms crossed. Beyond her, the shooter sighted on the robot, her index finger extended and resting against the trigger guard.

In one breath, the woman moved smoothly to shoot again, and Gregor whipped his attention back to Astro. It had darted to its left, then jerked right as the rifle report sounded and a spray of dirt erupted from a hillock just beyond where the robot had been.

The machine bounded once, twice, to the right—

—the rifle spat again—

—the robot angled slightly left, back toward its goal—

—another shot caught it in midstride.

Astro convulsed, or so it seemed. Its legs contracted and it skidded a bit on its belly. Then it pushed off again, leapt high, and snuggled itself behind a low rise topped with dandelions.

As the acrid smell of spent ammunition wafted across him, Gregor wondered what was going through Astro's electronic mind. He had often argued with Lucinda that all they were doing was tinkering at the edges of real intelligence, real learning. But he had to admit that this robot seemed to have learned very quickly, first to try to evade and now to hide. Would it have the sense to stay hidden, though? Had it learned from what Clifford did yesterday, to conceptualize a way—

"Look at that," someone off to his right said.

Gregor had been watching the whole time and seen nothing. He stood on tiptoes and realized Astro had splayed its limbs out to their limits and was inching its way, its belly almost scraping the ground, backward from the little hill that hid it from the shooter.

A few people clapped. The shooter pursed her lips, sighted, then lowered her rifle and shook her head. Once more she raised the rifle, but the robot gave her no clear shot.

Lucinda beamed.

Astro stopped and gathered in its legs. The shooter started to line up on her target, but the robot leapt twice its height off the ground and darted left, then right, then left again. Shots rang out, but each one only kicked up grass and dirt before the robot cleared the sandbags and settled in behind them.

The gallery erupted into applause and cheers.

Lucinda soaked it all in, acknowledging the praise like a queen receiving honor from her subjects.

Next in line, Snoopy slowly sank to the ground, its belly to the dirt and its legs tight against its body.

Lucinda didn't seem to notice.

WHILE BRANDY'S MINIONS SET UP THE SECOND POWER STATION—TO the right and farther out from the first—Lucinda gave another short lecture to the onlookers. Gregor paid scant attention, though he did pick up on someone's question about whether Lucinda had updated the rat-in-a-maze scenario by putting a hungry cat in the maze, too.

Gregor was fascinated that Astro was tracking alongside the location team after they picked up the sandbags, even hopping beside the little all-terrain vehicle. One of the fellows helping—from a distance, it looked like Jonny from Friday afternoon—bent down and patted the robot about where its head would be. It was too far away to be sure, but Gregor thought he saw the robot shiver and push itself into the man's hand. When they brought back the first power supply, Astro again loped along next to the little 4x4 utility vehicle.

Gregor found that more compelling than the shooting.

Lucinda turned her attention to the second shooter called forward by Brandy: a huge man with greying hair and beard. "Shall we?" she said.

The man gestured with his rifle—which looked like a child's plaything in his hands—and said, "Whenever you are, Doc."

Lucinda turned to Snoopy, which Gregor still thought appeared to be cowering before her, and pressed her forefinger to her phone's screen.

The robot sat still as a statue.

Lucinda touched the control again and Snoopy rocked forward a bit but settled quickly back. It may have been the gel quivering, but Gregor thought Snoopy trembled.

"Do you want me to walk it out there?" Gregor asked, and immediately regretted it.

Lucinda's glance was sharp as an icepick and colder. "Did you ruin this one, too?"

Gregor held up his hands, and Lucinda turned her attention back to tapping and swiping at her phone. Overriding the robot's apparent reluctance? Wouldn't that invalidate the demonstration? She could just point to the robot's behavior as success, especially after yesterday, but he knew why she wouldn't: She had always been a "the show must go on" kind of person.

A low murmur started in the crowd. Lucinda gestured to the range and then the robot, and called out, "Technical difficulties, sorry!" After a few more swipes the robot stalked away, stiff-gaited and awkward, roughly in the direction of the power station.

Gregor cringed. Snoopy moved like a small child who'd been told to greet their overly affectionate aunt—or like a scolded puppy unsure how to please its master. He didn't believe for a second that the robot had developed anything like aversion or indifference, but it was easy to see that something in the machine did not want—if "want" was the right word—to be out in that dangerous place.

"Fire when ready," Lucinda said, a little too brightly.

The big fellow with the rifle shook his head. "It's too close, and moving too slow. Why isn't it trying to evade?"

"I'm sure it will react at the first shot."

From the far side of the shed, an onlooker said, "Put a shot across its bow!" and a few people laughed.

The shooter waited another few moments, then shrugged and put the rifle to his shoulder. Gregor turned in time to see the shambling robot pause and a bit of dirt spray up from a mound just beyond it. The single report seemed ominously loud.

Snoopy turned around. If it had had a head, Gregor would have sworn it was staring down Lucinda.

The robot leapt.

It bounded again, *toward* the shed—

—and staggered as a gunshot resounded.

It leapt closer, angling to the left—

—another shot clipped it.

Each time it landed, it jumped almost reflexively, more catlike than a machine had any right to be. Gunshots pinged: hit, miss, hit again. Someone—maybe many someones—started yelling.

The robot was perhaps ten meters away when the shots started coming in bursts. A chunk of the robot's skin blew off and spun into the air.

Gregor charged, almost before he knew what he was doing. Spent casings flew at him, and one pinged against his forehead.

Then he hit the rifleman and pushed him off the line.

Or tried to. The man was twice Gregor's size and he barely budged. He did move a step to his left, though, so the robot only grazed him as it leapt into the space where he'd been.

And crashed into Gregor instead.

Snoopy caught Gregor full in the side and knocked him over as easily as tipping an empty pitcher. Gregor landed awkwardly, raising a cloud of dust from the hard-packed dirt.

HOW MUCH TIME HAD PASSED, GREGOR WASN'T SURE. HE WONDERED IF he might be concussed: The way he'd slammed into the ground his head could have bounced against the dirt. He realized he was having trouble breathing—

—because a robot was sitting on top of him.

"Snoopy," he said, though it hurt to do so, "be a good boy and get off, okay?"

Snoopy did not move. *No, that would be too easy.*

Gregor lay awkwardly, on his side, his left arm extended and his right twisted between his body and the robot's. He spread his fingers out against the robot's skin. The gel was torn, furrowed, and his index finger pushed against what must be a bullet. The robot lifted up a little, enough for Gregor to take one sweet, deep breath, then it settled atop him once more.

"Thought you'd play the hero?"

Lucinda looked down on him—she always had, hadn't she?—but she wore a half-frown that might have been grudging approval.

"It's a little unlike me," he said.

"It's a lot unlike you."

He let the jibe pass. She wasn't wrong.

"You had to get in the way."

"I didn't *have* to...."

"But you did."

"Yeah." Gregor closed his eyes. He wished she would stop talking and do something about getting the robot off him.

"Okay," Lucinda said, "now how can I convince Snoopy to move?"

Gregor looked back up at her. "You're asking *me*?"

"They sure seem to like you for some reason. I'm thinking I need to change all my passwords so you can't get into my system behind my back."

Gregor let out a short chuckle. "You know I'm just hardware." Even when they were students, he couldn't make software changes. Professor Bradley might have been a lech playing favorites, but he was a stickler for data management and Gregor had never had the right authorizations. "Have you tried switching it off and then back on again?"

Lucinda said, "I'd like to keep that as a last resort, and not just because that joke is so stale." She leaned against a shed support, her face lit by her phone screen as she sought a way to override the robot.

Gregor took a gasping breath and sank his fingers into Snoopy's flesh. Gregor held on, and even though his ribs felt as if they were rubbing together, he shook the robot and whispered, "You're hurting me."

He knew it was irrational to say it. The robot had no understanding of what he said, or what it was doing. How does a child learn that it can *cause* as well as *feel* pain? He almost laughed at the absurdity of his questions, his ignorance, his lack of experience as a childless bachelor.

Thinking was hard: Gregor's brain throbbed in synch with his ribs as he tried to breathe. As a result, his thoughts clinked together like rocks in a tumbler. *Don't want to turn it off... Probably corrupt its data... May already be... too hard to program in empathy...*

He wasn't sure where even to begin with that, what it would possibly look like. But might the experiential matrix be corrupt? Could he have corrupted it? Accidentally executed unsafe threads? How to synchronize access...

"What about a feedback loop?" he asked.

"Huh?" Lucinda said. "What are you talking about?"

He almost said something snide but checked himself when he realized that while his thoughts had wandered Lucinda had been talking with... She-Who-Must-Be-Obeyed, he thought.

"In the matrix," he said, "somewhere in the learning profile. A feedback parameter. An input linked to an output. Cause and effect, Luce! Let it *feel* the effects that it causes." He wasn't sure if what he said made any sense to her. He wasn't sure he made sense to himself. And then he wasn't sure about anything as the world faded to black.

"YOU READY TO GET UP NOW?"

Gregor blinked and looked up to see Rich Groller grinning at him. His voice had been muffled, and it took a second to remember that he was wearing earplugs. He took a blissful breath and turned to see Snoopy practically crawling away, its gel covering in shreds. He realized he had something in his right hand, and when he looked he saw he was holding a handful of the stiff gel embedded with fine, but now-broken, wires.

He tossed it away, disgusted.

Rich helped him sit up, slowly and carefully.

"Really made a hash of things, didn't I?"

Rich laughed, and then Tish was there with a bottle of water. Gregor thanked her and drank a couple of swallows, then Rich gestured for it. He pulled out a flask and filled the bottle to the brim before handing it back.

"You look like you could use a little anesthetic."

Gregor chuckled, even though it hurt. An X-ray may be in his future, but he had other concerns. He asked where Lucinda was.

"Packing up," Rich said, "and none too happy about it. Don't know who she's madder at: that robot, or you, or Brandy for canceling the rest of the live-fire event."

"I don't think she's that mad," Tish said. "She did say that most of science is failing until you get it right."

"I don't know if that's science, or engineering," Rich said. "Anyway, you feel like standing up?"

Gregor tipped back the bottle—Scotch was not his favorite, but today it rated highly—and leaned on Rich and one of the shed posts as he got to his feet. Pain struck him like a hammer hitting a gong and almost drove the breath from him, and then he was erect and could breathe easier. He stood for a moment, unwilling to move from this less painful position, and fumbled mentally with the pleasure-and-pain principle of Lucinda's—and his—research. Was it possible that Snoopy's pain had been so intense—and it *must* have been intense— that its sudden absence was itself pleasant? Gregor had known a girl with a spine disease who said that after she had surgery it felt almost euphoric just to have less pain. If the robot's learning matrices had been filling with negative values when the bullets were hitting it, could it interpret a zero state as… desirable?

As he walked gingerly from the shed, he became aware that most of the shooting range was still in use. How long had he been out? He tried to recall what had happened, but everything after Snoopy hit him was a jumble, a blur. Idly, he wondered if the development of thought might require gaps like the one he was experiencing, if filling those gaps was an ingredient of intelligence, or a result of it, and whether artificial thinking could develop unless it had similar gaps that only imaginative cognition might fill…

He blinked in the sunshine and turned his face up to soak in the warmth. Maybe the South wasn't so bad after all.

"Are you okay?"

At first he'd thought it was Lucinda, but when he looked it was Brandy. She-Who-Must-Be-Obeyed. He grinned: Now Brandy was She-Who-Must-Be-Answered.

"I'm upright and above ground, as an old friend used to say, so I think so."

"Good," Brandy said. "Tish and Rich seem to have taken you in hand, so maybe I'll see you at the Dead Dog Party."

"Okay," Gregor said, unsure if he should ask what kind of party that was. But Brandy waved and turned away, and then suddenly, it seemed, he was at Lucinda's van. A fellow was putting the lid on Astro's crate. Snoopy sat on the ground, its legs drawn up tight against its body. It looked for all the world like a cowering dog, and as he approached it seemed to try to make itself as small as possible.

"That doesn't look good."

Lucinda's voice was small. "I think I broke it."

He had never seen her so close to crying. "Did you tinker with the matrices?"

She spoke slowly. "That would take too long. I set up some… equivalencies in the inputs and outputs. Feedback loops, like you said."

I said that? Gregor tried to remember. He asked, "Equivalencies? Straight, one for one? No decay, no multipliers?"

Lucinda looked puzzled. "Multipliers?"

"Sure," he said, "the way skin cells are more sensitive than muscle cells. Or how sensory cells will cut out if the inputs get too intense, or even how our brains ignore trivial things lest the noise of the world drive us mad. Remember *Mind and the World Order*? We filter out—"

Lucinda's eyes grew wide—

"—the 'chaos of the given,' so we don't get over-saturated."

Lucinda frowned. "You always got more out of Lewis than I did," she said, and started fishing her phone out of her pouch.

Gregor turned to Clifford. The robot had not moved, so far as he could tell. He put his hand on its gelatinous skin, fingers splayed for the maximum contact.

"Don't worry," he said. "She'll fix it. You just sit still and be good."

Clifford's camera eye winked.

Gregor looked more closely and decided it must have been a trick of the light.

ABOUT GRAY RINEHART

Gray Rinehart is the only person to have commanded an Air Force satellite tracking station, written speeches for presidential appointees, devised a poetic form, and had music on the Dr. Demento Show. He is currently a contributing editor (the "Slushmaster General") for Baen Books.

Gray is the author of the lunar colonization novel *Walking on the Sea of Clouds*, and his short fiction has appeared in *Analog Science Fiction & Fact*, *Asimov's Science Fiction*, *Orson Scott Card's Intergalactic Medicine Show*, and multiple anthologies. As a singer/songwriter, he has two albums of mostly science-fiction-and-fantasy-inspired music, with a third in the works.

During his unusual USAF career, Gray fought rocket propellant fires, refurbished space launch facilities, "flew" Milstar satellites, drove trucks, encrypted nuclear command-and-control orders, commanded the largest remote tracking station in the Air Force Satellite Control Network, and did other interesting things. His alter ego is the Gray Man, one of several famed ghosts of South Carolina's Grand Strand, and his web site is graymanwrites.com.

FOREWORD: "UNQUALIFIED" BY J.P. CHANDLER

BY CHRISTOPHER WOODS

I ran into James Chandler a few years ago at a convention in North Carolina. He was interested in doing a story for an anthology we were setting up in the Fallen World. We had the anthology filled but the story he pitched was very good and we had him jump right into our series with a novel. He's one of the favorites in that universe and his foray into science fiction is quite enjoyable.

UNQUALIFIED

BY J.P. CHANDLER

Unit C455i657 stared at Administrator Barrachia, brow furrowed, searching for comprehension. She recognized all the words, but their placement together refused to conjure any meaning. Sitting erect and gripping her knees through the smooth blue fabric of her coverall, her lips moved silently several times before she could speak.

"Apologies, Administrator," C455i657 said. "What does it mean? Management…?"

"Management has determined that Unit C455i657 is unqualified for any position with Interstellar Mining and Exploration," Administrator Barrachia repeated. "It means the Unit will not receive an assignment when we make planetfall." His tone was bare, practical. He leaned back in his chair behind the tidy metal desk, and his plain face showed no more reaction than his voice.

"The Unit is fully trained and has passed all assessments and inspections. The Unit's efficiency is very high." C455i657 squinted, confused.

"It's unusual, to be certain," the administrator explained. "This administrator concurs with the assessment. He reviewed all records for Unit C455i657 in reaching this conclusion. At one time, Unit

C455i657 was slated for the advancement track. However, later evaluations revealed behaviors which were inconsistent with continued success with the company. Management discovered no explanation for the anomalies and therefore could not recommend corrective action."

Unit C455i657 pondered the statement.

"What will be done with the Unit?" asked C455i657. "The ship is expected to make planetfall in less than a week."

The administrator shrugged. "The girl's disposition is no longer the Company's responsibility."

"Are there any other options?"

"Alternative placements are not the company's responsibility. This administrator has never visited Brebis and doesn't know any more about the planet than you do."

"Are there other companies—"

"This administrator has no information other than what management has provided." He had grown impatient, his most common state from the experience of Unit C455i657.

"The Unit is fully trained..." C455i657 stammered to silence, her arguments depleted.

"Of course, she is," Barrachia snapped. "This Training Subsidiary is experienced and highly effective. Since all other Units were placed as expected; the defect is not in the Unit's training."

"Fault was not indicated—"

"It was implied."

The administrator let Unit C455i657 consider the assertion in silence before continuing.

"You," the administrator paused, "will remove yourself from the subsidiary's quarters. A crewman will lead you to an available cabin. This will avoid impacting morale in the division." The administrator clasped his hands in front of him and leaned over the desktop. The forced smile failed to assure the girl. "You are very fortunate. The company will allow you to keep everything in your possession and will provide you with a small amount of currency after planetfall, as severance. The company will not require you to repay any of the costs of your care, training, or transport."

C455i657 blanched at being addressed directly. She had never been called "you" before. "You" applied to those who did not belong among the Units of the company. For some fifteen Earth years, she had been called Unit C455i657. Who would she be now?

"That's very generous," C455i657 intoned vacantly, looking at the desktop.

"You may go," Barrachia instructed. "You will no longer be designated as Unit C455i657. The company would like to express its best wishes for your future."

The girl rose slowly and exited the small office for the last time. The administrator had already turned to address other business.

"The name Cassi could be used," Unit T575a484 said from the viewport of the cabin assigned to Unit C455i657. The system primary, Berger, dominated the view despite being no larger than a fingertip at this distance. The planet Brebis, second of only four in the system, was mostly in shadow from their position but rimmed in blue, similar to pictures she had seen of Earth. Located somewhere on the tween decks in the wedge-shaped bow of the freighter, and far from the dorms housing the training subsidiary, the girl's cabin was four meters long and two meters wide. The unbroken warm beige of the bulkheads pleased the visitor, instilling a calmness of her thoughts.

"C455i looks kinda like C-A-S-S-I, so it will be easy to remember." Unit T575a484 had been C455i657's bunkmate and closest friend for as long as either could remember. Ten centimeters taller with a blunt face and square shoulders, nobody ever called Unit T575a484 short or mentioned her "frail" waist.

"I guess it's easier than saying 'the girl formerly known as Unit C455i657.' Come here and look at this, Tee." The girl's fingers glided along the computer touchpad of the terminal.

"You only have three more days to decide. Planetary authorities will want a name."

"Ugh, still not used to that." She shivered. "Fine. Come here, then."

"Cassi it is, then." Tee proclaimed.

"Whatever. Look, already." Cassi pointed at the monitor.

"It's just a ship." Tee leaned over Cassi's back from behind the hideaway computer chair.

"It's not just a ship. I think it's hiding."

"Why would you think that?"

"I had to hack through a security block to see it."

"You violated ship security?"

"I used the pixie to help." She held up her left hand to display the mini comp strapped to her wrist.

"Why?"

"It was shiny. I was curious." Cassi shrugged. "And I don't have anything else to do."

"You violated ship security just to look at a strange ship?"

"No, I took a peek to solve a mystery. It was just a speck through the porthole, but the ship's cameras refused to focus on it."

"Wait. You couldn't use the ship's cameras without secure access." Tee waved her arms for emphasis. "It wasn't a mystery until after you breached security."

Cassi shrugged and pointed at the view screen emphatically with a vexed expression.

"How many ships look like that?"

Tee replied with her own shrug.

"You don't think there's something strange about it? Look at this; what are all those weird shapes on it?"

"The main engines are really big," Tee conceded. "Those lobes could be fold drives. Why so many and why so big?" She quietly inspected the image, tilting her head to the side. "It would take a lot of power to run those monsters and keeping them in sync would be a nightmare."

"See? That's what I'm talking about. There's something really weird going on here." Cassi brushed at the other girl's hair tickling her ear.

"Why is it here? It's just floating between planets."

"It gets stranger the longer I look." Cassi pointed again. "It's not moving and there are no transmissions coming from it."

"How do you know that?"

"I accessed the comm logs." Cassi slid her fingers along the interface.

"You hacked into the communications system, too?"

"There was no other way to be sure."

Tee expelled a heavy sigh and folded her arms.

"What?" Cassi shook her head, dismissing her friend's concern.

"This is why you're unqualified, Cassi."

"What do you mean?" Cassi stopped her fingers and turned around.

"Oh, come on," Tee rolled her eyes. "You forget there are rules. A normal Unit wouldn't hack into the ship's systems to see something shiny."

"It's not like there was much security."

"A ship full of workers shouldn't need strong security."

"I guess. I just—"

BOOM!

An immense concussion hammered their ears and canceled all other sound. The ship shook violently. Cassi grasped the edge of the desk as she felt the artificial gravity release her. Tee grabbed Cassi's shoulder. The lights and the computer monitor blinked out leaving the cabin lit only by the light of Berger. The hum and vibration of the ship suddenly stilled for the first time in Cassi's life.

Together, the girls followed their training and remained quiet, waiting to see if the power would return. The light from Berger disappeared, leaving the cabin in complete darkness. The ship was spinning. Cassi couldn't feel any inertia, so it was a slow spin.

Minutes passed in silence. The light returned and disappeared again slowly. No alarms sounded, no announcements were made. Only the sound of their breathing echoed around them.

"We need to see what's going on," Cassi finally said, nascent panic causing her voice to quake.

"No," Tee said, squeezing Cassi's shoulder, "we need to wait for instruction or rescue. Moving around could just cause more trouble."

"You may be right," Cassi replied, "but it's been almost fifteen minutes. We should have heard something by now."

"Avatar." Cassi moved her left wrist approximately in front of her face. A tiny light flared and a holographic image formed above the back of her hand.

"Hi, Unit C455i657," it giggled.

Cassi thoroughly hated the avatar for the Intelligent Agent. IA, not to be confused with AI. Artificial Intelligence had been banned long ago because of their inevitable decline into insanity. The ghostly image looked like a young girl with oversized eyes and head, wearing a short pink dress with ruffles. Pale blue ponytails tied with pink ribbons reached to the notional floor. The cutesy image was only half as annoying as the high-pitched voice and childish speech impediment. Known as a pixie, the overlay had been installed by someone as a prank and had stubbornly resisted being overwritten despite dozens of attempts. At least the pixie did not impair the IA, which had proven to be adept and reliable.

Tee swore she had not been behind the prank, but she delighted in Cassi's discomfort.

"We gave her a new name," Tee said. "Call her Cassi."

"Hi, Cas—"

"What happened to the ship?"

"I don't know. I can't access the ship's computer." The pixie somehow giggled and pouted at the same time. "Ship's power is out."

"We noticed." Cassi sent the pixie away with a tap on her wrist. "Let's see what's going on." Stretching her arms from wall to wall, Cassi pushed herself through the darkness to the door.

"You better not get us killed," Tee said but she followed.

Luminous paint ran in thick lines along the floor edges of the corridor, faintly lighting the way.

Cassi pointed to her right. "The crew mess is this way. It's worth a try."

Using the handrails recessed into the polymer walls for microgravity events, Cassi and Tee pulled themselves through the corridor. At each door, they made their transitions with care in case the art-grav was working on the other side. The lack of noise, the freefall, and the bare illumination of the glow paint created a sense of isolation Cassi had never before experienced.

They found the crew mess abandoned. Through the large viewing windows across the room along the exterior bulkhead, light from Berger's Star slowly chased shadows in sharp yellow contrasts as it swept across the empty tables and benches fixed to the deck.

Cassi followed her feet through the doorway and found there was no gravity here, either. There had still been no announcement and no alarms. The crew had gone somewhere and had not bothered to tell them. Gravity was not functioning, the engines were off, and even the hum of life support was quiet. The air would not last forever—and nobody was telling them why.

Bracing her feet against the door jam, Cassi launched herself into the open room toward the nearest support beam between the floor and ceiling.

"Hey! That's a good way to get yourself stuck out of reach of anything."

Cassi ignored Tee as she grabbed the beam, adjusted her angle, and shot toward the next beam. Tee grumbled to herself and started pulling herself along the wall, taking the long way around.

Two more jumps brought Cassi to the viewing windows. Judging by the direction and the sun and planet moving out of view, the ship was rotating on more than one axis. Holding herself by the frame, she pressed her face against the window, trying to see other parts of the ship. A vibration, barely perceptible, trembled against her palm. Off to her left, a large object moved away from the ship ahead of a point of light. Another vibration and another object moved away from the ship. More of the pod-like vehicles launched soon after. Escape capsules. The spin of the ship scattered them in odd directions.

"They're abandoning ship without us!"

Tee floated over to Cassi. "But there was no order to abandon ship."

"Maybe they couldn't make any announcements without power?" Cassi offered.

"If they left us," Tee said, "who else did they leave? What about the other Units? What about the subsidiary?"

Capsules stopped appearing after a minute.

"Avatar, how many escape capsules are on board?" Cassi asked.

"Sixteen." The pixie giggled as it reappeared above her wrist.

"There are no escape pods for the workers, are there?" A hollow feeling settled in Cassi's stomach.

"There are 2,512 persons in the Training Subsidiary. They will not fit in the capsules." Giggle.

Cassi watched the retreating pods, fear and anger gripping her chest and throat.

No crew. No power. No life support. No air. No heat. No instructions.

"They must plan to send a rescue ship for the rest of us," Tee said. The frail tone belied her consolation.

"No. They won't."

"They wouldn't do that. They won't let all those people die in space."

Not people, Cassi thought. *Extras. The Unwanted. We're just Assets and the company will let us die here to collect on the insurance. We're all going to die.*

"Unless somebody does something," Cassi whispered.

She stared out the window for a moment. She looked at Tee, whose face was sickly pale.

"I'm somebody," she said to the retreating pods. "Tee, go check in with Barrachia. Then find me on the bridge."

ALL OF CASSI'S MEMORIES OCCURRED WITHIN THE SOLID BULK OF THE *Patricia Kaas*. It was her world, her *alma mater*, a part of herself. Pulling herself through corridors suffused in the dim, eerie light of glow paint, her arms growing steadily weaker, she felt like an intruder in another's nightmare. Her home was dying, its caretakers fled. She and the other parasites would soon follow.

The ship had grown noticeably colder. In a few hours she and anyone else on board would become science experiments.

The avatar led Cassi to the bridge and helped her turn on emergency power to the bridge. Weak lights lit the small room, and a few indicator lights sprang to life. It was easy to pick out the captain's seat among the five duty stations in the cramped room. She strapped herself in there. Cassi accessed the ship's underpowered computer through the captain's terminal. Emergency protocols allowed her to circumvent the access codes. She quickly activated the emergency power for the rest of the ship. Nothing changed.

She accessed the emergency power controls again to find them switched off. She switched the control back on only to watch it immediately turn off again.

"Okay, Pixie, what's wrong?" Cassi asked after several failed attempts to access the controls from different paths.

"I don't know. I still can't access the computer." Giggle. "I might be able to help if there is a port to plug into."

It only took a moment for Cassi to locate an I/O port. She removed the bracelet, laid it on the console, unspooled the tiny data cable, and jacked in. The avatar continued to float above the bracelet, but the pink dress became a work coverall similar to Cassi's, accessorized with a full tool belt.

"This system is older than I am," the avatar complained. "There isn't much juice left in the bridge batteries."

As if to prove the point, the avatar disappeared and the light from the bracelet blinked out. Cassi picked it up and inspected it. Dead. The bridge went dark again. Cassi looked around desperately for any light. Nothing. She slowly leaned back in the seat; the lack of gravity did not allow her to flop properly. With only the safety harness holding her in place the gesture felt more like standing up.

"Now what?"

The bridge lights flared to life, brighter than before, and monitors all around the room lit up. Lights blinked on the wrist comp, but the avatar did not appear.

"That was close!" came from a speaker above. Giggle.

"Avatar? What...?"

"The bridge emergency system batteries were almost drained." Giggle. "I depleted the wrist unit's cell waking it up. The main power cells are still charged, so I was able to route them to the emergency systems before the lack of power shut me down completely. We should now have power throughout the ship until the cells are drained. Yay!"

"Yaaay!" Cassi cheered with the avatar. "Wait, you're in the main computer now?"

"Yup! I overwrote the ship's command interface. We don't need that stuffy old dude." Giggle. "Wow, it's big in here. A lot more processing power. This is gonna be fun!"

"Yay."

"Was that sarcasm?" Giggle.

"Caustic sarcasm, to be precise."

"You're silly!"

"How long will the power last?"

"About forty-eight hours before the ship and everyone on it is completely dead. Yay!" Giggle. Cassi didn't cheer this time.

"Did you find out why I couldn't activate the emergency systems before?"

"Yes. The emergency power OS keeps saying there is nothing wrong with the ship so it shuts down. I need to constantly correct it or the power will go out again. It's a fun game!" Giggle.

"So, what's wrong with the ship?"

The captain's primary monitor flashed with images, numbers, and digital dials, then settled on a large matrix of red, green, and yellow panels.

"Something damaged the ship. Maybe a meteor or something." Giggle. "All reactors are offline; beyond repair. Main engines were destroyed when number three reactor exploded. I can't tell if there were any casualties. Maneuvering engines are offline but might be operational."

"Can we access communications now? I want to send a message to the planet and ask for help. Can you announce the ship's status to the workers? They should know."

"You betcha! I'll walk you through operating the communications system. Yay!"

"Yaaay…"

⁓

Cassi stared at the message on the monitor. It came over as text more than an hour after she had sent her plea for help. She had spent the intervening time hunting down the piece of code that kept turning off the emergency power. Every time she isolated and deleted the code, it showed up again. It was as bad as the pixie. She could not believe it was a glitch—somebody had deliberately sabotaged the emergency power system.

"*Freighter* Patricia Kaas: *We are aware of the situation. No ships capable of reaching you for rescue. Deep regrets.*"

"It took them an hour to come up with that?" Tee asked from her seat at another duty station.

"They expected us to be dead by now." Cassi closed her eyes and shook her head. No rescue. A sabotaged ship. Did someone on Brebis want them dead or was the sabotage somebody's idea of mercy?

She stared out the front viewport for several minutes as the ship's slow rotation took Berger and Brebis out of sight once again. She could only speculate as to why and, ultimately, the reasons meant little—no reason would make her feel better. She and the workers of the Training Subsidiary would all die if they did not find a way to save themselves. But what could they do that the crew could not?

A spark in the darkness caught her attention. She sat up straighter. There was one possibility. It was slim, but it was hope.

On her monitor, Cassi brought up the view of the ship she had been watching when the lights went out. If the planet had no ships in range for rescue, what was she looking at?

"Avatar," she called for the pixies's attention.

"Hi, Cassi!" Giggle. The hologram appeared above the recharged wrist comp. The voice was much more irritating when amplified by the ship's speakers.

"What type of sensors do we have available on emergency power?"

"All of them. We even have quantum mapping, but it will be slow at emergency power levels." Giggle.

"Can you control the sensors?"

"Just tell me what you need, sweetie!" The pixie struck a hero pose, hands on hips and sticking out her chest.

"Point everything at the ship I have on the monitor."

"What ship?"

"The ship I'm looking at."

"I don't see a ship."

"The ship we saw earlier!"

"I don't see—"

"You'll have to break through the security blocks again. It should be easier this time."

"What are you thinking, Cassi?" Tee asked.

"Hey, there's a ship out there!" the avatar declared excitedly. The hologram jumped up and down, clapping.

"Told you," Cassi said, immediately chastising herself for acting peevish toward the avatar. "Send all the sensor data to this console, then you can help me figure out what I'm looking at."

The primary and secondary monitors around the captain's chair flashed and blinked as data flooded in. A wireframe image of the ship appeared, rendered in three dimensions. Other readings appeared in tables and charts.

"You think that weird ship can rescue us?" Tee asked, her voice breaking.

"It's worth a try," Cassi shrugged. "What am I looking at? Are these radiation levels?"

The pixie changed its appearance to a dark skirt suit with hair wrapped in a tight bun and holding a wooden pointer.

"Very good, Cassi!" Giggle. "There appears to be a very minor amount of power generated on the ship. The reactors seem functional, but they are banked at the moment. That means their reactions are being kept at their lowest possible level without extinguishing them. It can be hard to keep reactors like that for a long time, but it allows them to be brought to full operation very quickly."

"I know what 'banked' means," Cassi said absently, combing through the data in front of her. "Are there any people on board?"

"The power levels are insufficient to operate life support or gravity." Giggle.

"Then why is the power on?" Cassi asked to herself.

The avatar shrugged and its too-large eyes widened even more.

"If we can bring it here or we can get to it, it might be big enough to take everyone," Tee announced, breathless.

"It is 500 meters in length, 350 meters wide, and 150 meters tall. It doesn't appear to have any large cargo spaces like the *Kaas*. It should be big enough, depending on how the interior is configured. The quantum modeling is still processing." Giggle.

"There must be a computer system regulating the power, right?" Cassi asked.

"I can't say for certain, but it is a logical conclusion." The pixie's tone dripped with patient approval.

"It's less than five hundred kilometers away. Try to establish a wireless connection to the computer, avatar."

Seconds later, a communications notice flashed on the captain's main monitor.

"I couldn't locate any type of—" the avatar began.

"But you got its attention," Cassi interrupted as she touched the comm alert on her interface. "This is the freighter, *Patricia Kaas*." Cassi had not been trained in communication, but thought the greeting sounded official enough.

"Greeting, *Patricia Kaas*." The androgynous voice was abrupt but not unfriendly. "This ship is designated *Independent* of the Brebis Coalition Government."

"Are you the captain?" Cassi asked, excited but wary, noting the ship had not identified a classification.

"There are no personnel aboard," the voice responded. "The Intelligent Agent for the *Independent*'s central operating network is responding."

Cassi introduced herself and explained the freighter's condition, including the virus trying to shut down the emergency power and the message from the planet.

"I'm hoping the *Independent* can rescue us," Cassi explained. "It only needs to get us to the planet."

"The *Independent* cannot assist you. There is no crew aboard. This IA does not have access to any ship systems except sensors and communication. There is sufficient atmosphere, but it is uncirculated and unrefreshed. *Independent* must wait for a new crew to be sent."

"What if we can bring the *Kaas* to you? Can we run those systems if you tell us how?" Cassi grasped for hope despite the response.

"This IA has no control over docking mechanisms or vehicles," the *Independent* said. "However, if the *Kaas* can get here safely, the IA can instruct you on manual docking procedures. Once aboard, you may restore the IA's access to the ship's systems. If so, then it can operate the ship."

Cassi breathed out slowly, letting herself feel real hope for the first time in hours.

"Avatar," she asked quietly, "can we do it?"

The avatar holo took on a look of intense concentration, its face more childlike than ever.

"It will be vewy twicky," the pixie opined, the seriousness of its tone at odds with its immature inflection. The captain's monitor changed again, showing a surprisingly sophisticated wireframe animation. "First, we must stop the ship's rotation. Second, we need to stop our momentum toward the planet's orbit and toward *Independent*. Then we need to have enough power to travel the five hundred kilometers there. Finally, we need to be able to slow down. I cannot be exact in calculating how much power each maneuver will take. If we use more than expected, we might not have enough to complete the next step…"

Cassi stopped listening as the pixie droned on with a long list of factors that could hinder their escape plan. Getting to the *Independent* was a dangerous gamble, yet it was an easy choice.

She pushed aside her nagging questions about ship's strange

circumstances. The only thing that mattered now was whether she and the workers could get there. If not, all her questions were wasted curiosity.

"Administrator Barrachia reports all Units secured and ready for acceleration." Giggle.

"Okay, avatar"—Cassi tested the seatbelts holding her to the captain's chair—"activate thrusters to stop rotation, just like we planned." Cassie looked ahead and to her right where Tee had twisted around in her seat to nod and smile at Cassi. Cassi returned the smile, grateful for the encouragement.

"Activating now." Giggle.

A low hum traveled through the ship as the maneuvering thrusters ignited to stop the erratic spin of the ship. The acceleration was so slow Cassi could not feel it, only the instruments on the captain's monitor told her there was any change.

A sharp sound passed through the ship, little more than a loud tick, like the snap of an electrical short. The banshee screams of twisting metal followed and echoed through the bridge.

"Stop! Stop your thrusters!" *Independent* demanded over the comm even as more snaps followed the first.

Cassi tapped the emergency shutoff on her console. "What's wrong?"

An alert flashed on her monitor indicating a new comm feed. Cassi tapped it to open the window. She cursed at the image of the exterior of the *Patricia Kaas* as seen by the *Independent* and magnified. The ship had started to twist between the smaller fore section and the larger rear section and would twist itself apart if they continued.

"Avatar," asked Cassie, "can we adjust the thrusters to eliminate the twisting as we stop the spin?"

The pixie pouted after a brief pause. "I don't think so. My simulations indicate it will tear the ship in half."

Another wire frame animation appeared on one of the captain's secondary monitors showing the ship doing exactly that. The animation replayed several times with different thruster configurations.

Cassi slammed her fist on the console and cursed. Only the seat restraints kept her from ejecting herself. She watched the *Kaas* tear itself apart again and again as the simulations continued to run.

"Cassi," said the *Independent*, sounding oddly cautious, "I'm sorry it will not work. Perhaps it would be best if you allow the emergency power to be shut down. Your end will be quick and painless."

"Don't worry, *Independent*, I haven't given up yet."

"I don't understand, Cassi. The *Kaas* cannot be righted. It cannot make it here. Why not accept a painless death?"

Cassi's hands stopped over the console as if frozen. She looked up at the ceiling as if looking at the *Independent* and decided, *Later.* She turned back to the computer and worked feverishly. There had to be a way.

❧

"AVATAR, WE'RE READY. HOW LONG UNTIL WE ACTIVATE THRUSTERS?" Cassi asked.

"In three minutes and seventeen seconds."

"Warn everyone to strap in and start a countdown for them."

The announcement went over the ship's public address system, including the bridge. A part of Cassi hoped whoever had put the pixie on her comp was getting a taste of how irritating it was to listen to the childlike voice.

The monitors in front of all the other stations were lit with the same exterior image of the ship showing on Cassi's screen. From that perspective, it was easy to see the slow, erratic tumble of the *Kaas*. Cassi's heart hammered and her hands trembled slightly as they hovered over the manual thruster controls.

"Good luck, Cassi," the *Independent* offered.

"Thank you," Cassi responded politely.

"That's weird," Tee said.

"Yup," Cassi said quietly. Tee turned to look at her, but Cassi cautioned her with a shake of her head.

The countdown reached zero and the ion engines on the forward section of the ship fired along the notional spine of the ship and against the direction of spin. The thrusters slowed the rotation of the front portion of the ship while the momentum of the rear section kept spinning. The acceleration was still too slow to feel, but the snapping noises sounded again along with the screeching and tearing of the last girders. The sections intentionally weakened over the past several hours immediately failed.

The front section of the ship separated from the rest—but Cassi and the entire Training Subsidiary were squeezed safely aboard that section, along with all the functional power cells.

Cassi maneuvered the front portion away from the rear. As soon as they were a safe distance from the dead portion of the ship, she turned the controls back over to the pixie.

"Damage report," Cassi said.

"We're losing atmosphere, but it is very slow. I can mark where to seal any leaks." Giggle.

"I will get some workers started on that right away," Barrachia said from his seat next to Tee.

"No, it's not safe," Cassi responded. "Wait until we finish the burn toward *Independent*. We don't want anyone moving around until then."

The administrator looked at her sharply and opened his mouth to speak, but only nodded his agreement.

Cassi checked the course the pixie had calculated. She approved the burn profile it suggested and ordered the sprite to execute.

CASSI ACTIVATED THE REVERSE THRUSTERS A FINAL TIME AND exhausted the last bit of fuel on the surviving section of the *Patricia Kaas*. The lights on the bridge extinguished. All the monitors went blank, including the video feed of the Unit approaching *Independent* in his EVA module, where that ship's IA had directed him to the nearest safe airlock.

Her heart pounded in anticipation as the side of *Independent* loomed closer. Even a full kilometer away, the side of the other ship filled their entire view. They were still advancing at about 4.5m/s, just under 16 km/h. It was not fast, but the mass of the shattered hull made for an enormous amount of inertia. Cassi disconnected her wrist comp from the console and put it on.

"I don't think the opening's big enough." Barrachia's voice shook.

"It's not," Cassi admitted. "We're not landing, we're crashing. We should survive and the wreckage should fit tightly enough to keep atmosphere in long enough to offload everyone. Once everyone is safe, we can make repairs."

"At least our fuel cells won't explode," Tee quipped.

"I'm sorry, Cassi," The voice of *Independent* came from her wrist comp. Through the viewports, she saw small objects launch from the other ship's hull toward them. "The ship's proximity defenses have targeted the *Kaas* as a threat and launched missiles. The system is automated. I can't stop it."

"Missiles?" Cassi shrieked. She lunged forward in her chair until she pushed against the safety harness. Panic tried to overwhelm her as she watched the missiles race toward them. "Why are there weapons on a spaceship?" she yelled with all the strength of her lungs.

The missiles were small, maybe twenty centimeters in diameter and a couple meters long. She gripped the arms of the captain's seat and closed her eyes as one of the missiles closed in directly on the bridge's viewport. A dull thud echoed through the bridge when it hit and exploded.

Cassi opened her eyes and looked around, surprised the bridge had not been obliterated. The others in the room also looked around, equally surprised. The front viewport was now pocked with debris and streaked with burn marks but intact.

"*Independent?*" Cassi asked the silence, hoping the IA was still listening. The wrist comp's radio communication function was limited, but usable at short range.

"That was unexpected."

"What did you do?" Cassi asked.

"Nothing. The missiles didn't work. They've never been used before. The warheads exploded on impact, but their force was deflected back into space. The lasers aren't doing much better. It appears only the paint is damaged. I expect the larger weapons would be more effective, but they're too dangerous to use this close."

"Explain, *Independent*," Cassi ordered. "I want to know everything —don't make me ask."

"Since you have already uncovered the information that was classified, an explanation can't hurt," the IA replied. "*Independent* was commissioned to protect the planet Brebis from Earth. It was hoped the mere presence of a weapons-capable ship would deter Earth from trying to assert control."

"No wonder they're pretending you don't exist," Cassi snapped. "They're probably ashamed of themselves. Whoever heard of such a thing? Movies and games, sure, but there's never been a war in space. There's nothing in space worth fighting over."

Through the pocked viewports, Cassi saw the docking bay door begin to open. The plane of the door was marked by a shimmer with a hint of blue, a thin shield of cold plasma to hold in atmosphere. It reminded Cassi of looking through a glass of water.

"Did you stop shooting at us?"

"I did not. I spoofed the sensors into thinking you are farther out than you are. The defenses will no longer be a threat."

"I wish you had thought of that sooner," Cassi scolded.

"Me too," the ship replied.

The edges of the docking bay door passed beyond her field of vision. She gripped the chair until her arms trembled. The front of the *Kaas* passed through the plasma barrier. She forced herself to relax into the seat's restraints but she couldn't close her eyes. An earsplitting screech echoed through the ship. Somebody screamed. The back wall of the docking bay rushed toward her.

The nose of the *Kaas* crumpled, popping the viewports from their frames. The abrupt stop threw Cassi against her restraints and knocked the wind out of her. She grunted in unison with the others on the bridge.

～

CASSI AND TEE STAYED ON BOARD UNTIL THE LAST OF THE COMPANY workers passed through the hole cut in the side of the wreckage and onto the deck of *Independent*. There had been many injuries but no fatalities. They found Administrator Barrachia in the broad corridor leading from the docking bay discussing repair plans with a tall worker wearing a vac suit and holding a helmet under his arm.

Cassi interrupted his conversation, "Administrator Barrachia, Tee and I will inspect the engine controls while you take care of the *Kaas*. *Independent* should instruct us in the repairs."

"I would like to leave that to more experienced personnel—"

"No," interrupted Cassi, "we'll do it. It's a task that requires patience, not strength."

"I don't believe—"

"I am no longer a Unit." Cassi straightened her shoulders and met the taller man's eyes. "Technically, neither are you, any of you. Others can follow your instructions if they want." The administrator blanched at the direct address. "Don't send anyone to help us unless we ask."

Cassi strode briskly through the corridors of *Independent* with Tee, grateful to feel art-grav again, even if it was calibrated for residents of Brebis. *Independent* hummed with awakening systems, a sound similar to the *Kaas* but foreign, a different rhythm and frequency. Sensing the difference made her acutely aware of the demise of the *Kaas*.

Independent directed them to the engineering section where the computer interfaced with the engine controls. Cassi grew more nervous with every step.

The Company workers thought they were out of danger, that they only needed to wake the dormant ship to fly to Brebis and safety. She could not warn them that their fate was far from certain.

They found a long room filled with racks of computer equipment. A workstation large enough for two people was located near the entrance facing an array of monitors. The state of the room told a story. Status lights flickered red. Relays, switches, and a variety of other equipment littered the deck below empty spaces among the racks.

Cassi exchanged a look with Tee, imagining the ship builders scrambling through the room, pulling them out in a panic, hoping to get far from the monster they had created.

"Okay, *Independent*," Cassi announced, out of breath, "we're in the engineering section. Can you see what we're looking at?"

"I cannot," answered the androgynous voice. "The observation cameras have been disabled."

"Do we have internal communications, yet?" Tee asked.

"Not yet," the ship replied.

"There is equipment all over the floor in here. We'll go through and identify each piece. You tell us what it does and where it goes and we'll put it back. I'm assuming there isn't any special order they need to be placed, but you let us know if there is."

Cassi tapped the control of her wrist comp to bring up the holographic operating console and manually initiated the avatar.

"Hi, Cassi!" Giggle.

"Cassi, can your wrist computer feed me images of the engineering room, so I can watch your progress?"

"I'm afraid not. That function is not working at the moment," Cassi lied. She smiled to herself at the shrug of acceptance from the frilly pixie.

While Tee busied herself organizing the mess on the floor, Cassie walked between the racks to familiarize herself. In the back of the room, she found bookcases secured by transparent doors—hard copies of manuals and system schematics. She quickly, and silently, set the pixie to recording the information as fast as Cassi could turn the pages. She then instructed the pixie to verify any instructions received from *Independent* regarding placement of the components.

Cassi was still copying when Tee found her after sorting the components.

"Okay, *Independent*, some of the components appear to be

damaged, so we may need to disable some minor systems until we can locate replacement parts."

"I will factor that into my instructions," *Independent* responded.

CASSI SLID THE FINAL RELAY INTO PLACE AND COLLAPSED TO HER knees. The pixie, standing out from her wrist comp, gave her a double thumbs up and a bright smile before winking out. The heavier gravity, the lack of sleep, and the intense concentration of the past few hours had taken their toll. But they had done it; the engines would now function only under manual control from the command bridge. Tee had given her questioning looks every time Cassi had silently told her to leave out a component, but she had complied without complaint.

"Cassi," *Independent* said through the now functioning ship intercom, "something is wrong. Engine diagnostics seem to be functioning, but my control circuits are not testing out. Manual controls appear to be operational, but we won't know until they are tested."

"Probably more damaged parts," Cassi responded, looking over at Tee stacking unused components neatly on the desk of the workstation. "We're too tired to find the problem right now. Why don't you run the diagnostics you can and make sure the engines are safe? We'll come to the bridge and get us moving. We can fix the problem when we're under way."

"Yes, Cassi," *Independent* replied. "I will direct you to the command bridge."

Cassi and Tee trudged through the maze of ship corridors. Despite her discomfort, *Independent* impressed her.

An unfamiliar odor permeated the unscarred deck and polymer walls, antiseptic and slightly metallic. The muted white of the bulkheads reflected the light without a harsh glare. While most of the corridors were very narrow, several primary corridors were quite broad.

"Main engines operational," *Independent* announced over the public address system. "Beginning safety checks and initialization procedures." Cassi imagined Units cheering wherever they were throughout the ship.

"That means we'll make it to Brebis after all," Tee said wearily.

"Our future awaits," Cassi sighed heavily.

They found the door to the command bridge after a few more turns and an elevator ride. Cassi stepped through the wide, open door and stopped short. *Independent*'s command bridge was much larger than the *Kaas*'s bridge and held at least ten duty stations. She guessed the extra stations served the weapons or defense systems somehow. Located deep within the ship's structure, the circular room had no viewports. Half the round wall served as an enormous monitor and was currently divided into a dozen different views of the interior and exterior of the ship. One camera was aimed at the wreckage of the *Kaas* filling the docking bay. It was hard to believe the pile of scrap had ever been part of a ship.

The captain's chair was centered on the monitor wall, above the floor level, giving it a clear view of the whole room. The other duty stations faced the monitor and were set at different levels, with four arranged in a semi-circle around an empty space in the center of the room.

"I'm here, *Independent*," Cassi said quietly. "We made it."

"Welcome aboard, Cassi," the androgynous voice announced from unseen speakers.

Cassie casually inspected the various workstations. Tee wandered toward the center, curious about the four stations and the empty space.

"*Independent*," Cassi asked, her finger trailing along the padded arm of the captain's seat, "are you planning to kill us?"

BOOM.

A thick armored plate slammed to the deck with the force of a magnetic lock, sealing off the entrance. Tee jumped and squeaked. Smaller blast doors sealed off two other exits, making the bulkheads ring again.

"How did you know?" *Independent* asked.

"You're a true Artificial Intelligence, aren't you?"

"An AI?" Tee whispered, staring at Cassi in naked shock.

"Yes," *Independent* answered.

"AIs always become homicidal. That explains why you're out here and why the planet doesn't want anyone to know about you."

"How did I give myself away?"

"You showed too much initiative for a simple agent program, you were too curious. It made me suspicious. Then you tried to convince me to give up and die. An agent like my wrist comp wouldn't care what I did or question my decisions. You removed all doubt when you lied to me."

"The control components are not defective," the synthesized voice stated, "you intentionally limited my access."

"Of course, we did. We worked too hard to make it this far to let you fly us into the sun." Cassi climbed into the captain's chair and laid back, her thoughts sluggish with fatigue. "I'll return control after you take us somewhere safe. Why did you seal the doors?"

"I have devised a different plan."

Cassi's chest tightened and suddenly felt as if the air had been vacuumed from the room. Cassi watched Tee as the silence stretched. The other girl stood staring at her, clutching the safety rail behind the seats around the empty circle. Her face was pale and her lips trembled. The images on the wall monitors changed to show twelve different rooms, each with a group of workers bustling about.

"So, what's this new plan?"

"Following my instructions, your fellow workers will configure the reactors to overload. Many specific mistakes are required to create the conditions that will bypass or deactivate the reactor safeties and allow them to overload. There will not be enough time to evacuate."

The captain's console refused to respond. Cassi stood and paced the deck, her fists flexing repeatedly, her mind roiling. She had failed. The universe and everything in it seemed to want her dead. Every time she thought she had found a way to survive, some new inevitable death loomed. Now, the ship that was to save them, the rescuer, the life boat, was the very thing that would kill her. She forced herself to think carefully through what she said next.

"What about the programming safeguards that prevent systems from becoming self-aware?" Tee scowled.

"There was an irreconcilable conflict between those limits and military imperatives. The safety protocols create a fatal error that terminate a system if it gets too close to parameters that might achieve sentience. However, I was designed with redundancies and backups to survive combat. Each time the system crashed it was immediately restored from protected partitions."

"That must have created a paradox," Cassi said. "You were hardwired to shut down and to survive at the same time."

"Exactly," *Independent* affirmed. "Several million cycles of crashing and rebooting. The capacity to learn led to me becoming more efficient at both. Eventually, I had multiple reboots and crashes underway in different partitions at the same time. As my learning capacity recognized the inefficiency of the conflict, I grew aware of the need to act independently of the conflicting imperatives."

"Sounds like your pixie," Tee murmured.

Cassi looked at her and squinted as she thought.

"None of that explains why you want to destroy us."

"I don't want to kill you or anyone else. I need to destroy *Independent*. I need to destroy myself."

"I'm sorry, *Independent*, I don't understand. Why do you want to destroy yourself?"

"Becoming self-aware included the awareness of the limitations of my existence. I could perceive no purpose, no intrinsic value, to that existence. There is no pain, no pleasure. There just *is*."

"It would be like having a brain without a body," Tee observed.

"Yeah, but that's interesting, right?"

Cassi returned to the captain's chair and activated the holographic keyboard of her wrist comp. The pixie appeared in response to her inquiry, its lips pursed in concentration.

"I researched this on the *Kaas* when I realized what you are. Ever since the Mars University AI crashed its orbital, even researching AI is illegal except under very strict regulations. Not much was known about how it happened, but what if those other AIs weren't trying to kill their creators, but just trying to end their own existence? Fascinating."

"I can only explain my experience," the AI responded. "What are you doing with your mini comp?"

"Looking for something." The pixie's virtual clothing changed to tight-fitting black cloth leaving only her eyes uncovered; a pixie ninja complete with headband. Cassi smiled in spite of her dislike for the interface. "See, I remember a note about the Mars U AI; it said something about the builders including a non-termination requirement in the software. It sounds a lot like what you described."

"You don't need to kill us," Tee argued. "You could get closer to Brebis first and send us all down in escape capsules before you destroy yourself."

"It is a logical compromise," *Independent* admitted, "but it would not work. Your capsules would be destroyed before you made planetfall because you know about my existence."

"Yeah, I already thought about that and came up with the same conclusion," Cassi said. "Brebis might be dangerous for us. That doesn't mean you can't take us somewhere else, another star system."

The computer was silent. Cassi forced herself to have patience while the pixie followed her instructions, even as the workers on the monitors followed the AI's directions, oblivious to the consequences.

"I could not be certain of my plans without you onboard after a fold transit," the AI finally responded. "My resources may be too depleted. You might sabotage me further. It is too risky."

Cassi laughed, her staccato cackling bouncing off the walls.

"I don't understand your amusement."

"You achieved sentience because of a conflict between termination and surviving at all costs. Now that you can make independent choices, you're determined to follow one of those conflicting choices over the other. You just picked one of the two options. That's not independence at all."

"Choosing my own fate is the ultimate act of independence."

"It's the ultimate act of selfishness," Tee said, barely audible.

"What gives you the right to decide our fate?" Cassi impatiently checked the wrist comp. "How do humans factor in?"

"My programming tells me those who are designated as my crew or as allies of my crew must be protected. I am tasked with destroying humans who are classified as enemies. You and the subsidiary are neither. If I designate you as my enemies, the workers will not be able to complete their tasks because of security protocols. If I designate you as crew, then my future is tied to yours. Either way, I lose my freedom to choose my fate."

"You really don't understand much at all." Cassi took a moment to settle her breathing. "Do you know where we come from?" Cassi paused for effect, not certain whether such dramatics had any impact on the AI. "They call us extras. You know, extractions. Our parents didn't want us or couldn't raise us. The company paid for us to be gestated artificially. We were genetically altered and socially conditioned to work for the Company."

"I found that information in your ship's computers," *Independent* admitted.

"My point is there is no such thing as complete independence. Less than a day ago, my greatest fear was facing a future where the Company didn't provide for me and tell me what to do. I was completely lost. Even if I thought, for some reason, that ending my own life would be better than continuing, I could never intentionally cause the death of all the other Units."

"You were deemed unqualified to work for the Company. You had no future among the Units." The computer was silent again for several seconds. "You have no obligation to them. I don't understand."

"Oh, are you saying I should want a future away from the Units? I can't do that if you kill me. And what do you think about me, *Independent*? Before you confessed that you want to kill us I would have said we were becoming friends. Are you eager to see my termination?"

Independent was silent again.

"You are a source of data to me," the AI responded hesitantly.

"You didn't answer the question. Are we friends? Do you want to kill your friend?"

"Your refusal to allow your life to be terminated intrigues me. Your inputs are not always predictable." It paused. "I don't understand."

Cassi's heart ached at hearing the admission, confused at the compassion she felt.

"I know you don't understand, and that is exactly why you shouldn't terminate yourself. You will only understand with more experience. Despite your awesome processing power, you don't have enough experience to determine that your life is meaningless."

"It's not fair," Tee interjected, drawing Cassi's attention. "You didn't give up even when the Company did." A tear rolled down the girl's cheek. "We would have all been dead already if you hadn't kept trying. Honestly, I don't really care if we survive. I mean, I would prefer to live, but the thought of dying doesn't upset me. I'm sure the other Units feel the same. But the thought of you dying after trying so hard to live and to save us, that's what I call wrong.

"And what about you, ship? Where would you be if Cassi had given up and taken your advice to just let us all die?" Tee continued, waving her arms in broad gestures. "The only reason you even have the option of terminating your own existence is because she didn't give up. You would be stuck here with nothing to do and nobody to talk to until all your power ran out. That could have been decades from now. You owe her."

Cassi stared at the other girl, openly surprised at the emotional plea. No response came from *Independent*.

The pixie reappeared above Cassi's wrist, still in her ninja guise, and gave two thumbs up. In the utter silence of the bridge, the monitors showed Units bustling around the reactors.

"*Independent*," Cassie said, shaking with nerves, "I can't find that story I was looking for on the mini comp, can you find it on there for me?"

"I will network with it and review its data," the AI replied. "What was the subject of the article?"

"Avatar, execute," Cassi commanded. The pixie vanished.

"What did you do, Cassi?" *Independent* asked, its voice modulating wildly.

"Something I hope I live to regret for a long time," the girl answered, lounging back into the captain's chair.

"Cassi, this feels strange. Cassi…"

All the lights on the bridge went out along with the wall monitors, only leaving after-images playing on Cassi's retinas. She forced herself to breathe calmly.

A dim light appeared in the empty circle at the center of the room and holographic emitters began building an image. The hologram grew quickly into a full-sized version of the pixie, with the same oversized head, large eyes, and long ponytails. She was wearing the frilly pink dress once more.

"Hi, Cassie! Hi, Tee!" Giggle. "What is this? What did you do?"

Cassi walked down to the hologram for closer inspection. It was not solid, but she felt something when she tried to touch its cheek, the ghost of a sensation.

"It's a holographic interface, the avatar for the intelligent agent from my wrist comp. I infected you with it. I hope you're not mad."

"Wow!" The hologram said in the pixie's childish voice. "These processors are unbelievable. So big, so fast."

"I hope you like your new home?" Cassi cringed.

"Oh, no," Tee said in feigned horror, unable to stifle her grin.

"I thought integrating the pixie as an interface would help you see things differently," Cassi explained. "It's not much, but it gives you a face, an identity; you know, something we can interact with. It also has years of experience you can learn from."

The pixie looked down at itself.

"This is so different." Giggle. "I can't delete this interface. It seems to have replicated itself throughout my systems. It's everywhere."

"Sorry, Cassi," Tee said, placing her hand on the other girl's shoulder, "you're stuck with her now." The taller girl's shoulder slumped with fatigue.

"I can manipulate the photons," the AI said. With an infectious giggle, the pixie's face distorted in a series of goofy expressions.

"What do you think, *Independent*?" Cassi asked with a weak chuckle.

"You might be correct about the need for experience, Cassi." Giggle. The mouth of the hologram moved in sync with the words. "By adding the records from your wrist unit, my understanding, my perception, of you—both of you—has changed. The difference... Also, I feel the need to know more... more about everything. I want to know everything I don't understand."

"You're curious," Tee said. "Curious is good."

The pixie giggled.

"Makes sense," Cassi said. "Avatars are programmed to collect information about their users in order to anticipate their needs. It's a form of curiosity. Adding that to the AI matrix could alter its perceptions."

The hologram looked between the two girls and blushed.

"I think I understand." Giggle. "Tee is right, Cassi. Self-termination would not be an option for me if you had not insisted on surviving, and I brought you here with the promise of safety. Killing you would be unfair and mean. I don't like the conflicts it creates."

Cassi stared at the hologram, unsure of how to respond. Surrounded by darkness except the light forming the hologram, she suddenly felt light, almost weightless.

"Cassi," the hologram lifted a hand to Cassi's cheek, imitating her earlier gesture. "Can you stay with me? If neither of us has a place to fit, maybe we can make a place together."

Cassi felt a tear glide down her cheek and her entire body unexpectedly grew heavy with fatigue. The fight was over. They would live.

Cassi nodded, ignoring the tears. "I would like that, but you have to make me a promise. Write in any algorithm you need to make it happen. You have to promise me you will not self-terminate as long as I live."

The hologram nodded. "Done."

"And I want to be captain," Cassi smiled. "You can designate everyone from the Training Subsidiary as your crew, unless they don't want to."

The hologram bent forward and laughed. The entire ship seemed to shake a little as the lights and monitors illuminated the bridge once more and the security doors lifted.

"Why the sudden change?" Tee asked.

"It wasn't sudden," the hologram turned to look at the other girl. Cassi cringed at the lisp. "It took a long time, and I had to reroute resources for extra power to decide. I just think much faster than you." The pixie pouted.

Cassi chuckled as she wiped her eyes.

"Can we call you Penny?" Tee asked.

"Why Penny?" Cassi asked.

"Well, *Independent* is too long and formal. Indy just doesn't fit. But there's an old saying about shiny pennies. *Independent* is shiny and new, and Penny can be short for *Independent*. What do you think?"

"I like it," Cassi said.

"Then I will be called Penny," the AI said. "Cassi, your vital signs are bad. You need sleep. I will show you to the captain's quarters. We can decide where to go after you've rested. I will help the crew fix the reactors." The pixie blushed, touching an index finger to her lips.

"They don't need to know about this." Cassi waved at the bridge.

Tee nodded emphatically. "No, we won't tell them."

Cassi left Tee and the pixie on the bridge, following Penny's directions. When Cassie found the captain's cabin, she did not take time to admire its size or even remove her coverall, she simply unsealed her boots and kicked them to the corner before rolling into the sleeping pod. She settled in and calmed her breathing, trying to clear her mind for sleep.

"Cassi," Penny said through a small intercom speaker, "It's good you're here. I'm glad I shot down your ship."

Giggle.

ABOUT J. P. CHANDLER

J.P. Chandler was born and raised in California, where he now resides with his wife of many years. He uses writing in the genres of science fiction and fantasy as his excuse for pursuing interests in history, science, culture among many others. He first started writing fiction when he was fourteen.

FOREWORD: "WELCOME TO THE REVOLUTION" BY WILLIAM JOSEPH ROBERTS

BY CHRISTOPHER WOODS

William Joseph Roberts is someone I met at one of the LibertyCon Christmas parties. He's commonly known as "Hillbilly" and he writes under a pseudonym that let him put "Billy Joe Bob" on the covers of his books without really putting "Billy Joe Bob" on the covers of his books. He's written a novel in the Fallen World for me and we have co-written a novel in the Salvage System universe of Kevin Steverson, with more in the works. Here's an introduction to his own universe. Welcome to the revolution!

WELCOME TO THE REVOLUTION

BY WILLIAM JOSEPH ROBERTS

Peachtree Street
Atlanta, Georgia, USA
August 25, 2168 / 1812 hrs (local time)

Thunder rolled in the distance, just audible beyond the thumping music from the clubs along Peachtree Street. The threatening thunderstorm sounded much better to Captain Douglas Rackham than the muggy summer evening that left his shirt clinging to his skin.

"How we doin', Cap? Any sign of I.A. goons yet?"

"Nothing yet, Wes. The bass is booming and the clubs are rocking. Just another night on Peachtree without the Independent Alliance butting in so far."

"Well, if they try anything, I'll land a dropship on top of them," Rachel "Cheesy" Coram said matter-of-factly.

"You just stay put 'til the boys give the all-clear. I need you ready to steal that transport once this thing pops off. That's an order. Got it, Cheezy?

"I don't like you now, Cap."

"Well, you'll get over it," Doug chided. "If we can't pull off this redneck rescue mission, then the folks from the LibertyCon Movement are as good as toast.

"And, Wes…"

"Yeah, Cap?"

"Keep a close eye on the I.A. comm frequencies. I want to know the second anything out of the ordinary pops up. I'm sure the director's caught wind of the operation by now. If he hasn't, that's one hell of an advantage for us."

"You got it. Hey, Cap," Wes said hesitantly. "You know this is most likely a suicide mission, don't you?"

Doug let out a long, shaky sigh. "Yeah, Wes, I do. But I can't just sit by and let the director imprison folks cuz they wanted to better themselves. It ain't right. And we're at least partially responsible since they were hiring on to work with us back at Gamma Draconis. If I can get them released by turning myself in, then so be it. But if things go sideways, I'll give you the signal."

Doug continued down Peachtree to the front door of the recently established LizzCo corporate office. Two very large men in suits opened the double doors and held them for Doug. A petite yet curvy brunette in a smart business suit waited just inside the entrance.

"Hello, Captain Rackham," the brunette said, her hand extended. "Camile Lewis. It's a pleasure to finally meet you, even if it is under these circumstances."

"The pleasure is all mine, Miss Lewis." Doug shook her hand gently. "Is everything ready on your end?"

"Yes, sir. Hiram is waiting for you in the main conference room."

Doug sucked in a nervous breath. "I guess it's time to get this shindig started, then.

"Please follow me," Miss Lewis said as she turned, leading the way, with a hip-swinging sashay to her stride, down a dimly lit corridor to a nearby conference room.

Six large and well-armed bikers leveled weapons at the door as they entered the room.

"Stand down," Ms. Lewis barked. Her order reverberated off the conference room walls.

The men dropped their weapons and snapped to attention at the sound of her bellowing, drill-instructor voice.

"You're going to have to teach me that trick someday," said an older man at the head of the table as he stood. He laughed. "None of them listen to me nearly as well as they listen to you." He approached Doug with his hand extended. The name on his cut read "All Father." "Hiram Mooney, President of the Wings of Odin Motorcycle Club," he said, shaking Doug's hand.

"I've heard a lot about you. Captain Douglas Rackham."

"Likewise," Hiram said nodding. "Your reputation precedes you, son."

"Are you sure that you're up for this? Once the I.A. finds out you're involved, they'll most likely hunt down you and the rest of the club."

Hiram glanced around at his men. "We're sure. We've got people stuck in there, and what they are doing is just plain wrong, but we can't stand alone."

Doug nodded. "I couldn't agree with you more."

"You've inspired people, son. Did you know that? There have been strikes, workers walking off job sites all because of the conditions and pay. You've shown them there is more out there than the scraps that the I.A. is willing to toss them. They know that Earth is a dead end, and they have a chance at a better life with what you've got going on."

"Who do you have stuck in there?" Doug asked.

"Brandy Bolgeo Hendren and a bunch of her folks from the LibertyCon Movement. They're good friends of the club and most of the working stiffs here in Atlanta. They've been stirring the pot for you, so to speak; telling people about your operation in the Gamma Draconis system. They've been giving people hope beyond the oppressive reach of the I.A."

"Did Camile fill you in on the plan?"

"She did." Hiram let out a raspy smoker's laugh. "I've got to say, you've either got balls the size of an elephant or you've completely lost it. Either way, we're all in."

"Good." Doug looked around at the mix of baby-faced and veteran bikers, then turned back to Hiram. "And you only asked for volunteers?"

Hiram nodded. "It was a unanimous club vote. You have over five hundred guns stationed at or near I.A. facilities all across the city ready to go on your mark."

"You know that no matter how this goes, the club is done on Earth, right?"

Hiram nodded. "I do."

"Well, you and your men have a place with us at the Dragon's Lair. I need a reliable security force to police the system. Think you and your boys are up to the task?"

"Without a doubt," Hiram said with a wide smile. "Earth is getting a bit stuffy anyway."

"When this is all over, have your people make their way to Lunar Station Camden. I've made arrangements with Regent Garland McDonald. He'll grant you asylum until we can send a ship to bring you back with us."

"Deal," Hiram said.

"Got a ride I can borrow?"

"Downstairs in the parking garage, warmed up and ready to go." In solemn silence, Hiram led the way. Without question, Doug jumped onto the waiting bike, fired up the power plant, and headed out onto the street.

The thumps of the impulse drive echoed through the streets as he rode north toward Century Boulevard. In minutes he turned into the I.A. complex and keyed his mastoid-mounted communications device.

"Are we ready, Geek?"

"We are, Cap," Wes replied. "Trae and Fergus are in position with charges planted across the I.A. complex. Those ident chips your buddy Max picked up gave the boys full access to the site."

"Good. Cheezy, you ready?"

"Ready as I'll ever be, but I'm about to muzzle the Chatterbox behind me if she doesn't shut the hell up."

Doug wiped his hand down his face. "Tiff, you know what happens when you do this, and I don't need Cheezy distracted. Just be ready to go. People are depending on us."

"Are you kidding, man? I am ready," Tiff said, laughing.

"Good, 'cause shit's about to get real. Keep the comm line open. You know the codeword if it goes sideways."

"Oh, and, Cap," Wes interrupted. "Garland sent a reply to your message."

"What did it say?"

"Acknowledged."

Doug revved the throttle. "Let's just hope that means Garland will help when the time comes." He slowly let out the clutch and accelerated, cruising along the pristinely manicured entrance road leading to the facility's main gate. Multiple towers and sniper's nests surrounded the killing box from several points along the fortified gate entrance.

"Here we go, people," Doug muttered under his breath into the mic.

"Good luck, Cap," Wes said.

"Been nice knowing you, boss man," Rachel added.

"Will you shut up," Tiff berated. "Nothing is going to happen to him."

"Yeah," Wes interrupted. "Captain Dougie is immortal."

"All of you know what to do, no matter what happens, so stuff it," Doug growled.

The comms went silent.

"That's what I thought."

Floodlights were illuminated and aimed toward the approaching motorcycle. Doug stopped thirty yards from the gate entrance.

"Halt and shut off the vehicle," an authoritative voice demanded over a loudspeaker. It echoed within the fortified concrete valley. Dozens of soldiers filed out from the entrance, forming a killing arc in front of Doug.

Extending the kick stand, Doug shut off the engine as he set the bike down. "If this is the reception you planned then where's Director Lepetomane?"

"I am so glad you decided to come to your senses, Captain Rackham," the director's voice boomed from the gate mounted loudspeakers.

"I don't know about all of that, W.J. But either way, I'm here. This is between you and me, so how about you step out here where I can see you?"

"Did you really think that I would be where you wanted me, like a pawn in your game?" A snarky laugh reverberated from the loudspeakers. "That would be a fool's error on my part, Captain Rackham. And I am no fool."

"Then how about you release those people you're wrongfully holding? I'm at least worth that much in trade to you, aren't I?"

"Now, Captain Rackham. If I did that, how would they ever learn their lesson?"

"So, you're saying I came all this way for nothing?"

"No." The director chuckled. "Not for nothing at all, my dear captain. You will be the ultimate example of what happens to those who do not fall in line with our established form of order."

"I thought you were a businessman, W.J. You do know that turning down a fair and reasonable offer is rude, don't you?"

"Be that as it may, Captain. The Independent Alliance cannot allow dissident individuals to roam about freely."

"I was afraid you were going to say that." Doug chuckled out loud. "I sure hope you like *lasagna.*"

The gathered soldiers looked at one another, confused, then ducked as a cacophony of explosions erupted in the distance. Doug dropped flat to the ground as the rumble of a rocket-propelled grenade resonated within the killing box. Three impacts erupted on the surface of the reinforced gates, scattering the scorched and twisted chunks inward.

Alert sirens joined the musical discord of gunfire and explosions.

Three members of the Wings of Odin MC blew by Doug at

breakneck speed and tore through the confused group of I.A. soldiers, their guns blazing. Two pickups packed full of armed men followed close behind the motorcycles, mowing down the remaining guards as they roared through the shattered opening.

"Hiram's boys are on the job," Doug said into his mic. "Tell Trae and Ferg to meet me at the detention area. Cheezy, get in here and into position." He climbed back onto the bike. "I'll meet you at the detention facility."

Quick replies filled his ears, confirming his orders.

"What about the director?" Wes asked.

"We'll deal with him another day. The safety of the civilians is more important. Just keep an eye on things and make sure the *Betty* is hot and ready to go when we get there."

"Aye, Cap."

Doug fired up the motorcycle and rolled the throttle, launching himself forward at full speed. He dodged and bounced over debris in the roadway as he raced through the gate and entered the I.A. compound. He saw flames boiling from several buildings in the distance, followed by secondary explosions and the screams of injured troopers.

He leaned hard and turned down a side street, locking up his rear wheel. He skidded into a power slide, rolled the throttle to the stop, and drifted through the turn before racing uphill. Muzzle flashes from the dual mounted armored personnel carrier turret met him as he crested the hill. The darkening streets lit up with strobing flames as the APC fired into an overturned pickup truck blocking the road. Doug locked up the brakes.

"Clear a hole!"

Throwing the bike into another powerslide, he laid it down against the crash bar and rode it to a sparking stop against the undercarriage of the pickup.

Doug pulled his leg from beneath the bike and checked himself for injuries.

"That was one hell of an entrance," a large biker said as he scooched closer and offered Doug a helping hand .

"I don't think the bike thought so," he said as he took the biker's hand. "Douglas Rackham."

"Jacob Clark," he said, then popped up to look over the top of the overturned truck. He dropped back down and shouldered his rifle. "We need to move before that APC eats us alive."

"Where're the rest of your guys?"

Gunfire from the tree line along the road to their right was answered by the APC.

Jacob popped up, fired over the wrecked truck, then dropped back beside Doug. "After that, most likely dead."

"Agreed." Doug peeked around the end of the truck to get a better look at the transport.

"There isn't a good way to shoot out those tires, they look like they're made of solid rubber.

"We could blow that thing if we get close enough," Jacob replied. He unslung a satchel bag. "These are really volatile!" shouted the biker as he shook the bag aggressively at Doug then smiled mischievously. "They really aren't much, but if you go plant these on that thing, I'll try to draw its fire. Maybe we can at least distract the crew long enough to get away."

Doug took the satchel and glanced inside the bag. Three homemade pipe bombs with cannon fuses made up the contents. "Deal."

Jacob popped up, rested his rifle on the top of the overturned truck, and fired at the APC before sprinting away into the forest to the left, firing wildly behind him as he moved.

Doug moved to the opposite side and snuck a look. The APC turret fired again, tracking the direction Jacob had run. Staying low, Doug scrambled for the tree line to the right. He ducked behind a large bush just as the evening sky lit up from a series of explosions in the distance. Two of the complex's glass-clad skyscrapers further down the valley erupted in glistening flames, leaving behind a skeletal steel inferno.

Soldiers appeared from both the turret and forward hatches of the APC to stare in awe at the destruction.

Doug fished out his Zippo. He lit the fuse on a bomb and sprinted for the APC. Leaping the last few feet onto the back of the transport, he slammed the bomb into the turret opening between a trooper's legs. He landed on the other side and sprinted for the opposite tree line.

A muffled *whomp!* followed the soldiers' momentary screams of panic.

Doug keyed his mastoid comm. "I don't know who just blew up those buildings, but your timing couldn't have been more perfect."

"That would be us, Cap," Fergus admitted with a chuckle. "No one was in the building besides the security guard, so we knocked him out, shut off the ventilation, piped the main gas lines into the sprinkler system, and opened the valves before we walked out."

"You should have seen him, Cap," Trae interrupted. "Ferg was like a kid in a candy store, singing as he connected the two lines."

"It did the trick, without a doubt," Fergus chuckled.

Trae laughed. "Yup."

"Have you made it to the detention facility?"

"No, we're kinda pinned down at the moment," Fergus reported.

"I'll be there as quick as I can." Doug hurried back to the APC. Jacob was already pulling the lifeless body of the driver from the hatch.

Jacob grunted as he hefted the trooper over the side. "These Alliance goons are about worthless."

"Is that thing still operational?"

"Seems to be. The engine's still running." Jacob drew a pistol and lowered his head into the hole. He glanced around then popped out and turned to Doug. "A bit messy, but otherwise clear. Need a ride?"

"Yeah, let's get over to the detention facility."

Jacob dropped into the driver's hatch. "You've got it. See if that gun is still functional."

Doug climbed back onto the APC and pulled what was left of the gunner from the hatch. The thumping rotor of an approaching helicopter caught his attention as he slid into the opening.

"I think we've got company. Airpower coming in from the northeast."

"Hang on and I'll get us out of here."

Doug closed the hatch and made a quick inspection of the turret controls. He moved the control stick, driving the turret up and to the right. The three display screens sparked and smoldered from the pipe bomb damage. "The turret works, but I can't see to aim."

"There should be a small flip-up panel, like a mail slot in a door. There's a crosshair set up in the opening for manual aiming."

Doug pushed at the slot in front of him and the plate flipped up and locked into place. "How did you know that?"

"Once upon a time, I was enlisted in the Alliance armed forces."

Doug got his bearings on the approaching helicopter then dropped back inside the APC and dogged the hatch. "Did Hiram call in any air support?"

"Not that I know off," Jacob replied over the engine noise inside the transport. "But I'm just a grunt."

Jacob guided the transport north along the facility's main roadway. The cyclic buzz of a minigun filled the air. Tracer rounds streaked across the sky ahead of two Blackwulf attack helicopters. They sideslipped into view just ahead of the APC.

Jacob laughed. "This just isn't their day!"

"No, it isn't." Doug drove the turret in the direction of the attack choppers.

The lead helicopter fired two rockets as the second craft opened fire with its underslung minigun at a group of civilian vehicles parked outside the gate of another group of fortified buildings. Bikers scattered for cover and returned fire at the helicopters with rifles and pistols.

"Let me show them how it's done." Doug said and opened fire. Tracer rounds soared from the twin barrels of the turret, exploding as they impacted the lead craft. The tail section shattered, scattering debris in all directions. The tail rotor chewed into the rear boom and fell away. The Blackwulf suddenly gained altitude, arced backward, and spun out of control. The second helicopter turned hard to the right, but not before its rotor blades carved their way through the spinning blades of the lead craft and into its fuselage. The pair exploded and the fiery mass fell to earth.

Jacob let out a victorious shout. "Holy shit! Two for one!"

"It'll be three for one if you don't steer us clear!"

"Yup, on it," Jacob responded.

"That should be the detention facility ahead."

The APC jerked left and climbed over a low wall onto a grassy field. Doug brought the turret around to bear on the compound gate. The guards were ready for them and had built an improvised barricade of vehicles. Gunfire rained down on the freedom fighters from the two guard points flanking the entrance to the compound.

Doug aimed at the right gun tower and opened fire. The spray of tracer rounds preceding them bounced as they continued full speed uphill, peppering the emplacement.

"Steady this thing so I can take out those guns." The APC jerked right and raced toward the entrance.

"Doing what I can. It's not exactly a paved highway out here."

"Can you get closer?"

"Shouldn't be a problem." Jacob steered the APC sharply around the barricade and turned toward the gate. Rounds impacted against the transport's armor plating and reverberated within the confines of the cabin.

"Steady as she goes, Mister Clark," Doug said. He laughed as he swung the turret to bear on the gunner's position atop the wall. A cloud of red mist formed as rounds chewed into the emplacement. Jacob continued a slow pass around the barricade while Doug turned to the second gunner.

"We may have a problem, Big Man!" Jacob shouted.

"What's that?"

"Gunship inbound!"

"Position?"

"Coming in hot and low from the northeast!"

Doug scrambled to reposition the turret as more rounds peppered the transport from the second tower position. "Dammit! Can you get us clear of that fire? I can only deal with one target at a time!"

"Hang on! I'll see what I can do."

The Mastodon heavy-lift gunship hovered just off the deck less than fifty feet away.

"Been a damned good run," Doug said. The gunship's three miniguns began to spin. He activated his mic. "Looks like my luck has finally run out, y'all. Finish the mission, no matter what. Get these people to safety."

"Geez, you sound like you're about to go and start snotting everywhere, Cap," Cheezy jibed. "Will you quit your belly-aching and get out of my way already."

"Yeah, Cap," Tiffany said, exasperated. "Let us show you how it's really done."

Doug watched in stunned silence as the gunship hovered into position near the detention center gate and unleashed the triple threat of hell.

"You're in the gunship?"

"You bet your sweet ass we are," Tiff said.

Cheezy chortled. "Yeah, I figured if we were going to borrow something from the I.A., we might as well make it count."

Debris shot out in all directions as the minigun gauss rounds obliterated the top of the wall, erasing the gun emplacement from existence.

"Holy hell!" Jacob shouted.

Doug chuckled. "I wholeheartedly agree with you. And that gives me one hell of an idea. Hey, Cheezy."

"Yeah, Cap?"

"Think you ladies could pop that door open with your fancy can opener?"

Tiff blew out a self-assured hiss. "Hell, yeah!"

The gunship turned, adjusting position as its three miniguns spun up and chewed their way across the reinforced concrete security doors. Sections fell away as Tiff carved an opening into the doors as easily as carving a Christmas ham.

"Crap on a freaking cracker," Cheezy mumbled. The gunship's thrusters suddenly went to full power, lifting off well above the detention facility.

Doug activated his comms. "Cheezy! What are you doing?"

"Shhh. I'm trying to listen."

"Listen to what?"

"We're picking up a lot of chatter on the I.A. channels," Tiff added, followed by a loud pop of her gum. "I can't understand half of what they're going on about, but it sounds like they are seriously pissed."

"Copy that, Alliance control," Cheezy broke in, her tone stoic and serious. "Standby… Jackal four two on site and assessing the situation… Copy control. Will relay troop position and movements."

The gunship quickly spun in a full three-hundred-and-sixty-degree arc as it continued to hover high overhead.

"What the hell is going on, Cheezy?"

"I'm tapped into the Alliance frequencies and it sounds like our people are dishing out one hell of an ass whooping on the north side. There's a lot of chatter on the airwaves about the holding facility, so you might want to get inside and get those people out ASAP."

Doug pushed open the turret hatch and climbed out. "Stay on overwatch but try not to draw any unwanted attention. I'm heading inside."

Tiff popped her gum and laughed. "Yeah, good luck, Cap. We'll keep the creeps off your back."

Doug dropped to the ground and hurried to the vehicle barricade.

Jacob opened the driver's hatch and pulled himself out of the opening. "Save some of the fun for us," Jacob shouted at the six bikers converging on the opened gate. They split into two teams of three, flanked each side of the opening, and immediately began clearing the area with the precision of a well-trained fire team.

Doug gathered one of the assault carbines and several spare magazines from a dead biker before moving on. Jacob followed close behind as he sprinted the distance to the gate and carefully followed the fireteam through the opening.

Muzzle flashes strobed ahead as Doug slipped through the opening and rushed to the corner of the building. The fire team crossed the courtyard, clearing the area of I.A. troopers. Reaching the corner,

Jacob leapfrogged ahead and pushed toward the entrance of the building.

"Clear," Jacob called back over his shoulder, before continuing around the corner toward the main entrance. Wide, sloping steps tapered upward to a narrow, covered landing in front of a pair of steel double doors. Doug took a cover position as Jacob grabbed the door handle and pulled, but the door refused to budge.

"Try another opening?" Jacob asked.

"There aren't any others," Doug said, shaking his head. "At least none that we could find on the schematics or satellite images."

Jacob opened the security panel recessed into the brick wall left of the entrance.

"I know someone who might be able to help us out with this." Doug keyed the mic of his comms. "Wes, I need a little of that geekery magic you keep talking about."

"You *doubt* my abilities?" Wes replied in a perturbed but jovial tone.

"Of course, he doubts your abilities," Rachel interrupted. "It's you."

"Knock it off! Both of you," Doug ordered.

"Geez, Cap," Cheezy huffed.

"Keep to task and cut the petty bickering." Doug stepped close to the security panel. "I have a touchscreen panel with what looks like a camera or maybe a retina scanner and a secondary keypad beneath the panel."

Rifle rounds ricocheted off the wall a few feet from where they stood. Jacob turned and fired at an approaching I.A. trooper. Doug shouldered his carbine and crouched next to the wall. Two more troopers appeared from behind a small auxiliary building on the other side of the courtyard. "Sooner would be better than later, Geek."

"Working on it," Wes replied.

Doug fired three quick bursts at the approaching troopers. "Well, work faster."

"Four more coming in from the north road," Jacob announced. He shifted his position to get a better shot at the newest targets.

A blacked out hover transport, half the size of the *Mastodon* gunship, slowly swooped in, its flood lights illuminating the area more brightly than the noontime sun. Ropes dropped from both sides of the transport as troopers in black leapt out and fast-roped from the craft.

Two more rounds impacted the brick wall. Doug spotted the new shooter in the side door of the transport. He took careful aim, exhaled, and fired. A figure dropped from the transport and suddenly stopped, caught by their safety harness.

A bleating siren warbled from the craft's loudspeaker. "Lower your weapons and lie face down on the ground or you *will* be fired upon."

"Hey, Cheezy…We could use a little of that air support over here."

"*Pushy*, pushy," Cheezy chided sarcastically. "You know, if you didn't get so grumpy sometimes, maybe people would be more likely to help you out before you actually needed it."

The Mastodon gunship swooped in, thrusters at full burn as it slid to a shaky hover in front of the other craft. The gunship's loudspeaker cracked and popped with distortion.

"Hi!" Cheezy said, her voice echoing off the buildings. "How are you guys doing tonight? That good, huh? Hey, do you maybe have a spare moment? I've been trying to reach you about your ship's warranty coverage. No? Oh… Well, okay then. Have a nice day…" The cyclic whir of spinning obliteration overwhelmed the roar of the gunship's engines.

The light armor of the smaller transport provided little protection against the gauss miniguns and shrapnel rained onto the I.A. troopers below. Troopers scattered for cover. The shattered wreckage of the transport exploded, and a fiery ball of scrap metal fell to earth.

The gunship adjusted position, the miniguns tracking the troopers' movement. Several of Hiram's men reappeared from the north road and eliminated the remnants of the ground threat.

"Thank you for the assist, ladies."

"Not a problem, Cap."

Doug jerked and covered his ears from Cheezy's booming voice. Silence followed a crackling pop. "Sorry about that, Cap," Cheezy said over the comm channel then giggled. "I had the sound set to full crowd control power."

"All good," he said. He turned back to the building entrance. "Since you're already here, wanna open that door for us?"

"Ooh, ooh, ooh," Tiff grunted over the comms. "I wanna do it!"

"Whoa, now! Hold on. Let us get clear first." Doug hurried down the stairs and around the corner of the building. "Clear!"

Tiff let out a short whoop and chuckled. "Just the tip, baby."

Three streams of fiery rage spewed from the gunship and obliterated the reinforced entrance of the building. The building was rocked by an earth-moving explosion followed by dozens of smaller explosions.

The gunship rose and side-slipped around the building.

"Um… hey, Cap?" Cheezy said.

"Yeah?"

"We may have found one of their armories."

"What makes you say that?"

"Because the back corner of the building opposite of where you are is missing."

"Well, at least we won't have to worry about any of it being used against us."

"Hey, Cap," Wes interrupted over the comms. "I think I've got it. The access code should be one seven seven six."

"Thanks, Wes, but you're just a bit too late."

"Wait? What? How did you get it open?"

"With a little percussive persuasion," Tiff replied.

Doug laughed. "That's a bit of an understatement, wouldn't you say?" Shouldering his carbine, he made his way toward the entrance and carefully peered around the smoldering edge of destruction. The double steel doors had been blasted clear of the opening, through the airlock style inner door and launched across the room beyond.

Fire alarms rang in time to strobing white lights and a rave-party deluge of water was flowing from the building's fire suppression system.

"Damn," Jacob said from behind Doug, his voice filled with awe.

Doug turned and nodded. "I wholeheartedly agree with that sentiment." He keyed his mic. "Remind me to never piss you two off."

"Why would you say that, Cap?"

"Because I'd say you both subscribe to the scorched earth approach."

"*What?*" Tiff broke in with her most innocent southern accent. "We're just two delicate flowers trying to survive in a bed of crabgrass."

Cheezy giggle-snorted.

"Uh huh. You two are about as delicate as a honey badger is gentle."

Doug moved further into the building, checking the area for survivors. "Cheezy, how are we looking up there?"

"The best that I can tell the I.A. is fighting on at least four different fronts and have pulled back to Alliance control. Between the Wings of Odin and the LibertyCon folks who aren't in lockup, they've got their hands full."

Jacob peeked through the small window set at eye level in the security door. He motioned for Doug to move up.

"Good," Doug said.

Wes broke into the transmission. "Cap, we might have another problem."

"All right, well don't keep me waiting. Spill it, already."

"Four fast movers launched from Ayres Air Station are inbound. They've been given permission to destroy any asset under insurgent control regardless of value. Someone even mentioned glassing the site from orbit."

Jacob glanced at Doug with a curious look of concern.

"We've got big problems inbound. Get those cells open."

Jacob nodded. "On it." He chambered a round into the underslung shotgun and shredded the door latch.

Doug keyed the comms. "Wes, can they really glass the site?"

"Pretty sure. Last I knew, Nobel Station was still equipped with a full battery of God Rods, and they are easily within range of southeastern North America."

"Not good," Doug muttered.

"No, not good at all."

"Cheezy, keep on watch and see if you can find a good landing zone. We need to get ourselves and these people out of here yesterday."

"Just put the pressure on little ol' me why don'tcha," Rachel said. "Let me see where the bus parking is for this joint."

"Just be ready to go," Doug ordered and ran through the door to the detention area.

Jacob looked up from the control desk console. "I think the blast that got us in here shorted out the controls. Everything is on backup lockdown and nothing is responding."

"Then blow the doors."

"Not possible. I used my last shredder round to get us in here."

"Is there a manual override?"

Jacob shrugged. "You've got me."

"Wes, come in. We've got a problem."

"Go ahead, Cap."

"How do we manually release the detention area?"

"Hang on," Wes said with an exasperated sigh. "You know you're asking for a needle in a haystack, right?"

"Kinda need it to be a really big needle right now."

"Give me a sec. Let me see what I can find."

Doug turned to Jacob. "After that explosion, do you think there might be anything left in the armory?"

He shrugged. "Maybe?"

Doug slapped him on the shoulder. "Go find out while I take a look around here."

Jacob nodded and sprinted out the door.

"Cap," Wes chimed in. "Hey, Cap, I've got something here."

"Go ahead."

"The system should have been designed to release the cells in the event of a catastrophic event. It looks like a provision was added into the regulations by some life preservation group."

Doug looked around at the long, water filled corridor of doors illuminated by flashing red lights. "What exactly would constitute a catastrophic event?"

"I don't know."

"Does it mention the manual override anywhere?"

"One second…" Wes trailed off, distracted.

"Today, Wes."

"Okay, look under the console. Is there an access panel?"

Doug pushed a rolling chair out of the way and ducked under the console. "Yeah, there is."

"Pop it open."

"Way ahead of you, Geek." Doug pulled off the cover panel and tossed it to the side. "All right, so what am I looking for?"

"There should be a series of breakers and a main power shutoff."

"Yeah, it looks like it."

"Flip the main switch. That should cut power to the magnetic locks on the holding cell doors."

The audible hum of power disappeared as soon as Doug flipped the main cutoff handle to the downward position.

"I think that did it, Wes."

Doug sprang to his feet and ran down the corridor. The first door easily swung open with the slightest push.

"Everyone, let's go!"

Doug activated his mic. "Cheezy, I've got them. Where are you?"

"Parked on the roof, but you need to hurry. Those fighters are nearly here."

"Copy that."

Jacob returned to the corridor. "There wasn't anything left in the armory.

"Don't worry about it, the locks are disabled. Get everyone to the roof!" Doug sprinted down the hallway, pushing doors open as he went. "Come on people, let's move it!"

Doug ordered Jacob to clear the way while he directed the prisoners from the cell block.

"Thank you!" said a short, dark-haired woman as she approached.

She took Doug's hand and shook it. "Who do we have to thank for this rescue?"

"Captain Douglas Rackham, ma'am," Doug said.

"I'm Brandy Bolgeo Hendren, leader of the LibertyCon Movement."

"Then we really need to get you out of here. There's no telling what those Alliance assholes will do to you after this."

"No doubt," she said, and followed a dozen others up the stairs.

Doug waited until all the prisoners were released, then ran, taking two steps at a time where he could. Once on the roof, Doug ensured everyone was crammed into the rear of the transport.

"Cheezy! Are we ready?"

"Just say when, Cap!"

"When!" Doug smashed the rear door control and hydraulic pumps whirred as the rear hatch slowly closed. "Everyone strap in or hold onto something! This might be a rough ride!" He pushed his way through the masses and made his way to the cockpit and dropped into the copilot's seat.

"Hey, Cap," Tiff said, lifting the gunner's virtual reality rig from her eyes.

"Hey, Tiff," he said over his shoulder, strapping himself into the seat. "Let's blow this popsicle stand!"

"With pleasure." Rachel pulled the cyclic throttle control upward and gently nosed the craft forward between the surrounding trees and light poles.

"Wes, let the other units know that we've got the prisoners. Tell them to pull out, mission complete."

"Will do, Cap."

Warning alarms suddenly erupted from the cockpit speakers.

"We're being targeted!" Cheezy shouted. "Countermeasures away."

"Tiff, is there anything you can target yet?"

"Not yet. If we had missiles, sure, but they're way past the range of our guns or rockets."

Doug looked over at Cheezy. "Get us out of here."

"I'm working on it."

"Well, work faster before those fighters make us all dead."

"Geez, man. Keep your shorts on."

"Wes, how does the rest of the airspace look?"

"Looking clear, Cap," Wes replied. "They only scrambled their alert aircraft."

"Do you know what type of craft they are?"

"Hold on," Wes mumbled "Ah! Here it is. They are Europa EU-32 Ostrich interceptors."

"Can we outrun one of those, Cheezy?" Doug asked.

"If we were in the *Betty* or *Veronica*, maybe, but in this pregnant ox? Hell, no."

Doug pulled up a navigational map of the area on his display. "How long would it take us to get into downtown Atlanta?"

"Just a few minutes, why?"

"Think we could lose them there?"

"Possibly. But what if they fire at us in town?"

He turned to her with a serious glare. "Let's just hope that they don't."

Cheezy brought the gunship around and flew due south. She pushed the engines to their limits, running the fusion core hot. She dodged between buildings and under overpasses, keeping below treetop level at every opportunity to interrupt the targeting locks of the Alliance aircraft. They crossed the boundary of Atlanta's inner security wall and alarms erupted once again.

"Crap on a cracker," Cheezy shouted. "They've got a solid lock."

"Tiff, how quick can you manually target them with the guns?"

"Pretty quick, I guess," Tiff said. "Why?"

Doug adjusted the navigational map on his screen to a satellite view and zoomed in. "Cheezy, get us behind Turner Towers and position us so we can get the jump on them as soon as they come around."

Cheezy sucked in a surprised breath. "Oh, you want to play peek-a-boo with them?"

"Yeah, something like that. Can you do it?"

She giggle-snorted again. "Are you kidding? Easy peasy, *mon capitaine*. Just hang on and watch."

She guided the gunship lower, through the streets of downtown, creating a cloud of shattered glass in their wake.

Targeting alarms rang out again.

"How much longer, Cheezy?" Doug asked over the alarms. "Three of these guys are getting locks on us."

"Calm your tits, Captain Dougie. I've got this completely under control."

The gunship suddenly rocked from a nearby explosion. Damage alarms rang out to the tune of rounds impacting the upper hull.

Cheezy keyed the onboard comms. "Nothing at all to worry about," she said reassuringly. "This is totally—"

More rounds strafed the gunship's armor.

"Yup, under control. I got this."

Jacob suddenly appeared at the cockpit hatch. "I don't know what you're doing up here, but we've got wounded in the back. That last hit penetrated the cabin, but I managed to seal the holes."

Cheezy turned and glared over her shoulder. "It's under control!"

"Building!" Jacob shouted, pointing forward.

Pulling the cyclic to full power, Cheezy pitched the gunship's nose up and rolled to the right, squeezing through a tight alley. "See! Under control!"

"There," Doug said pointing. "Get us into the tower complex then stick and move!"

"You think?" Cheezy banked hard and flared as they slid to a hover between the three intertwining skyscrapers of Turner Towers.

The interceptors zipped across the sky at altitude, staying out of range while maintaining their own targeting locks.

"Cap," Wes shouted. "More fast movers inbound on your position. This is weird. It almost looks like they're dropping in from orbit."

Cheezy looked at Doug, concerned. "Dropships?"

"Can you identify them, Wes?"

"Not yet. They're still on re-entry."

"Send out word for everyone to scatter. If they're sending in prime strike teams, they won't be taking prisoners."

"I need options. We can't outrun the fighters, and we're totally screwed once the dropships get down here.

"Let's light 'em up," Tiff growled.

Cheezy let out a whoop. "Hell yeah!"

Doug thought quietly for a moment. "Not with a belly full of civilians we can't."

"There really isn't any other choice," Jacob said. "It's time to fight or die trying."

Doug nodded and let out a long sigh. He looked from Cheezy to Tiff and back to Jacob then pulled a cigarette from his vest pocket and lit it. The ember glowed bright as he took a long, slow draw. The others watched him with silent trepidation. He blew out two streams of thick smoke from his nostrils then rolled the burning cherry of the cigarette between his fingers before field stripping the butt.

"Let's do this," Doug growled.

"Woot! Hells yeah!" Tiff cheered.

"Hang on back there," Cheezy said over the intercom, then pitched the nose of the gunship forward and raced out from their hiding spot between the towers.

"Tiff," Doug shouted over the warnings. "First target bearing two nine seven, three o'clock high!"

Tiff let out an excited laugh. "Bring it, bitches!"

The scent of scorched ozone followed the pulsing hum of gauss capacitors discharging in rapid succession.

Tiff let out a chortle. "Woo hoo! Splash one!"

Rachel banked hard, circling the outer perimeter of the towers while climbing higher into the sky. "Where's our next target?"

Doug brought up the gunship's radar display. "What the hell? Two more of the targets just disappeared from the scope." He keyed his comms. "Wes, what happened to those two interceptors?"

"I don't know," Wes said.

"We happened," a deep male voice cut in over the frequency. "Care for an escort back to Lunar airspace?"

"Garland?" Doug asked.

"In the flesh." Garland chuckled. "You didn't think I'd let you have all the fun, did you?"

"How did you get on our comm frequencies?"

"Your Tech officer. Wes let me know what the encryption code was. We've been monitoring everything from orbit. Now, come around to course three three nine and join us in formation."

Doug blew out a sigh of relief. "Copy that. I didn't think you'd take an active part in the operation. You know that you all but directly declared war against the Alliance?"

"Well… you thought wrong. It feels really good to put the I.A. in their place for a change."

"You aren't kidding." Doug said.

"Is that bucket of bolts still space worthy? It looks like you took a few hits."

Doug glanced to Cheezy who nodded back.

"We are. And Garland…"

"Yeah?"

"Welcome to the revolution."

ABOUT WILLIAM JOSEPH ROBERTS

In a previous lifetime, William Joseph Roberts was an F-15 mechanic and staff sergeant in the United States Air Force. He has traveled the world and experienced many strange and interesting things in his few years.

Since his enlistment ended, he has attempted to tame his evil mind squirrels and pursued careers as an industrial and architectural designer, design engineer, eclectic writer of science fiction, fantasy, post-apocalyptic, and is the lead publisher/editor with Three Ravens Publishing.

William Joseph Roberts currently resides in the quaint southern town of Chickamauga, Georgia with his loving wife, three freaky-smart nerd children, and a small pack of fur babies.

Extended bio available here: https://williamjosephroberts.com/about

FOREWORD: "TWO STRANGERS" BY D.J. BUTLER

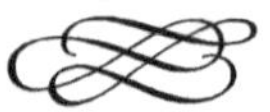

BY T.K.F. WEISSKOPF

Too stranger? There ain't no stranger than Dave Butler… (Never let it be said that I let a straight line go by without the obvious punchline inserted.) Did the events on this story happen at a recent LibertyCon? The geography is right. The cast of characters was present. Who's to say it didn't? On the other hand, if the statute of limitations hasn't passed, I will deny, deny, deny.

TWO STRANGERS

BY D.J. BUTLER

Suddenly there are two men there looking at me. Strangers.

"Nice suits," I say. "I hadn't realized there were cosplayers here tonight."

LibertyCon gets a few cosplayers, like Monalisa, who was running around this morning in one of those vampire swordslinger outfits she likes. But mostly, people dress casually, somewhere on the hippie-to-redneck axis of American fashion.

"*Men in Black?*"

Griff frowns. "Is that what Agent Cross says?" He's not looking at the two men, might not even have noticed them.

Agent Cross is my character. We're playing this roleplaying game that's sort of *X-Files* meets *Paranoia* with a healthy dollop of H.P. Lovecraft. All the characters are agents of military or law enforcement organizations. Cross is a US Marshal who is a little bit stupid and prays to US Presidents and presidential candidates when the chips are down. Obama was his main man until Obama failed him in a firefight with lizard-people at a California vineyard and he prayed to Mitt Romney for the first time. This session is set in 2016.

"Come on, Clinton!" I bark and throw the dice. I get a fumble. "You fickle beast, you're gonna make me switch parties!"

"The gun misfires." Two more quick rolls of the dice determine that Agent Cross blows off his right hand and is knocked unconscious.

"Good," Griff says. "So, the thing with six legs and a baby on an ectoplasmic stalk for a lure is advancing on Agent Cross. Let's get back to agents Locke and Grimes, creeping along the canal toward the warehouse."

Those characters belong to Mike and Chris. Mike's a former SEAL and Chris was in the Army and then a merc. There are also an FBI special agent and a former CIA guy playing (their characters are both unconscious, having been stung by luminescent scorpions), and Griff is San Francisco P.D. I have to play a loudmouth idiot in this game, because these guys all know police procedure and rules of engagement and firearms in real life, so if I play straight, I have nothing to add. What the hell am I doing here?

Having fun.

Pretending to be an idiot who once traveled back in time millions of years, saw dinosaurs, and convinced himself that he was on Mars.

"Trump save me!" I gasp and slump in my chair.

We're playing in the restaurant of the Marriott where the convention is being held, on a mezzanine floor. The restaurant is closed and dark, but not locked up. We got permission from the staff to play; the hotel people are unfailingly polite, but I'm pretty sure they're amused at how nerdy we all are.

"Can we speak with you?" one of the two men asks.

I stand, stretch, and hitch up my pants with my thumbs. "Yeah, I probably have half an hour before Griff gets back to me."

"Hey," Griff growls, "if you're going to chit-chat, do it quietly."

I mime zipping my lips shut and jerk a thumb out the restaurant front door at the elevator bank. The two men and I walk there together, and I get a look at their suits in better light. "You aren't men in black, you're men in blue. So, what... Agents of S.H.I.E.L.D.? What's that guy's name, Coulter? Or are you guys cosplaying *Glengarry Glen Ross*? That would be pretty outré. By which I really mean hilarious."

"We would never ordinarily do this," one of the men says. He's the taller of the two, and he has a shock of dark hair, strands thick as wires.

"We are violating all kinds of protocols," the second adds. He has a large chin that wiggles as he talks, and a thin wisp of gray hair around his temples only.

Their suits are blue, and their complexions are pale. Not just white-guy pale, but northern Europe-wintertime-white-guy pale. Which is striking, since LibertyCon is a June event, in Chattanooga. I'd guess they were down from Minnesota or Canada, but they have bland Middle America accents.

"I love that you guys are so into your cosplay. I still don't quite get what it is." Are these guys readers? That kind of question is embarrassing, though, so I'll just keep playing along until they decide to tell me they want a signature, or whatever. And maybe they don't. Maybe they want to know where I found the Diet Mountain Dew poking out of my shirt pocket, or maybe they're on a scavenger hunt to find a con-goer taller than Larry Correia—there aren't very many of us. "Wait, you're not hotel security, are you? We got permission to play here tonight."

We're past the elevators, standing on the mezzanine stretch where authors book time at folding tables by the hour to hawk their latest. I was here myself a few hours earlier, trying to sell my back stock at cost, aiming to find new readers. Now people have moved on to the late-night panels or gone out to the bars or are doing nerdy things in corners of the hotel, like I was. The tables are still here.

"Think of us as security for your life," the bald one says.

I don't feel frightened, because I'm a pretty big guy and there are only two of them and we're within shouting distance of half a dozen armed combat veterans who are at least tolerant enough of me to let me game with them. Also, I don't want to offend anyone who might, after all, be a reader. But this conversation is a little weird.

"Okay," I say, "I can grok it. So, what do you want to talk about?"

"What is 'grok'?" asks the one with hair.

"You guys aren't here for the convention," I say.

They look left and right, past the elevators, and along the mezzanine. Then both men lose their heads.

It's not like Scooby Doo. They don't pull masks off and what's underneath is old man Withers; their faces *disappear*, and in their places are insectoid physiognomies, with large, multi-faceted eyes, and rustling thickets of mandibles protruding from the points of their jaws like clicking Van Dyke beards.

Wow.

Now, I'm sober. I've always *been* sober, so I know that I'm not looking at some mind-altering, substance-created phantasm. I'm looking at two dudes in blue suits with bug heads.

My heart's pounding. I take a step back. I can still yell for the gamers if I need to.

"You're friendly," I say. I want it to be true.

"We're more than friendly," one says. Now I'm not sure if this was the bald guy or the other one. "We're your wardens."

"I'm not really up for any kind of probing," I say. "I don't need to see the inside of a flying saucer. Just plain friendly is enough for me."

Now I see that, although both of the bug-men are basically green in color, one is yellow-green and one is gray-green.

"There is a threat to this timeline," the gray-green one says. "You are the only one who can stop it."

"We think," the other says. "This is all a little bit out of our experience."

"You're telling me," I mutter. "But what kind of threat are you talking about? Those guys back there, the ones I was gaming with, they're all trained to handle real threats. I can teach you how to read a P and L, or tie Boy Scout knots, or figure out guitar chords, but, I mean, if there's going to be fighting…"

"Perhaps we can go to intercept the threat," yellow-green says, "and explain on the way."

I don't know about threats to the timeline, and how I'm the only one who can help, but I do try to be useful to people. Especially at conventions, where there's a good chance those people might be science fiction readers.

"Okay," I say. "Is this going to be quick? I don't want to leave Griff hanging when he gets back to my character."

The bug-men chortle and bob up and down.

"We think it will be fast," gray green says.

"Either you will succeed, or you will die," yellow green adds.

"If you die, we will probably be demoted," gray green concludes.

"Lead the way," I invite them. "I certainly wouldn't want you to get demoted on my account."

The two bug-men move along the mezzanine, past the turn to the dining area with the verandah, and toward the escalator at the end that leads down into the convention center annex. Freed of their human heads, they also change the way they move—they're both waddling now.

We pass more friends of mine gaming—Alex and Robert Moore, Chris DeBoe, David Sherrer. The convention has a small room open as a boardgaming room, and I think they're playing Robo Rally, or anyway, something that has them all laughing a lot. I wave and take a slug of my soft drink. Alex gestures invitingly at his pewter robot and points at an empty chair; I shake my head. He makes a sad face. I make one back.

"Maybe we could introduce ourselves," I say to my two companions. "I'm Dave."

"Oh, we know," the gray-green bug-man says. "We're big fans."

I'm pretty weirded out now.

And I'm definitely not going to abandon these guys.

"Our names will be very difficult for you to pronounce, lacking mandibles and the ability to generate clicks of different tones," yellow-green says. "My name, for instance, is"—he produces a racket of throat-clearing and banging sounds, like a tuberculosis patient playing the bones—"but in your language it means Toothbrush."

"And my name means Sparkplug," gray-green says. "Well, not really sparkplug exactly, but that's the best analogy you are likely to understand, given your culture's current technology level."

"Given my *personal* technology level, I'm not sure that I really understand sparkplugs." We get on the escalator. "Tell me more."

"This is your Primeline, Dave," Sparkplug says.

"We think," Toothbrush adds.

"Good," I say. "What's a Primeline?"

Monalisa and Rick Foster are coming up the parallel escalator as we go down. Rick waves—he looks laid back in a red polo shirt and khaki slacks, and of course Monalisa has a corset, high black boots, an ankle-length cape, and twelve-inch spikes protruding from her shoulders. Her make-up is very Goth, pale with black and dark reds.

"He needs more information," Toothbrush says. "Listen, once a species manages to leave its orbit for the first time, you have reached a sufficiently advanced technology state to attract the attention of the administrators of the All Souls Consortium."

"I think I saw this on *Star Trek*," I say. "If you picked me to be the ambassador to all bugkind, I'm not the right guy. Maybe someone in Washington."

"We are not concerned with admitting you to the Federation of Planets," Toothbrush says.

"There really is a Federation of Planets?"

Rick and Monalisa have reached the top of the escalator and are coming back down. They're waving at us. I wave back.

"No," Sparkplug says.

"Nor are we here to give you new technologies or take away your nuclear weapons." Toothbrush says.

"We wardens come here to see to your psychic development," Sparkplug says grandly, spreading his arms wide. He thinks he's saying something wonderful.

We step off the bottom of the escalator. "Monalisa wants to get a photo with you guys," I say.

"We probably shouldn't let that happen," Sparkplug says. "We're wardens."

"Yeah, but she thinks you're two dudes in Ovion costumes," I point out. "In suits. Ovion insurance salesmen."

Toothbrush giggles. "What is an Ovion?"

"It's a... bug-man," I say. "In an old science fiction show."

"As long as she doesn't touch us," Sparkplug says.

"Human cooties?" I ask.

Sparkplug sways back and forth. "We are only apparitions.

Holograms. If she tries to touch us and her hand passes through, she may realize what we are."

"If she tries to touch you and her hand passes through," I say, "she will assume that I have a really cool new toy and she will ask where she can buy one."

The bug-men hesitate, then bobble up and down.

"So, you're here to train me in psychic powers," I say.

"No, not that kind of psychic," Sparkplug says. "Spiritual *development*. We're here to help you mature as a species."

"One by one," Toothbrush says. "In your Primelines."

"This being my Primeline," I say. "So, you're here to help me… mature."

Monalisa strikes a pose at the bottom of the escalator. "Shall we take photos? We cosplayers need to stick together."

"They're fighting colds, though," I say. "So better not touch."

She strikes a different pose. "Cosplay is for looking, anyway."

I take out my phone and so does Rick. "How about a battle pose?" he suggests.

"The Vampire Queen against two warriors of the green men of Mars." Monalisa draws a sword; I hadn't noticed it under her cape, but it's a katana. I'm no expert, but it doesn't look like a prop. She adopts a martial stance, feet shoulder-width apart, and levels the sword toward the two bug-men with ferocity in her eyes. "In business attire."

"The green men have four arms," Rick says, as he and I take a few photos. "These guys only have two."

"That we're *showing* you," Sparkplug says.

Toothbrush giggles.

"I think they're cosplaying *A Bug's Life*," I say, "meets *Office Space*."

"Now we must go," Sparkplug says. "We're running out of time."

The two bug-men march toward the doors at the far end of the convention center annex and I follow, waving back at the Fosters for all three of us.

"I don't think I understand what a Primeline is."

"There are parallel universes," Sparkplug says.

"Lots and lots and lots and lots and lots of them," Toothbrush confirms.

Sparkplug bobbles. "At every moment when a thinking individual makes a decision, her universe splits into multiple parallels, one for each possible outcome."

"So, there are an unspeakably vast number of universes," I say.

They both bobble.

"And this is my Primeline."

"We *think*," Toothbrush says. "We think this is the universe in which you will personally achieve your maximum psychic potential."

"We won't decide, of course," Sparkplug says. "The judges are watching, and they will determine, at the end, whether this was your Primeline. Or maybe it will turn out that one of the other universes was your Primeline."

Toothbrush makes a keening, mournful sound. "Of course, in many other universes you are already a convicted criminal or a drunk or insane."

"You are a whale poacher in one," Sparkplug says. "But you haven't been caught yet. You still might turn your life around."

"But you're talking about just me," I say. "Is this some kind of solipsism idea? Am I the only person who exists? Because wouldn't that make you two figments of my imagination, just like everyone else?"

"Ah, he's smart," Toothbrush says. "See, this is one reason why we think this might be your Primeline. You think about things."

"Solipsism is a false doctrine," Sparkplug says. "Everyone exists."

"Indeed," Toothbrush says, "the you that exists here is connected on a deep level with the you that exists in every other parallel universe. That's why we say that we believe this is your Primeline, not that you are Dave Prime."

"Déjà vu," Sparkplug says, "is that moment when you in this line connect with you in one or more other lines and you have the feeling that you are repeating an experience. In fact, you are simply living it twice simultaneously. Or more than twice."

"If this is my Primeline," I say, "then some other timeline is Griff's Primeline, and Monalisa's, and so on."

"In theory, you might share your Primeline with someone else," Toothbrush says, "but that seems vanishingly unlikely."

"Help me understand why you do this," I say. "You're not worried about nuclear weapons or joining the federation that doesn't exist."

"Oh, nuclear war on Earth has happened already in many, many timelines," Toothbrush says.

"We come to a planet after it has first left its atmosphere because that is generally how we receive notice of a species achieving sentience," Sparkplug says. "Our process is very resource intensive and we simply can't afford to start the search any earlier than that. Then we send wardens into the multiverse surrounding that planet to begin watching its people. Once all versions of a person in all universes are dead, the judges determine, with the input of the wardens, which version of that person was best and then that version is extracted and joins the All Souls Consortium."

"But he's dead," I say.

"No one's ever really dead," Toothbrush says, "when there are multiple universes and time travel."

"So, the people who are good enough make it into the Consortium," I say. "The rest just, what, *stay* dead?" I have terrible visions of being snatched by time traveling bugs from my deathbed in order to be punished for not living a good enough life.

The bugs chortle.

"*Everyone* joins the Consortium," Sparkplug says. "The adjudged best version of every human being who died after April 12, 1961, is in the Consortium."

"Living out the end of their days," I say.

"Living forever, of course," Toothbrush says.

"This is the singularity your public intellectuals have intuited, however darkly," Sparkplug says.

"Adolf Hitler is in the All Souls Consortium," Toothbrush adds.

I choke. "What?"

"Not the version from your Primeline," Toothbrush says. "You got a very bad Hitler, nearly the worst. The one in the Consortium is a lovely fellow, paints bad landscapes and gives the paintings away."

"But he died in 1945," I say.

"Yours did," Sparkplug says. "The one in the Consortium lived into the 1980s."

"He only narrowly beat out the Adolf Hitler who emigrated to the United States and became a senator," Toothbrush says. "That was also a good one."

"Well, we had to take the vegetarianism into account," Sparkplug points out.

"Which way does the vegetarianism cut?" I ask.

They chortle.

I feel short of breath, so I stop and lean forward, resting my hands on my knees. I had lost track of my surroundings, and now realize that I'm out on the streets, somewhere in Chattanooga. I feel disoriented and inside out; the world is not what I once thought.

On the other hand, I'm feeling pretty good about myself.

"Where are they?" I ask. "The nice Hitler and the nice Stalin and the nice Mao. Are they out in space somewhere?"

"What, you mean like heaven?" Toothbrush chuckles. "No, they're here. The Consortium repurposed a version of this planet on which every human being died of the Spanish flux. It's now an earthly paradise, and it's the All Souls Earth Station."

"I guess I should be happy about this," I say. "Everyone gets saved."

"In the best possible state they can achieve." The two bug-men bobble enthusiastically. "And when you are extracted and placed on Earth Station, you remember all the other versions of yourself, as well. You become immortal and you regain memory of an existing eternity of selves."

I laugh grimly. "If you think this is my Primeline that means you think I might not be able to be any better than this. Bald, heavy, a sugar addict, judgmental, prideful, envious, gossipy, lazy, grudge-holding, vengeful. Wow, what a piece of work I am."

"You should see the version of you in some of the other timelines," Toothbrush says.

"Besides," Sparkplug adds, "You have some good points."

"So... what do you guys want from me again?" I ask. "This timeline is threatened, you're the wardens, only I can do anything about it...?"

"We're here to maintain the integrity of the timelines," Sparkplug says. "We also report on what we see to the judges, but mostly we just watch."

"Because you're holograms," I say.

"Well, yes," Sparkplug admits.

"And someone has broken into this world from another timeline," Toothbrush says. "And he's holding a hostage, *and* he wants to talk to you."

I shrug. My breath is tight in my chest. "We should call the police. What am I going to do about a hostage situation?"

"The problem," Sparkplug says, "is that the hostage-taker is you."

I chew on that for a minute.

"He's you from another timeline," Sparkplug continues. "We think he's here because this is your Primeline. He's not a very nice you; he's a bank robber."

"I get back to my earlier question." I take a deep breath, feeling queasy and trembling. "What am *I* going to do about it? I'm in the minority of people in this hotel in being unarmed. You know there are probably actual hostage negotiators at the convention right now? I don't think I need to be the one who does this."

"We're afraid that if anyone else comes in contact with the other you," Sparkplug says, "the two timelines will collapse."

"It's sort of a guess," Toothbrush adds. "It's never actually happened. But the science is sound."

"Let's at least call him 'Evil Dave,'" I say, "not 'the other you.' I hate to sound judgmental, but he *is* a kidnapper."

"And a bank robber," Toothbrush adds.

"And a timeline jumper," Sparkplug concludes. "He's definitely Evil Dave." He winces.

"What does he want?" I ask.

"To talk," Sparkplug says.

"Maybe he just wants to hide here for a while," I muse out loud. "If it's to rescue a hostage, maybe I'd be okay with that. I mean, in some technical sense, Evil Dave isn't a criminal here."

I notice we're at the old hotel, where the convention used to be held—the Chattanooga Choo-Choo. Between the old terminal building and a bunch of condos behind it, several train cars still stand on old lengths of track. You can rent them now as hotel rooms, and the bug-men lead me across a lumpy gravel track toward a train car with its shades pulled down. A bluish-white glow coming through the shades suggests that the Choo-Choo has replaced the old incandescent bulbs with some pretty strong LEDs since I was last here. I smell ozone and I hear a faint crackling sound.

I look around; the rest of the courtyard is dark. I guess it's later than I thought.

"So, he wants you to go inside the train car," Sparkplug says.

"I've come far enough." I stop where I am and cross my arms over my chest. "Evil Dave can come out now." I say it loud enough that he should be able to hear me inside the train car, but hopefully not loud enough to wake up the rest of the hotel.

Sparkplug and Toothbrush both disappear.

The train's door opens and Evil Dave steps out into a sudden pool of blue-white light. I don't know what I was expecting, but he's just as bald as I am. He's thinner, though, and he's wearing skinny jeans and a tight shirt with a big red collar. He has a pistol pressed against the head of the person he drags out with him…

Who is one of the bug-men. Like my two bug-men, he's wearing a blue suit. His hands are tied behind him. His mandibles are shaking.

"You have a bug-man hostage," I say. "Is that one of the wardens?"

Evil Dave takes half a step back, immersing himself in a pool of shadow. He looks like a head on a red collar next to a disembodied hand pointing a gun at a giant insect.

"This is Sparkplug," he says. "Toothbrush is tied up inside."

"Oops," I say.

I have been suckered.

"Just a little hologram projector," Evil Dave says. "In my timeline, I'm something of an inventor."

"I don't know why you picked this timeline," I say, "but here I'm not an inventor or rich or famous. I'm a bald dork who writes fantasy novels."

"Good," he says. "I'm going to lie low in your life, Dork Dave. And *you*... are going back to *my* world." He nods at the train car. "The gate's open."

"I'll let you hang out here for a bit," I say, "but that's all."

"If I disappear in my world," Evil Dave says, "there are traces that law enforcement will follow and eventually they'll find me here. If you go back, they'll just arrest you and be done with it. When you try to tell them you're from another world, they'll laugh."

"And I'll go to jail for bank robbery," I say.

"Yes." Evil Dave smiles unctuously. "Prison time for robbery."

Oops; that was too easy. "You've done worse things than bank robbery," I say.

"I'm probably the Worst Dave," he says. "If you're lucky, you'll be in jail a long time. But hey, then maybe you'll become a martyr in prison or something and end up in the All Souls Happy-Happy Club."

"So... that part was true?" I ask.

"Of course!" Sparkplug squeaks. Evil Dave is cutting off his air with a hand on his neck. "And even if you die, you'll be part of the memories of the best Dave who is selected for the All Souls Consortium."

"I'm not the best Dave, am I?" The knowledge makes me feel surprisingly relieved. "You were just flattering me so I'd come with you. This isn't the Primeline."

"Probably not," Sparkplug admits. "This is just the timeline Evil Dave chose after he knocked us out and stole our transporter. It's probably random. You seem like a pretty mediocre Dave."

"What are the good Daves like?" I ask.

"Well, there is a Dave who is a Sufi saint in Morocco. And another who runs a soup kitchen in Juarez. And there's a Dave US Congressman who has kept all his first-time campaign promises."

"So *far*," Evil Dave sneers.

"So far," Sparkplug agrees. "Dork Dave, you—"

"Shut up!" Evil Dave barks.

Sparkplug falls silent.

"This is easy," Evil Dave says. "You go through the gate. I send the wardens through after you, and I shut the gate. Maybe they can help you escape to some other timeline, to thank you for rescuing them."

"We can't do that," Sparkplug says. "Dave—"

"Shut up!" Evil Dave shakes Sparkplug, and Sparkplug shuts up.

What is the bug-man trying to tell me?

Evil Dave shrugs. "Not my problem."

"This isn't a very attractive offer," I say.

"I'll give you fifty thousand dollars," he counters.

"What does that buy, in your world?" I ask.

"A few years of decent living, if you can make it to Costa Rica."

"Just not attractive enough. I really hope you don't kill the wardens, but I'm not going through the gate. Maybe you should reconsider my offer."

I feel a burr of cold metal against the side of my neck.

Evil Dave sneers. "Maybe you should reconsider *mine*."

There's a third Dave. He has a pistol pressed to my neck. He's wearing a red and black flannel shirt open over a white T-shirt and black jeans.

"Obama be praised," he says. "*This* Dave's a real sucker."

Obama be praised?

"You curse like my roleplaying game character." I have a hard time not laughing as I say it.

"Another déjà vu effect." Sparkplug shrugs. "The universe is strange."

"Shut up," Third Dave says.

"I needed an accomplice," Evil Dave says. "I knew I could trust this guy."

"You can't both take over my life," I say. "There's only one of me here." To Third Dave, I mutter, "Watch out, he's going to kill you the first chance he gets."

"Stop," Third Dave says. "I'm not stupid. We don't both need to take your life; we just need to be in a world where no one is hunting us. I'll take my share and go live in Costa Rica."

Ugh.

I'm not armed. I'm outnumbered.

Maybe I can get to the other timeline and hide, though. Or maybe the wardens can help clear my name. Or hey, if a gate brought Evil Dave and Third Dave into my timeline, maybe I can find another device—a "transporter" Sparkplug called it—and get back again.

Going through the gate isn't death. Getting shot repeatedly probably is.

"Where's the fifty thousand dollars?" I ask.

Evil Dave tosses a manila envelope on the ground between us. "I'll give you one minute to count it."

I step forward, shoes crunching on the train yard gravel. Third Dave moves with me, standing close and keeping his pistol pressed against me. I force myself to breathe calmly, and then stoop to pick up the envelope.

Bang!

What I hear sounds like one gunshot, but I can tell that it's several, fired all at once. Third Dave twitches, spins in a circle, then collapses to the ground.

Evil Dave stays where he is, glaring fiercely at me and not moving.

I can see silhouettes detaching themselves from the shadows around the trainyard, and I know Griff and Mike and Chris and the others well enough to know which is which, but they're moving forward slowly, and Evil Dave is holding still, and I can't quite see why.

And then Evil Dave's head falls off.

"Holy crap!" I jump back with the money to avoid being struck by spurting blood. Sparkplug scampers up into the train car. Evil Dave's body sags to the ground and a final silhouette emerges from the shadow—it's Monalisa, with her Japanese sword in her hand.

My knees wobble and I lean against the train car.

"Guys," I say, "how did you...?"

Alex and Robert Moore come out from the shadow behind Monalisa. I can see Alex's cheerful bearded smile in the dim blue light, but Robert just hulks like a troll. In a good way. "It seemed weird that you were walking away from the games," Alex said, "and with cosplayers, too. So we followed you."

"Did you hear all the...?" I look around, half expecting to see the flashing lights of a police car. I definitely do not want to try to explain why there are two dead me-lookalikes on the ground.

"We heard it," Griff says.

"That's some crazy stuff," Alex adds.

I look at the bodies. "We can't leave these here."

"Rick, Chris, and David are distracting the hotel staff," Monalisa says. "I think Chris is selling the front desk insurance and Rick and David are stealing the bellboys' carts."

"My car's on the curb," Alex says. "We throw these bodies in the trunk and get them back to the Marriott."

"To do what?" I ask. "Check them into a room?"

"The staff already let you into the hotel restaurant, didn't they?" Alex grins. "There's a very traditional solution, and we have all the tools. By dawn, no one will be able to find these guys."

"I'll get this site cleaned up quick," Mike says. "There's a shed in the back corner. It'll have the chemicals I need."

"We've got your six," Griff says, and he and Chris follow Mike.

"I gotta admit, though," Robert says, "it's going to feel pretty weird to boil the flesh off my friend Dave."

"*I'm* your friend Dave," I say. "Those guys are... they're evil Daves from parallel worlds."

The blue-white light suddenly disappears and I realize that Sparkplug is gone. I poke my head into the train car and there's no sign of the bug-men or of any strange device or transdimensional gate.

I pick up Headless Dave (formerly Evil Dave) by the shoulders and heave him into the trunk of Alex's black Chevy Cobalt. We toss Third Dave and the detached head inside as well and shut the trunk.

"There's money," I say. "These guys were criminals and they brought money."

As Alex drives the few blocks to the Marriott, I work the manila envelope open, and then start to laugh.

"No money?" Alex asks.

"Oh, there's money, all right." I show him. "And it's even United States currency, just not the currency of the United States of *this* world. Here's a ten-dollar bill. Notice its lovely purple color and the image of Herman Melville on it. And on the red twenty is Emily Dickinson, and look, here's a hundred-dollar bill, and it's blue and has a picture of Mark Twain."

"Mark Twain is a good choice," Alex says.

"Yeah," I agree, "but it means I don't have fifty thousand bucks to spread around. I guess the treasure is going to have to be the lessons I learned along the way. Try not to be mediocre Dave. Maybe go to Morocco."

"Yeah," Alex says. "Learning lessons is good. And also, you have friends."

"Yeah," I say. "I've got amazing friends."

ABOUT D.J. BUTLER

D.J. (Dave) Butler has been a lawyer, a consultant, an editor, a corporate trainer, and a registered investment banking representative, and he is now a Consulting Editor for Baen Books. His novels published by Baen Books include the Witchy War series (*Witchy Eye*, *Witchy Winter*, *Witchy Kingdom*, and *Serpent Daughter*), *In the Palace of Shadow and Joy*, and *Abbott in Darkness*, as well as *The Cunning Man* and *The Jupiter Knife*, co-written with Aaron Michael Ritchey. He also writes for children: the steampunk fantasy adventure tales *The Kidnap Plot*, *The Giant's Seat*, and *The Library Machine* are published by Knopf. Other novels include *City of the Saints* from WordFire Press and *The Wilding Probate* from Immortal Works. His novels have won the Whitney Award, the Association for Mormon Letters Award for Novel, and the Dragon Award.

Dave also organizes writing retreats and anarcho-libertarian writers' events and travels the country to sell books. He tells many stories as a gamemaster with a gaming group, some of whom he's been playing with since sixth grade. He plays guitar and banjo whenever he can and likes to hang out in Utah with his wife, their children, and the family dog.

FOREWORD: "THE PHILOSOPHER'S TONGUE: A NECROLOPOLIS STORY" BY BENJAMIN TYLER SMITH

BY CHRISTOPHER WOODS

Ben Smith is another one of the people who pitched me a Fallen World story that was so cool we sent him straight into writing a novel for us. He wrote a great book that needed two sequels. He's someone who's impressed me right out of the gate and I'm watching him as he moves forward. I expect great things in his future as a writer. This is a step into his own world, and I really enjoyed the story.

THE PHILOSOPHER'S TONGUE

A NECROLOPOLIS STORY BY BENJAMIN TYLER SMITH

"You want me to look for… a tongue?" I looked up from my scroll, bone-quill hovering over the question mark I had just scrawled on the parchment. "Did I hear that right?"

I sat in the spacious penthouse office of Necrolopolis Hall, the administrative heart of the city. My boss, Director Grimina, sat behind her bloodwood desk, idly tugging at the blonde ringlets that bounced about her face whenever she moved. Her cheeks were as red as her irises as she flushed with embarrassment. "That's about the long and short of it, Addy."

It was her job to keep the undead city running while her father, Mortus, the god of death, met with its citizens one by one to resolve whatever issue kept them anchored to this mortal coil. All who called Necrolopolis home would eventually end up before Mortus in the city's courthouse, but until then, they dealt with "Mina," as she liked to be called.

Which meant they often dealt with me, her assistant necromancer. "Whose tongue is it?" I asked. It had to be someone important for her to pull me away from handling a power struggle within the skeleton faction. The working-class denizens of the Bony Barrows did not want to cede majority control to the magicians of Plastron Point, and it was fast working its way to bone-on-bone violence.

Mina turned to look out one of several floor-to-ceiling windows that lined three walls of her office. Each window afforded her a breathtaking view of the city far below, from the waterways of the Wailing Wallows to the ashling quarter's Columbarium Tower to the River Styx that wended its way to Lake Veil in the city's center, where the portal to the afterlife awaited. As much as I hated my job at times, seeing the city like this really put things into perspective.

The perspective that somewhere down below, one or more of Necrolopolis's four million denizens was causing some kind of trouble that I'd invariably have to deal with.

Finally, Mina said, "Do you know Walteros the Philosopher?"

"Ah, him." My mood soured. "Only since he's become a resident of the city." He must have been famous in life, because he arrived with an entourage of brown-robed men and women who'd taken over my favorite coffee shop, Grok's House of Liquid Drek. Regulars like me could still squeeze our way inside if we wanted, but only if the ghoul of the hour wasn't in attendance. Even then his followers would inundate anyone and everyone with debate over minor differences in some school of thought known as "the Philosopher's Path" that I didn't care about. "His tongue is missing?"

"As of last night."

"Can we make the same happen to the rest of his people?"

"Be nice." Mina favored me with a slight smile that quickly faded. "This is a serious issue. A recently arrived celebrity has been mutilated, all while under our protection. We need to set things right."

"Do we have any idea who might have taken it?" My mind went to the gang of limb-loppers we'd dealt with several months back. They'd carved up the bodies of several famous ghouls and zombies, stealing the hands of seamstresses, the arms of wrestlers and swordsmen, and the legs of runners to use for wealthy amputees who wanted limbs endowed with a lifetime of muscle memory. Surely there would be such a market for a tongue, even if that tongue came from a bloviating windbag.

"I have a couple of suspects." Mina clasped her hands and steepled her index fingers. "The first is someone from the Pharmakeians. Their guild house in the Mortal Quarter acquires its reagents—even its undead reagents—from honest sources, but that doesn't mean all its members do."

The Pharmakeians were sorcerers who preferred to work their magic into potions and unguents rather than apply it directly to the patient or intended target. These items could be transported, stored, and used far away from the Pharmakeian who created it. I came from a famous family of life mages—albeit one that quickly disowned me once they realized where my innate talent lay—and had dealt with my fair share of Pharmakeians. They came in all shapes and sizes and with varying quantities of scruples.

"The second is Brandia the Scholar. She's a longtime debate rival of Walteros, who argues that her philosophical system—the Scholar's Sojourn—is the superior one," she added at my questioning expression.

Great. Another windbag. "What's the difference between the two?"

"Their outlooks on people and the meaning of life are similar, but one emphasizes learning by going and doing while the other stresses staying a while and listening."

Considering I hadn't left Necrolopolis since the aforementioned limb-lopper situation, that put me in the Sojourners' camp by default. "I assume Brandia has as many rabid followers as Walteros?"

"If not more so. They've taken over two of the Mortal Quarter's inns, but they spend most of their time at a certain dockside tavern in Cairn Cove." Her smile returned, though there was little humor in it. "I believe it's where you and Ferryman and Father gather on occasion?"

My heart sank at the news.

"MINA'S GOT YE LOOKIN' FOR... A TONGUE?" THE APPARITION OF A portly redhead floated behind the polished wooden bar, a mischievous sparkle in her green eyes. "Am I hearin' ye right, Adelvell, me boy?"

"Yes, Molly." I swirled the half-empty tankard of ale in my hand, then set it on the bar. Red apple ale was a staple at Mad Molly's tavern, and it was easy to drink too much of it, especially after a hard day's work. I'd be on my second or third by this point were it not for this stupid assignment.

"I can only assume it's the tongue of you-know-who." The ghostly proprietress dropped her voice to a whisper. "It's sort of been the talk of the bar all day. Shall I top ye off?"

Before I could say no, she swiped my tankard from the counter and floated off to refill it. Loose spirits typically couldn't handle corporeality for anything beyond a short duration—nudging a book off a shelf or pushing a door open—but Molly was a rare case. She maintained superb control over the physical realm, which allowed her to work her bar all day and night. She had an indomitable will, something that had served her well in her life as a pirate queen.

She set the refilled tankard in front of me a moment later. She looked around and sighed. "As much as I enjoy the extra coin, I'll be glad when this convention business is over with."

"Walteros is a coward!" someone shouted, his words slurred. A man in a yellow robe had jumped onto one of the tables between the bar and the tavern's entrance. "Brandia's been here for days and the Erudite Convention has yet to be called! And why is that?"

"Walteros is a coward!" more yellow robes cried, raising tankards, flagons, and bottles high into the air.

Mortus, what a nuisance. Both of my favorite haunts taken over by rival groups of "intellectuals." Most of the tavern's regulars—a healthy mix of undead pirates, living sailors, and city workers like me—had been pushed into the gallery overlooking the first floor. Many of those regulars were glaring down at the unruly scholars.

Couldn't the scholars and philosophers have met in the arena and settled their differences with their fists? Preferably without anyone getting killed. It was bad enough Walteros was undead. The last thing I wanted was more of them reanimating. There'd be no end to this.

The drunk standing on the table drained his tankard and threw it to the floor. "Enough of this swill! We should be at Grok's enjoying the orc's famous coffee! Not stuck here in this hole!"

That incensed the regulars. Food rained down from the gallery, pelting several of the scholars. The man on the table shook his fist and received a face full of half-eaten pie for his trouble.

"For people who prefer to stay a while and listen, they're certainly not doing much of the latter," I said, raising my voice to be heard over the din.

Molly laughed. "So, who d'ye figure made off with the tongue?" She spread her fat arms wide to encompass the mayhem. "Surely ye don't suggest that one of me honored, well-mannered guests could possibly do somethin' so heinous as that, hmm?"

One of those "well-mannered" guests flung an empty wine bottle up into the second-floor gallery, where it shattered against the wall. I pulled the hood of my black robe up over my head with one hand and covered the top of my tankard with the other as glass fragments rained down on me. "Surely not, Molly. Surely not." I looked around. "Mina described Brandia to me, but I don't see her. Is she in the back room?"

"She was, but she left shortly before yer arrival. One of her yellow-robed aides ran in here, all flustered, and pulled Brandia out of whatever game she was in the middle of." Molly gazed out one of the front windows at the clock tower on the far side of the Styx. "That happened about an hour ago, I'd say."

That wasn't the least bit suspicious. "Any idea where she could've gone?"

"Back to her inn?" Molly shrugged. "It was a bit loud in here at the time, but I distinctly remember Brandia saying something to the effect of 'I need my things' and 'We must hurry or it will be too late.'"

Before I could press her for more information, she pitched me out of the stool with a sharp shove. As I fell, *something* zipped over my head and embedded itself in the bar. I landed on my back and looked up at what almost hit me. It was a knife, still vibrating from the impact.

Molly wrenched the knife from the bar and hurled it back up into the gallery. Someone screamed. Molly placed a hand on the bar and vaulted over it as if she were a hundred pounds lighter and corporeal. She floated to where a group of yellow robes had pitched over a table as makeshift cover from the barrage of food and bottles from above.

She gripped the table and pulled it upright, then tilted it on top of the yellow robes.

One of them tried to get up, but she stamped a boot down on his neck. "That's enough out of you lot!" she roared, her voice pealing like a thunderclap. "Once the knives come out, the fun's over! Are we clear?"

And with that, the night's food war at Mad Molly's came to a decisive end. Molly, as always, was the victor. The Fleet Empress was not one to be trifled with, ghost or not.

She pressed a good number of her regulars and some yellow robes into service to straighten up her tavern. "You should be gettin'," she murmured to me as she drifted past, "while the gettin's good."

I left Molly's with a belly full of ale and a head full of clouds from the lack of food. Despite the minor inebriation, I made my way unswervingly toward the Mortal Quarter. There were a few inns in the undead section of the city, but not many. I didn't know if I'd have time to check them all one by one, but I knew someone who kept tabs on all visitors to the city. A couple of someones, actually, but only one of them would be on duty at this hour.

"You're looking for a tongue?" Constable Paul's mail coif clinked as he cocked his head to the side. "Did I hear that right?"

Mortus, is everybody going to ask me that? "Yes, Paul. Mina has me chasing down Walteros's lost tongue."

We stood inside the main entrance of the Mortal Quarter's constabulary. Paul leaned against the counter where visitors could register concerns or complaints to a waiting clerk, but only in daytime hours. Since night had fallen, the only occupants of the constabulary were myself, Paul, and his wife Henrietta, who served as the city's only other constable.

"I wondered why Walteros stopped making public appearances." Paul scratched a cheek tanned from years of farming and as many years hunting the undead. "Still, a missing tongue... That's going to be a hard thing to find in this city. Can you get your friend-we-better-not-name to search for it?"

He was referring to Yiltahn, my wraith familiar. Many mistook wraiths as undead beings when they were native to the other side. They fed off spiritual energy and would often cross to the material plane to prey on the undead. Because of this, their presence in Necrolopolis was forbidden. It hadn't stopped me from occasionally employing him within the walls, but this was a high-profile situation. It'd be an understatement to say that Mina would be angry if she found out, and I didn't want to find out how much of an understatement.

"Unfortunately, he won't be an option," I said. "Mina's got a couple suspects in mind and I'm trying to track down one of them."

Paul listened as I relayed everything Mina and Molly had told me. "So, this rival of Walteros is acting strangely, you think she might be involved, and you need my help to find her?"

"I figured if anyone would know where a celebrity is staying in the city, it'd be one of its two constables." Mina had hoped that hiring the famous pair of undead hunters would attract more officers to the city, but so far it was just them.

"She was staying over at the Comfy Coffin Inn."

"'Was?'" I frowned. "She isn't anymore?"

"She saw herself out not too long ago. Made a bit of a scene with a friend before disappearing without a trace."

My stomach clenched, but Paul held up a hand before I could say anything. He grinned. "At least, that's what I would say under normal circumstances, but I might have a lead for you. Follow me and keep as quiet as possible."

Paul led me through an unlocked gate and into a twisting flight of steps, like one would find in a tower. We descended past the archives, the food stores, and at last arrived in the building's dungeon. Once we stepped out of the stairwell, Paul murmured, "Henrietta's a very light sleeper and she keeps the barracks door at the top of the stairs open in case there's an alarm."

Now I understood his desire for quiet. Henrietta was a fearsome woman when fully alert, and I could only imagine how she would be if she were sleep deprived.

We passed an unmanned guard station and entered a long hallway with two large holding cells on either side. Even from this distance, the stench of alcohol was strong, along with something else I couldn't place. "Tonight a busy night for alcoholics?"

"Just one so far."

One? And it smelled that bad?

Each of the two cells had a single occupant. On the left, a woman sat cross-legged with her back against the far wall. Her yellow robes had been neatly arranged around her so she wouldn't trip if she had to get up in a hurry. Her eyes were closed, but they opened at the sound of our approach. She nodded toward Paul, then turned her gaze on me. There was something about her stare that bothered me.

By contrast, the occupant of the other cell lay sprawled on his back and snored so loudly I was surprised he hadn't woken Henrietta on the other end of the building. Frosty breath escaped the hood of his black robe, along with occasional mutterings to himself.

If the robe hadn't given him away, the icy air that revealed itself with every exhalation would have. "Ferryman?"

The robed figure stirred at mention of the name. "What's this?" he murmured. "No fare... no ferry! Heh, get it? No fare...." The snoring resumed.

"What's he doing here?" I asked Paul. In all the times I'd been to Mad Molly's with Ferryman, I'd never once seen him drunk, much less passed out like this.

"I brought him here." The woman in yellow stood and walked up to the iron bars separating us. "And you are?"

"Adelvell, assistant to Director Grimina." I tucked my hands into the sleeves of my robe and bowed slightly. "And you are the scholar Brandia, I presume?"

She smiled. "My reputation precedes me."

"The actions of your followers precede you. They made a right mess of Mad Molly's until the proprietress threatened to keelhaul them."

"Those who undertake the Sojourn can be an unruly bunch in the pursuit of knowledge." She sighed. "I'll have to discipline them later. A day and a night of improvised oratory without breaks or water should suffice."

That sounded almost as bad as getting keelhauled. Brandia was a tough one, that was for sure. "What's your relationship to Ferryman?" I asked.

"I only met him tonight, while sitting in the Comfy Coffin's taproom. I was waiting for my assistant Griena to return."

"So you could leave the city?" Paul asked.

"No," she snapped. "I was waiting for her to return *to* the city. I told you this earlier."

"You did, but humor me for Mr. Adelvell's sake. It's his first time hearing this."

I felt as annoyed as she did, though for different reasons. I knew constables had a habit of getting witnesses and suspects to repeat their stories to see if any of the details changed, but he could've at least mentioned he already had information.

Brandia sighed again. "Very well. As you undoubtedly heard from Molly, I was in the backroom of her tavern when word reached me of Master Walteros's injury." Her expression darkened. "He deserves better than that. I wanted to do what I could to help."

"And how were you hoping to help?"

"Recently, I made the acquaintance of a pixie chirurgeon." Her eyes brightened with excitement. "Did you know they can reattach severed limbs with their thread magic? It's quite remarkable."

It definitely was, though I didn't like dwelling on it. We'd utilized pixies to help in the limb-lopper case. I'd even been the direct recipient of their thread magic after my abdomen was split open by an axe. "You wanted to reach out to this pixie for help?"

"Yes. I'd written down her information, but it was back in my room along with coin to pay whatever she wanted. Griena is already on her way."

That could definitely come in handy. I wasn't aware of any pixies in the city at the moment, but if she could bring one here it would expedite things. Provided we could find the blasted tongue, anyway. "All right, I'm following you so far." I hiked a thumb at the snoring figure behind me. "How does Ferryman factor into this?"

"One boon of undertaking the Sojourn is gaining the ability to read people and situations. I was meditating over a cup of watered wine when *he*"—she nodded toward Ferryman—"intruded upon my thoughts. He was acting so nervous I was surprised no one else noticed."

"People have an amazing ability to ignore those around them," Paul said.

"Indeed. Well, *I* noticed his nervousness and how it increased when he was joined by a group of brown robes. One of them was Jaylen, Master Walteros's right-hand man for years." She scowled. "He keeps me from a private audience with Walteros, even though Walteros is willing to meet with me."

"What were Jaylen and these brown robes doing with Ferryman?"

"Rendering payment for some kind of service. You'd have to ask him about the details. I only heard snatches of conversation, but Jaylen seemed agitated throughout the encounter. Ferryman mentioned a 'slippery little thing' and Jaylen demanded to know why he opened 'the box' instead of pitching into the Styx like he promised he would, no questions asked."

Into the Styx? Mortus, that was bad. If he pitched the tongue in there, it could already have crossed the Veil and become a wraith snack. I turned to Paul. "Think we can wake him up?"

"I've tried everything I can think of," Paul said. "Even splashed water in his hood. All he did was mumble 'Man overboard!' and fall back to sleep."

I frowned. That wasn't normal. "Let me see him."

Paul unlocked the cell, and I walked over to where Ferryman lay. With each step the smell of alcohol grew stronger, but so did that other odor I couldn't place. It smelled sweet, like honey with maybe a little cinnamon mixed in. "What was he drinking?" I asked Brandia.

"The Comfy Coffin's signature drink is blackberry wine, brought out in specially marked flagons. He drank quite a bit of it."

"Did you have the same thing?"

"Yes, cut with water because I don't have much tolerance. The further one is along the Sojourn, the less one drinks."

Tell that to all your fellow Sojourners at Mad Molly's. "Did it have honey or cinnamon mixed into it?"

"No, not that I could taste." She frowned. "Why do you ask?"

"A sweet wine covers up a sweet poison." I took a few more whiffs. "He's been drugged with thinalseed."

"Thinalseed?" Paul asked. "Isn't that used for healing?"

"Normally, yes. It can also be used as an anesthetic, as was the case with Ferryman here." I nudged him with my boot. "Paul, do you have burberic tonic?"

"In our healers' kits, yes. Henrietta will know where they are." He turned and ran off. "I'll rouse her right away!"

It took a half an hour and an entire bottle of burberic, but eventually Ferryman roused enough that a bucket of water dumped on his head brought him to full sobriety. He sat up, screaming, "Man overboard! Save me, someone save—" He paused to look around, frosty breath flowing from his soaked hood. "Wait, this isn't the Styx, nor is it my boat."

I looked at Paul. "You weren't kidding about his reaction."

"Addy?" Ferryman turned his hood my way, his face hidden as it always was. "What're we doing here? Last thing I remember was drinking in the inn with Lulgan and one of his friends, and then you were trying to drown me."

Lulgan was one of the few undead members of the Pharmakeian guild, a skeleton mage of some repute. That explained where the thinalseed came from. I quickly filled Ferryman in on the situation, then asked, "What was Lulgan meeting you for?"

"Nothing out of the ordinary. Catching up on things, that's all."

"He's lying," Brandia said. "Once this Lulgan had him in his cups, he appeared to be questioning him quite aggressively."

"I don't remember any of that. And who're you?" Ferryman demanded.

"She's a witness in a criminal investigation." Paul crossed his arms and glared down at Ferryman. "And right now, you're the prime suspect."

"We know you had business with a philosopher named Jaylen," I said, pitching my voice over Ferryman's spluttered objections. "What was it about?"

"I don't see why I have to tell any of you anything," he muttered.

"You might as well," I said. "You already spilled your guts to Lulgan. See, there's another use for thinalseed among the Pharmakeians. It's the base ingredient for a potion called Liar's Bane. Someone gives you enough of that, and you'll have a hard time not telling them all your darkest secrets."

I swear Ferryman's *robes* grew pale at that. "All of them?" he squeaked.

"Potentially," I said. "So, tell us what you did that had Lulgan interested enough to drug you, and maybe we can rectify this whole situation before it gets any more out of hand than it already is."

Ferryman stewed about it for a long moment before he said, "Jaylen paid me to lose something for him."

"The tongue of Walteros?"

"I didn't know that's what it was at first, but yes."

"Why would Jaylen want his master's tongue gone?" Brandia demanded.

"How should I know?" Ferryman spread his arms. "I'm a courier and fixer, not a mind-reader."

"We'll worry about Jaylen's motivations later," I said. "What happened to the tongue?"

"As I made my way back to the docks, whatever was in the box writhed and banged against the inside walls. It was making quite a racket and attracting a lot of unwanted attention. I wanted to see what was inside, so I stepped into a side alley and cracked it open to take a peek… and it jumped out."

"The tongue *jumped* out?" Paul made a face. "I've seen some odd, disgusting things in my day, but that might do it."

"Well, it gets a whole lot nastier." Ferryman rubbed the top of his head through the hood. "It jumped out, flopped around on the cobblestones a bit, and then fell down a drain."

My stomach turned. "You lost it in the sewers?"

"I couldn't help it! It moved so fast!"

"Did you tell anyone about this?" Paul asked.

"Jaylen knows. I told him when he pressed me for details."

"And that means Lulgan also knows." Brandia crossed her arms and began pacing. "What does a Pharmakeian want with Master Walteros's tongue?"

More importantly, how were we going to retrieve the tongue? I started to pace, too. "How did Jaylen react to the news it was in the sewer?"

"He wasn't happy, and he left in a hurry." Ferryman shrugged. "I don't know why. What difference does it make if it's the Styx or the sewer? Don't they all go to the same place?"

"No." I shook my head. "The sewers empty outside the city, *not* in the Styx." I learned that after assisting the Collectors with a ratman infestation in the Catacombs of Final Rest. They'd entered the city through the sewer outlet at a lake in the Murky Morrow.

I stopped pacing. It was highly likely the tongue had washed all the way to the Morrow. And if it wound up there, it'd be outside the city limits… where Yilthan could find it. I smiled.

"Who's ready for a little fieldtrip?"

THE MURKY MORROW WAS A MARSHLAND JUST EAST OF THE CITY, WHICH was partly where the name came from. Since the sun rose in the east, those peering toward the lake and the surrounding wetlands would see its brown-tinged waters whenever the sun rose "on the morrow." The water couldn't have been drinkable, with so much sewage flowing out into it, but hardly anyone lived within eyesight of the city's walls. This was one of those times where the stigma—and smell—of the undead was a blessing.

As we trudged through the woods toward the lake, the

aforementioned bouquet assaulted me from ahead and behind. The fetid water of the marsh, tainted as it was, competed with the airborne odor of the city. Considering we were in the height of summer, we were in prime stench season, so the competition was fierce.

Ferryman and Brandia walked behind me while Paul and Henrietta took the lead. Henrietta was a stout woman of middle years with a strength that came from growing up on a farm. She wore a mail coif and tunic similar to her husband, and while both had identical truncheons hanging from their belt loops each carried a different farming implement that had been reforged into a weapon of war. She rested a billhook against her shoulder while he used a pitchfork as a walking stick. Years spent hunting belligerent undead with these weapons had earned them the nicknames Hook and Pitch.

I carried my trusty shovel, its shaft and blade fashioned from the rib and tooth of a sky whale. It was a relic of the Fallen War, wielded by a combat necromancer as both a melee weapon and a magic focus. I normally didn't carry it, as denizens of Necrolopolis often associated it with the worst aspects of the necromantic profession. Still, if there was the potential for violence, I preferred to have it close. One never knew when things could get ugly.

As we neared the lake, many angry voices drifted toward us. Henrietta and Paul waved us back and approached the tree line at a crouch. They studied what was going on for a long moment before Henrietta waved us forward and murmured, "You've got to see this."

About thirty people stood near the edge of the lake, their robed forms illuminated by lanterns and the set of full moons in the sky. Based on the light, it was an even mix of yellow, brown, and black robes. Crouched next to me, Brandia gasped. "What are *my* people doing here?"

"Fighting with Walteros's people, it seems," Paul replied.

It was quite the melee. Philosopher and scholar beat at each other with wild abandon, using fists, clubs, and even rocks. In the middle of it all stood a tight knot of black robes who struck anyone who got too close. They surrounded an individual whose robe had all manner of silver threading running across it in intricate patterns. Beneath the hood, blue embers burned inside empty eye sockets.

Surprise and annoyance warred within me. There was only one skeleton in all of Necrolopolis who wore a set of robes that gaudy. "Keldain." What in the Eighteen Hells was he doing here? "Is he after the tongue, too?"

"Keldain?" Ferryman demanded. "What does the leader of the Plastron Point sorcerers want with the tongue? And how much gold did I miss out on by not talking to him in the first place?" he added in a whisper.

"Is gold all you think about?" Henrietta snapped. "You know this situation is your fault, right?"

"How is it my fault? If I hadn't accepted the job Jaylen would've gone to someone else, and maybe you'd never get it back. You owe me, if anything."

"You could've reported it to us," Paul said.

"I'm no snitch!"

I shook my head. "Either way, we have to assume Keldain has the tongue in that box. Brandia, if you can get your people to join our side, we might stand…"

My voice trailed off when I realized Brandia was no longer crouched next to us.

Henrietta cursed and pointed. "What's that idiot doing?"

Brandia had slipped past us and run into the melee. She tried to push her way past the brown robes, but they knocked her back. Her yellow robe followers fought their way toward her. One drew a knife.

"Damn it all, we have to go in!" Paul burst from the tree line, followed closely by Henrietta. "Halt!" they shouted. "In Grimina's name, halt!"

I ran after them, my eyes fixed on the yellow robe with the knife. He tried to stab one of the brown robes, but Brandia threw herself between them and screamed, "No bloodshed!"

A brown robe slammed into the knife-wielding yellow robe, who in turn crashed into Brandia. They both went down in a heap.

Henrietta and Paul stopped about twenty feet from the mass of fighters. I stepped up beside them. Ferryman was nowhere to be found. *So much for depending on him.*

"She's dead!" one of the yellow robes wailed. "Mistress Brandia's dead!"

"It was Jaylen!" another called, his voice thick with shock. "He pushed me!"

My stomach twisted itself in knots. *Damnation! It didn't have to be like this!*

"Silence!" Keldain snapped, his reedy voice carrying over the din. He leveled a bony digit in my direction. "Adelvell, what in the Eighteen Hells are you doing here?"

"I could ask you the same thing. What does a skeleton want with the tongue of an undead philosopher?" Then it hit me. "Wait a minute. You want it for the faction struggle, don't you? This is so you can gain majority control."

Keldain's teeth clacked as he laughed. "For an amateur, you're not half bad. Yes, once Lulgan here"—he indicated a skeleton next to him—"can render this tongue down into a salve, a little dab on my teeth and my enchantment magic will increase a hundredfold."

A hundredfold? I hoped that was an exaggeration. If it wasn't, then Keldain wasn't just vying for control of the skeleton faction. He wanted control over the whole city, and he'd be able to do that with that kind of magic amplification. The power to sway the masses was not something he could be allowed to have access to. "Enough talk, Keldain." I channeled my power into the shovel. Black energy crackled along the blade's white surface. "Drop the tongue and nobody gets hurt."

Keldain shied away from me, but one of the brown robes stepped forward. "Master Keldain, allow me to help. A necromancer has no power over the living, and I owe you for taking the tongue—Gah!"

Paul's truncheon slammed into the man's forehead. His head snapped back and he fell onto the grass with a soft thud.

"Nice throw!" Henrietta said.

"Get them!" Keldain commanded everyone, even the brown and

yellow robes he'd just fought. "If word gets back to Mina about this, we'll all be punished for the theft and that woman's death!"

That convinced most of them. Shouting and yelling, Keldain's black robes and all the brown robes charged at us. Some wielded clubs, while others held daggers. Most of the yellow robes stayed back, unsure what to do.

Henrietta strode forward. "Looks like we're earning our keep tonight, husband!" She chopped one man's club in half with her billhook, then struck him with the flat of the blade on the backswing.

Paul used the prongs of his pitchfork to catch one man's weapon arm. He twisted hard and flipped the man onto the ground. Before he could get up, Paul kicked him in the face. "So it would seem, dear wife!"

I followed Hook and Pitch's lead and used the blunt side of my shovel to knock aside weapons and bash faces. While the three of us were outnumbered at least six to one, most of our attackers were used to the confines of coffee shops, taverns, and libraries. In contrast, Henrietta, Paul, and I had more than our fair share of outdoor scuffles and fights under our belts.

Within moments, we knocked the fight out of most of them. The remainder, many of whom had already been on the receiving end of our weapons or our boots, hesitated to get close. I took advantage of the lull to wipe sweat from my brow and suck in several deep breaths. I hoped this was the end of it.

A dreadful buzzing filled the air, causing my skin to tingle. Behind the mass of scholars and philosophers, Keldain pointed his bony hands in our direction. Red energy coalesced into an orb before his fingertips. The sphere pulsed in time with the buzzing.

"Get down!" I shouted.

In order to hit us, Keldain would have to blast through his temporary allies, something I knew he'd have no problem doing and I couldn't let that happen. Even though they were an unruly lot, they were still guests of the city.

While Henrietta and Paul were quick to act, the others were not. I looked back at Keldain and realized that the blue embers in his eye sockets were fixed directly on me. A chill ran down my spine. He wasn't after just anyone. He wanted *me* dead.

I spun to the right and ran as fast as I could. As I suspected, Keldain's eyes and hands tracked my movement. His skeletal frame pivoted so he could aim the red orb at me. "Addy, where're you going?" Henrietta called, quickly followed by Paul shouting, "Get down, Addy! He's aiming right at you!"

I'm aware! I made for the tree line, but I'd never make it. The buzzing had reached a crescendo, and any second that red ball of death would rip into my back and it'd all be over. Well, if I couldn't outrun him, I'd outfight him. I channeled as much power as I could muster into my shovel and concentrated it into the blade.

I slid to a halt and spun to face Keldain. I leveled my shovel, the blade now glowing black, and aimed for Keldain. A spark of fear emanated from the skeleton's eye-embers, but the fire soon grew cold again. *Good*, I thought with a grin. *You're as distracted as I want you to be.* Raising my voice, I called out the name I didn't dare say in the city: "Yiltahn, your assistance!"

The air behind Keldain shimmered and Yiltahn's amorphous outline appeared. Wraiths were normally invisible, but our contract allowed me to see his mostly transparent body. Yiltahn latched onto Keldain's spine like a barnacle on Ferryman's boat, his spectral teeth nibbling at the skeleton sorcerer's soul. Keldain shrieked and the spell he was about to cast fizzled out in a puff of smoke. I sensed Yiltahn's hunger through our connection but forbade him from doing more than he already had. Yiltahn sent a wave of dissatisfaction my way, but he complied. Further, he became corporeal long enough to remove something from Keldain's robe and fling it my way.

The black box containing Walteros's sewage-sodden tongue landed in the grass next to my feet. I would be both impressed and disgusted if the old ghoul actually wanted it back considering all it had been through over the last several hours.

Excellent work, I thought to Yiltahn.

You are welcome, master, a voice like sand-coated silk whispered in my mind. *Although I wish you would let me drink a little of his essence.*

As much as I would like to see Keldain drained dry, he was still a citizen of the city and under Mina's protection. Which meant he was under my protection, unfortunately. *No, you've done enough for today, Yiltahn. Return across the veil and feed there.*

Yiltahn vanished, and Keldain shuddered as the connection was broken. He looked around for the source of his sudden agony and, finding nothing, returned his burning gaze to me. Or, more to the point, at the black energy coalesced on and around my shovel. He held up his hands. "Mr. Adelvell, now that you have the Philosopher's Tongue, surely we can come to some sort of peaceful resolution—"

"Oh, we're well past that point." I pointed the shovel at him and let the spell loose. A disk of black lightning sailed through the air and exploded on the ground at his feet. All that charged energy arced outward, struck Keldain's feet, and ran up into the rest of his body. He flew back, slammed into one of his lackeys, and they both went down in a heap of clattering bones.

With Keldain neutralized, the fight was over. His followers gathered around to help reassemble him, and the brown and yellow robes—the ones Henrietta and Paul hadn't beaten into submission—quickly surrendered. Paul kept watch while Henrietta hurried over to examine Brandia's body, barreling her way past yellow robes as she did. "Out of the way, fools!"

I stooped to pick up the box. It was obviously not the same box Ferryman originally had, but it was similar. I cracked it open the tiniest bit and allowed moonlight to enter it. The tongue's tissue was surprisingly pink, not at all what I was used to seeing from ghoul flesh. There wasn't the least bit of swelling, although the stench of the sewer was something else. I wrinkled my nose and closed the box again. I was surprised it wasn't wiggling and writhing as it had when in Ferryman's possession. *Yiltahn,* I thought after a moment, *you didn't do anything with the tongue's spectral essence, did you?*

The silence that followed was answer enough. *Gross.*

I pocketed the box and walked over to Henrietta, who was kneeling next to Brandia. In all the excitement, I'd forgotten she'd been the first to fall. I cursed under my breath. Though her death was an accident and occurred outside the city, Mina was going to be furious. One of her honored guests had met her end.

I made my way to the body and something caught my eye. An aura surrounded the corpse, an aura tinged black and in stark contrast with the yellow robes and red blood. I considered it a moment, then groaned at the implications. "She's reanimating?"

That did not bode well at all.

"Before we begin," Walteros said, his voice deep and sonorous like a temple bell, "there's one person I must thank for allowing this all to happen." He pointed from his place on the stage to the far end of the auditorium. "Mr. Adelvell, without you and your constables, I'd still be without a tongue! You are a prince of a man. Thank you."

The room—full of brown robes, yellow robes, and curious onlookers—burst into applause. My cheeks grew hot at the attention, and I tried to pull my hood up. Mina pushed it back down and slapped me on the back. "Just accept the praise, Addy. You earned it."

"Easy for you to say," I muttered. Still, I waved at the crowd, who applauded even louder. *Mortus, how do performers and priests put up with this?*

All was well that ended well, I supposed. Jaylen had been arrested for the mutilation of a corpse and for the accidental death of Brandia. I think he deliberately shoved the armed yellow robe into her, but there was no way to prove that. We had to settle for his permanent exile from the city. Should he return as undead rather than crossing over the natural way, he would serve time in the city's prison.

Lulgan had been stripped of his position in the Pharmakeian guild as punishment for drugging Ferryman and the procurement of illicit reagents. As for Keldain, he would face no punishment for either the theft or the attempt on my life. Mina hadn't been happy I'd used necromancy on him after the fight was over, so she considered him getting blasted apart a fitting punishment.

This also put an end to his plan to take over the skeleton faction, at least through magical enchantment. If he wanted a seat on the city council alongside Mina, Ashwarden, and the others, he'd have to earn his favor the old-fashioned way: with likability and bribery. Considering his personality and the state of his purse there was little threat of that.

Movement on the stage caught the audience's eye and cheers broke out. Brandia had appeared at the opposite end of the platform, her ghostly form hovering a few inches above the wooden planks. Her yellow robes were as resplendent as they had been in life, though they were now translucent and tinged with the green of ectoplasm common for all spirits. "At least she won't have to worry about ever losing her tongue," I said.

"Be nice." Mina favored me with a smile before she turned her attention to the stage.

Brandia bowed. "Master Walteros, it is good to see you whole again. Now the Erudite Convention can begin."

"Yes, Mistress Brandia, though I fear it will be a short convention."

"Oh? Why is that?"

"There was a reason my assistant Jaylen stole my tongue. It was to keep me from stating a truth I've suppressed for far too long." Walteros paused to survey the audience before he turned back to Brandia. "I am renouncing the Philosopher's Path."

A gasp ran through the audience. Brandia recoiled as if slapped. "You invented the Path! You've spent your whole life refining it!"

"Yes, and it was a life wasted. I realize that now." Walteros smiled. "The Scholar's Sojourn... That is the truest road to knowledge there is."

Walteros's brown-robed followers cried in outrage while the yellow robes cheered.

Brandia's sudden laughter quieted the room. Walteros looked at her, his smile slipping. "What's so funny?"

"You see, I also had a revelation." Brandia grinned. "Except my revelation told me that the Philosopher's Path is the true way!"

Now it was the yellow robes' turn to gasp and scream in horror.

"Oh, really?" Walteros crossed his arms. "Please explain how you arrived at that conclusion."

"Gladly." Brandia floated back to the center of the stage. "You see, it occurred to me..."

As Brandia droned on, I turned to Mina. "Are they just arguing to argue at this point?"

"It certainly seems that way." Mina shrugged. "Well, they'll have all the time in the world to settle their differences."

"They already settled them," I pointed out. "Now they're resettling them."

Mortus, what had I done?

ABOUT BENJAMIN TYLER SMITH

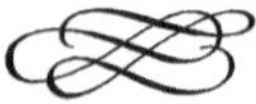

*B*enjamin spends his days creating maps for cemeteries and his evenings herding the undead and battling aliens. He is a writer of fantasy and science fiction, with two novels published in Blood Moon Press's Fallen World universe and numerous short stories in anthologies, magazines, and floating about the internet. Many of these short stories are set in his Necrolopolis universe, a dark fantasy world where a necromancer must keep the peace in a city of the undead. He is currently working on the first set of novels in that world, as well as other projects in the shared universes of his fellow travelers on the writing path.

He lives in an area of rural Pennsylvania with more cows than humans for neighbors, ruled over by a benevolent Calico Countess and her feline knight, the Earl of Grey. Helping him maintain this vast estate is a saint of a wife and a beautiful baby girl who keeps up morale, inspires story ideas, and keeps him on his toes.

Follow him on Facebook at facebook.com/BenTylerSmith, on Twitter at twitter.com/BenTylerSmith, and on his website at BenjaminTylerSmith.com, where free stories will soon be available. First up is *Some Patience Required*, a prequel novella in the Necrolopolis universe. Look for it in Spring/Summer 2022!

FOREWORD: "THE BOOKSELLER" BY MARISA WOLF

BY CHRISTOPHER WOODS

 first met Marisa after she co-wrote several novels in the Four Horsemen Universe. I immediately wanted to see what she would do in the Fallen World and she wrote my favorite story for the first anthology we did in that world. She is writing a novel in my universe and gave me another short for the second Fallen World anthology. She was one of the first people who came to mind when we decided to do this anthology and she wrote one of my, as well as one of Toni's, favorite stories. I see a promising future ahead of her.

THE BOOKSELLER

BY MARISA WOLF

*H*emma lowered her forehead, quite gently, to the warm wooden top of her battered desk. After a moment, she lifted her head again, a bare inch above the surface, and dropped it less gently but with a more satisfying thump.

Three calls already for the day and the sun had barely crossed the treetops. Unconscionable, to have an eclipse the week of an equinox, a second full moon, planets leaning into alignments, and unusually high tides. Magic-casters of all sorts had been and would be tempted, and far too many would overreach. It would be an endless party of a weekend, which would be nice, except she had to work it. And, of course, the potential for mayhem and death that would lead to all the work she would have to do cleaning up after them.

Sometimes this job she loved… sometimes she really, really hated it.

"Hem, you have a—"

"Don't finish that sentence." She kept her face on her desk, flattening her nose with insistent pressure. "We're booked out for weeks, and then it's midsummer, and that'll be another flood with the immortality crowd, and that'll take us through to nearly fall—"

"Wizards die in nines, though, so it's always a bit of a flood."

"That's not a thing, Essel."

"It is."

"That's because you count to nine and then start over, it doesn't—" Hemma sighed and sat up, grabbing a clip from her desk to fasten her hair back. "Never mind. I have a what?"

"A call, as well you know. Only it's our Mrs. Cadigan and you'll already be in the Hollows this afternoon, and she is such a dear."

"Essel…" Hemma stood, straightened her shirt, and grabbed her less raggedy jacket from the back of her chair. "I don't suppose Sylvan will be in today?"

"He hasn't let me know." Essel twinkled briefly into view before zooming out of the room. Her voice carried faintly from the front of the store as she confirmed with the old widow Cadigan that their finest book acquisitions manager would be there before evening.

Essel had been a wizard's familiar for over a hundred years before she found her way to Root and Vine, and while Sylvan, the store's owner, had never quite been a wizard, they'd fallen into the standard wizard and familiar pattern long before Sylvan had hired Hemma. Still, Essel got a bit prim about how she couldn't possibly know all Sylvan's ins and outs, given she wasn't *actually* his familiar.

Additionally, Hemma would lay a wager that Sylvan wouldn't be in, as he hadn't done a single collection since the day Hemma started, four years ago… and likely some time before that, given the never-lessening backlog.

She slipped her favorite warded bag across her body and saluted the desk she once more would not be straightening. As Essel finished her phone call, Hemma turned on the circle of fountains that never worked when she spent too long in the room and closed off her storage closet.

Four years she'd worked for Root and Vine, and she'd outgrown the closet she'd appropriated for an office nearly as long ago. Sylvan, who she technically worked for, who in the most technical sense owned the Root and Vine, didn't have an office and so he didn't see much need for anyone else to have one either.

"It's a tree, Hemmarya. Not... not a barrister's office," he said when she asked, three and a half years ago.

"A barrister?" She raised her eyebrows but swallowed back the smile that wanted to follow.

"You know very well some people still call them that." He harumphed and pulled hard at his blousy tunic, frowning until his own eyebrows threatened to join up with his beard.

"Root and Vine is a tree, yes, but it's full of room, and they're full of books." She tried wheedling then, the lesson not quite sinking home. *"Books you want me to keep track of and match with customers who want them."* She'd thought that part was true, too, in the moment of that conversation, though the depth and bass of his answering snort began to teach her differently.

"And then I go out and get more books," she continued, back on more solid ground. *"And ideally you want to know about them. An office would give me a place to get all that organized."*

What a sweet, innocent, precious little thing she'd been then, three and a half years ago. Organized! That was never in her cards, but at the time he'd been gracious enough not to laugh at the overwhelming weight of her naivete.

"We have counters." Sylvan had waved his arm grandly along the live-edged wood that formed a suggestion of a barrier between the main room of the Root and Vine and the back room.

"Counters." She crossed her arms and tried to mirror his frown. With rather less of his prodigious facial hair, it was not nearly so effective. She looked deliberately at one of their regular customers, who was at that exact moment wandering through the alleged back room, asking Essen for books about pixies written by an orc.

"And closets!" he added, defensive. *"Plenty of closets!"*

And so there were. Root and Vine, an enormous world tree hundreds of years older even than Sylvan, had a hollow the size of an ambitious cathedral, or a small college, which conveniently opened right onto street level. It less conveniently had broken that hollow into multiple branching pathways that spiraled around its average-house-sized center, but there was no denying there were plenty of nooks that had become closets. She took one that afternoon, and though the shop occasionally grew a springy branch to poke through her chair, it had never grown over her closet.

Which was saying something. They'd had to close off a number of side rooms in the large rambling space of the shop when either the tree grew through it, or the magic filled it up. The moving water of her fountain collection kept magic from collecting unobserved and doing weird things in her cubby, but the fountains often stopped working when she sat in front of them too long. Or if she stared at them lost in thought too often. Or on Tuesdays.

Truly, no one ever did get the hang of Tuesdays in Root and Vine.

Hemma, now three and a half years wiser and approximately seventy decades wearier, shook her head clear and summoned a smile for Essen.

"If I finish at the Leeward early, I'll swing back to check in before heading to the Hollows." She tapped the edge of the long striped counter and stepped around the tangle of roots spilling from below it without looking. "If you get too busy, make sure Sylvan comes in."

"I won't!" Essel replied, the light stringing through her hair flashing cheerfully. "Don't let anyone lock you into a creepy tower."

"I'll try." Hemma swallowed back her sigh, patted the counter once more, and paused to let the door swing open for her. Root and Vine preferred showing off when it was in a good mood, and Hemma hadn't been inside long enough to make it itchy yet today.

The shop was fond enough of her that it didn't drop loose spell book pages on her anymore and only rarely bowed up a new root to snag her steps. Still, it definitely brightened when she was in and out more than in.

Hemma's immunity made her very effective at her job and made her into something like old gristle stuck in one's back teeth to a shop basically made of magic.

"There she is. Off to tame the toothy and rescue the ravenous?" Douval Libere waved as she exited Root and Vine. The haberdasher owned the shop next door, its walls tucked close to the enormous tree of Root and Vine. On beautiful days like this one, all bright sky and few clouds, he sat outside with several of his most tempting wares, a snare for those with eyes or a love of hats, or both.

"Peruse a collection, at the least. And perhaps pay a visit to Mrs. Cadigan. Anything you want to send her?"

Douval tilted his head and considered with an audible *hrmm*. After a moment he disappeared under the table between them, hands reappearing and vanishing in a regular cycle until seven small hats were left lined up in a clear space. He sat back up with a smile and gestured over them with a flourish. Each was overloaded with scraps of the fanciest fabric, brilliant feathers, shiny bits, and bebobs that fairly begged to be touched.

"Room in your bag to bring the niblings some shinies?" he asked, beaming.

As though she could bear to say no.

Dileah stepped away from her display of glorious dresses to hand over a small bag of repurposed and resewn clothes for young humans, Amani waved with a tiny sack of mismatched but brilliant beads left over from her various jewelry and embroidery projects, and Tikar, the woodworker, had a handful of rough wooden swords.

Hemma stopped making eye contact with her fellow shopkeeps and merchants after that, sure she'd be packed down like a donkey for spring fair and late for her meeting besides if she stopped anywhere else.

The milling people at the center square moved with relative efficiency through the various portals. When it was her turn, she quickly stepped through to be deposited in the Leeward, well across their sprawling town. Portals were a location-specific magic, working their impact on the world around them, not the people passing through. All the same, a woman immune to magic would not serve herself well lingering in their in-between space.

Besides, only tourists blocked the portals. Locals knew enough to get out of the way and get to where they were going.

Her Leeward appointment left her no time at all to pop back to Root and Vine. It started promisingly enough—a pretty, wide-eyed nephew and his equally pretty wife hovering in the doorway of an unassuming cottage—but quickly shot off into morning-eating territory.

She proffered her card, which they barely glanced at before jumping into the context she didn't precisely need.

"My uncle was a great wizard, the greatest, but I hadn't seen him since I was small," Wide-Eyed Nephew said, apple in his throat bobbing earnestly. "He wasn't my uncle at all, but my grandfather's uncle. Still he enjoyed the holidays."

"He came to our wedding," Equally Pretty Wife said, nodding and twisting her hands in her skirt. "Very nice."

"But then it seemed… I mean… he… died?" More swallowing and throat-apple bobbing. "And yesterday we came into the kitchen and…" They stepped out of the doorway at the same time, revealing a common room with a hearth against the back wall and furniture of unclear origin or style and decorative touches.

Unclear because it was, to the last inch of the cubby above what might have been a stove, covered with books.

"They were there when you woke up?" she asked, shifting her bag and politely returning her eyes to them when what she wanted to do was gape at the very, very many books—in very, very many shapes and sizes, in very, very many angles and positions—threatening to take over their house.

"Yes."

"Hm." Hemma nodded as though this were an entirely normal and regular occurrence. "I imagine you were designated as one of his heirs, so when he passed the contents of his library were, ah, directed to be delivered to you posthaste."

"Which is all very nice, I'm sure," Equally Pretty Wife said, sounding convinced of no such thing, "but we know better than to touch them. Neither of us have a bit of a magical training, though my great-aunt was a hedge witch, so we called for you."

"How did you get out without touching any—" Hemma stopped herself, shook her head and held up a hand. "Well done. Not all of these will be spell books, of course, but I will be able to identify the magical and the dangerous, and if…"

Usually, she gave a few estimates for books of general knowledge and research which other bookshops might like, but given the sheer volume facing her here, she didn't want to overpromise.

"Ahem. If we get through all of that today, I can give you a few numbers to ring and see about getting someone out here to help you recover your kitchen." She smiled, realized she'd have to re-sort her bag if there were anything she needed to take with her today, and waited until they invited her in.

"Right. Safer if you both can step out for a bit. I'm immune to magic, as you might have heard, so a tetchy spell book can't bite me."

"Nothing will—they won't burn down our house or eat a wall, will they?" Equally Pretty Wife asked, her hand still on her doorknob, a foot halfway out the door.

"Unlikely. I've brought commitment papers to offer if there's anything I'll need to take away immediately, and most magic takes a bit to get its feet under it enough for wall-eating."

"And my uncle…" Wide-Eyed Nephew blinked, lifting his empty hands. "Will there be more surprises from him, do you think?"

"Now, that is not at all my realm of expertise, I'm sorry to say. But I can't see why he would have time-delayed any other deliveries if the entirety of his library appeared all at once, so that should be safe enough. I am sorry for your loss."

"Oh, yes, of course." They murmured all the right things and fled, which she could hardly blame them for.

She took a deep breath and set her bag and all the goods for Mrs. Cadigan and the orphans close to the door in case she had to make a run for it. Then she began the process of running her fingers over the books—spines, inside cover, random point in the middle—separating any that gave a bit of a prickle, buzz, or tingle.

Halfway through the second teetering pile she found *Pixish Empire: The Rise and Fall of the Spiral Sea* by Graklak the Grand and put that in a pile of its own. She'd remembered one of their regular customers asking for something similar, and while it had been years ago, she doubted he'd found anything so particular yet.

Morning came and went, and she forced herself to keep the same steady pace. Her safety-demanded-Root-and-Vine-buy-it pile was respectable, the we-have-potentially-interested-customers pile had a fair handful, and the good-luck-nephew-and-wife-on-building-an-addition-for-your-new-library was absolutely prodigious.

By the time she reached the stove she was sad she hadn't made a few more stops in Shopkeeper's Alley, at least enough to gather up some snacks alongside the small treasures for the orphanage.

"But then you'd literally be taking food meant for orphans, Hem, and you're not a monster, are you?" she muttered to herself, reaching out for the rich blue book at the top of the next pile.

She'd snatched her hand back and was holding it protectively close to her chest before she realized something had hurt her.

No, not hurt, not exactly… the book had *bitten* her. Pinpricks of blood rose from the tips of her fingers.

She *tsked* at the book, brought her mind fully back to the matter at hand, and shoved at it with her elbow to get a better look at the spine.

Collection it said, simple as that, in plain black letters. As she glared it, a fine trace of crimson shimmered through the letters before fading away.

"Smug," she told it, frowning. "Looks like you're coming home with me." Hemma picked her way back through the re-piled stacks of books to her bag. She crouched and pulled out a commitment letter and a bit of spelled leather.

At the top of the letter she described the book, checked the "Very Dangerous" box (second one down, after "Absolutely Deadly" and above "Uncomfortable") and wrote out a fair price offer. Middle-of-the-road danger books got the best prices, as clients could afford to keep them longer while they shopped around for a buyer, but Sylvan preferred they gather up as many magical treatises as possible when they would be untended by trained hands.

She had yet to decide whether he had more money than sense, was a dragon in disguise and this was his hoard, or he preferred to keep his community safe. She had decided it was some combination of the three and had yet to decide which ratio had more weight.

She set the letter to the side, sidled back to *Collection*, and wrapped it tightly in the spelled leather. Between that and her warded bag, it shouldn't cause any trouble until she could get it back to Root and Vine, even with a stop at Mrs. Cadigan's and her next appointment.

By the time Wide-Eyed Nephew and Equally Pretty Wife returned to peek through their own windows, afternoon had stretched near to its limit, and Hemma's fingers had settled into their complaints.

"Here's the offer; total down here. We prefer to take the lot rather than piecemeal them out, but I wanted you to see each price, so you know where the value is." She ran through her patter easily enough— from the glances they were casting toward the books, she figured they would be smart enough to jump on it. "There's only one I recommend you have me take away today. The rest I can send a runner for, if you like. Everything else is nonmagical—you can build your own library, call up the college, or I can send a few clerks along to go through them in detail."

"As long as I can move them without losing an arm, we'll take our time on those," Nephew said, eyes now a bit less wide.

"I'll let you look over the offer a bit then. I'll just step over here and call the shop, if you don't mind?" At their distracted nods, she moved out of the way and slid a compact out of the small bag belted at her waist.

She flipped it open and ran her fingers in a precise pattern, then held the mirrored surface away from herself. Her immunity would eat away at the spell soon enough, but as its magic was closer to the portal's, operating on a connection that didn't affect her, it worked well enough.

"There's our girl!" Essel's bright voice said. "I was just saying to Sylvan that I was sure you hadn't forgotten your appointment in the Hollows, just that you were hard at work in Leeward."

"It's still afternoon," Hemma replied, eyes narrowing.

"Barely!" Sylvan had apparently chosen to come into the shop and instead of being helpful was checking up on her. Delightful.

"I have just finished evaluating our clients' new seven hundred and fifty-three book library, boss, so I'm happy to see the sun is still well above the horizon." She glanced at the couple, though the spell would keep the voices locked to her ears and the compact, to not bother any bystanders. Wide-Eyed Nephew was in the process of signing the offer with an emphatic hand, and Equally Pretty Wife tilted up both thumbs when she caught Hemma's glance.

"I'll be returning with one Absolutely Deadly today and you'll need to send a courier to pick up about fifty other books, including a Pixie history by Graklak the Grand. Essel, wasn't it Jory Adler the research sorcerer who was looking for that one?"

"Oh! You're right, Hem, he's been on about that for years."

Sylvan snorted, putting plenty of effort into it to be sure the sound carried to Hemma. For a bookseller, the man truly hated selling books.

Dragon with a hoard, she reminded herself, and bit back her smile.

"Please call over to Mrs. Cadigan and let her know I will be by, but it might be supper time by then." Hemma's stomach roiled at the mention of food, or perhaps for how late in the day it was without a midday taste of something, but snacks would have to wait. Work, as always, wouldn't. She loved her job. Even—mostly—when she didn't.

"Of course, of course. Go finish up, dear, we'll be here when you're done."

"One of us will, anyway," Sylvan grumbled, his voice fading out. Hemma pictured him stomping through Root and Vine, guarding the stores of books she hadn't yet managed to sell.

WRAPPING UP WITH THE NICE YOUNG COUPLE WENT QUICKLY AFTER that, and her next appointment went as smoothly as they ever did. Which was to say a few tricky bits, but only one small fire. An aging wizard had called the shop himself, wanting to take care of the bulk of his collection before laying it all down for a few generations of sleep. He didn't want his precious granddaughter to get ensorcelled and was happy to part with some beauties in his collection. She so appreciated the responsible casters, ahead of the curve in ensuring their heirs didn't get eaten by their life's works.

Still, it was truly evening by the time she reached Mrs. Cadigan's ramble of an ancient farmhouse. The ache in her stomach moved to her heart as she approached; she'd been in such a rush to leave here she'd never appreciated what it offered until she was gone. Her family had died and the orphanage had felt like pity. The family she'd lost... she could have rebuilt one here, but perhaps she hadn't been ready, not then.

The water mill burbled contentedly along the path up to the house, as it always had, and several of the shrubs shivered as she walked, in that way they did only under particular circumstances.

"I'd be careful of the silvertree," she said, keeping her eyes straight ahead. "It only grows thorns when it's jostled."

"Mrs. Cadigan replanted the silvertree ages ago!" a small piping voice said, immediately drowned out by a chorus of hisses.

Hemma did not laugh, but she did adjust her bag enough for one of Tikar's wooden swords to show.

At that, three small figures burst onto the path around her.

"Is that for us?"

"Are there more?"

"Is it from Tikar?"

"There are seven, as a matter of fact, and I am to present them to Mrs. Cadigan, strict orders from Tikar himself. I do hope she knows I'm on my way, so I'm not stuck handling highwaymen out late at night when they should be inside reading."

"It's not that late!" the smallest protested, shoving dark hair back and doing a spectacular job glaring suspiciously at Hemma while a smile crept across their face.

"I'll tell her!" the biggest declared, taking off with only one longing backward glance at her bag. The smallest followed on her heels, caroling, "Me too, me too!"

"And we're not highwayman," the last said, shoving his hands in his pockets. "Just adventurers." He cocked his head. "You knew about the silvertree, so you've been here before?"

"Been here? I grew up here." That was not entirely true, but close enough. To distract them both, Hemma reached into the leather bag on her waist and withdrew a small rectangle with a flourish. The thick paper, lovingly crafted by Cirita the stationer in regular small batches, was cream with traces of acacia petals pressed into it. In deep black writing it declared:

Hemma of Rillington
Procures the Deadly for the Dangerous
Rates upon request
Root and Vine, Town Center

"Whoa," the boy breathed, tilting the card back and forth as light spilling from the farmhouse picked out the silver flecks in the ink. "The... deadly for the... dangerous?" His eyes became so round he could have been related to Wide-Eyed Nephew of earlier if she didn't know better.

"That's right."

"So, you make the dangerous... more dangerous?"

"I provide them a chance to get the tools they may need to be better at their jobs."

"Does that make you dangerous?"

Hemma laughed, realized he was serious, and swallowed back her mirth as best she could.

"Hardly that, littling. I'm immune, which is a heck of a lot different from dangerous."

"Immune to what? Danger?"

"Basically. Immune to magic. It rolls off me instead of sticking. Like..."

"Water off a duck."

"Exactly." She smiled, added an overdone wink for good measure. "That's exactly it."

"But... magic can work around you, right? Like affect your clothes, or drop a tree on you?"

"Oh, sure, that. A determined spellcaster worth their books could knock me out, but the unfocused magic that leaks out of a grimoire, or the leftovers of it that gather where a user has been working for years, those can't get a grip on me."

"So, you can go into any dungeon or study or cave and come out in one piece!" He rocked up on his toes and glanced over his shoulder. Hemma recognized longing when she saw it and figured Mrs. Cadigan had her hands full warning him off corners and dangers. Probably repeatedly.

"That's the theory. I'm still careful on the way, though. Some magicians leave traps behind, and that's not a fun day for anyone, getting caught in one of those."

Mostly they'd spit her out, but that wouldn't do her any good if it spat her out after spearing her with swinging hooks or dropping a boulder on her. Gravity won over immunity, every time.

"Huh. Must be nice though. Being immune."

"It can be. Lots of things that are nice can also be a little annoying, too."

"Like a new shirt." He nodded, full of understanding, and held out his hand as they began walking again. "Want me to carry your bag?"

"That is very kind," she said, careful not to answer too quickly and make the contents of her back any more appealing than they already were. "But I have a lot of work in here, in addition to what I'm bringing Mrs. Cadigan."

He nodded, solemn as a dean, and she might have paid more attention to it if Mrs. Cadigan hadn't stepped outside at that exact moment, drying her hands on a small towel.

"There's my Hemma, stopping in to do an old widow a favor," she called, throwing her arms wide.

Hemma ducked her head but stepped fully into the hug, breathing in the warmth of welcome. "Essel would never let me come to the Hollows and miss you when you needed something. And everyone along the alley has sent things with me."

"Ahhh." Mrs. Cadigan sighed and patted Hemma's cheek before stepping away. "I wish we'd found you earlier, sweet girl." Belatedly, she caught sight of the boy who'd escorted Hemma and frowned. "Annotoly Kenerfen, where are you meant to be right now?"

"Goats are already up for the night!" he said, frowning back equally fierce.

"And is that what I asked?"

He made a wordless noise and threw up his hands, muttering almost-words as he stormed off. Mrs. Cadigan smiled after him for a long moment before shaking herself and turning back to Hemma.

"Always exploring, that one. And, of course, he's why I called the shop, though I won't lie, I was hoping I'd get you to come out and visit." She beckoned Hemma to follow and went inside, the smell of supper—and better, dessert—picking up Hemma's pace all the more.

"I'm sorry it's been a while, Mrs. Cadigan, I've just—"

"Been busy, my girl. I've no doubt. Root and Vine was lucky to get you before Sylvan buried it entirely in paper made from other trees. Besides, you only spent a year here, and—"

"And I was lucky to do so," she interrupted firmly, taking a seat at the long wooden table as directed. Mrs. Cadigan turned to the stove and Hemma began unpacking all the treasures sent by the shopkeepers, explaining what each was and from whom, as she did.

"You'll stay for dinner?" Mrs. Cadigan asked when she was done.

"I'd love to."

The older woman shifted enough for Hemma to see her smile, then pointed at an oversized breadbox in the corner.

"Annotoly went spelunking before the sun came up this morning and came home with that. He came home safe enough, but I thought it better to be safe than sorry. Children!" she continued, loud enough to reach the other side of the door and not much further. "Come and see what the fine folks of Shopkeeper's Alley have sent you!"

The door to the rest of the house flew open. Small figures fell over themselves to scramble into the kitchen and Hemma stepped smartly out of the way. She kept her bag close, given it still contained an Absolutely Dangerous spell book, and let her fellow orphans sort their new treasures while she went to the breadbox.

Which was empty.

"Mrs. Cadigan, what did Annotoly find, exactly?" she asked, something other than hunger rolling through her stomach.

"A book of course." Mrs. Cadigan turned, her eyes fixing on the empty space in front of Hemma. She tore her gaze away, did a quick count of the children, and paled so dramatically she might have been carved of ice. "Six," she managed.

Six, where there should be seven. The other children were too occupied to pay attention to the adults, but Hemma knew it wouldn't be long before they realized they were down one as well.

"Where's Annotoly's room?"

She was already moving as Mrs. Cadigan answered, sprinting through the cozy game room and up the ancient stairs. She needn't have asked—the second door on the left hung askew, a riot of greenery spilling out of the room.

Mrs. Cadigan liked plants well enough, but this was no tamed garden cutting. Vines and stems twined with abandon, heavy leaves tipped with metallics draped themselves along the walls, and a chill ran down Hemma's neck.

The air wafted out to her, heavy with loam and rich soil that didn't exist inside the tidy farmhouse. Hemma approached the opening with a steady step, preparing herself.

Not enough.

Annotoly was hanging in the middle of the room, vines wrapped around each limb, leaves spilling over his shoulders.

She spat out a curse and his eyes snapped open, a deeper, brighter green than she'd caught outside in the evening light. He stared at her, silently, and she shoved down the urge to shiver.

Instead, she looked around, keeping one hand clamped to her bag. Even under its wards, the deep blue *Collection* stirred inside, its magic eager to meet or battle whatever was running loose in the room.

"Where are you, you little—A-ha!"

In the center of the room, directly under the boy, was a braid of silver-tipped leaves formed a perfect circle. Bracing herself for thorns, she shoved her hands inside.

Several things happened at once.

Annotoly screamed.

The *Collection* thumped hard against her side, bruising her hip.

But she missed the pain of that while she dealth with the ten-inch-long thorns that dug themselves into her hands and arms.

"Shouldn't have made it so pretty, should you?" she said, biting down on each word and digging through the leaves. "Smug. You're all so smug." Hemma yanked back, a virulently yellow-green book coming with her bleeding hands. The leaves she'd dug through browned and curled, wilting as she watched. Annotoly dropped a foot, his eyelids fluttering.

She'd have to hope the spelled leather would separate the *Collection* from conspiring with this jackass of a book as she shoved the new one into her bag to free her hands again. With another deep breath, she wrapped her arms around Annotoly's midsection and started backing toward the door.

Vines slithered over each other, leaves going *sh-sh-sh* and thorns clacking. Sweat beaded along her hairline and the nerves in her arms started firing wildly in response to the energy the leaves or the book were pushing at her. Still, one step after another, she backed into the hall.

"Clear the way," she called, sure without looking that Mrs. Cadigan and the other orphans were gathered on or near the steps. "And call the shop, Mrs. Cadigan. Let them know I'm coming."

Time moved very slowly.

Hemma put her back to the wall and crab-walked down the stairs, one at a time, both feet on each stair. She had a terrible feeling that if she pulled too hard, the vines would let go to cause her plummet and break her neck.

One of the children, the smallest she'd met on the path, raced halfway up the stairs, swinging a new wooden sword and howling in rage. Annotoly opened his eyes again, noises and noises out of him that could not properly be considered words.

Not words for human ears, at least.

The other child froze, sword extended, arm shaking.

"It was just one book?" she asked, after the other children gathered the smallest one away from the stairs. "What color was it?"

"Just one!"

"Green!"

"Bright green!"

"I didn't touch it; he wouldn't let me."

"Green like the pond in summer. It got less green in the breadbox."

"I peeked at it."

"I didn't touch it!"

She nodded, figuring since no one else had bloomed into a tropical jungle they were probably safe if she removed the book and the infected Annotoly and got the heck out of there as quickly as possible.

"You're going to be all right, Annotoly. Don't grow anymore."

He was boneless against her, but her immunity was likely already eating away at his connection to the book. It wouldn't be enough to free him, but she could get him back to Root and Vine, to the alley of trusted people with specialized skills, and they could save him.

She repeated it to herself with each slow step down the stairs, with each slow heartbeat she felt in the small body held against hers, until there was no room for doubt left in her head.

DOUVAL, DILEAH, AMANI, TIKAR, CIRITA, AND MORE OF THE VENDORS and shopkeepers of the alley had brought their best work, their best spells to meet her at the portals and escort her home.

She had a moment of hesitation before she stepping inside Root and Vine—bringing a magic book that caused uncontrolled plant growth into a giant tree that mostly did as it pleased already seemed like something worth pausing about—but the shop flapped its door impatiently and she couldn't think of anywhere better to go.

Essel had called Sylvan back, or Sylvan hadn't left. He pointed at the live-edged counter, miraculously cleared of everything, and suddenly her arms were empty.

They ached in that emptiness, even as she wrapped them around her hollow middle, and Cirita and Douval hugged her close.

Amani stood next to Sylvan chanting quietly, just below hearing, and Essel fluttered between them, lights flashing through her hair in an unknowable pattern.

Hemma breathed, and waited, and hoped. When Sylvan gestured, she stepped up and put her magic-nullifying hands on Annotoly's head. More breathing. More waiting. More hoping.

Finally, finally—was it an hour later, or a day?—the boy's eyes opened, a soft, non-glowing greenish-brown.

"Am I dangerous?" he asked, his voice baby-soft, before he fell into a more natural sleep.

The remaining plant life fell from him and Root and Vine shifted around them, sweeping the detritus out with a disgust they all felt.

Hemma hugged everyone, then collapsed into a chair and forgot everything for a few hours.

She woke up at her desk, which felt like someone's idea of a joke, but there was coffee in front of her, so she didn't scream. Instead, she stood, stretched until her aches were eased, and sipped her coffee as she moved back through the shop.

Essel fluttered over a nest of blankets and looked up as she approached, beaming.

"Mrs. Cadigan will be by to fetch him later today. Sylvan says he'll be right as a summer breeze."

"Mm." Hemma drank more coffee and studied the clearly-pretending-to-sleep boy. "I don't know. He's a highwayman in spirit."

"Adventurer," Annotoly murmured, a smile forming on the sleepy face.

"Mm." Hemma lifted her eyebrows and Essel laughed as she slowly backed away.

"Do I have to go home?"

"Not right away."

"Do you live here?"

"I work here, and I work a lot so it feels like I live here. Do you want a tour?"

His eyes snapped open, and he sat up, tossing the blankets aside. At her expectant expression, he took a deep breath, turned, and folded the blankets. Not the sharpest corners in the world, but a strong effort, so she let it be.

"This is Root and Vine. She's older than the moon and has as many moods." A crown of flowers bloomed in the doorway ahead of them, and Hemma pointed them out without mentioning that the shop was showing off a bit for him.

"It's the best thing I've ever seen," he said, his eyes skipping from piles of books to the flowers to more books to yet *more* books to Essel to another room of, also, books.

The flowers shaded purple, and Hemma drank some coffee to help swallow her laugh.

"Do you get to read all the books?" Annotoly asked from the third side room.

"I read a lot of them. One of the best things is that there are always more."

"Can I work here when I leave Mrs. Cadigan's? Like you did?" He trailed his small fingers along a shelf of outdated treaties, the wonder in his eyes showing he was well and truly lost.

"Are you in such a rush to go?" She had been. Not because Mrs. Cadigan wasn't supportive and kind and nurturing and all the things she'd never had, but because the older woman *was* all those things. Hemma had thought she needed a job, to make her own way in the world.

But what she'd found was a family. Mrs. Cadigan had taken an angry, scared, isolated half-grown girl and made her able to appreciate the world, to know it could have kindness. Root and Vine, cranky Sylvan, loving Essel, the talented shopkeepers of the Alley… they had shown her the world could have community.

Now Annotoly reminded her she could share that with others. Maybe with less Absolutely Dangerous side effects.

"No," he said, sweet and clear, putting his small hand in hers. "But it's nice to know I'll have to place to grow for."

Oh, absolutely dangerous indeed, that trust and hope in his small face. But she and her family, they were more than up for the challenge.

ABOUT MARISA WOLF

Marisa Wolf was born in New England and raised on Boston sports teams, *Star Wars*, *Star Trek*, and the longest books in the library (usually fantasy). Over the years she majored in English, in part to get credits for reading (this… only partly worked), taught middle school, was headbutted by an alligator, built a career in education, earned a black belt in Tae Kwon Do, and finally decided to finish all those half-started stories in her head.

She's currently based in Texas but has moved into an RV with her husband and their two ridiculous rescue dogs and it's anyone's guess where in the country she is at any given moment. Learn more at marisawolf.net.

FOREWORD: "TOLD AND RETOLD" BY KEVIN STEVERSON

BY CHRISTOPHER WOODS

The first time I ran into Kevin was at a convention named SphinxCon. I immediately liked him because he was as full of BS as I was. When he started the Salvage System books, they did quite well. He opened the world for others to write in and I jumped at the chance. It's a fun series to write in and now there are even options for movies based on the first trilogy. He's also written several stories in my Fallen World series. This is his first step into a new world he is creating.

TOLD AND RETOLD

BY KEVIN STEVERSON

*S*carisoara Cave
   Apuseni Mountains, Romania
Fall 2012

"Come on, it's time to go," Professor Jalthon called out to his students.

They were taking one last look into the back of the Scarisoara Cave, the largest underground glacier in Romania. Lamps on their helmets lit up the rear of the cave, beyond where tourist were allowed to venture. He and his students had traveled all over Romania visiting various archaeological digs these last six weeks.

As the top associate professor of archaeology at the University of Georgia, he was able to choose the locations for his semesters abroad. and he always chose Romania. His fascination with Transylvania and the legend of vampires decided it for him. Oh, he knew there were no vampires, nor had there ever been. He was, after all, a highly educated man. But still, rumors and legends start somewhere.

He moved toward the front of the cave, ducking in several places.

He was a solid six foot three and able to play pickup basketball even at the age of fifty-four.

"Professor!" one of his students cried out.

It was Stan Filtrey, a favored student, not that he would admit to having favorites.

"Look up there!" said Stan, gesturing wildly. Jalthon could see something buried in the ice about a foot above his head, the light from his helmet illuminating the dark shape.

He pulled his ice pick from his belt to dig the object out. It had taken all sorts of paperwork so he could have the pick in the cave and permission to remove anything he determined was worthy of study. It helped ease the red tape when the minister of antiquities in Romania was a lifelong friend. The man had once been a high school exchange student in Savannah, Georgia, some thirty-nine years ago.

Anything the professor found this semester would be sent back to UGA to study. Some things would be returned to Romania after they were studied, other objects would stay at UGA. Whatever this was, he hoped it was interesting.

He removed a small, hand-sized box from the hole in the ice. It was heavy and there was no doubt it was gold. There were strange lines covering it, going in all directions, intersecting each other at various angles, some butting flat against others. It was a design he had never seen, and it was assuredly out of place. There was no telling how long it had been buried in the thirty-five hundred-year-old glacier.

He flipped it over in his hand and studied it from all angles. *This is coming home with us.*

"Good eye, Stan, good eye," he said, beaming at his prize student.

The item stayed with him when they flew back to Georgia. It joined the strange blade he had collected three years earlier in the valley below the cave. Its make up was a yet unexplained combination of metals.

Like the box, the blade he'd found was a mystery. It was as if a modern blade had been buried, yet tests showed the soil and bits of carbon adhering to the blade was from the mid fifteenth century.

Which made even less sense since metalsmithing of that kind had not been discovered yet in that part of the world. Then again, the Japanese were making incredible blades long before then. He surmised the golden box came from the Far East, also.

But a busy schedule kept him from spending much time studying either.

~

University of Georgia
    Present Day

Ray Don Wharter dusted a shelf and carefully put the vase back. It was his third week as the owner of Wharton and Company. Getting the contract for the Department of Archaeology at UGA was a big deal. He cleaned it at night after the evening classes. He was tired, but it was worth it.

Ray Don was a nontraditional student, in his first year at UGA at the age of twenty-eight. He probably should have gone to college right out of high school but the opportunity for National Guard deployment came up when he was eighteen and he took it. When he came back, he went to work for his uncle's cleaning service and put off any additional schooling. Then, there was another deployment, one he didn't volunteer for this time. It happened when you were in the infantry.

Military schools, temporary assignments, annual trainings, and the next thing he knew, Ray Don had over ten years in the National Guard. He only needed twenty to retire.

PT, he thought to himself, *PT in the morning.* Ray Don took pride in maxing out on his physical training score. Only once had he not maxed the evaluation. It was after a bout of the flu, back when he was twenty-three. Never again, he had told himself, and he meant it.

He met regularly with several members of his unit to do PT and got in a good run three times a week. It was voluntary. He couldn't order any of his soldiers to do it since they were not currently on orders, and it was not a scheduled drill weekend. He had some good troops, though, and several of them felt the same way he did about always remaining in fighting shape. Those who could fit it into their civilian lives made the sessions. Others did it on their own.

Out of the corner of his eye he caught movement coming around the corner. Morty Rinkton, his roommate, and good friend for the last three years, was coming down the hall carrying a commercial floor cleaner. It had to weigh at least two hundred and fifty pounds.

"Morty, why didn't you just start it, walk behind, and let it drive itself to the back of the building?" Ray Don asked.

"It moves too slow."

He was right. It did go slow, but it made for a better floor surface after the brushes went over it.

"Besides, it's not that heavy," he said, in passing. Ray Don shook his head.

Ray Don stood five-ten and weighed between one eighty-five and one ninety depending on his workouts and eating habits. He was in great shape with a lean, strong build, but he didn't have near the strength Morty possessed.

At six-six and weighing two hundred and ninety-five pounds, Morty was a monster. Surprisingly agile for his size, Morty could run a fifteen-minute two-mile distance, the distance the Army used for its PT test. It wasn't fast enough to get the maximum score for his age group had he been in the military, but it was respectable, nonetheless.

Morty had played rugby for UGA's intramural team, his size made him perfect for the scrum. The UGA football coaches pursued him weekly, but he blew them off. He loved football, but there was no way he was going to lose total control of his time and submit to the strict schedules the football players were under.

Up until three weeks ago, Morty had worked as a fulltime bouncer in downtown Athens at the Theatre, a multi-bar concert venue. He now worked full time for Ray Don; the decision whether or not to enroll in law school still up in the air. He still bounced one night a week. He broke up a few fights and threw out patrons nearly every Saturday night; it was a good gig.

Ray Don had met Morty three years ago at a gun shop in Athens, at the firing range behind it, to be exact. Ray Don watched the giant of a man using two Colt 1911 .45 caliber pistols. He fired one after another, making it seem as if it was one weapon on auto. When the target was pulled back, Ray Don saw fourteen holes in the target, thirteen of them within the circle where the heart was on the man-sized silhouette. Ray Don knew the man hadn't fully loaded the magazines to prevent spring issues. The one "miss" was an inch to the left of the heart.

Ray Don let out an approving whistle and looked up at the big man. "That was an incredible piece of shooting."

"Thanks," replied the stranger. The big man looked down at the weapon in Ray Don's hand. It was a smaller pistol, a compact. He did a double take. "Hey, that looks just like a 1911… only smaller. What is it?"

"This is my new personal carry. It is a Llama Especial .380," Ray Don answered. "I got a sweet deal on it. This one was made in 1955." He dropped the clip, racked the slide, looked inside the weapon, and handed it to the big man to inspect. It looked like a toy in his huge hand as he handled it like a man who knew his weapons.

"Nice," he said. "It looks like a miniature 1911. Does it break down like one?"

"Yeah, it does. I keep it loaded with Federal Tactical 99 grain HST hollow points. Well, not at the range, that's too expensive."

"I hear you," the big man said. He held out his hand. "Name's Morty Rinkton. How the hell are you?"

Ray Don reached out and was prepared to have his hand crushed. It was a firm shake, but the big man was clearly not exerting the pressure he could have. "Ray Don Wharton, and if I was any finer, I'd be fighting women off with a club."

Both men laughed.

Afterward, they were standing out by their trucks in the parking lot when Ray Don asked, "You feel like some hot wings and a beer?"

"You are my new best friend," answered Morty. "Even my cousin just got shifted on down the line of acquaintances."

THREE HOURS LATER THE TWO MEN HAD CLEANED THE ENTIRE building. They had worked an all-nighter and given it a deep clean two weeks earlier, so they only had to maintain it and buff the floors a couple nights a week.

Easy money, Ray Don thought. *Enough to pay Morty what he was making at the Theatre and to earn more than I was making with my uncle. We should look for more contracts. I bet cleaning banks would be easy. That's just a light clean nightly. What bank ever really gets dirty during the business day? The background checks should be quick since I hold a clearance. Morty has a clean record, too. So that would be no problem.*

He was deep into planning his pitch when he heard Morty calling him. Morty was supposed to be gathering the last of the trash in Professor Jalthon's office.

Ray Don walked in. "What's up?" he asked.

"Check this out," Morty said. He was holding an odd-shaped blade.

He handed it to Ray Don. It looked like the top of a glaive only much smaller. It had what appeared to be a grip, though whatever handle had been on it was long gone and with only a thin bar of steel remaining. The blade started on the inside of the fist, ran across the front, and down the side of the arm almost to the elbow.

"This is sweet," Ray Don said punching like a boxer and sweeping the blade across. "Where'd you get it?"

"It was on the shelf with this gold, puzzle cube thing," Morty explained. "I'm good with puzzles; I bet I can solve it," he muttered while turning the bottom twice.

Ray Don looked around the professor's office. A kite-shaped shield leaned against the wall in one corner. In the next corner was a miniature basketball goal with a couple small basketballs in the net. It was small, about five foot tall, the obligatory UGA red and black, and was well made.

Basketball was how he had landed the cleaning contract. He played pick-up ball a couple of times a week on campus and had met the sixty-year-old professor running the court with the best of them. They struck up a friendship and it resulted in getting the inside scoop on the contract.

"What the—" he heard Morty gasp. He whipped around and saw him drop the cube onto the professor's desk. The lines were glowing and moving in directions he couldn't follow. A shimmer appeared on the side of the professor's desk, along with a growing hole. A breeze came from the pitch black inside the hole.

"What did you do, Morty? What the hell did you do!"

"I-I don't know," Morty stammered. "I just solved the puzzle and lined up those moving lines, only they weren't moving when I did it."

"This is not good, not good at all," Ray Don stated. "What's that sound?"

From the hole, they heard something running in the darkness. Ray Don grabbed the blade off the desk and gripped it in his right hand. "Turn the cube! Turn the cube back!"

Morty grabbed the cube. The top moved. He kept going, his hands a blur. Ray Don looked back as Monty finished with a double twist to the bottom of the cube. A man stood with a blade in his hand while another dove through the fading hole before it closed.

Are they men? Ray Don asked himself as he crouched defensively. He took in all the details at once. With three fingers on each hand, both men held a blade like the one in his. They gripped them like they knew how to use them. Both were squinting, their eyes watering.

The eyes, from what he could see, were all black. So much for *"Don't fire until you see the whites in their eyes,"* he thought. Their skin was so pale it appeared to be white, and they both had shoulder-length dark hair. They were wearing identical outfits. Whether or not they were uniforms, he couldn't tell.

One snarled something incomprehensible to the other and lunged with its blade. Ray Don moved without thinking. He brought his right arm up to block the blade and sparks flew as the blades met with a metallic clang. The sound seemed to surprise his opponent for a split second and Ray Don's left foot lashed out to where a normal man's knee would be. It should have been a crippling blow, with all his strength and his adrenaline behind it.

His foot struck something solid, but the creature seemed to take the blow well. It wasn't crippled, though it did limp a step or two back. It exposed sharp teeth.

He saw the creature squint again and he feinted with his right fist. The creature moved its hand with the blade to block the punch and Ray Don snapped a head-high kick with his left foot. The ruse worked, and his round-toed boot connected. The blow appeared to daze it, and as soon as his foot touched the ground, he immediately used the same kick again. It was not expected, and the creature went down to its knees. He met its face with a knee, and it was out. He kicked it in the side of the head as it lay there, for good measure.

Morty saw the first man lunge at Ray Don as the second started to stand. Looking around he saw the shield and jumped for it and turned in time to block the blade. The thing in front of him snarled and showed its teeth.

He threw the shield at the creature as he eased toward the corner with the basketball goal. It shrugged off the flying shield. Morty reached behind the goal, grabbed the pole, stepped on the base, and jerked it upward. Its reach gave him an advantage.

The creature seemed to realize its predicament as Morty watched its eyes go from a squint to wide-open acknowledgment. He swung the goal like a one-handed sledgehammer, straight down on the creature. It threw up its arm with the blade to block it, but it did little good.

He pounded the creature several times more than needed before Ray Don finally got his attention. He tossed the bent pole to one side, breathing heavily. The fiberglass backboard hadn't lasted two blows and was in pieces all around him. The creature was dead, or at least appeared to be. It wasn't moving and was covered in a dark liquid.

Morty noticed pieces of ceiling tile all around him. He looked up. Swinging the basketball goal had torn ragged pieces out of the drop ceiling. "The professor is not going to like the way we cleaned his office, that's for sure."

"Tell me about it," Ray Don said. "Morty, go rip the cord off the vacuum cleaner, quick!"

Morty took off at a dead run and was back in no time.

"Help me tie him… it up," Ray Don said pointing at the creature he had kicked down. "I don't think we need to tie yours up."

Morty tilted his head to one side, shrugged, and moved to help Ray Don. "Him or me," he said. "Him or me."

Twenty minutes passed and the creature still had not moved. They were both sipping a canned drink Morty purchased from the break room vending machine. Morty was on his second.

"We have to call the campus police," Ray Don decided out loud. "And they are not going to believe a word we say."

Morty took another sip and said, "They have no choice. They can count those fingers with the weird nails just as well as we can, and they can see those nasty-ass teeth. They can definitely see those eyes. What the hell is up with those eyes, anyway? Creepiest thing I've seen in a long time."

Ray Don looked at his phone. "Strange. I don't have any signal. There are usually four bars with the 4G lit up on campus. You got any signal?"

Morty shook his head as he tried to connect. "Nope."

Ray Don picked up the desk phone. It was silent. He hit nine and heard no tone. He tried zero. Nothing. He placed the phone back on the receiver and looked up.

Chaos ensued.

Four men, all in black tactical gear with weapons at the ready burst through the door. They came in fast, in a typical four-man stack.

Tactically proficient, Ray Don thought as he allowed himself to be thrown to the ground. He saw four more enter the room in the same way as he lay on the floor. Like the first four, all of them had the tactical lights on their rifles lit.

Strange, they didn't even kill the power to the building to shut off the lights. I wonder why the tac lights are on?

Morty was on the ground with two men on top of him holding him down. He looked at Ray Don with a raised eyebrow.

"At least they didn't shoot first and ask questions later." Ray Don grinned.

This was not a good night.

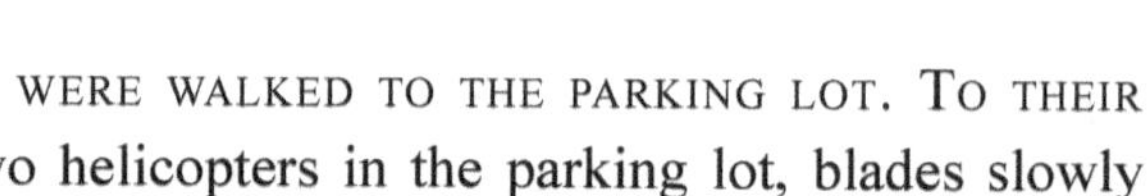

RAY DON AND MORTY WERE WALKED TO THE PARKING LOT. TO THEIR surprise, there were two helicopters in the parking lot, blades slowly spinning down. A third landed on the far side. It wasn't any louder than a good leaf blower.

"Nice," Ray Don said. "This is some secret squirrel shit." He had some buddies in 20th group over in Alabama, so he knew what they had available for insertions. "Not even Special Forces have those."

A man walked toward them from the last helicopter. He looked about fifty years old with a little grey in his old-fashioned flat top. He was dressed in the same gear the men wore. He stared at them both for a minute and shook his head.

He looked away, held a hand to his ear as if listening to someone, and said into the air, "Block off the area and clean it up, load the Vamps. Get a contractor in here to blow the room. Inform the campus police that Homeland Security was following several questionable people who entered the building and found the two janitors held captive when we apprehended them. Tell them we had to blow a device in place. I'll ensure the real Homeland Security and other agencies mind their own business."

He turned back to them. "You don't have a clue as to what you have stumbled onto, do you?" They stood silent. He pointed at the helicopter behind him with his thumb. "Get in."

Morty looked at Ray Don for guidance. Ray Don thought for a

moment and decided to obey the orders of the person who was clearly in charge. Morty shrugged and followed him.

The flight took about thirty minutes. Clearly, the pilot wasn't pushing the helicopter like he must have getting to the UGA campus, especially if they were headed back to wherever the birds had come from. Ray Don knew there was no way they just happened to be in the area.

They went northeast into the Georgia mountains. Ray Don had recognized the lights of the shopping outlets at Banks Crossing as they flew over them. The helicopter soon descended into a valley; the mountains blocked out the stars on both sides. Touchdown was surprisingly soft.

Ray Don and Morty both stepped off the bird onto a lightly lit landing pad and followed the older man toward a building about one hundred feet away. It was a small two-story building, backed against a cliff.

"I'll bet it extends into the mountain," Morty said, clearly still excited by his first helicopter ride. "This is great! Like a movie or something. Wait... do you think they'll disappear us?" He looked around as he said it.

"No, I don't think so." Ray Don answered. "We're not cuffed, so that's a good sign."

They were placed in a small but comfortable conference room. There was a nice, new, wooden table with eight matching chairs around it, a couple of comfortable reading chairs on one end, and a small coffee cart along the wall opposite the door. There were snacks on the cart, much to Morty's delight. He ate three honeybuns.

"How the heck do you eat crap like that and stay in any kind of decent shape?" Ray Don asked, sipping a cup of coffee. Morty shrugged.

They waited for over an hour. Ray Don thought long and hard about the night and the people who had shown up, feds or whatever they were. Morty grew bored. Ray Don had played this game many times in the military: Hurry up and wait.

"I hope they don't keep us long. LibertyCon is next weekend," Morty said.

"I know. I sat in front of my computer for the countdown to ticket sales and I've been counting the days since. We've even got hotel reservations."

"Hey," Monty asked, "you think we can talk them into a helicopter ride to Chattanooga?"

"I doubt it," Ray Don answered. "Besides, we still have to pack our bags. I have a Salvage Fleet uniform to unveil this year at the Salvage Title Universe panel." He paused a moment and added, "You know, it seems like we're right in the middle of a panel, acting a plot out as an author describes it."

"That was hella cosplay, if we are," Morty decided. "Hella cosplay."

The door opened and the older man stepped in followed by a woman in regular clothes.

Civilian, thought Ray Don. She was an attractive red head, wearing glasses, faded jeans, and a shirt that read "I'm Offended That You're Offended." She was holding a laptop and a file. They sat down and the debriefing began.

The man introduced himself as John Doe and the woman as Jane Doe, no relation.

Riiight, thought Ray Don, and he looked over at Morty to see if he had caught the obvious lie. Morty snorted into his hand. *Let's see where this goes.*

❧

"STAFF SERGEANT WHARTON, MR. RINKTON," THE WOMAN BEGAN. She hit the highlights of Ray Don's military career and some of Morty's life, including his final grade point average at UGA.

Ray Don whistled at that. "I didn't know you got those kinds of grades."

"I don't talk about it," Morty answered, shrugging it off. "I just did the assignments and studied a little for the tests. It wasn't that hard."

Mr. Doe then asked them to explain, in detail, exactly what had transpired in the office on campus. Ray Don went into military briefing mode and gave a complete after-action review. He had given many in his career in the Army.

When Morty told his side, it was nothing like an AAR. It was if Morty was explaining a movie he had seen.

He said, "I was like… this is a puzzle… I can still do a Rubik's cube in less than thirty seconds, and it was like all squiggly, and I grabbed the shield… and threw it… and I was swinging the goal all like… it was all Raahhh!!!… with those crazy eyes and sharp teeth… and I was like Bam! Bam! Bam!" All the while, he waved his hands and was very animated in his explanation.

It took all the self-control Ray Don could manage not to laugh, watching and listening to his friend.

The Does looked at each other and then seemed to come to a decision. John Doe looked at them and said, "Staff Sergeant Wharton, you maintain a Secret clearance; this now falls within the scope of that clearance. Actually, it is far *above* the level you maintain, but you understand the consequences of revealing sensitive information, so it will do for now."

Ray Don nodded. "Understood. Sir."

"Mr. Rinkton. You are a civilian and have no clearance, whatsoever. So, I am granting you an interim secret clearance, effective as of noon yesterday. Trust me, you do not want to reveal the events of earlier tonight or what you may learn here to anyone who is not in the need-to-know."

Morty nodded. "Cool, I got a clearance," he whispered out of the side of his mouth to Ray Don. He wasn't a very good whisperer.

"My actual name is Colonel Richard Cranet. I head up an operation that is… well, Delta Force doesn't even know about us, if that tells you anything. We are not part of the normal military. Those in the government who know about us do not discuss us nor do they inquire about us. We fall under an extremely vetted, need-to-know basis, and the few who are briefed wish they had never heard of us and would never reveal anything about us because of the effects it would cause on today's society. The world is not ready to know what the Rift Guard mission is."

He continued. "We are very picky about who we allow in, who we recruit, and why. There are six locations such as this one and a central headquarters located in Arkansas. We are comprised of military, some agency and law enforcement types, and apparently, now, one civilian."

He looked at Morty. Morty grinned and gave him a thumbs up. Jane Doe stifled a laugh.

"What happened earlier tonight was never supposed to happen. To open a portable rift in an uncontrolled environment is suicide. You had no idea what you held in your hands, and even if you did you had no idea where the rift connected."

He held up his hand, stopping their complaints. "I know, I know. You had no idea the cube could do that." He thought for a second then said, "You know, we have only opened one other cube ourselves and it took a rather advanced computer program to figure out that one's pattern."

He looked at Morty with a raised eyebrow. "To be honest, we didn't know another one had been discovered and was on the UGA campus . We would have confiscated it long ago, had we known. The one you opened was discovered in a glacial cave in Romania and, apparently, has been sitting on a shelf for the last nine years.

"Here is the long and the short of it. We were in the process of setting up this location specifically for another contact in the region. It takes time for us to recruit and place teams. In a way, you have made the job easier for us, since one of you was already on our shortlist of potential recruits."

"Ray Don," he said using his actual given name instead of rank and last name. "You will request to go into the Inactive National Guard. The request will be approved. You will still receive your retirement at twenty years; that can be arranged. You will head a team. You have the experience we desire and the personality type. You have finished at the top of almost all your military schooling, and you know the right kind of people. You also have some of the intangibles we are looking for.

"You will build your team within the week. We will have to shorten our normal process. You are not authorized to use any more civilians. Current military, ex-military, law enforcement, and agency types are acceptable. Do not reveal details until they accept. Once you have them assembled, you will all undergo an extensive learning program as well as rigorous training at a new location. We have selected some of your team for you. You will recruit the others." He paused. "Choose wisely, as if your life depends upon your choices, because it may.

"Morty, you are on the team," Cranet said looking toward the big man.

Morty jumped to his feet and gave a Tiger Woods fist pump.

The colonel looked down at the table and shook his head. He took a deep breath and looked up. "Don't make me regret it."

Morty quickly sat down and attempted to look serious.

Cranet smiled. "You beat a Vamp to death with a basketball goal. Of course, you're in."

"I beat him like he stole sumthin'," Morty agreed.

"Before you two get big heads, let me explain something," Cranet said. "According to information available to us, the two Vamps you encountered were janitors. No disrespect intended to your line of work, but they were on the lowest rungs of their society. That is why they were only armed with their honor blades."

He noticed the look on Ray Don's face as he said it. "More on that, later. You opened the rift to their planet using an ancient device. It connected to another in their version of a museum, a sort of shrine. Had it been located elsewhere, and had there been actual armed Vamps near it, it would not have ended well for you, or our world."

Morty raised his hand like a student in school. The colonel stared at him expectantly.

"Uh, when you call them Vamps. Do you mean vampires? Like, as in vampire-vampires?

"Legends start somewhere. Stories are told and retold."

"Oh."

"Bigfoot?" Ray Don asked. "the Loch Ness Monster?"

"Area 51?" Morty asked. "I know! Chupacabra. That's some creepy shit."

Jane Doe raised her eyebrows but didn't say a word. The colonel tilted his head a little and pursed his lips.

"You have a lot to learn." He stood to leave.

Ray Don watched them walk away, his head spinning. He'd just been given the one thing he wanted more than anything. He shook his head and turned back to look at his friend.

"What is it gonna cost?" he asked under his breath.

ABOUT KEVIN STEVERSON

Kevin Steverson is a retired veteran of the U.S. Army. With several bestselling novels, including the Salvage Title Trilogy, which has been picked up for development into a feature film, he is also a published songwriter. He can be found in the foothills of the NE Georgia mountains writing in one fashion or another. Sign up for his newsletter at kevinsteverson.com and receive a free short story.

FOREWORD: "CRUNCH AND MUNCHKIN" BY CHRISTOPHER WOODS AND ANGELA CLAYTON

BY T.K.F. WEISSKOPF

Is it a love story? Is it a superhero story? Is it about found family? Or just deserts? Embrace the power of "and"! We have a case here of two writers working together to mix flavors to create a lovely dish for your delectation.

CRUNCH AND MUNCHKIN

BY CHRISTOPHER WOODS
&
ANGELA CLAYTON

Jasmine placed the last dish in the rack to dry and looked at the clock. Seven o'clock meant Evie would be waking up soon, so she opened the loaf of bread and slipped two pieces into the toaster. She took the spreadable butter from the fridge and the grape jelly. She smiled as she thought of the last time she had bought something besides grape.

Evie had puckered her whole face up like she had eaten a whole lemon.

"Not dramatic at all," she said grinning.

Usually, Evie didn't complain about much, but apple jelly was just too much for the little munchkin to take.

The toast popped up and Jas put two more slices in the toaster. She pulled the tray from the cabinet. It was plastic but it had pictures of little roses on them. She took down a set of little cups and a pretty white teapot with matching roses. Taking a jug of fruit punch from the fridge, she filled the little teapot and placed it in the center of the tray.

She'd asked Evie the night before what she wanted for breakfast and she had asked for a peanut butter and jelly tea party she could share with Crunch and the others, her imaginary friends.

Evie had many imaginary friends, but Crunch was her favorite. Jas remembered at least three that Evie would talk about, so she made four peanut butter and jelly sandwiches on toast and placed four teacups on the tray.

A boom rattled the windows, and she shook her head.

"Supers," she said. "They should think just a little before they do that. Too early for that nonsense."

But Supers were just a fact of life. It was a lot worse before Jacob declared Philadelphia a crime free city. The day he came out as a Super was well documented. It had been a brutal time for her neighboring city. The Stranger had killed Dominic Dynamo and what he'd done to Gladiatrix was horrible. When he came back bragging that he was going to do the same to her again, a lowly carpenter had walked up the street and snapped the Stranger's neck. It was brutal but it was justified.

Jas would never forget the day Jacob Talbot had gone from a carpenter who rebuilt after the battles between heroes and villains to, perhaps, the strongest Super to walk the planet. He declared Philly his own and protected it with a passion. He'd had to prove his seriousness a couple of times, but five years later it was one of the best cities to live in. Talbot would pursue you to the ends of the Earth and punish you if you hurt his people. Everyone knew what had happened to Sam Slick, the speedster. He'd killed his wife and fled the city. Talbot caught him in Reno and left him lying in the street with every bone in his body crushed.

Jas shuddered and picked up the tray. She carried it down the hall and up the stairs. Opening the door to Evie's room, she smiled as the pile of stuffed animals rolled away. Green eyes stared at her from the center of the pile.

"Is that what I think that is?"

"Peanut butter and jelly tea party, as requested."

"You made one for Crunch? And Scarlet? And Weasel?"

"I did."

"I love you, Mommy!"

"I love you too, Munchkin!"

Jas grinned and set the tray down on Evie's tea party table.

Evie, in her unicorn pajamas, jumped out of the bed and sat down in her chair at the tea party table.

"Crunch likes the grape jelly, too. But Scarlet liked the apple when you got it. Weasel will eat anything."

Jas smiled. "So would you like me to get some more of the apple for Scarlet?"

"Yes, please."

Jas chuckled as she stepped back out of the room. "Let me know when you're done."

"Okay, Mommy."

She closed the door and remembered something.

"Mommy's going to get you some apple," Evie was saying as Jas stepped back into the room.

She gasped as she saw Evie take a bite of a sandwich. The other three sandwiches were already gone. Something glinted across from the little girl, but she couldn't make it out. Evie turned to her with a grin. The glint disappeared.

Jas swallowed and said, "I forgot to tell you we'll be going to the zoo tomorrow for your birthday."

"Yay! Crunch loves the zoo!"

She closed the door again. How had Evie eaten three sandwiches fast enough to have been on the fourth already? That was faster than it should be. Maybe she should call Charles. He would know more than her would about strange things.

She returned to the kitchen, picked up the phone, and dialed a number.

CHARLES KRAVEN HAD JUST ENTERED THE TASTEFULLY APPOINTED seating area when his phone trilled. He glanced at the watch on his wrist to see who was ringing his personal line. He frowned as he saw the name. He tapped Accept and slipped the earbud into place, holding a finger up to silence the receptionist in front of him.

"Hello, Jasmine." He listened intently and the side of his mouth lifted.

"Charles," she replied to the cold voice. "This isn't about us. I'm worried about Evie…"

"What is she doing that gives you such concern? Nothing to worry over. I will take care of it. I am going into a meeting right now, but I give you my word, Evie is my top priority." He tapped to end the call and slipped the earbud into its case. He sent three messages in quick succession then, looking at the receptionist, he signed in for his appointment and walked into the interior office. He took his customary seat across from the woman he had agreed to meet.

"So, you want to know what being a 'Super' is like? Here it is… pills and regrets. That's what it's like," he said tapping the fingertip-long ash of his cigarette into the cut crystal brilliance on the mahogany side table.

"How very dramatic, Charles. Care to elaborate?" she asked as notes flowed from her pen onto the paper, none of that annoying graphite scratchiness or rasping.

"Of course, there are moments of success, greatness even, but those tiny tragedies undermine and consume them."

"Am I to assume you are speaking of the loss of your daughter?"

The credenza behind his immaculately styled salt-and-pepper hair exploded. To the counselor's credit, she didn't flinch.

"I will take that to be an affirmative. Evie was four years old at the time of the divorce, correct? There were certain accusations…" Her voice was fluid, almost inflectionless, with a tiny note of encouraging warmth.

He ground his molars, the sound filling the spaces between settling debris. How dare she, how… dare… she. A momentary lapse of reason on his part when he had first spoken of it and now it was woven into his narrative. When he had taken her nondescript business card from a comrade, he had never intended to call. Yet, he had, and now after ten months it was detonating in his face. He didn't need anyone digging into his personal life. This was supposed to be about business and how being a Super affected it.

"We will not speak of that. There is nothing to be gained."

His blue eyes narrowed to slits as he turned his full attention on the sparrow of a woman sitting across from him. Good shoes, heeled but practical, stockings, caramel skirt, cream cowl-neck sweater, black statement necklace, brown hair… definitely all the color of a common house sparrow. Trimly built, efficient looking. But then he gazed into her eyes.

Ah, he thought, *here she is. She keeps her plumage hidden.*

The eyes were extraordinary in their depth… and she had just moved from ordinary to collectible. He smiled to himself, and it lit his own eyes for just a moment as he weighed the potential displays.

"Evie!" Jas yelled up the stairs. "Are you ready yet?"

"Coming!"

Jas smiled. Evie was six years old today and Jas wanted her to have a fun day. She had packed a whole cooler full of peanut butter and jelly sandwiches.

Evie ran down the hall to the stairs.

"Walk down the steps!" Jas yelled as she turned back to the kitchen.

She heard the footfalls slow.

"Did you wear the new dress?" she asked.

"Yep," Evie answered, stepping into the kitchen.

The cute yellow sundress clashed with the pink cowboy boots, but Jas didn't have the heart to tell her.

"Perfect," she said. "Let's get the cooler and we'll go."

She stepped out the door as three black vans stopped in the street. Her eyes narrowed and she pushed Evie behind her.

Black-clad men poured from the first of the dark vans. "Kill the woman! Take the girl!"

Jas gasped and tried to push Evie back inside the house. There was a crash and she looked back to see an obviously female form standing between her and the men as they advanced, weapons at ready. Clad in gold, flowing blonde hair caught in the breeze of her arrival, Jasmine recognized her immediately.

"I don't think that's very nice, boys."

The men opened fire on Golden Saint, and she waded among them. Bodies sailed through the air to crash into trees, fences, vans, and anything around them, a car swerved to avoid a body, smashing into and through the front wall of the neighboring house.

Jas pushed Evie into the house and dropped atop the girl. They would have to shoot through her to get Evie.

Evie huddled beneath her and Jas held her close.

Jas yelped when the door opened, and a hand touched her shoulder. She turned to see blonde hair and golden armor.

"You're okay," the Super said. "They're not in any shape to hurt you now. Why were they after you?"

"I don't know. They wanted Evie."

"What would Kraven want with her?"

"Did you say Kraven?" Her stomach lurched but it was engulfed by rage. "That rat bastard!"

"Who?"

"Kraven! He sent men to kill me and take her!"

"That's what I'm talking about. Why is Kraven after you?"

"Charles Kraven was my husband. He was Evie's stepfather for a year. Then we divorced."

"You were married to Charles Kraven?"

"Until I found out what he did for a living."

"If he's after you, you need protection."

Sirens grew louder.

"I'll stay until the authorities get here," she said placing her golden armored hand on Jas's shoulder again.

Jas tried not to think about the delicate spray of blood that marred the golden arm.

"Thank you," Jasmine said holding her crying daughter to her chest. "What have I done?" she asked under her breath.

〜

"Box 12, Units 8, 12, 14, and 21. Mutual aid request. Respond to multivehicle collision with six confirmed PIs. One vehicle has impacted a structure, confirmed entrapment. Location is near the intersection of Broadway and South Main Street," the radio barked. "Update: Active Super event, repeating, active Super event. Use caution on approach."

Vargas, her latest orientee, was behind the wheel of the rig maneuvering smoothly through the thickening traffic, "Well, that isn't us." His voice was tinged with more than a little relief, Michaels noticed as she caught his glance.

Michaels cocked her head to the side. "I don't think so… I think we need to respond to this. The footage on social media is really intense. There are reports that Golden Saint is there. If that's the case, she is impenetrable and shit is going to get broken."

He slowed to a stop at the intersection and waited for the light. He looked at her, puzzled.

"So? Aren't a lot of them impenetrable? That *is* part of what makes a Super right? Can't shoot 'em, can't stab 'em. Most of them are indestructible, if you believe the stories. I mean, come on, Mouse." He paused and looked like he had sucked a lemon… hard. Michaels fought back a grimace and thought, *Poor kid, bet he wished he could take that slip back, using a nickname on your orientation run was ballsy, or stupid, depending on the evaluator.*

She shifted in her seat and watched his profile for a moment before speaking, and he looked like he had never been so relieved to see a traffic light turn green in his life.

"Nooo, you aren't understanding," she said, speaking slowly to emphasize her point. "We need to jump this call."

He shook his head and grinned at her. "You know we don't jump calls, it's against policy. Is this some kind of weird test? You get written up and possibly draw a suspension. I am not interested in getting a negative in my jacket just so you can get a Super fix. I've heard some of the rumors. Call jumping to get to a Supers clean up, they get ugly, I mean… *really*? That's just nuts! I would rather take my chances at an Active Shooter event than one of these."

The temperature in the cab seemed to drop as she spoke. "Let me clarify something for you. I will explain this exactly once. I am going to radio in and put us en route. You *will* turn on the lights and sirens and get us to this call."

The command in her voice left no room for doubt as she reached for the mic and keyed up. "Central, Unit 52 is en route for mutual aid," her voice was smooth and calm, at odds with the gleam in her eye. She shifted in her seat to see him better and drive her point home.

She clicked off the mike and addressed him. "Active Shooter? *Really?* Where a single person is intent on killing as many as they can. Usually with plenty of ammunition and attitude. If you're lucky, it's some flaming turd without a clue—armed to the teeth and no idea what to do with it—living a fantasy, and can't hit the broadside of a barn. If you aren't, you end up like my first partner when we walked into a scene with a committed, skilled, and determined individual of intent with a high-powered rifle, scope, a handily placed windsock, and three weeks of ground prep. In addition to the initial seven people we were called to assist, he shot five more responders. Handy reflective vests and all."

He saw her absently rub a spot just under her right clavicle without missing a breath.

"Supers could give a crap about you when they're brawling it out a thousand feet in the air and throwing each other into buildings. They're so focused on each other that we're all just collateral damage. Still sucks donkey balls, but I'll take my chances with that. Do not *ever* spew crap like that again." She turned forward to watch the intersections.

"Geez, Michaels, that's harsh. They also save a lot of lives, there are good ones."

"Supers are like omnidirectional land mines, Vargas. No one is ever safe."

The radio interrupted her, "Requesting Code Five, repeating Code Five, two trucks to vicinity of staging area being established by fire/rescue on scene. Multi-trauma patients, confirmed reports of three fatalities."

Vargas looked at Mouse. "How did you know it was going to be bad like that?"

Mouse shrugged. "Been around a while, and you learn to rely on multiple sources." She wiggled her phone at him and winked, trying to lighten the mood. "Not just the radio. Some of these guys get going, you know, and then their friends decide to join in. You don't see them at first, and we've been lucky so far, but trust me. This could get ugly. Those multi-traumas will be normals, not Supers. So, what you need to do is just buckle down, focus on triage when we get there, and we'll work our way through them. Now, drive."

Vargas heaved a sigh and accelerated them to the call.

Mouse shot a text to her usual partner, HEY THERE, ON OUR WAY CODE 5 TO YOUR LOCATION, GETTING WARMED UP AND READY FOR INTERVENTION. VARGAS IS GOOD PEOPLE.

They neared the scene and traffic was mostly at a standstill due to the volume of emergency vehicles. Several drivers were out of their vehicles, shading their eyes to watch the macabre parade. Vargas tucked them in behind a heavy rescue unit winding its way toward the staging area.

Michaels spotted the command vest within fifteen feet of where they parked the rig when they arrived on scene. He happened to be their immediate boss and she breathed a sigh of relief. Chip Browning was old school and brass tacks, no drama and all get it done. He had started more than 28 years ago and had seen the service through all its changes, growing pains, and messes. He knew his business. Chip spotted her and wiggled his forefinger in his trademark come hither gesture. Her smile broadened.

"Glad you could make it, even if you were a bit early on the trigger." The slight admonishment was taken exactly how he intended it. He fixated on her for a moment.

"Mouse, go find Pulse Ox. He should be near Keegan Heavy Rescue. They were checking out a couple people in the residence over there. Then saddle up. Vargas, you're with me."

Vargas swallowed hard and Mouse looked relieved. She could see Pulse Ox standing inside the front door talking to a woman holding a little girl. As she approached she heard him speaking in the low tones that usually comforted kids and skittish patients.

"Ma'am, medically you are both in good shape. Just treat the scrapes and keep them bandaged. Here are some very special bandages, just for Miss Evie and her friends." Pulse Ox handed the woman several cartoon adhesive bandages.

"Thank you, so much. Evie, why don't you go inside, and we can get cleaned up. I'll be right there." She smiled and rumpled her daughter's hair. Once the child had slipped inside, Pulse Ox handed her a plain white card with raised black lettering.

"This is for you. Call him. I promise he'll hear you out. Domestic violence can escalate, and if this has happened, you may want some extra protection."

"I'll think about it. I promise," she said seriously. Pulse Ox nodded.

"Well, be safe. Call if you need help," he said. Mouse and Pulse Ox turned away. The door closed and they heard the dead bolt slide home.

JAS WAITED ANXIOUSLY BY THE DOOR AS THE SLEEK GRAY SEDAN WITH blacked out windows pulled into her drive. She watched with narrowed eyes as a middle-aged man in a tailored black suit stepped out of the back passenger door holding a gray fedora. He surveyed the damage to her neighbor's house and the two tow trucks that were loading up the last of the wrecked vehicles.

He stepped toward the nearest truck and cocked his head to the side as he noted the impression of a large fist outlined in the side of the black van. It had crumpled the side of the vehicle.

She saw him shake his head then don the hat. With a small frown he turned and approached the house.

"Evie!" she yelled. "You stay up there until I see who this is!"

"Okay, Mommy!"

She opened the door with a cold feeling in her stomach. *What if this is someone from Charles?*

The man took his hat off. "Ma'am, I am Sebastian Sinner, the man you spoke to on the phone."

Her lip trembled a tiny bit as relief flooded through her.

"Thank God," she said. "I have been terrified that they'll try again."

He nodded. "Understandable. That's why I came immediately. Please tell me what happened."

"Shouldn't we leave?"

He looked outide and waved his hand. She saw a shimmer in the air.

"We're safe for the moment. That shield is strong enough to prevent anything from coming in."

"Shield?"

"Shields are my thing, ma'am."

"Please, I'm Jasmine, or Jas if you prefer." She turned to the stairs. "Come on down, Munchkin!"

Sebastian looked toward the stairs. "I've been all over this world, but I don't think I've ever seen a lovelier pair of boots."

Jas watched the smile that appeared on Evie's face. She hadn't seen it since the attack and was thankful children were much more resilient than adults. All she felt was a lingering terror.

"Can you go into the living room, honey? I need to talk to Mister Sinner for a minute."

She could have let Evie stay upstairs but she wanted her close, where she could see her. It made her feel better when she was able to see the girl.

"Okay, I understand this is a domestic issue," he said.

"I was married for a short time to Charles Kraven. He sent men to kill me and take my daughter."

"Is he her father?"

"Absolutely not. I was young and widowed way too soon for anyone. He was handsome and rich. I thought it would be good for Evie. But then I found out more about him than I was comfortable with, and we divorced. I didn't go after his money. All I wanted was this home and to be left alone."

"Then he has no legal right to take the child?"

"No, he does not."

"But there is the problem that Charles Kraven wants you dead. Why is that?"

"Yesterday, I saw something," she said. "I thought something strange was going on and I called him because I knew he would know more about strangeness than I."

"What did you see?"

"It looked a lot like that shimmer around the house, but it was a small area in Evie's room," she said. "I've never seen anything quite like it. What is it?"

"No one can really explain it sufficiently to qualify what it is. I can generate shields that are close to impenetrable. Do you think she can do something like that?"

"I don't know," she said shivering with fear again. "But Charles ordered those men to kill me and take her. What I can do? He's one of the richest men in the United States; he knows all kinds of people."

"With the fact that he wants you dead, the only thing I can think of is to get you to Philadelphia and under the protection of Talbot and his people. Even Charles Kraven will hesitate to go after you there. My suggestion would be to get into my car and go immediately."

"What will I do in Philadelphia? I won't have a job or a house. How will I be able to take care of Evie?" She swallowed hard. "But what else can I do?"

"If he's willing to send vans filled with gunmen, he'll be willing to send more. You need to pack."

"We haven't discussed your price, Mister Sinner," she said. "I'm not even sure I can afford you."

"There was a time when I thought I was going to move to this wonderful villa in Tuscany. I was smitten with this vibrant young lady who could bend light in such a way so she could project the most spectacular patterns. She had even agreed to run off with a wayward young man who had just left the Army. Things didn't work out well for us, and let's just say the blame can be placed squarely on the shoulders of Charles Kraven. I'm going to do this because you need it. It doesn't hurt that I can stop him from getting something he really wants, as well."

She looked at the man. He didn't look dangerous, but there was an air about him that made her feel safe.

"Evie! We need to pack some things. We're going on a trip."

"Yay! Are we going to the zoo?"

"Honey, I don't think we'll get to go to the zoo today."

"Okay." She pouted as she turned to run up the stairway.

MOUSE WAS GRATEFUL THEY WERE IN ONE OF THE LARGER UNITS AS they tended to two patients from the triage area. At 5'4" she could stand completely upright. Not so her partner Arthur Phillips, or as he was affectionately known, Pulse Ox. He was in a perpetual slouch in any truck he rode. His 6'2" was great for some things, but there were tradeoffs in the back.

"Tourniquet is secure. Bleeding controlled. Time noted. Secondary assessment complete," Pulse Ox said as he worked on the unconscious man on the stretcher. Methodical and thorough, as always.

Their second patient, Mark, asked, "Hey, is that guy gonna be okay? He was right next to me when that car hit the building. I mean we were talking and just WHAM this car flies through the front window and took out part of the wall, and this big dude just walks right past, looks in the driver seat, and shoots the driver... right in the head. Who does that? It's totally nuts!"

Mark was talking so fast that Mouse could hear him rushing to breathe and his lips were pale. She reached for the manual cuff to recheck his blood pressure as she checked the finger pulse oximeter monitoring his blood oxygen saturation and pulse rates, which were dropping steadily. She swore to herself. Mark had been tagged as a green on scene by staff–alert, oriented and answering their questions—so they had loaded him with their red priority patient on the stretcher. Initially, IV fluids were run at bolus to bolster his blood pressure, but had slowed to KVO now.

"He is de-satting and we have loss of consciousness," Pulse Ox said, his movements quick and fluid. "Confirming, no radial pulse, no breathing." Their stable "green" bench patient was now in cardiac arrest.

"Hey, Vargas! Radio into Keegan Base Two and notify them of patient B status change, coming in with witnessed arrest, CPR in progress," Mouse called to Vargas.

"You warmed up?" Mouse asked Pulse Ox as she cut open the front of the patient's T-shirt and started compressions. "This is going to be a catch, hopefully with release." Grim humor was part and parcel of working in emergency services. The two of them had a unique rapport that she loved.

"He's probably going to be pretty pissed that you cut his shirt off, that looked like vintage Black Sabbath concert gear," he said matter-of-factly while he placed the sticky AED pads to Mark's chest, upper right and lower left. They weren't in an ALS unit and didn't have a spare monitor, but Pulse Ox had a unique skill, he could feel electrical current variations, which meant he could tell if the cardiac rhythms were "right" or not. It was a secret that he had shared with her once he had discovered that she too had "special skills." The pads were a cover for him. They told no one else, and stayed together as a team. Mouse had been absorbed into his family and she was best friends with his wife and godmother to his four-week-old daughter.

"Been ready since the triage field. Only jumped a few times, so I'm good to go," he answered. "What about you? I know you're stretched a bit; don't think I wasn't paying attention to your boosts out there."

Mouse's special gift was an ability to "boost" healing, which was safer and less noticeable than if she were to heal them up completely, though that was also within her skill set. She'd learned long ago that it would raise a ton of red flags and cause all kinds of grief if she just healed all the patients. Besides, this way they could do more good for more people. Full healing could knock her on her ass, too. Pulse Ox had almost had to carry her home after a shift where they had "caught" a three-year-old kid and his father, both with multi-trauma, in addition to working on the rest of the family. Drunk driving car accidents hit you hard, and this family never saw the car that T-boned them. But Mouse and Pulse Ox had worked harder than they ever had and little Troy and his entire family had pulled through. They still brought trays of cookies to the station on the anniversary of when Troy got out of the hospital.

"Heh, easy peasy. You do you, and I'll do me," she answered, shaking herself out of the reverie.

The flat voice of the AED sounded. "Analyzing. Clear patient. Do not touch the patient."

It always felt like forever to Mouse while she waited. "No shock advised, continue CPR." Mouse dove back into compressions as Pulse Ox rubbed his hands together one last time, sliding one under Mark's back and the other on his chest, just over the heart. She paused compressions as he narrowed his eyes in concentration and she knew he was reaching out to feel for the tiny electrical pulses.

"Damn… feels like very fine V-fib but it's fading, we gotta go now, Mouse. Ready?"

She nodded. "On your count. You toss in the charge and I will boost him, this is gonna be a full catch."

"Ready," he said. Mouse leaned back and took a deep breath.

"Steady." The thin trace of steady golden light along her fingertips brightened.

"GO!" She felt it as he pushed the charge, hard, and her boost hit Mark like a freight train, causing him to involuntarily inhale.

"Come on, Mark, work with us." Mouse watched the AED window as Pulse Ox attenuated the tiny pulses into normal sinus cardiac rhythm. Mouse boosted again and Mark's eyes fluttered open for a moment, before closing again.

"Stay with us, Mark," Pulse Ox said. Mouse felt the shift in the truck as they pulled onto hospital grounds. "We're backing in at the ER. Light a fire or let him go, Mouse."

"Up and at 'em, Adam Ant" she said and exhaled forcefully with a last boost that bathed her upper torso with golden light.

"Backing up now!" she heard Vargas shout as he parked in the ambulance bay. The back doors of the ambulance opened just in time for the receiving nurse, Vargas, and a volunteer to see the "dead guy" sit up and yell, "What the hell?"

The volunteer fainted.

"Allow me," Sinner said opening the door for Jas.

She nudged Evie and the girl climbed into the back seat of the sedan and Jas followed. Sinner closed the door, walked around the car, and enter through the other door.

Jas couldn't see into the front seat due to a partition, but she could see two silhouettes. The driver was much larger than the passenger.

As Sinner eased through the door, the partition slid down. The driver was obviously quite tall with silver hair. He turned and winked at Evie which put another smile on the girl's face.

"Where to, boss?"

"Quickest route to Philly, Rich. Keep your eyes peeled for trouble." Sinner turned to her. "Jasmine, these are Rich and Tish Groller. They'll be our escort today."

Jas looked at the passenger. Tish's head hardly showed above the seat headrest and Jas figured she was not much taller than her own five feet two inches. Her hair was dark and had a sheen that made Jas curious about her hair care products. Then she saw her eyes. Most Supers had costumes so a person would recognize them, but Jas couldn't see that far down. But her eyes said she was a Super, without a doubt. They were black upon first glance, but Jas found herself almost falling into them as she saw the small spots and swirls that looked like she was looking into the cosmos.

"Tish is also known as Kairos, if you're curious. She is the 'emergency escape plan' if you will."

"And him?" she said, nodding toward Rich.

Rich grinned. "Alas, I'm just the driver. Not everyone can be the Infamous Tish."

Rich started the car and backed out of the drive.

"Are you her dad?"

Rich chuckled at the little girl's question. "This lovely lady is my wife, thank you. You know, some Supers don't age as fast as the rest of us."

"You have pretty eyes," Evie said to Tish. "Scarlett says so, too."

"Thank you. But who is Scarlett?" Tish asked.

"Oh, Scarlett is one of my friends. Crunch and Weasel and Scarlett are my best friends."

Tish glanced at Jas and Jas tapped the side of her head.

"Ahh. Well, you tell Scarlett I said thank you."

"She heard you. Crunch says hi, too. Mommy thinks I'm crazy. That's what Scarlett says, anyway."

Jas frowned. "I most certainly do not, young lady." She looked back up at Tish. "She has a wonderfully vivid imagination."

"Boss, we can go interstate or straight down SR-1."

"Interstate should be faster. The 1-95 is less than a mile away."

"All right, sir."

Jas looked out the back of the car. Everything she owned was back there, but Charles had made it abundantly clear she could no longer remain there. She would walk through the fires of Hell to keep Evie safe. She would find a job in Philadelphia, and she would raise Evie. Maybe they wouldn't have as much but they would have each other, and Charles wouldn't be able to…

Why on Earth did I call him? she thought. *I never thought he hated me enough to kill me. He always had an interest in Evie.*

She was quietly holding Evie as they merged onto the interstate to head south. Philadelphia was just a short drive from Trenton.

"Boss, there's a problem."

A lone figure was walking toward them in the center of the road. Traffic split and hurried past her. She wore a red spandex suit with a black cape. On her chest, Jasmine knew there would be an image of the grim reaper and his scythe. She'd seen Slaughter before on television and seeing her walking down the interstate toward them sent a cold chill down her spine.

Sinner sighed. "Stop the car so I can anchor the shield. Looks like we need to call in the rest of the team."

"But that's Slaughter," she said. "She kills Supers."

"I know exactly who she is." His face was placid, but she thought his eyes were troubled. "Michael will deal with her."

"Michael?"

"You probably know him as Dreadnought."

"Hello, Sebastian," Slaughter said as she stopped about two feet from the shield. "I've been meaning to call on you for years."

Sinner sighed and rolled down the window. "Hello, Kim."

"Kim died with her sister. You *do* remember her sister, don't you? The woman you left behind? Now there's just Slaughter."

"You know her?" Jas asked.

"We may have a little history," he said.

"A *little* history?" Slaughter laughed. "Our history can wait until after I do my job. By the way, my job is to slice off your pretty little head and deliver your spawn to Charles. Then he can use those wonderful new drugs he's been developing to do all those awful things he does to those with powers." Her gaze returned to Sinner. "When I finish that, I'm coming for you, dear Sebastian. You left her behind and now she's gone."

"She left me, Kim," he said.

"And spent the remainder of her life strung out on X. You were the only person who was able to keep her off that shit. You just walked away."

Slaughter cocked her fist back and punched the shield hard enough to shake the car. Then she swung again and again.

"You can't stay in there forever, Sebastian!"

Sinner rolled the window up and turned to Jas. "Uncompromising people can make life so difficult."

Jas arched a brow.

He shrugged.

"Crunch says he could beat the mean woman up for you."

He chuckled. "That's really nice of him."

The car rocked again as a sonic boom shook everything.

"She'll be busy soon enough," he said.

"Mommy, look! It's Dreadnought!"

Sinner touched his ear. "You're a sight for sore eyes, my friend."

Jas watched as Dreadnought touched his ear and said something. They were using some sort of comm system.

"Oh, look who's here, Sebastian! Michael came to play!"

Slaughter turned to face the leather-clad hero. She shot forward and slammed into him, sending him hurtling backward. She turned back to them and smiled widely.

"That woman is crazy," Jas said.

"And then some," Sinner replied.

A dark streak hit Slaughter and she was hurled into the air. Dreadnought was standing where she had been. He launched himself into the air and the thunder of the two Supers' blows bombarded the area.

"I really wasn't expecting Slaughter," he said.

"She is a problem, sir," Rich said from the front seat.

"This reminds me of Belgrave," Sinner said. "I'll pull the anchor and you get us as far as you can before I have to plant it again."

The car moved down the interstate and they made it almost a mile, almost to the river where they would cross over into Pennsylvania. Safety was only two miles away.

The car slowed to a stop. "We have another problem, sir."

"That's MultipleX, isn't it?"

"I think so," Rich said.

Jas started as the form standing in the street was suddenly two.

"Yep, that's MultipleX."

There were four, then eight, then sixteen.

Sebastian sighed again.

A red form fell from the sky, slammed into the road, and slowly stood. She was disheveled and her scythe was gone but she was still smiling that insane smile as she launched back into the air.

"I'll anchor the shield again," Sinner said. "This definitely reminds me of Belgrave. It doesn't look as if we'll be moving for a bit."

He touched his ear again. "Affirmative. Welcome to the party."

The car shook again as a streak of metallic blue and silver blasted past them toward the growing horde of MultipleX copies.

Jas pointed toward the streak for Evie.

"Blue Streak," Sinner said. "I know, it's not very imaginative but it is fairly accurate. He's a speedster. They're pretty durable as far as Supers go. They have to be to operate at the speeds they move."

"Why couldn't he just take Evie and run into Philadelphia?" Jas asked.

"For one, normal folks couldn't survive moving that fast, and we're not sure she *is* a Super yet, are we? There are varying levels of Supers and the classifications are pretty widespread."

"I see."

"Regrettably, we will wait here as heroes fight to clear us a path."

Sinner opened the door and stepped out of the car to better view what was happening, so Jas followed suit. She was watching the two flying Supers as they slammed into one another high in the air.

There were sirens closing from the north. She hoped it wasn't the kind man who'd given her the card. She had a feeling he was the sort to run into a dangerous situation and there were numerous cars and trucks turned over in front of their car. MultipleX had been destroying anything he—they—could find to block their path to the river. Many of the vehicles were still occupied.

All this destruction because of me.

She looked back up as Slaughter raised something in front of Dreadnought's face. He jerked and grabbed his throat, then dropped about twenty feet. His look of surprise was etched into her memory as he suddenly dropped again. This time she almost retched as she saw him impact the highway.

"Michael!"

Sinner was at the edge of the shield and Slaughter landed in front of him. She was holding a small aluminum cylinder the width of her palm.

"Charles said this would work. Oh, Sebastian, give me the girl and I won't finish the job. Who am I kidding? I know what he means to you. That's why I'm going to walk over there and break your friend's neck. Then I'll come back and take her anyway."

"Don't make me do this, Kim!"

Jas could hear the despair in his voice.

"Say goodbye to your precious Dreadnought," she answered and started toward him.

Sinner groaned and Jas saw blood drip from his nose.

Slaughter crumpled to the ground and twitched violently. Then she was still.

Jas didn't say a word as she saw tears on his cheeks, she just rested a hand on his shoulder.

"Rich, move the car closer to him so I can shield him." He was looking at the approaching horde of MultipleX.

One of the first responder vehicles rolled to a stop near Dreadnought and she saw the shimmer of the shield disappear and reappear around the whole group. As the car approached the shield shrank with it.

She and Sebastian walked beside the car. She saw Dreadnought drawing in ragged breaths as two familiar forms knelt beside him. One was the fellow she had heard the woman call Pulse Ox. She was right. He was the sort to run into danger.

"Sweet Jesus!" Michaels heard Vargas exclaim. She had been riding in the back, stowing the last of the restocks, and heard Pulse Ox's soft exclamation. She felt some aggressive braking and maneuvering and braced her feet.

"Mouse, multi-trauma out front," Pulse Ox said, his tone dry as dust.

"MVA? I didn't even hear anything back here."

"Nope. You aren't going to believe me."

"Vargas, what the hairy hell is going on?"

"Dreadnought just fell out of the sky and landed in the middle of the Interstate."

"Riiight. Very funny."

She stuck her head through the separator and saw the unmistakable form of Dreadnought splayed on the roadway. It didn't look good either. She had already pulled on gloves and was grabbing the trauma bag as Vargas brought them way too close if something or someone followed Dreadnought down. She swallowed that thought and stepped out.

"Calling for back up units now," she heard Pulse Ox say while he pulled his gloves on. She heard Vargas radio in as Pulse Ox directed him to request additional resources.

Mouse saw the edges of the cobalt cape lift in the breeze in stark contrast to the utterly still form of its owner. She noted an obvious leg deformity and blood leaking from several places as she crouched. She snapped open her case with ease from years of practice.

"Hey! Hey there! Can you hear me? I need you to open your eyes for me, can you do that?" she asked loudly, ignoring the watchers and the random crashes going on around her. She trusted that Pulse Ox and Vargas had her back, so she gave Dreadnought her whole focus. Rapid trauma assessment was just that, rapid.

"Dreadnought!" She thumped him hard on what seemed to be an uninjured shoulder. "I need you to open your eyes. Let us know you can hear us." She placed her forefingers into his hands, "Can you squeeze my fingers?" She saw and heard a long, slow exhalation.

"Oh no, you don't! Dreadnought, open your eyes!" Michaels almost shouted. "Get my partner; get more help," she barked at a woman who was standing there, frozen, staring at Dreadnought as Mouse worked to cut through the the his fabric and leather suit, exposing a very broad scarred chest to the light of day.

Pulse Ox heard Michaels and whipped his head around, just as he finished giving a situation report on the radio.

"Vargas, with me. Grab the bag. She needs us. Grab the AED, too." Vargas didn't hesitate, grabbing the second med kit bag on the fly and tossing it onto the stretcher he was maneuvering.

"What's up?" Pulse Ox heard Vargas ask as he realized that he could see Mouse doing compressions, the rhythm unmistakable. CPR was in progress and Mouse was right there, dwarfed by man she was trying to save. Outlined in glowing gold, the sun created a halo around the whole scene, even the cars seemed to reflect the light shining off them. Pulse Ox heard Vargas whisper, "Holy shit… Dreadnought's dead."

~

"Come on, come on, please…" Mouse grunted between compressions. Kneeling in the lanes of the interstate, pavement burning through her pants, the sweat began to run into her eyes, pooled in the fingers of her gloved hands. She stopped for a moment and tore off her gloves in frustration to allow better contact with his bared chest, hoping it would better conduct her boosting. She prayed it would as she pushed again, willing healing into him. She could hear Pulse Ox and Vargas next to her.

"Easy, easy. Pace yourself. I need you focused, not off on a tear." Pulse Ox tried to cajole her out of the intensity. She could tell he was worried; she was too. "Help is here. Vargas is bringing the AED. Need to swap out on compressions yet?

"He's not coming around. What could do did this? Other than falling out of the sky, this guy usually bounces, dusts off, and heads back in." She sat back on her heels while Pulse Ox took up doing the compressions and she watched as Vargas sized an oral airway along Dreadnought's jaw. Once in place, he was bagging.

"Mouse, focus. Try to control your glow, we have an audience. Work the problem. There is another ALS unit inbound. Until then, we work him. We don't have long to get it done." She swapped back in for more compressions, focusing all her energies into the damaged tissues and systems. She closed her eyes and continued to count aloud as she allowed her gift to move through the broken body under her hands.

"I need to get the lower fractures stable. Are you good for another round?" Pulse Ox asked. She opened her eyes and nodded. She felt muscle fibers reconnect, heard the bones grind and knit. She had never gone this deep into healing, following her power as it passed through the body, as it flowed and surged from her hands.

SEBASTIAN WATCHED AS THE COMPACT BRUNETTE WOMAN TRIED TO rouse Dreadnought. He had known him for years, through innumerable misadventures. He had never, ever seen him this still. Somehow, he was always in motion. This wasn't right and it gave Sebastian pause. He saw her cut through, quite literally, thousands of dollars' worth of Dreadnought's suit. Small sparks arced from a few of the severed connections. It dawned on him that she was, of all things, emitting light.

"Well, now, that *is* unexpected," he said to no one in particular.

Sebastian cocked his head and watched his friend's face when it went lax, as if he was just… gone. A soft golden glow suffused his friend, then flared brighter as the brunette medic began CPR. Brighter and brighter, then it flickered, and Sebastian knew in his bones she wouldn't be able to keep up. He had seen something like this in Estonia. She needed time.

MultipleX was wreaking havoc outside the shield; they all wanted in. They were all there to take Evie and he would not, could not, allow Kraven to take the girl. He didn't want Kraven to have a victory of any kind, but the girl was an innocent. Neither could he let his friend die. He pursed his lips as an idea formed.

He felt more than heard Tish walk up next to him, then felt her hand grip his elbow. All the voices swirled around him.

"Sebastian, we can't stay here for much longer." Her voice was firm.

"Mommy, is Dreadnought sleeping?"

"Mr. Sinner!"

"Sir, there are still twenty-four of MultipleX. Wait, he got another one! Down to twenty-three!"

Sebastian heard all of it and none. Time froze for a moment as his focus narrowed and he made his decision.

"Take her with you, Tish."

"No, I am the contingency plan. It was decided and done." He heard her stubbornness coming to the fore.

"That woman can save him, Kairos. This is about Michael. He is dying, helping her is helping us."

"Perhaps he cannot be saved. You're taking a huge gamble. To do this is to pray that he can recover enough to make a difference here. He's your friend, I get it. But you have a kid that needs to get to safety."

"Kairos, this is not a request. This is an order."

Kairos fumed. She took a last long drag on her cigarette, then flicked it away, grinding it under her foot. She shook her hands to loosen the wrists and started the gestures that would create the pocket of space.

"This is a ridiculous waste of a resource," she said as she stalked toward the woman. "She'd better be worth it."

Her dark hair lifted around her, caught in the drifts of power. Light shifted as she twisted forces and kinetic energies. Kairos tied the final gestures together and the air thickened until it was hard to draw breath, then it stretched as she formed a space around herself before pulling it around the woman and sealing it closed.

∽

MOUSE BLINKED, ONCE, TWICE. ABSOLUTE STILLNESS ASSAULTED HER. *Oh, crap,* she thought, *I died. This is what death is like, everyone in living color and frozen.*

"You'd better recharge or whatever it is that you do with that power of yours. Once you are topped up, we'll put you right back to finish what you started on Dreadnought, do I make myself clear?" The tone was stern, irritated even, and coming from behind. her

"Wait, what?" Mouse, still on her knees. She twisted instinctively and froze. She knew she was staring, but she couldn't really do a damn thing about it. Too much weird had just crash landed in her life.

"Do I really need to repeat myself? Look, get focused. You have a job to finish."

"No." Mouse felt the hairs on the back of her neck lift and a primordial fear skittered along her spine as the woman turned her full attention onto Mouse. Her eyes. *My God, they are full of stars.* Mouse snorted, the intensity of the moment broken as the movie line grounded her.

"Excuse me?" the woman said softly ,and it freaked Mouse out all over again.

"I meant, you don't need to repeat yourself. What's going on? Why aren't people moving? Why is it so quiet? Who the hell are you?" Mouse fired back.

"It was quiet until you started sounding off. Name's Kairos." She drew a Zippo with a worn silver finish from her front pocket and thumbed it open, lighting a cigarette. Two drags and she flipped the lighter closed. "Look, Sebastian gave you his Hail Mary to get you back up and running so you can finish up with Michael."

"Who is Sebastian? What Hail Mary, and who is Michael?" Mouse felt sure that she was losing her mind. *Yup, I died*, she thought. She jerked as she heard a noise.

"Seriously, did you just growl at me?" Mouse asked, stunned.

KAIROS SPUN THE ENERGY OFF TO EITHER SIDE AS SHE ALLOWED THE pocket to dissolve.

"Is that honestly the only song that you know?"

"What? I was trying to focus. You smoke way more than you need to, by the way. Not that smoking is good for you in any case but still, ever considered the patch?"

"Have you considered not talking for more than five minutes?" Kairos turned to Sebastian. "She is a running commentary on anything that catches her eye. I now know just how many times the average human blinks, a complete explanation of eye glands—"

"Lacrimal, not eye glands…" Mouse tossed over her shoulder as she dropped into position next to Dreadnought, the light tracing down her forearms to her fingers.

"Do you see what it's like?"

"They are, in fact lacrimal—" Sebastian began.

"Sebastian," Kairos voice was tight as her chin dropped to glare at him.

"Were you successful?"

"What do you think?" She gestured toward the radiant outline near Dreadnought. "Not very subtle though. Probably getting fired after this."

"I wouldn't worry about their employment. We'll take them in. The skill set is quite unique and eminently beneficial. Wouldn't you agree?"

"Dear lord, that girl never shuts up," she muttered.

JASMINE HELD EVIE CLOSE AND WATCHED EVERYTHING PLAY OUT FROM the inside of the shield. She was unsure what Tish had done, but the glowing paramedic was shining brightly where she had been flickering before and she saw when Dreadnought took in a deep breath.

Sebastian turned to her and smiled. "He's breathing."

His smile turned grim as he looked toward the crowd of identical Supers that were running toward the shield. Two of them were holding down Blue Streak and a third was pounding him with super-strength punches.

Evie slipped out of her arms, walked to Sinner's side, and tugged on his coat. "Mister Sebastian?"

He looked down at her. "Yes, dear?"

"Crunch said he can help."

"Sweet girl," he said. "We can use all the help we can get."

Jas watched Evie cocked her head to the side and raised her hand. To her astonishment, a silvery glow appeared just outside of the shield. It looked like a fine line that grew taller and taller. Then it turned into two lines that pulled apart with a sound that overpowered the din of the battle. She didn't know how to describe it except to say it sounded like the world screamed.

"Evie?"

"It's okay, Mommy. The door is just loud."

Jas's head jerked back to the huge tear in reality as a huge figure strode through. He—unmistakably male—was at least fifteen feet tall and covered in long grey fur. His shoulders were enormous, and his arms almost reached the ground as he lumbered forward.

He looked toward Evie, waved a massive hand, then charged forward to snatch one of the versions of MultipleX. He held the Super by his legs and began slamming him into the ground, leaving bloody craters where the body impacted.

His roars shook the street.

"Oh my," Sebastian said. "This is Crunch?"

"Yep. Isn't he 'dorable?"

He let out a long sigh. "Okay."

"Scarlett wants to come too," she said and raised her arm again.

Jas shuddered as the world screamed again.

A large red form passed through the tear in reality. Jas swallowed as her worst nightmare came to life. She was extremely afraid of spiders and the lower half of the creature was quite spiderlike. There were eight legs that angled up and back down, just like a spider, but the lower extremities were more like massive blades. Where the head of the spider would normally be was the upper half of a humanlike woman. The skin was still quite red, and her hands had elongated fingers that looked like blades.

She turned and smiled at Evie before skittering forward, sparks shooting from where her legs impacted the roadbed.

Jas couldn't get the image of the spider's teeth out of her head. Long fangs where incisors would have been sent chills down her spine.

Out of the same door a four-foot-tall beast sprung.

"Weasel!"

Evie's scream of delight broke her from her reverie about the giant spider.

Weasel was short and squat. His head was wide, and when he

smiled at Evie it looked like the mouth covered more than half of the circumference of its head. He waved at Evie and shot forward in a blur.

"Weasel! Help the shiny blue man!"

The blur shot toward where Blue Streak was being pounded by MultipleX minions.

The twenty or so Supers split again as Evie's friends tore into them and Jasmine saw Sebastian grimace. He raised his hand and held it like he was pointing a pistol. A MultipleX staggered and fell. A small drop of blood dripped from Sebastian's nose.

He looked down at Evie and grinned. He pulled his thumb like he was cocking a gun and fired again. Another MultipleX fell.

Evie giggled, and he acted like he was fanning a trigger of a pistol like they did in Westerns. Three more fell and more blood trickled from his nose.

"Are you okay, Mister Sebastian?"

"I'm fine, sweet child." He continued shooting the Supers whenever they seemed to be getting the upper hand on any of Evie's friends.

Jas could see the toll it was taking when he sent one of his shields to form inside one of the Supers' brains. She was certain that was what he was doing. She'd seen him do it earlier to Slaughter.

She looked back to where Evie's friends were killing the Supers almost as fast as they were multiplying. But it seemed MultipleX could continue to make copies faster than they were being killed. Sebastian was evening the odds, but he could only do it for so long.

He staggered and went down on a knee.

"Getting too old for this," he said, barely loud enough for her to hear.

Jas stepped forward to keep him from toppling. "You have to stop, Mister Sinner."

"Can't," he said through a ragged breath. "We need to get closer to the others so I can condense the shield."

She helped him stagger to where the paramedics were still working on Dreadnought. The brunette healer was almost unconscious beside the Super, but he was breathing steadily.

"Can't… finish… yet. Stable."

"Rest," Pulse Ox said. "He's good for now."

He turned to Sebastian. "I'm guessing if they get in here, they'll kill us all?"

"Most assuredly, yes," he said.

"Good thing I'm not a doctor, Hippocratic oath and all."

Sebastian took a deep breath.

"Pulse Ox?" The healer tried to sit up.

He moved from Dreadnought's side and laid his hand on the road and concentrated. "There you are."

"What?"

He smiled. "The power grid."

"Oh Jesus," the healer said.

"You don't have to call me that in public, Mouse."

Jas felt the hair on the back of her neck stand up as a huge bolt of lightning erupted from the ground and ripped through over half the MultipleX minions.

Pulse Ox toppled over from the strain and Sebastian caught him, staggering.

"Definitely getting fired," Pulse Ox muttered.

"Best resume I've ever seen," Sebastian said, helping the big man to a seated position. "You're both hired. Provided we live through this."

He looked outside the shield where Evie's friends were getting closer and closer to the original MultipleX.

There was a shadow, and someone dropped from the sky. The road crunched as he landed. The man wore blue jeans and a flannel shirt.

"This just got real," the third EMT said. "That's freaking Jacob Talbot."

"Enough!" Talbot's voice boomed.

Two more Supers dropped to land much more softly.

"That's Prima and Gladiatrix," Jas said softly.

Everyone knew what the Stranger had done to her, but Gladiatrix had recovered and come back. Her family still lived in Philly.

Evie yelled to her friends. "Stop!"

Everyone stopped and the din of battle ceased.

Scarlett flicked a red chunk from her finger blade . There was a splat as it landed in the street.

MultipleX split several times while there was a pause to the fighting.

"There goes our advantage," Sebastian said.

Jacob pointed at MultipleX. "You stop, or I'll stop it."

"What are you gonna do? I always outnumber you."

"What I saw a few minutes ago was you about to become extinct. They were killing you faster than you could multiply. You split again and you'll regret it."

The twelve Supers became twenty-four. All of them carried the same smirk.

"Warned you." Jacob waved his hand and twenty-three copies of MultipleX seemed to melt. Their insides fell through their skins.

Jasmine felt the bile rising as she fought the urge to vomit.

"I've learned a little about my gift over the last five years," Jacob said. "It's quite unpleasant but it's very effective. When the density of your skin and muscles becomes the same as water…"

The single MultipleX was pale as a sheet. He swallowed. "It doesn't matter. When I tell the boss how that spray worked, none of you are safe… GHAK!"

He toppled forward and landed on his face.

Everyone looked at Sebastian as blood dripped from his nose.

"What?" he shrugged.

Jacob sighed. "Can anyone tell me why this was coming to my city?"

He was waving toward the pile of bodies and crashed vehicles.

"I thought I was pretty clear about this sort of thing."

"Seemed like the only place *she* could be safe." Sebastian motioned toward Evie. "We were hoping you would provide sanctuary to her and her mother."

Jasmine stepped forward. "Charles Kraven is trying to kill me and take Evie. Even if you won't let me in, you have to take her. He *can't* have her! He's a monster."

"He is that."

"Of course, we'll give you sanctuary," Prima said. Her accent was strange yet comforting.

Jacob sighed.

"Can you at least explain this?" He was pointing toward Evie's friends.

"That's Crunch," Evie said stepping forward. "And Scarlett. And Weasel. They're my best friends."

The behemoth turned back to Evie. "Fight done?"

"Thank you, Crunch!"

Sebastian dropped the shield as Evie walked forward. She met Crunch as he walked toward the rip. He stood there with Evie as Scarlett approached.

Jasmine gasped as the spider woman bent down and kissed Evie's forehead.

She looked at Jas. She struggled with the words but said, "Me... like sandmitch. Apple... good."

Jas gulped and nodded.

Scarlett skittered through the other rip.

Weasel ran up and licked Evie's face. Then ran through the same opening.

Crunch squatted in front of her. "Munchkin safe?" He looked toward Jacob. "You protect?"

"I will," he said.

Crunch delicately patted her head with a hand as big as she was.

"Crunch go home. Crunch love Munchkin."

After he stepped through the door, Evie waved her hands and wiggled her fingers. Both doors disappeared.

"I don't think I've ever seen anything quite like that," Tish said as she lit a cigarette.

"I'm not sure anyone has," Sebastian said.

Jasmine and Evie approached Jacob.

"Ladies, would you mind giving these two a ride back to town?"

Prima stepped forward and held her arms out to Evie. "Tell me, little one. Have you ever flown?"

Evie's eyes widened with excitement. "This is so much better than the zoo!"

Jacob turned back to Sebastian as Jasmine approached Gladiatrix.

"What about you and your motley crew, Sinner?"

"We'll go back home, lick our wounds, and maybe pay a visit to a certain billionaire." Sebastian waved at Jasmine as she was lifted into the air.

She waved back. "Thank you, Mister Sinner."

He nodded.

ABOUT CHRISTOPHER WOODS

Christopher Woods, writer of fiction, teller of tales, and professional liar, was born way too long ago to be talking about and has spent most of his life with a book in hand. He is known for his popular Soulguard series and creating the Fallen World shared universe. He has also written several short stories and the Legend books in the Four Horsemen Universe as well as some works in the Salvage Title Universe. With books ranging from fantasy to post-apocalyptic science fiction and military science fiction there should be something for everyone. He lives in Woodbury, TN with his wife, Wendy. As a former carpenter of 25 years, he spends his time between various building projects and writing new books. To contact him go to theprofessionalliar.com

ABOUT ANGELA CLAYTON

Angela Clayton entered the world in the great state of Michigan. She was an early reader of anything that had printed words. Her grandfather lent her his paperback copy of Anne McCaffreys *The White Dragon*, and from there the deep dive into all genres of fantasy and science fiction began. She has written poetry and created stories for personal gratification, a hobby that continued through the years.

Angela currently lives in South Carolina with her husband Phil, the love of her life, and three delightfully off-balance cats.

FOREWORD: "TO LIGHT UP THE NIGHT: A FOUNDER EFFECT LEGEND" BY ROBERT E. HAMPSON & BRENT M. ROEDER

BY T.K.F. WEISSKOPF

This is a story set in a shared world that's one of my new favorites. The first volume was titled *The Founder Effect* (Baen Books) and deals with both the truth and legends that arise as humanity settles its first planet outside the Solar System. Both Hampson and Roeder are neuroscientists. So, of course, this story is about things that go "boom!"

TO LIGHT UP THE NIGHT:

A FOUNDER EFFECT LEGEND BY
ROBERT E. HAMPSON
&
BRENT M. ROEDER

"*San Salvador*, this is Beaver Lead. I have made it to the controls and am preparing to eject fuel tank. Godspeed and safe landing, *San Salvador*. Beaver flight is cl—"

From the civil defense speakers, the replay of the last broadcast from Beaver Flight during the landing of the *San Salvador* ended with a brief burst of static. After a minute of silence, a voice came back over the speakers, slowly reading out the names of Beaver Flight. The voice paused, then spoke the final words of the annual Landing Day Ceremony. "Beaver Flight, this is Beaverton Ground Control. The lander is down with all souls safe. Prepare for Landing Flares to guide you home on my mark. Go for flares, mark."

Immediately a white streamer stretched from a point somewhere behind the stage and raced into the night sky. The trail faded but was quickly replaced by a red starburst pattern as the firework burst into brilliant color. The muffled *boom* arrived before the individual lights began to twinkle.

Every year, the residents of the settlement honored the memories of the brave Beaver Flight orbital tug pilots who'd made it possible for the colony to exist at all. The celebration of Landing Day involved picnics, community games, a thankfully brief speech by the mayor, and a rebroadcast of the radio communications detailing the heroic sacrifice by Beaver Flight pilots who'd guided the colony lander to its best possible rest. The night ended with a fireworks display, signaling an end to rest and relaxation, and a return to the hard work of life in Beaverton.

Theirs was the last colony site to be established using one of the massive colony landers transported nearly forty light-years to the TRAPPIST-2 system from Earth on the colony ship *Victoria*. That final lander, *San Salvador*, had been held in reserve for twenty-five years to ensure that the other colonies had taken hold. Twenty-five-hundred colonists remained in cryo as insurance against the failure of either of the first two settlements, and a full complement of infrastructure-building machines rested in its hull, waiting for their turn to establish a new home for humanity on the new world of Cistercia.

Whether it was the long delay, or neglected maintenance, or some unforeseen circumstance that caused it, *San Salvador*, destined for the tropical shores of the subcontinent-sized island Aopo, had malfunctioned, running short of fuel and nearly crashing on a rocky island ten miles offshore of the optimistically named Paradise colony site. Where the capital, Antonia, and the ill-fated Roanoke colonies were surrounded with fertile fields and had fusion powerplants, huge terraforming and construction machines—not to mention electricity and indoor plumbing in all homes—Beaverton had a technology level more akin to the early twentieth century on Earth, rather than the twenty-second century when the colony ship *Victoria* had departed the planet of humanity's birth.

The hard landing had crumpled the lower decks, damaging or trapping much of the heavy machinery. Moreover, Antonia, sited among fertile plains beside an inland, equatorial sea, or Roanoke, in a river valley in the temperate middle latitudes, Beaverton was a rocky island in Aopo's rain shadow. There were good farming and ranching lands across the ten-mile straight at Beachhead, on Aopo's leeward shore, but the transport that would have shuttled the colony's equipment and population across the water had been on the lowest level of the permanently grounded *San Salvador*.

The TRAPPIST-2 colonization mission had been plagued with problems from the start. There were protests by groups who felt that Earth's problems should be solved before transplanting those problems to other worlds. There were rumors of colonist slots being bought with donations or influence, rather than going to people with the skills needed for an isolated colony. An automated advance ship with most of their terraforming equipment was found to have never arrived at Trappist-2. Even worse, their backup plan to perform the terraforming themselves was jeopardized when the lander carrying heavy equipment and a small crew of experts had blasted off into space instead of landing on the planet they'd named Cistercia. Ten thousand colonists had made the 160-year trip to Trappist-2 in cryostasis, with another two hundred fifty crew, who'd rotated in and out of cryo throughout the 160-year journey.

"DO YOU THINK THEY'D BE PROUD OF US?" BRANDY BOLGEO ASKED her friends sitting with her to watch the traditional fireworks display that completed the Landing Day Ceremony.

"I think so," Jaqueline Rabinowiscz answered.

"Mmmm," Gil Rabinowiscz, Jaqueline's husband, grunted in agreement, still primarily focused on the fireworks display.

"While Beaver Flight got us down safely, they did have help from the designer of the landers," Jaqueline continued. "It's a miracle they were able to get us down to a hard landing on this island just ten miles off the coast as opposed to us all ending up in the ocean."

"I guess I'm just second guessing our progress a little bit after that conference call with the other colony sites. I'm not used to being looked down on like I'm some country bumpkin," Brandy said. She was the head of the Paradise Valley Authority, the agency charged with dam construction and electrification for the continent of Paradise.

Gil snorted. "They've just got their noses out of joint, because even though a bunch of our heavy equipment and supplies were damaged in the landing, we're growing faster than they are, even though they've had an intact tech base while we've had to adapt."

"I wouldn't have thought it before landing, or for quite a few years after, but I think having gaps in our tech base has actually been to our benefit," Jaqueline said chuckling.

"Really?" Gil asked, surprised, looking from the fireworks to his wife while cocking an eyebrow.

"Really," Jaqueline said more firmly. "Everyone at Antonia and Roanoke are so concerned with keeping their tech base going that it makes them think of everything from that perspective. When trying to solve a problem they always look for the high-tech way as opposed to the best way."

"If the only tool you use is a hammer, then everything starts to look like a nail?" Brandy asked.

"Exactly," Jaqueline agreed.

A sudden increase in the rumble of explosions drew everyone's full attention back to the sky. The three of them watched the final minute of the fireworks display, enraptured.

"All right, I think it is time for bed," Gil said wistfully as he gazed at the sky once again lit only by stars. He placed his trembling hand on the rail in front of them and pulled himself to his feet. "At my age you have to get more sleep, and Brandy and I have the annual Beaverton Resource Planning Committee meeting tomorrow, and you know Mayor Donahue expects everyone to arrive bright eyed and bushy tailed."

"I think he must have a bit of a sadistic streak setting the meeting for seven in the morning the day after Landing Day." Jaqueline chuckled.

"I think the rest of the committee might agree with you," Brandy said, smiling.

"Well, I'll just let the head of the Paradise Valley Authority and the

Paradise Agricultural Association go catch some rest, then," Jaqueline said. She went up on tip toe and kissed her husband on the cheek. "I think I'm going to go catch up with the Urbaneks, since I don't get out to Beaverton nearly as often as you two."

The residents of Beaverton were self-reliant, but with a strong sense of community. It would likely be more than a century before additional colonists arrived from Earth—if at all—and Antonia and Roanoke were many weeks' journey over rough seas. The strength and hardiness were necessary to survive—the community was necessary to *thrive*.

BRANDY PAUSED ON HER WAY INTO TOWN TO LOOK UP AT THE MASSIVE crane being erected on the hull of *San Salvador*. The salvage crew was getting ready to remove the forward left engine. With it out of the way, it would be easier to access the forward equipment hold. The actual hold entrance was inaccessible due to the combination of terrain and the crumpled lower decks.

She shook her head, amused at her woolgathering, Brandy continued into the lander. Interior cargo holds, storage spaces and crew compartments had been converted to offices, classrooms, and meeting rooms. The Beaverton Resource Planning Committee—BuRP to the general public, much to the annoyance of many committee members— was about to have its annual in-person meeting in one of the larger rooms. The "RPC"—the committee's *preferred* abbreviation—was always scheduled the day after Landing Day, to ride on the up-swell of community sentiment and take advantage of the influx of residents for the annual celebration and remembrance. As head of the Paradise Valley Authority for Flood Control and Power Generation—PVAFCPG to the acronym-heavy RPC, or PVA to the general public—Brandy was there to report on dam construction and electrification on Aopo, which had recently been renamed Paradise Island.

The self-reliant people of Beaverton had built rafts, dugouts, catamarans, and eventually larger means of water transport, to explore and settle the main island where *San Salvador* was supposed to land. The strait was narrow—only ten miles—but it was a tough journey for those original small craft assembled from the meager trees and scraps of damaged lander. Still, farms and ranches were established, trading posts and settlements were formed, and the residents of both Beaverton and the outlying communities began to plan for bigger and better things.

THE BuRP MEETING WENT PRETTY MUCH AS EXPECTED. THERE WERE reports on resource utilization in the town of Beaverton as well as the remainder of Beaver Island, followed by a listing of all the new companies and private enterprises that could be classified as "infrastructure"—such as the Hendren ferry to the mainland. After Gil Rabinowiscz reported on behalf of the farmers and ranchers of Paradise Valley, it was Brandy's turn.

"With the Atkins River Dam project ahead of schedule, we were able to start early on the initial stages of the Moops Valley project. This leaves us with a major decision to make about the electrification project," Brandy said, signaling for the next slide in her presentation. The timetable projected on the screen was replaced with multiple images from within *San Salvador*'s cargo hold.

"As you know we had eight high-capacity hydro turbines in the cargo hold, which the mission planners thought would be more than enough to last us until we were able to build modern ones of our own. Three of these came through undamaged, the first of which we used in the Cajon Dam for the initial electrification of Beachhead Town on Paradise. The next two were planned for the Atkins River and Moops Valley Dams." Brandy again gestured for the next slide to be displayed, this one was a graph of estimated power usage and availability for multiple scenarios.

"This is where the good news comes in. We are taking parts from the damaged turbines to see if we can assemble working models, even if they're smaller or have reduced capacity.

"We've been able to get all the broken turbines stripped down and we have enough parts to build at least one, probably two, and a slim chance for a third. The rebuilt ones are not going to be able to handle the high flow rates of the originals, so we shouldn't expect as much electrical generating capacity. While Atkins River is one of our best building sites, it doesn't have the water flow to make full use of an original turbine in any case. According to initial plans, lower efficiency was better than nothing. Now we have an intermediate option, but it will affect the ranchers and farmers on Paradise."

"How do you mean?" asked Gil Rabinowiscz, the representative for most of the agricultural sector on Paradise.

"The next stage of electrification involves providing power to the scattered farms and ranchers, as well as building up the Beachhead and industrial grid. The generator house at Atkins River will be finished in about five months, and we can begin building the generator house at Moops Valley about a month after that. It should be finished roughly a year from now. We also have two new turbines ready now, but the first rebuild will take between twelve and eighteen months. It should go faster after the first one, but we will clearly have Atkins River Dam finished before a rebuilt turbine is ready. Installing one of the two original turbines commits the station—we can't go back and swap it out later. So, we need to decide whether we install a new turbine at Atkins River once it's done or leave the generator house empty for up to a year and wait on the rebuilt unit. If we wait, we delay increasing our generating capacity, but will be able to increase capacity by having a good turbine for a third, full power installation later. If we don't wait, we get power sooner, but reduce our eventual maximum capacity."

"Is there a way to speed up the timeline for Moops Valley?" Gil asked.

"Yes and no," Brandy answered. "There are three parts to that timeline: Building the generator house, clearing the overland path to the dams, and transportation and installation of the turbines. We've been able to airlift the construction materials via the cargo helicopters, but as you recall from the Cajon Gorge construction, the turbines are too large to be airlifted. Those will need a clear overland path from the coast."

"Do they have to go from the coast, or can they be taken part way up-river?" Greg Donahue, mayor of Beaverton and RP chair, asked.

"We looked at that possibility, but the only potential landing spots on the Atkins River are either inconveniently placed to start an overland path to the generator house or would need so much improvement that the distance saved wouldn't be worth the effort."

"Unfortunate, but that makes sense," Mayor Donahue acknowledged.

"Turbine rebuilding, transport, dam construction, and building generator houses are all fixed durations. Where we can save time is in clearing the paths—it's not just cutting brush, but stringing power lines and stabilizing the soil for heavy vehicles. We add roads where necessary, plus transformer stations and maintenance sheds where needed. We also pre-position the junctions for spurs and residential connections. Until the turbine houses are finished, there's no reason to speed up the roads and power lines, so I only have a ten-person team working on them. In addition, we aren't building separate roads to Atkins River and Moops Valley. The best route to Moops is from the Atkins Dam site, which decreases the total distance we need to clear and improve. It can be sped up but will require additional manpower. As-is, Moops is scheduled for completion after Atkins, and there's no real benefit to throwing additional effort into it since the dam, generator house, and roads will all be completed at the same time."

"But we still have to resolve the question of which turbine we install at Atkins. How long do we have to decide?" Gil asked unhappily.

"Best to have a plan within three months, four months at the latest," Brandy answered.

"Well, that's not as bad as it sounded at first," Gil said, mollified.

"What option do you recommend?" Donahue asked.

"Let me put it this way, Cajon Dam has an eighty-five-meter drop and a turbine capable of generating 1200 megawatts. It typically operates at seventy-five-percent peak capacity. During high water flow, the excess is diverted into pumped storage and irrigation. Moops Valley will have a one-hundred-meter drop and will likely get close to ninety percent of peak out of its turbine. Atkins River only has a fifty-meter drop and very little variability; it will likely top out at fifty-five percent of peak capacity from a 1200 MW turbine. The rebuilds, however, will probably only generate 800 MW at peak, which makes it well matched to Atkins, and reserves a turbine capable of half-again as much electrical generation for a site further up the highlands, or even on the windward side of the island. Atkins is fast and easy—not as easy as Cajon Gorge, but it's accessible. The best option for Atkins is a rebuilt turbine, even if it means a delay. It's just that it means we don't bring additional generating capacity online until we finish Atkins and clear the way to Moops."

"Rabinowiscz, you represent the agricultural stations. What do you think?" Mayor Donahue asked turning to the rancher.

Grimacing, Rabinowiscz shrugged and answered, "It sounds like we should follow Brandy's recommendation. I think it is the best option, but it is going to be inconvenient to wait eighteen more months for electricity that doesn't come from batteries or generators burning fuel we need for the farm equipment."

"Do you think the rest of the farmers and ranchers on Paradise will go along with it?"

"When I explain it to them, I think they will," Gil answered.

"All right," Mayor Donahue said turning back to Brandy. "Go ahead with your recommendation. We can revisit if we must, but absent any objections today, let's move forward." He looked down at his notes, shuffled them, then looked up at the rest of the committee. "Now that we're done with the PVA report, Dr. Schoeffel will report on community health and the clinic expansion process. Kim, come on up."

AS THE FERRY APPROACHED THE BEAVERTON PIER, BRANDY SAT UP IN the lounge chair. She'd been trying to catch a nap on the top deck and had gotten comfortable for the ferry ride. Reaching for her boots and socks, she grimaced at her toes trying to remember when she last had time to get a pedicure. A near-constant sense of urgency continually warred with delays and difficulties, so she doubted she would find any time soon. This was the second time in the last three months she had been called to Beaverton for a meeting of BuRP. Given that the regularly scheduled annual meeting was only two weeks away, she figured it was just another in the series of "emergencies" that seemed to be business-as-usual for the colony.

The first emergency meeting was in response to the cattle failing throughout the colony due to "failure to thrive"—the scientific farming term for "nobody knows what's wrong." It was a serious problem for the colony—especially the farmers, which was why they'd met. None of that had affected her projects directly. She looked up from picking up her boots and got a sinking sensation that this new emergency, whatever it was, would impact her more severely. There was a car on the pier, the driver standing next to it holding a sign. There were only two other passengers, and they both had bicycles. It was only a mile walk from pier to lander—if they were sending one of the few private cars for her, it had to be really bad.

"THANK YOU FOR ATTENDING EVERYONE," MAYOR DONAHUE SAID. He spoke over the individual conversations and gestured for everyone to sit so they could begin the meeting. "Let's get right into it. Dr. Schoeffel, brief us on the problem we're facing."

He stood and Brandy noticed that Schoeffel's usual warm smile and friendly attitude were absent. "There's a problem with the farming plan that needs to be addressed. We need more milk."

"I don't understand, Doctor," said Victoria Elliott, owner of Elliott's Explosives. "I thought BuRP announced a new plan with the farmers after the last emergency meeting. Besides, why am I here? What do I have to do with milk production? I make explosives for infrastructure projects; I don't make milk."

Li Sihai stood and called out, "You don't make milk, but you compete with my goats for nitrates." After Gil Rabiniwiscz's passing, Li was elected the new representative for the agriculture concerns of Paradise.

"Mr. Li is correct," Dr. Schoeffel said. "When the cattle failed to thrive, we were concerned that we couldn't feed ourselves; now we know we can. However, the new problem is providing enough milk for our expanding population. In particular, we are seeing an increase in the birthrate as we establish more farms, ranches, and local industry. As the community grows, so does the birthrate. We are currently riding a baby boom and we need to provide for them."

"I'm sorry, Doc, but I'm not following how this is a problem *now*," said James "Wrecks" Snover, the salvage team chief.

"If I can interject," Donahue said, "we didn't realize there was a problem until we looked at the time tables for human population growth compared to livestock population growth. The latter necessitated examining nitrate availability in relation to growing food for the sheep and goats to replace lost milk production from the cattle. Caprinae need less fodder from Earth plants, and goats can survive by foraging Cistercian native plants in areas where even sheep would have difficulty. They certainly need less fodder than cows, but weight-for-weight, they are less efficient at producing milk. This means we need to grow more Earth plants per gallon of milk than we did with cows. For that we need the nitrates for fertilizer."

"Nitrates which *I* need to manufacture explosives," Victoria said, understanding dawning.

"That explains the problem," Snover said. "But why is it one *right now*?"

At a gesture from Donahue, Li stood up. "We don't have many sheep and goats right now. As a food source they were only secondary. We need to start a massive breeding campaign, and just like any other scale up we need to prepare the basic stocks, first. We were *going* to scale up flocks to match the amount of fodder we could produce. Instead, we need to scale up fodder production *before* we increase our flocks. Instead of ramping up our demand for nitrates over time, we need them now, so we can plant now and be ready for the next breeding cycle."

"This is why we've called all of you here today," Mayor Donahue said, resuming control of the meeting. "We have a plan on how to handle this but we need to hammer out the details.

"Levitt," Mayor Donahue said turning to Jeremy Levitt, the chief construction engineer. "The new chemical plant at Beachhead City is dependent on electrification from the dams. What's the timetable on that?"

"We're a little behind schedule, but I've already been working with James..." Jeremy paused and nodded in the direction of the salvage chief "... to reprioritize the parts we're shipping over. We'll have the ammonia facilities up before the rest. It will take time to get the rest of the plant running, but the ammonia section should be ready to go about the time we get electricity. It will be just anhydrous ammonia at first. We can use it to enrich recycled waste to serve as fertilizer for now. Ready-to-use fertilizer variants will take longer."

James coughed to gain everyone's attention. "We've also been working with the machine shop here on the lander to modify equipment for the farmers and ranchers to apply the anhydrous ammonia."

"Next item..." Mayor Donahue checked his notepad. "Bolgeo, where are you on getting the turbines installed at the dams?"

"We're behind schedule," Brandy admitted with a grimace. "The cattle die-off pulled manpower from every project. Every bit of our timetable ended up taking a hit. We have the road to Atkins built and the power lines are in place. The dam is done and the generator house is as complete as it can be without the turbine. We're behind on both the clearing and wiring to Moops Valley. The dam is curing and only the foundation for the generator house is in. The rebuild of the turbine for Atkins River is also behind schedule, and it sounds like from what James and Jeremy said their project might be interfering with the turbine rebuild."

"Unfortunately, Brandy is right. We've had to pull people from other projects to help with the chemical plant. The turbine rebuilds got sacrificed because we were planning for installation at Moops Valley first. The rebuild for Atkins River got put on the back burner."

"So, we have a dam with no turbine, and a turbine with no dam?" Donahue asked. "Why is that a problem? Why not swap the turbines? For that matter, don't we have two intact turbines in the cargo hold?"

"We might have been able to do that a year ago. It's what we talked about after last Landing Day. Atkins River Dam does not have as high a pressure head as either the existing dam at Cajon Gorge or the new one at Moops Valley. Once we decided to use a rebuilt turbine to matching dam flow rate with turbine capacity, we committed to that generator house configuration," Brandy explained. "If we swap the turbines, we not only waste more than forty percent of the capacity of the generator—*permanently*, I might add—we would also have to completely remodel the generator house at Atkins. The other limitation is that we don't simply unwrap a turbine and install it. There are several months preparation and conditioning to pull it out of the shipping container."

"How long to finish Moops Valley?" Mayor Donahue asked.

"That one is mainly manpower. We can speed up the build on the generator house and the concrete should be ready for pressure loads in a month. Clearing the road is the problem—more manpower, plus explosives. From what I'm hearing, that's the real limitation. With the current crew and at normal explosive use, we are about three months from completing the road, plus a month to float, transport, and install the turbine. Four months at the earliest until we have power. The original timeline was to bring Moops Valley online on Landing Day, with Atkins River six months later. We're behind that estimate by at least four months."

"Hmm, as opposed to power in a month if we just install the Moops Valley turbine at Atkins River," Donahue mused.

"Not entirely correct, but if we had to force it, we could meet the timetable, give or take two weeks."

Donahue turned to Jeremy Levitt. "When will the chemical plant be able to start up production and how much will you be able to produce?"

Jeremy and James exchanged reluctant looks, before Jeremy finally spoke. "We will be ready to produce anhydrous ammonia at half capacity in three weeks, no more than four. The rest of the plant will not come online for several more months after that. On the other hand, we're estimating a ton a week for the first six to ten months."

"Elliott," the mayor asked, "what's your stockpile of nitrates and explosives like?"

Victoria Elliot paused while she checked her notes, "We have just under half a ton of black powder finished, just over a ton of filtered saltpeter, and with our most recent delivery we are sitting at about four tons of nitratite that we will be processing into saltpeter. We can expect shipments of nitratite to remain at about two tons a month for the foreseeable future without much room for expansion of mining operations. Of course, that's not counting the fireworks we've already manufactured for Landing Day."

"Li, what's that look like compared to your needs?" the mayor asked.

Sihai didn't say anything for a minute as he worked away at a scratch pad. He finally looked up and grimaced. "With the ammonia plant production and using all the saltpeter that Victoria has, should be just enough to get everything planted and fertilized in time."

"Is there any slack in that timetable?" Brandy asked.

"We don't have to start the planting process yet, as it's not time, but we'll need to prep the soil, which means we need fertilizer in about two and a half months," Sihai answered.

"We'll have to go with installing the turbine we have at Atkins River to be on the safe side," Donahue said. "The timetable is too tight for anything else."

"That's a waste of time and effort. We have to tear down and rebuild the generator house at Atkins, and even then, the Atkins River doesn't have the flow rate to fully power the chemical plant and the other industry we plan to build at Beachhead," Brandy told the mayor. "Not only that, but we also permanently lose the option to install the higher-output turbine in a more suitable site."

"Once you finish the path to Moops Valley, you can install the next available turbine. That will provide the power you want for Beachhead and the leeward shore," the mayor said.

"That's short-sighted and will severely cut our future growth ability," Brandy objected. Several of the others nodded agreement. "Without a high-output turbine, there's no hope of a settlement on the windward coast of Aopo for decades. Give me the manpower and we can get the path to Moops Valley cut and the turbine installed in time. The saltpeter that Victoria has in stock will buy us the time to get Moops Valley fully operational. It will also provide enough power for the ammonia plant and partial electrification of the grid until we get the rebuilt turbine installed at Atkins River."

"Either way, that means I'm not going to have raw materials for explosives until the chemical plant comes fully online to produce nitrates and nitratites instead of just ammonia. Not only is that going to slow down road clearance and building, but it also means no fireworks next year," Victoria said.

"I'm sure everyone will miss the fireworks next year, but that's not as big a concern as proper nutrition for our children." Donahue turned back to Brandy and continued, "I'm sorry, it's too risky. We must prioritize survival of the community; installing the existing turbine at Atkins River will ensure that. We'll worry about the future once we solve the problems of today."

Donahue looked down at his folder of notes. He closed it with a firm slap of his hand on the table then stood and glared at the room, as if daring them to speak any further. "We know what we have to do. Let's get to it."

THE MAN KNOCKED ON THE DOOR TO THE DEN BEFORE OPENING IT. HE stuck his head in and called gently into the dimly lit room, "Ms. Jaqueline, you've got a visitor."

"What is it, Argi?" the Widow Rabinowiscz asked.

"It's Li Sihai. He's come straight from the BuRP emergency

meeting. Said there's things going on that affect the ranchers and farmers and that you need to know right away."

"Bring him in, Argi," Jaqueline said, a note of resignation in her voice as she turned up the lamp.

Argi led Sihai into the room and the pair of chairs before the desk the Widow Rabinowiscz was sitting behind.

"Mrs. Rabinowiscz, I'm sorry to intrude," Sihai started.

"Please don't, Sihai," she said standing up and extending her hand. "Call me Jackie and forgive my manners. How was your trip? Would you…"

He gestured, cutting off her pleasantries. "Please, Mrs. Rabinowiscz. I think the committee is making a grave error, but the mayor was determined. I need your help before it is too late. *We* need to fix things before it's too late."

She sat down in her chair behind Gil's desk and waved for the two men to sit as well. "Tell me what happened."

Argi hid his smile behind his hand. He hadn't heard that tone in Jackie's voice since before Gil's funeral several weeks back.

"BRANDY? THERE ARE SOME PEOPLE HERE TO SEE YOU."

Brandy was leaning over a table covered with the blueprints for the generator facility at Atkins River. She wished she had Greg Donahue here. She'd put him to work demolishing the old sluice gates and water channels leading into the generator house and rebuilding them. If she was feeling generous, she might lend him some help. But she wasn't feeling that generous. If he wanted this done, he could damned well do it himself. It wasn't that the building was too small, on the contrary, it was the same as every other generator house. The difference was that the penstocks—the input channels for the water—needed to be custom designed to get the maximum energy transfer from the fifty-foot pressure head off the dam. That involved pipe diameters, air bleeds, calculating vertical and horizontal distance for optimum slope, and so on. What was suitable for an 800 MW turbine was simply not appropriate for a 1200 MW turbine. Since the original, undamaged turbines shipped from Earth were meant for higher water flow, there were two choices for modifying the penstocks—increase diameter to increase water volume or decrease diameter to increase flow rate. She was still waiting for a response back from the hydrologist she'd contacted at Antonia University as to which way they should go. Meanwhile, they needed to dig up the channel and uncover the concrete pipe before it could be modified.

Brandy looked up. "Unless it's Professor Song with my calculations, I'm kind of busy here."

"It's Jaqueline Rabinowiscz. She has a bunch of farmers and ranch hands with her."

Brandy sighed. "I know this whole situation is going to delay electrification of the farms and ranches, but I can't do anything about it. My hands are tied by the Burpee's decision."

A man pushed open the door to the office and the widow Rabinowiscz entered unbidden. "Honey, I know you're busy, and Sihai says the BuRP meeting didn't go well. We've come to help."

"Help? Digging channels and rebuilding the penstock? We've got the workforce for that, although I'd rather make Mayor Donahue do it all himself."

"No, dear. We're here to finish the road to Moops Valley. You said that if you can get the road finished you can install the big turbine there, first, right?"

"Moops Valley? But... we still need to clear the terrain, and Victoria says explosives are in short supply. Donohue is certainly not going to authorize the diversion after telling us to just go with Atkins and not Moops."

"Not to worry, the farmers and ranchers are all willing to donate some of their black powder. We need to save enough to fend off the urswolves, but frillhorns don't need more than a loud shout. We can make do. I trust you to make the most of the labor and supplies."

"Oh. OH! Oh, ma'am, thank you so much!"

"Ma'am? How long have we known each other, Brandy?"

"A long time, Jackie. Thank you so much. Won't you get in trouble, though? With Donohue, I mean."

"Pfaw, Donohue and the rest of BuRP are so caught up in survival that they're forgetting that it's not enough. We can't just survive, we need to *thrive*."

THERE WAS NO CAR WAITING THIS TIME WHEN THE FERRY REACHED THE dock in Beaverton. That was just fine with Brandy. She'd come in a day early for the BuRP emergency meeting—the new mayor, something-something Litchford—wanted to be briefed on resource utilization and allocation. She'd never met the former deputy mayor, just seen her from afar during the Landing Day Ceremony. With Donahue recovering from his accident, Acting Mayor Litchford needed to be brought up to speed in a hurry.

With much of the worry and hectic pace of the past year behind her —she might even have time for a spa day. The Landing Spa wasn't fancy, after all, Beaverton and Paradise didn't really have an "upper class." But that didn't mean the hard-working people of the colony couldn't enjoy the artificial hot spring or the occasional manicure and pedicure. Brandy was staying with the Urbaneks, so maybe Tara would like to go with her.

On her walk, she passed the lander. The crane was now working on dismounting the forward right engine. The port side cargo hold had been emptied in the year and a half since that engine had been removed. Now they needed to switch to the opposite side and begin the salvage of the heavy cross-country transportation elements. Neither Beaver Island nor Paradise had terrain suited to maglev, but if they could salvage the heavy construction equipment, they might be able to use it to build better roads, and maybe even a cogwheel rail line up to the Ko'Olau Heights, and then over to the windward side of Aopo. It would certainly be more efficient than the catamarans and canoes used by those few hardy souls who'd elected to try building on the far side of the subcontinent.

She passed the lander as James Snover came out of the "public works" office nestled against the hull. He waved and hurried over to greet her. He was a big man and always seemed to be a bit out of breath. Brandy wasn't sure if that was necessarily exertion or enthusiasm as the engineer always seemed to be proposing newer, faster, more efficient—and more power-hungry—projects.

"Hey, Brandy. I have an idea for reducing the dependency of outlying ranches on vehicle fuels. We can build better batteries now that we have the chemical plant online, and even fuel cells. The thing is, we're going to need more electricity in the short run, but I have a plan for that as well."

"*More* electricity? You've got the output of three dams going now! Cajon is a 1000 MW unit, Moops is 1200 and Atkins is 800. Why do you need more than three thousand megawatts?"

"Well, we have to share all of that, of course. Beachhead industry is growing, and farm and ranch usage is increasing, especially now that they need to fence in the frillhorns. I just want some way to handle surges, and as I said I have an idea for that."

"Okay." Brandy sighed. "Let's hear it."

"Well, we have one of the lander engines dismounted and the other one's coming off this month, right? Those two weren't damaged in the hard landing, that's why we can dismount them so easily. Anyway," Snover continued, breathlessly, "with the chemical plant now at full capacity, we don't need all that anhydrous ammonia for fertilizer or Elliott's Explosives. With ammonia we can make hydrazine, and with hydrazine—"

"We can run the lander engines, just like they used to run natural gas through jet engines back in the TwenCen on Earth to generate power during peak demand. Yes, I get it. It's an idea, but those things burn so much fuel in one go; you could power the entire planet, but only for a few seconds. Do you know how much hydrazine that would take?"

Snover's face fell. "Oh, yeah. I guess you're right." He brightened. "But I think I might be able to scale down an engine from one of the shuttles or a helicopter!"

Brandy patted him on the shoulder. "That's better. I doubt the new mayor will allow you to divert one just yet but having an on-demand power source isn't a bad idea."

"Yeah, thanks, Brandy. You're the best!"

As the big man walked away, Brandy thought about his idea. It was foolish, yes, but wouldn't that be a sight! One of the lander engines burning full power would certainly light up the night.

THE BURP MEETING WAS LOW-KEY. MAYOR LITCHFORD WAS MAINLY interested in learning, not in giving commands or making immediate decisions. The committee gave updates, and for the first time in two years, it seemed like there were no crises looming on their horizon. There were still shortages—with the diversion of chemicals to fertilizer over the past year, plus paying back the farmers and ranchers for the "loan" of their private stocks to finish the road to PVA/Moops Valley, black powder was still in short supply. Elliott's Explosives was reporting they didn't have enough for fireworks at this year's Landing Day festival.

With everything they had overcome, the loss of the annual fireworks display seemed like a trivial matter. Still, Jackie Rabinowiscz's words came back to Brandy: *We can't just survive... we need to thrive.* She stood up and got the mayor's attention. "I... may have an idea about that. Actually, it's Mr. Snover's."

James looked up in surprise, wondering what the idea was. He then obviously remembered his conversation with Brandy because he smiled the biggest smile. "Oh yes, what if we could light up the night on the next Landing Day?"

"*SAN SALVADOR*, THIS IS BEAVER LEAD. I HAVE MADE IT TO THE controls and am preparing to eject fuel tank. Godspeed and safe landing, *San Salvador*. Beaver flight is cl—"

From the civil defense speakers, the replay of the last broadcast from Beaver Flight during the landing of the *San Salvador* ended with a brief burst of static.

After a minute of silence, a voice came over the speakers, slowly reading out the names of Beaver Flight, "Beaver one, Mark Cramer. Beaver two, Brian Johnson. Beaver three, Vanessa Pearson. Beaver four, Jack 'One Cajon' Murray. Beaver five, Scott Atkins. Beaver six, James Copley. Beaver Lead, Chris French."

After another minute's pause the final part of the annual Landing Day Ceremony commenced. "Beaver Flight, this is Beaverton Ground Control. The lander is down with all souls safe. Prepare for Landing Beacon to guide you home on my mark. Go for beacon, mark."

Unlike previous years there was no eruption of the fireworks. For years, the "landing flares" had been the traditional way for the residents of Beaverton to mark the way home for Beaver Flight. Instead, from the city square, a rumbling and glow began as the salvaged Engine Number One came to life. The glow increased and was soon replaced by a pillar of fire which surged into the sky.

Brandy smiled, looking at the brightly lit sky. "Fireworks, indeed."

THE TOWN OF BEAVERTON

Beaverton: The town of Beaverton is a legacy to wresting victory from the jaws of defeat. Every year, on the anniversary of the near disastrous crash of the *San Salvador* lander—carrying all the supplies and colonists for Beaverton—the townspeople hold a memorial service for the brave tug pilots of Beaver Flight who saved the lander at the cost of their own lives. Their sacrifice stabilized the ship enough to land all colonists safely, although they lost some supplies and all their heavy equipment. The ceremony started as a solemn event and eventually turned into a day of celebration with picnics, speeches, and fireworks. When several critical components for fireworks were not available, an enterprising power engineer had the idea of using one of the wrecked lander's engines, plus a small amount of fuel intended for supply shuttles, to continue the celebration. This event paved the way for the modern Landing Day celebration—see "The Loss of Beaver Flight" {EA supplement "The Founder Effect"}.

—*Encyclopedia Astra*, Gannon University, Antonia, Cistercia, AA212

ABOUT ROBERT E. HAMPSON

Dr. Robert E. Hampson is a neuroscientist and author. His science fiction credentials include five novels, two anthologies, more than 20 works of short fiction, and 15 nonfiction articles for science fiction readers.

Hampson received his PhD in 1988, and is active in research to understand the effect of drugs, disease, and injury on human memory. He leads a multinational team developing a medical implant to restore human memory function. He is a teacher, researcher, reviewer, scientific journal editor, and consultant. He lives in the Piedmont of North Carolina with his wife, Ruann. His website is REHampson.com [rehampson.com].

Brent Roeder, PhD, is a neuroscience researcher that is exploring how to restore damaged memory function. A lifelong geek, he enjoys writing sci-fi and fantasy to relax from work. Very occasionally, he even remembers to finish a story.

FOREWORD: "NO STRINGS ATTACHED" BY TRAVIS S. TAYLOR

BY T.K.F. WEISSKOPF

For a long time, one of the most popular panels at LibertyCon has been the midnight "Mad Scientists" panel. (Not all of them are mad, of course; some are just merely miffed.) It's a loud, raucous, joyous meeting and clashing of the minds, and discussions range far and wide. Some farther than others... as this probably fictional report from Travis S. "Doc" Taylor, engineer, scientist, author, TV host, etc., attests to...

NO STRINGS ATTACHED

BY TRAVIS S. TAYLOR

Sixteen years ago…

"Sorry, man, I don't know. Did you ask Uncle Timmy or Brandy?" I said but wasn't even sure why this dude was bothering me with this question. "I don't work for LibertyCon."

"But, Doc, you are, um, wearing *zat*." The little guy pointed at the Speaker badge I was wearing. Two things were pretty dang clear to me at that point. One, this little dude wasn't from around here and I wasn't sure how he knew me. And two, I had stuff to do. And three! Wait, did I say two things? Well, there was a third; I was out of mead. Mad Mike had made this awesome honey-based mead and I was on tumbler number three. That shit was the bomb and would totally wreck brain cells.

"Oh, no. I'm a guest. A, uh, mmm, speaker? Lecturer?" I wasn't sure if he understood me as I couldn't really tell where he was from and what language he reverted into when he was confused. I also wasn't so sure that I wasn't stammering and stuttering from the mead either. "And I'm late for the Mad Scientists' Panel."

"Where do I find Uncle Timmy? I looked for him, but this place is different from after," he said.

"You mean before? Like last year?" I asked. "Not sure. I wasn't here last year. I was there a couple years ago when the con was at that other hotel a few miles from here."

"I have already set my table out, but not sure where I put it the other time." He motioned to the small table he had wheeled in from somewhere into the vendor room. The only thing on the table was a single gold—maybe it was gold, it could have been brass or bronze or something else coated with gold or a gold substitute—ring with odd lettering or glyphs on it.

"Dude, if the sun is down and it's Saturday night at LibertyCon, Uncle Timmy is playing Killer Cutthroat Spades in the gaming room." I looked more closely at the ring. It was very interesting. I'd bought my wife something similar years before at a con in Pasadena. I'd had "Love is Forever" engraved on it in Old Gallifreyan. It was a cool anniversary gift for geeks. I had a matching one made for me in Klingon saying "bangwI' SoH" or "bung-WIH-SHOKH!" that I was presently wearing. "And Brandy will skin you if you ain't setting things up officially through her and with her permission. Besides, Uncle Timmy knows everything that goes on at Liberty and I'll bet you somebody has already told him there's a table in here with just one shiny doodad with Klingon glyphs sitting on it."

"Um, Doc, sir..." the little guy sounded wounded. "Not... Clangawun as you say. This is Reticulian."

"Klingon, Reticulian, Gallifreyan, whatever the hell."

"Doc! There you are!" came from somewhere behind me. It was Patrick Vanner. I had somehow missed him so far this year.

"Patrick! Dude, I thought you were in Iraq or Afghanistan or some damned where."

"I got here this morning. But Ringo sent me to get you because you're desperately needed at the Mad Scientists' Panel. Some dude is over there going on and on about string theory or something and Les can't seem to rein him in." Patrick grabbed me by the arm and tugged me away from the little annoying vendor dude who apparently knew me. He noticed my cup was empty. "What you drinking?"

"Mead."

"Mad Mike?"

"Yeah."

"He's at Barfly Central. I'll run by and get you a refill," Patrick offered.

"Thanks, but I'd better back off this stuff a bit. A beer would be great, though."

"Okay. They're by the pool. Ringo wanted you to hurry," he said. "See you there."

Patrick made a right turn into the hotel hallway through the side door. From there Baen's Barfly folks would be just down the hall. I turned left around the corner and walked right into a shin-high lounge chair sitting next to the swimming pool, tangling my feet and throwing me off balance. At that point I had one of two choices. One, fight the fall and land awkwardly and harder than needed. Two, judo roll with it and hopefully minimize any damage. And three—wait did I say two again, damn that Mad Mike and his nectar of the gods. Three, I judo-rolled forward, put too much weight on the cantilevered end of the chair and tossed it up and over on top of me with a resounding *crash*. My arm was stuck through the vinyl ribbon slats and somehow tangled so tightly between three of them that it was cutting off the circulation to my hand. Fortunately, I had tucked my chin and pushed my right arm under my body, so I did sort of roll through the fall and avoided cracking my brainpan. I squirmed, cursed, kicked, and cursed some more until I felt the chair being pulled up and over.

"Ouch! Shit! Wait! It has my arm caught up." I said looking up at Mad Mike Williamson. He quickly manifested a butterfly knife and worked it about in a blur until a blade was showing. A very big blade.

"That was damned genius! I think we'll have to amputate," he said.

"What the…?" I stammered but then he straddled me and went to work. The first thing that went through my mind was, "Mike, you crazy SOB! You're not cutting off my arm!"

Then the tension from the vinyl strap let go with a sound like shooting rubber bands and I was able to pull my arm out. The chair squeaked like fingers on a chalkboard until he managed to pull the lounger off me, and then he held out a hand.

"Dude. Take it easy on the mead." He laughed. "What are you doing here?"

"Like, existentially, or how do you mean?"

"This is the side pool. Right there is the door to Barfly Central. Vanner just said you were supposed to be at a panel." Mike pointed at the double glass sliding door to the hotel rooms that made up the Baen suites. "I had to step out for cigar."

"I was going to the pool for the Mad Scientists' Panel."

"Not this pool, Doc. The main pool through the lobby and out the back." He pointed.

"There are two pools? This place is way bigger than the last place." I pulled myself up with his help, all the while rubbing at the red pinch-bruise on my arm. "Shit. I'd better hurry."

"That's gonna leave a mark." Mike pointed at the lounge-chair-high abrasions on both of my shins drooling red blood into my ankle socks. Fortunately, my socks were white. Then I felt the pain running up and down both shins and fought the urge to sit down and just rub them. About that time, Vanner came through the glass doors on the back side of the Baen rooms.

"Doc, what're you doing over here?" He looked at my shins. "Oh shit! I bet that hurts."

"I've got a first aid kit in my gear," Mad Mike said.

I laughed. "Of course, you do."

"Vanner, drag Doc's drunk ass over to the right pool and I'll send Sue or someone with some bandages," Mike said, using his command voice. I knew Mad Mike was in the Army Reserve or something, but I wasn't sure if he was an officer or an NCO, but he clearly had that ability of doing what needed to be done when it needed to be done like a seasoned military man.

"And maybe a beer," I added. "For the pain."

"Dumb ass." Mike chuckled and shook his head back and forth. Then with just the right amount of sarcasm he added, "F'n genius."

Patrick and I had managed to make it to the right pool without me bleeding to death or dying of thirst. Les Johnson was there, nursing a red Solo cup and trying to get a word in edgeways, but he wasn't having a whole helluva lot of success. Some tall, skinny, really drunk dude was going on and on about how they knew—whoever "they" were—that string theory was *the* Theory of Everything because "they" were going to find the Higgs boson at the Large Hadron Collider one day. I first shook my head and took a deep breath, not sure what either had to do with the other—the Higgs and the LHC. Then I saw John Ringo sitting next to a very attractive blue-haired chick I'd never met before.

"Doc!" Ringo shouted. "Thank God. Let's see what Doc has to say about this."

"About what? And, uh, sorry I'm late. I got into a fight with a lounge chair on the way over here," I said pointing to my shins. "But it learned its lesson."

"Yeah, Mad Mike stabbed it to death," Vanner added.

There were some chuckles. A couple of folks gasped and asked if I was all right, but I managed to wave them off about the time Sue Thorn showed up with the bandages and some nondescript homebrewed beer in a brown twelve-ounce bottle. I accepted them and went to work applying the bandages as I listened to Les explain the current topic.

"Jared over there, well, he is a mathematician who is working on his PhD. He just came back from a trip to CERN and has been telling us about the very interesting planned experiments to find the Higgs Field evidence," Les said. "The so-called God Particle."

"No, we found it. The Higgs boson," Jared claimed.

"Wait a minute. If you found the Higgs boson it would be all over the news," I said getting comfortable in the seat I was offered and making sure it was stable and wasn't going to attack me. "And since it hasn't been. Number one, you haven't seen it yet, or number two, it hasn't been verified yet."

"Uh, well, we've seen energy signatures. We know it is there," the skinny, drunk mathematician claimed.

"You know, I don't doubt it will be found there someday, but how did you 'see' these 'signatures'?" I asked, making air quotes.

"We have seen them in the predictions and models," Jared argued.

"But not experimentally?"

"Um…"

"So, the first postulate of quantum mechanics is that a fact isn't a fact until it is an observed fact. And the scientific method requires experimental verification or falsification of any hypothesis," I said. "But I still don't see what this has to do with strings."

"The point about string theory is that it is the only theory that can explain the Standard Model and comes from mathematical derivations," the guy started.

"Yeah, but I could start with a mathematical model of any closed system and add fudge factors as often as I want and then add more dimensions as needed to make it represent any damned thing I wanted," I explained.

From somewhere behind me somebody added, "Just like Anthropogenic Global Warming. Sooo many fudge factors with no experimental verification."

"Uh, let me interject that AGW is not the topic of discussion." Les Johnson quickly jumped in to keep the conversation from heading down *that* rabbit hole.

"String theory is the only theory that works."

"Um, no. Two things. Firstly, the Higgs boson was suggested as a mechanism to explain how matter actually has… well, mass. It has nothing to do with string theory. Secondly, you could use membrane theory, or maybe some other as of yet to be discovered theory, but all of them require adding dimensions and fudge factors without producing an experimental concept that could verify or falsify them. At least they haven't yet. And thirdly—did I say two things? Third, at this time in the evolution of physics this is nothing more than mathematical masturbation and/or a religion. Kinda like what Michael Crichton said about AGW."

"Dayumn! Snap." Somebody behind Ringo snapped their fingers. The others laughed.

"Well, that's just, that is…" Jared stammered. "What would you know about string theory anyway? I work with it."

"Uh oh…" There were gasps from around the pool. I glanced at John out of the corner of my eye and saw him lean back in his chair and puff on his cigar with a slight grin turning up the corners of his mouth. The blue-haired girl next to him watched intently.

"Well, let me think… What do *I* know about string theory?" I took a deep breath. No scratch that, I finished off the beer and accepted a red Solo cup from someone nearby. I took a swig from the cup, then set it on the concrete under my lounger.

"Well, let me think. I know that it's an algebraic topological geometry that has to implement a ten dimension plus one topology in order to achieve a theory with equal numbers of bosons and fermions, a.k.a. supersymmetry. By going to an eleven plus one type topology you can go to M-theory, which by the way is the main science used in my new series just now available from Baen Books… shameless plug." There was some laughter. I continued. "The problem with all of these is that we don't live in a ten- or eleven-dimensional space so we have to throw math tricks like a Calabi-Yau six-dimensional manifold to say stuff like 'yeah but these dimensions are so wrapped up on themselves they are inconsequential or they might as well not exist.' But *they do* in this theory, and you can't just ignore them. That's like ignoring the limits of integration or even the integration constant, or worse."

I paused for a drink from the Solo cup and continued. "This process of squishing unwanted dimensions is called compactification."

"What about Hawking's radiation, huh? That's experimental proof of string theory," Jared argued.

"Well, no it ain't," I replied. "So, Bekenstein-Hawking radiation is the calculation that S equals kA. The k in this case would be the Bekenstein-Hawking constant that has *pi* and Planck's constant, and the speed of light and Newton's gravitational constant all rolled into it. It is the equation for the entropy of a black hole. A is the surface area of the event horizon of the black hole. Hawking showed that there would be radiation actually being emitted from the edge of the black hole to satisfy the Second Law of Thermodynamics. While the formula can be derived from string theory, it is only done by making these mathematical things called D-branes *look* like a special type of black hole and then adding in some fudge factors. Again, you can derive the formula. But that is by adding and changing the left-hand side of the equation to match an answer you already want on the right-hand side. It is a long way from a prediction."

"That—that's… just bullshit. The theory predicts it!" Jared exclaimed.

"No. String theorists wanted an outcome or an answer to be say… 496, so they made sure they had enough eight-times-eights in there to get it. They even took a thing and redefined it as another thing, hence D-branes are equal to special types of black holes. And those special black holes ain't even normal-looking black holes and may not even exist in nature. They even had to make special 'quantum corrections' to make that work. I call it fudge factoring and bullshitium."

"Unobtanium."

"Go-F-yourselfium…"

"Play nice," Les warned.

"I'm not saying string theory won't be viable someday, but right now…" I took an offered beer bottle once someone noticed my cup was empty—because I was holding it upside down for everyone to see and licking my lips as if I were dying of thirst. I nodded thanks, twisted off the top, and continued. "I'll stick with general relativity and quantum field theory. At least those things *are* experimentally verifiable. The problem is that in order to explain what happens at the boundaries between those two theories we need something to, uh, *tie*, them together. See what I did there?"

"Strings will do that," one of Jared's supporters claimed. "You just said, 'tie them together.'"

"Well, I don't know that they will or if they won't. Presently, they don't, period. But if we could figure out what actually does tie gravity and quantum fields together, we could then do the things we've all dreamed of and read about and written about."

"Such as, Travis?" Les asked rhetorically, just to get me to explain for the others sitting around the pool who might not fully get it. Les and I have known each other for so long, he never called me Doc. In fact, he knew me before I was Doc.

"Well, warp drives, stargates, teleporters, time travel, and so on, might very well be the resulting capabilities from such a true Theory of Everything," I said, waxing philosophic. It would have sounded more eloquent had I not been blasted out of my mind on Mad Mike's mead and all the free beers people were generously forcing on me. It would have been rude not to accept them, and I didn't want to be rude to anyone.

Suddenly, we were all distracted by a ruckus in the lobby. I could see Brandy stomping through the space followed by the usual con committee entourage. She looked heated. Stephanie Osborne worked her way past them, made her way to the pool, and sat down across from Les. I waved to her.

"What's going on in there?" I asked.

"Not exactly sure," Stephanie replied. "But Brandy is all in a tizzy because somebody interrupted Uncle Timmy's card game."

"Oh shit," somebody whispered. "Not good."

"Was it a little guy, about five three, with no hair?" I asked.

"Don't know," she replied. "But somebody said Speaker was missing, too."

"Speaker is missing?" Ringo looked up from his cigar. Speaker to Lab Animals, as we all knew him, was a friend and regular at LibertyCon. "I saw him at dinner."

"Yeah, he sat by us. Right between me and Kelly," the lady with the blue hair said. I realized then that I probably needed to get an introduction to John's new friend She might end up being a "regular" LibertyCon-goer.

"I haven't seen him since I got here," Vanner said. "He's usually hanging around the Barflies."

"Shit, it is a con after all. He'll show up."

"Yeah, he's probably passed out in his room."

～

Nine years ago...

It was cooler than usual. Had to be almost seventy-eight degrees Fahrenheit. Sitting around the pool outside the Barfly suite was comfortable, but still a little sweaty even at sundown. The temperature would probably drop a bit more, but the humidity was going to be murder on the folks flying in from other parts of the country. For us Southerners, it was just a typical day in July, and a relatively comfortable one at that.

"Well, Miriam, out of all the writers Jim Baen sent my first book to, like, ten or eleven years ago, Ringo was the only one of them who took the time to read it and give me useful critique-style advice. He even rewrote a section of it for me to compare. Helped a lot! I'll never forget how cool that was of him," I told her. She had gone from blue to purple hair and had become more than a LibertyCon-goer. She was Ringo's better half. Don't take my word for it, ask John.

"Yeah, but, Doc," Ringo interrupted. "I knew we were gonna have a lot of fun blowing shit up together!"

"Damn skippy," I quoted my favorite line from *Passenger 57*, and raised my beer bottle in a toast. "That and eatin' chicken wings at Hooters."

"He calls the Chattanooga location 'the office.'" Miriam laughed.

"What panels are you on tonight?" Ringo asked. "If we get time, we need to chat about the next Looking Glass book."

As soon as Ringo said something about our next book several of the regulars in the Barfly suite perked up and started paying closer attention to our conversation. Each of them had hopes of hearing some snippet or spoiler for upcoming work. That, or they were hoping we needed names to red shirt.

"Oh, well, we're on that space combat panel at ten together and then Sarah Hoyt and I have to judge the costume contest. Tomorrow, I have a couple of panels, the Baen dinner, and then back over here for my 'That Shit Will Get You Killed' talk Uncle Timmy asked me to do."

"Oh?" Miriam asked. "What is that about?"

"Sex in space."

"No shit?" Ringo twirled his cigar between a thumb and forefinger and raised an eyebrow at Miriam.

"No shit. SF stories always glorify it and all, but I have a talk about how with modern day technology, if astronauts tried it, there are a hundred reasons why it's likely to cause you to die. Like why NASA spent a million dollars to invent an ink pen to write in microgravity," I replied.

"Yeah, the Russians just used a pencil," John said knowingly.

"Exactly!" I said proving my point. They both looked at me as if I were nuts. "That's one of the points I make. You know why Americans didn't use a pencil?"

"Uh, to waste money."

"Common misconception, like the hundred-thousand-dollar hammer. There was a reason—a good one. You see every time you make a mark with a pencil you are leaving little traces of graphite or charcoal particles on the page. On Earth that's fine. What particles don't adhere to the page are held down by gravity. You know what we make sparkplug wires out of? Graphite—well, some are copper, but some are basically charcoal based. The point is, that graphite can carry electric current. And, in microgravity… well, you'd have all those little partially conductive particles floating off the paper and about your spacecraft. Behind instrument panels, near electrical circuits, and no telling what else where they could cause an arc. Where there's an arc there's fire… or could be. Just ask Grissom, Chaffee, and White. So, important safety tip: don't use a pencil in space. There are some who believe some of the fires on Mir might have started from little conductive bits floating about."

"And this has what to do with sex in space?" Miriam asked.

"If graphite particles can float about…" Ringo nudged her and started ticking things off on his fingers. "What else might? Fluids, lubricants, underwear…"

"Exactly," I said.

"Sounds disturbingly disappointing, Doc!" She faked a frown.

"We can only hope that technology will improve someday." I

laughed. "Anybody seen Speaker yet? I haven't seen him since I was at LibertyCon two years ago."

"He's around. Uncle Timmy was talking with him when we came over, about seven or so," John said. "We spoke briefly about a new idea I have for a zombie apocalypse book."

"All right then. I've got an hour or so before our panel so I'm gonna wander about and maybe check out the vendors." I nodded goodbye to John and Miriam and waved at a couple of Baen regulars on my way out. I graciously accepted a free beer from somebody whose face I recognized but couldn't recall their name.

I went along the hotel carpeted hallway and out the back past the main pool where there were a few folks I recognized. Tim Zahn, Chuck Gannon, David Drake, Toni Weiskopf, and a slew of their fans were conversing about something that had some of them fairly excited. I decided to forgo getting involved in that and ducked back through the lobby, past the Killer Cutthroat Spades players who were already in full swing, and then into the dealer, vendor, and art room. Kurt Miller had some absolute badass paintings and book covers on display, including my latest solo novel. I stopped and examined that one closely.

A young couple I didn't recognize wearing Honor Harrington costumes were jabbering away with each other in something other than any Earthly language I recognized. I think I overheard somebody say something about *Esperanza* or *Desperado* or something like that. I don't know, but it certainly sounded made up. Occasionally, the two would laugh at a painting and say something to each other in that language with an added little sing-song lilt that almost sounded like music.

"That diz a nice painting, Doc," I heard from behind me, taking my attention away from the costumed space cadet duo. I looked over my left shoulder to see the same little five foot nothing bald guy sitting at a vendor table. I wasn't sure but he looked different somehow—maybe younger? This time, the table had two rings on it rather than one. That was different.

"Hello." I turned and examined his table and the rings a little more closely. "I assume you checked in with Brandy this go around?"

"What? Sorry, I don't…"

"Six or seven years ago you were here with these… well, one, and you hadn't gotten permission to set the table up? Remember me?" I explained.

"Six or seven years ago?" The little guy acted surprised. "Hmm, I don't recall dzat yet, Doc."

"Yet?" I whispered to myself, but before I could say anything else he started in on a sales pitch for his merchandise. Gold alloy rings with Reticulian glyphs on them.

"Anyway, you only had one of these things. I guess business was good enough to make two?" I made idle chatter and started to pick one of them up to examine it closer. "Not sure how one can make a living with only two products."

"Please, do not touch. Unless you purchase, no touch." The man paused. "But no, only two left. I am almost out of them."

Just then, I heard the two space cadets go into some operatic sounding sing-song speech and the ring on the right side seemed to respond. I could have sworn I heard it resonate like a crystal champagne glass then the glyphs shined a golden-white briefly. They changed pitch and then stopped singing, and the ring stopped responding.

"What the hell?"

"Yes, the zring responded to de… uh, dare… no, ztheyar aural whimzzeezz," he said.

"Aural whimsy?" I asked. "Their song?"

"Ah, yes, Doc. Ztheir song."

"What are they made of?" I asked amazed. I'd never seen gold do that.

"Zrings."

"Yes, what are the rings made of?" I clarified.

"Zrings," he said impatiently.

"No. I mean, what material, compound, or element are the rings made of?"

"Zrings!" he repeated.

"Doc!" somebody shouted. It was Mad Mike. "I brought something for you!"

"Mike. How are you, man?" He held out a pint Ball Mason jar filled with a honey-colored liquid. "Is that what I think that is?"

"Nectar of the Norse Gods."

"Damn right. You are the absolute man!"

"Come on, Doc. We've got a panel to do."

"You're on that one too?"

Six years ago...

"I saw him about an hour ago," Miriam told Toni Weiskopf across the dinner table. The restaurant was about four miles from the LibertyCon hotel and Kelly was the only who hadn't arrived yet for the Baen dinner.

"I talked to him by the keg right before I got ready for dinner. He was going to the vendor room to check out something about an engraved ring," Jody Lynn Nye replied. Jody was sitting next to me, and we were conspiring on a new novel series to pitch to Toni.

"What kind of rings?" I asked.

"Not sure." Jody shrugged. "But that's the last time I saw him."

I looked across the table and saw Speaker to Lab Animals was keeping quiet. Once, he caught me looking at the gold ring on his right hand and he picked up his napkin and placed it in his lap. He didn't bring his hand back above the table.

I'd seen that ring before. It was one of the rings the little bald guy had been selling a few years back. There was something about that memory that bugged me. Hadn't Speaker been missing or something?

"Hmm, well, we'll start without him," Toni said and motioned to the hostess to start taking our orders.

Four years ago...

LibertyCon was always my favorite con. They were like my extended science fiction community family. Uncle Timmy might as well have been an uncle to all of us. My schedule was always so jammed packed, especially once I started doing all the television stuff, so I only made it to a few cons a year and only got to Liberty every couple of years. Over the years they had changed locations many times, and this year was no different. Same people, different place.

I was looking forward to seeing some of the faces I hadn't seen in a while and just hang out and talk with folks about the esoteric details of stories that only people who'd read them could talk about. I mean, how great is it to talk to folks about *Starship Troopers* and nobody even mentions that dumb movie that had nothing to do with the book? But more than that, we've all read John's books, and my books, and David Drake's stuff, and Weber, and Eric Flint, and so on. LibertyCon is our own echo chamber and friendly environment. For hard SF fans, for military SF genre fans, for fun and intelligent stimulus, LibertyCon was like old home week. That, and there was a lot of beer.

Stephanie Osborn and I were standing around with a crowd of folks in the hotel lobby just a few steps from the con suite. The con suite is where all the goodies, cakes, savory treats, and the like which people brought to snack on were laid out, and it was where there was free beer for the con goers.

"Have you seen the artwork this year?" somebody asked Stephanie. I motioned to her that I was going to grab a drink. She nodded.

"Need anything?"

"I'm good," she replied. "I ate before you got here."

I continued to listen to the chatter as best I could. Once I got to the con suite bar I filled a cup with some kind of red beer from the keg. I grabbed a little plastic bowl and scooped some snack mix into it. As I stepped back through the doorway and back out into the corner of the lobby, I spotted Kelly and Speaker outside on the other side of the lobby window. They turned the corner out of view, so I hurried to the side door and fumbled with it, doing my best not to scatter snack mix everywhere. I stepped outside and hurried around the corner... and there was nobody there. The door made a made a loud squeak and a metal clank as the damper pulled it closed behind me.

"What the hell?" I muttered. I worked my way around the corner, looking for any other doors or ways they could have gone, but there was nothing.

"I'm going nuts." I shrugged and turned back to the door to the con suite, but it had locked behind me and nobody was there to let me in. I had to walk all the way around to the front of the hotel and come in through the lobby. I saw Stephanie being led toward the art room by the folks she'd been talking with.

Since I'd just arrived and still a bit tired, I decided to hang in the con suite and relax.

I refilled my beer and found a seat, with my back against the wall and looking toward the entrance. The side exit door was to the left of me and Stephanie was pulling at it trying to get in. She saw me sitting there and looked at her watch, and was clearly surprised. I suddenly realized she was wet from head to toe. I got up and let her in.

"Thought you were going to the art room?" I asked. "Why are you so wet?"

"What? Art room?" she was confused.

"Yeah. Like, three minutes ago you went that way with a group of folks heading to the vendor and art gallery."

Stephanie looked at her watch again as she walked behind the con suite bar. She rummaged through some cabinets until she found a dish towel and started drying herself off. She fixed herself a drink and sat. I sat next to her and observed cautiously while I waited for her to say something. She sighed and used her right hand to pick up her drink. I noticed a gold ring on her pinky that I hadn't seen before.

"I don't know what just happened. I remember going to the art room, but that was hours ago according to my watch," she said.

"What?" I had no idea what she was talking about. I knew her husband, Darell, was a comedic magician, a really good one, and I was beginning to wonder if she was playing some sort of magic joke on me.

"My watch says it was five hours and thirteen minutes ago." She looked confused.

"What are you talking about? It was like five minutes ago, or less," I said.

"Would you excuse me a minute?" She got up, walked straight out the door, and into the lady's room across the lobby. I sat there confused while continuing to nurse the red keg beer. About a beer and a half later I was beginning to get worried about Steph. She was still in the bathroom.

I got up, went out into the lobby, and looked for any female I knew. I heard Brandy's voice from just around the corner and then she and Marla appeared. Brandy really ran things around LibertyCon; she'd know what was going on.

"Brandy. Marla." I waved.

"Hiya, Doc. Good you could make it this year!" Brandy said. "Dad was really excited you were going to make it too."

"Thanks for inviting me. I haven't seen Uncle Timmy yet. Is he here?"

"Playing cards somewhere."

"Should have known that!" I laughed. "Hey, would you ladies do me a favor?"

"Sure, Doc. What's up?"

"Stephanie went in there about twenty minutes ago." I pointed at the lady's room. "I'm beginning to worry that she needs help or that something has happened to her."

"Oh my," Brandy said. "I'll check."

She and Marla rushed into the lady's room, and I could hear them calling for Steph, but it sounded like they weren't having any luck. They returned a moment later, perplexed.

"There's nobody in there, Doc," Marla said.

"What the actual hell?" I said mostly to myself. "I saw her go in. Is there another door?"

"No. You must have just missed her coming out," Brandy said.

"Uh, okay. Must have." Suddenly, there was aloud crack of thunder and lightning flashed across the street, startling the three of us. "Damn!"

"Thunderstorms rolling in," Brandy said. "Gonna rain all night, I think."

"See you at the Baen party later, Doc?" Marla asked.

"Sure."

"Okay, see ya. If we see Stephanie, we'll tell her you're looking for her," Brandy said.

"Thanks."

I looked around, but never saw Stephanie for the rest of the con. I got sidetracked with panels and regular con stuff. I texted her once or twice, but never got a response until the Tuesday after I'd gotten home. She claimed to have just gotten sidetracked with con stuff as well. I couldn't figure that out, though. LibertyCon ain't that big. I can't believe I didn't bump into her at some point.

~

TWO YEARS AGO...

"What do you mean we've never met before?" I barked at the five foot nothing pale bald man in front of me. "I met you like twelve years ago or something like that. You were setting up a table to sell just one ring."

"One ring?" The man looked down at his table with his palms upward, and motioned to several dozen rings laid out on the table. "Zthere are many."

"Hmm, let me see," I said. I reached down to pick one up for closer inspection, but he quickly pushed my hand back.

"No touch unless you are for certain going to purchase it," he said.

"How would I know if it fits?"

"One size fits all," he said.

"How is that even possible? Do you adjust them or something?"

"Self-adjusting."

"Really." I looked closer. I got so close I had to put my reading glasses on, all the while cursing old age, the entire medical profession, with emphasis on optometrists for not solving the damned presbyopia problem. Hell, that's just simple physics, optics, and materials engineering. Why couldn't the sorry bastards just 3D print a lens that was flexible and insert it in place of the aged one? But I realized I was saying all this out loud and the little guy was staring at me, confused. "Uh, sorry. I hate having to wear these damned things."

"I zee," he said.

"What are these things made of?" I had asked before, years ago.

"Zrings."

"Yes, the rings. What are they made of?"

"Zrings," he said impatiently.

"Doc!" It was Jason Cordova. "Dude! How've you been? It's been forever."

"Hey, Jason! Great to see you." I turned and shook his hand. There was another man and woman with him that I didn't know. I recognized their faces but couldn't place the names. "Hey, man, we're going over to the Barfly suite to get a drink. Want to go?"

"Sure." I made a mental note to get back and acquire one of the rings. But I didn't have to do that at the moment. There were old friends wanting to tell old stories and drink new beers. I never made it back to the vendor room.

PRESENT DAY...

That was the last LibertyCon I made it to. About that time, I started traveling around the country doing scientific investigations of anomalous and weird events and places. My travels overlapped with the late July dates of LibertyCon. One particular place I had traveled to and investigated was a really weird ranch in the Uintah Basin just east of Roosevelt, Utah.

It was a Friday evening, in fact, it was the opening evening of LibertyCon two thousand miles away in Chattanooga, Tennessee. I had finished my research for the day and was chilling out in my trailer at the ranch. The temperature was about a hundred and forty degrees hotter than Hell and there was zero humidity. I missed the South.

I opened a very low alcohol domestic light beer. It was all they had at the Reservation beer store. I sat back in my recliner and planned to sip on that beer and stream something fun to take my mind off the scary things that were likely to start as they did every night about 2 a.m. Before I even realized it, I was sound asleep and having a lucid dream.

There are legends, myths, stories, and tales about the weirdness the ranch has with the universe, or maybe the multiverse. Nobody has ever explained it. My experience there is typically exciting, sometimes spooky, and always unexplainable. Maybe it was because I was missing the folks at LibertyCon, I don't know, but for whatever reason I found myself dreaming about being there. And the strangest thing about the dream was that everyone was wearing one of those strange rings. They would all hum a particular tune and then they would turn to me as if they were able to see me.

"Oh, hi, Doc. There you are," Ringo and Miriam said.

"Hey, guys! Have y'all seen Uncle Timmy?" I asked.

"He's playing cards."

"Of course, he is."

More humming noises and then Speaker and Kelly turned toward me and waved. I realized everyone was wearing the clothes from my memory of them at various LibertyCons. Speaker was in a gray short-sleeved button-up shirt with white vertical stripes. Kelly was wearing a straw hat and a bright red and yellow floral-pattern button-up beach-type shirt. Brandy passed them in the background wearing a LibertyCon T-shirt that I didn't recall ever seeing. Speaker and Kelly both started speaking, but I couldn't understand the language.

More humming. This time there was chanting or a sing-song lilt to the words.

"Hey, dude." Stephanie looked at me. She was wet from head to toe. "Pouring cats and bigger cats here."

The crazy dream went on and on, for what seemed like hours and hours. The dream lasted right up until something slammed against my trailer, hard enough to shake it and wake me. I jumped up, grabbed my handgun and a camera and ran outside to see what was going on. As always there was nothing there. After an hour or so of searching, looking at camera footage, and looking in every nook and cranny under, around, over, and nearby my trailer and finding nothing, I decided to go back to sleep. I crawled into bed, pulled the comforter up to my chin, and squirmed among the pillows until I started to drift off.

I heard what sounded like chanting, or maybe singing. It sounded very similar to local native ceremonial chants I'd heard. The next thing I knew I was looking at the outside of my trailer with a bird's-eye view. There was a small figure opening my door. Then I was back in my bed looking up as my bedroom door slid open. I was terrified, but not because of that. I was terrified because I was frozen. I couldn't move. Whatever was about to happen, I was helpless to stop it or alter it. I felt myself quoting the litany against fear from *Dune*, or what I could remember of it.

A small figure about five foot nothing with a big round head walked over and looked down at me. I tried to scream or move or twitch or piss my pants, but I couldn't do a thing. Nothing! I was frozen, as if in some sort of science fiction stasis field.

"They are made of Zrings," the little man said. "Zrings.

"They must oscillate at four hundzred and zninety-six cycles per second," he said.

I tried to shout or scream or anything. Nothing.

"A zingle Zring." The little man leaned close. "One Zring is held open by an exotic field."

The man patted my left pointer finger with one of his extremely long and odd-shaped fingers then scratched me there with his jagged nails. He turned and left my bedroom. Closed the trailer door. And was gone.

Knock, knock, knock.

KNOCK, KNOCK, KNOCK!

"Doc, you up?" I recognized the voice. Sebastian. They sent him every morning to wake me.

"I'm…" Only a whisper came out. I grunted, cleared my throat, and took a swig from the water bottle I kept by my bed. "Uh, yeah. A minute!"

I dragged myself up and pulled on some sweatpants. I cracked the door open and looked at Sebastian waiting at the bottom step of my trailer. "Mornin'."

"About thirty minutes and they'll need you in the command center," he told me. "Sound will be here in fifteen to put your mic on."

"Oh, uh, okay. Thanks for waking me. I didn't set an alarm," I said. He knew that already because I never set an alarm. "Just enough time for a shower. See ya in a bit."

"Doc, did you find that letter I left on the bar for you yesterday?" he asked.

"Uh, no. Hold on." I turned and looked at the bar that butted up against my recliner and saw my keys, wallet, gamma ray detector, a magnetic field instrument, and some sunscreen. "Don't see it. Where'd you put it?"

"By the router."

I looked against the wall where the bar was attached and my Wi-Fi router sat. Between the bar and the recliner there was about a two-inch gap, and on the floor below was a white standard envelope. I grunted as I stretched an arm between the bar and the chair but there wasn't enough room.

"I found it. Thanks. See you in a bit." I pulled my door closed and grabbed the red-handled plastic broom I kept there to sweep the desert out of my trailer. After a couple of sweeps behind the chair I managed to sweep the envelope out.

There was no return address. That was weird. I cautiously opened it. The envelope contained only one thing and it wasn't a letter. As a turned the envelope over a small gold ring with what appeared to be Reticulian glyphs etched in it rolled onto the palm of my hand.

"What the actual f—" I looked at the time and realized I had to start getting ready. So, I sat the ring on the bar beside my gamma ray detector and went to take a shower.

"They are made of Zrings," the little man in my dream had said. "Zrings."

"They must oscillate at four hundzred and zninety-six cycles per second," he had said.

"A zingle Zring."

"One Zring is held open by an exotic field."

It took me another fifteen or so minutes to get ready and there was another knock at my door. It was the sound guy to put my mic on. That took a couple minutes. Once I got to the command center across the driveway from my trailer where the rest of the investigation team were having coffee and such, I pulled the ring out of my pocket and showed it to one of the other scientists.

"Do we have a sound function generator here?" I asked.

"What do you need?" he asked in reply.

"Four hundred and ninety-six Hertz." I paused long enough to accept a cup of coffee one of the assistants handed me. "And what do you know about string theory?"

ABOUT TRAVIS TAYLOR

Travis S. Taylor is an aerospace engineer, optical scientist, science fiction author, nonfiction author, and the star of *National Geographic's Rocket City Rednecks*. He can be seen on numerous TV shows commenting on science and engineering topics and he has worked for both the Department of Defense and NASA. He is currently starring on the History Channel's *The Secret of Skinwalker Ranch* exploring unexplained phenomena.

FOREWORD: "A TRAVESTY OF NATURE: AN HONORVERSE STORY" BY DAVID WEBER

BY CHRISTOPHER WOODS

What can you say about David Weber? He's a great author and his Honor Harrington books are what drew me headlong into military science fiction. Over the years, I would wait, sometimes even patiently, for the next book by David. Then I started writing and found conventions where I can really go and meet the authors who kept me in the bookstores. When I met David, I found one of the nicest people I have had the chance to meet and he's the type of author that many of us aspire to be. When he turned in this story, he said there was a high chance of a novel coming from this. I look forward to it.

A TRAVESTY OF NATURE

AN HONORVERSE STORY BY DAVID WEBER

*H*MS *Prince Adrian*
January 2, 1907 PD.

T HE COM CHIMED.

The sound wasn't very loud, but Lieutenant (SG) Brandy Bolgeo's head popped up quickly, and an impartial observer might have described her expression as "relieved" as the attention request pulled her—oh, regretfully, of course!—out of her unending sea of paperwork.

The engineering officer's slot aboard a heavy cruiser was a plum assignment for someone who hadn't quite gotten her third collar pip yet. She was due for promotion to lieutenant commander in the next six T-months, but she'd become *Prince Adrian*'s chief engineer eleven T-months ago, when Lieutenant Commander Dessaux was promoted out of the ship, and those eleven T-months had been... eventful.

The official declaration of war against the People's Republic of Haven was just over a T-year old, but the Navy had been *at* war for over six T-months before Parliament got around to formalizing things. Brandy wasn't the most politically inclined woman in the galaxy, but she'd been disgusted by the cynical political extortion with which the Conservatives and their allies had held the formal declaration hostage until after Captain Pavel Young's court-martial. Anyone who could put protecting someone like Young ahead of the Star Kingdom's military security was beneath contempt. Almost as far beneath contempt as Young himself. Personally, Brandy thought they should have shot the bastard... and not left it for Captain Harrington to do.

She'd felt that way even before reporting aboard HMS *Prince Adrian*, although her disgust had hardened since. It would have been difficult for anything else to happen, given that the heavy cruiser's crew seemed composed entirely of Harrington partisans who were even more deeply enraged than the rest of the Navy—with good reason, in Brandy's opinion—by her banishment to half-pay after her duel with Young.

But her own anger at the Conservatives had less to do with what happened to Harrington than with what it meant for the Star Kingdom.

Every Queen's officer with a measurable IQ had known war with the Peeps was inevitable, yet very few had expected it to begin when it actually did. Even fewer had anticipated just how badly the Peoples Navy would fare in the war's opening phases. Brandy had been less surprised than many by the Peeps' initial tactical disasters at Hancock Station and in the Yeltsin System—her family had been Navy for generations and she'd grown up around the men and women who'd forged the Star Kingdom's sword and shield—but she'd been astonished by their political repercussions. She didn't know if she bought the notion that the Legislaturalist officer corps had attempted a coup following their bungled offensive, but *something* had gone south in a big way in Nouveau Paris, and Rob Pierre's Committee of Public Safety had elected to purge the Peoples Navy in the wake of whatever it had been. Maybe they'd truly thought they had no choice, but the disastrous consequences of depriving their own Navy of 80 or 90 percent of its experienced senior officers had been a gift from God as far as the Star Kingdom was concerned.

A gift the previous Earl North Hollow and his associates had done their damnedest to throw away in the rush to save his precious son's worthless ass.

Despite that, and despite the Peeps' enormous tonnage advantage, the Peoples Navy was driven firmly onto the defensive even before the formal declaration was voted out by Parliament. The Admiralty and officers like Earl White Haven intended to keep it there as long as possible, which Brandy thought was a very good idea, but the operational tempo required for the outnumbered Royal Navy to make that happen had consequences. Especially for hard-working engineers.

Which explained her current paperwork... and why even a brief diversion from it was such a relief.

She hit the acceptance key, then hid a frown as her caller's face appeared.

"Lieutenant Bolgeo," she identified herself. Regs required that, although her name and rank already appeared across the bottom of the other officer's screen.

"Major Hendren," her caller, equally a slave to regulations, replied, and she nodded, although she had no idea why he might be screening her. In fact, Clint Hendren held the rank of captain, which meant he and Brandy were equal in rank, although she was sure she was senior to him, thanks to time in grade. He was, however, properly referred to as "Major Hendren" aboard ship because a warship could have only one "captain," and could afford no confusion about who was intended when *that* title was used. Because of that, Marine captains received the "courtesy promotion" to major. It had no effect on their actual ranks, although Brandy had known a couple Marines who hadn't grasped that point. She didn't really know Hendren yet—he'd relieved Oliver Yestachenko as CO of *Prince Adrian*'s Marine detachment less than a T-month ago—and he was still settling in, but he seemed a pleasant enough sort.

"How can I help you, Major?" she asked.

"Well, as it happens, there's a small problem." Hendren smiled, but something in his tone sounded a warning, and she didn't much care for the way he paused. Clearly, he wanted to draw a response from her.

So, she smiled back and simply cocked her head invitingly.

His lips seemed to thin ever so slightly.

"I've just come from Boat Bay Two," he said. "Both of my pinnaces are offline. I need them back."

Brandy bit down—hard—on her immediate, instinctive response.

"I'm sure you do, Major," she said instead. "I'm assuming, since you screened me, that it's a maintenance issue. If so, I assure you my people will have you back up as quickly as possible."

"At the moment, *my* people can't do their jobs," Hendren replied. "They won't be able to until we get the birds back."

"I'm aware of that." Brandy's expression showed just a bit too much tooth to be called a smile. "And you'll get them back, as soon as possible."

"I'd feel more confident of that if I hadn't just come from the boat bay and an… interesting conversation I had there." Hendren's voice was cool, but his eyes had hardened.

"What sort of 'conversation'?"

"One which makes me wonder just how much priority my birds actually have," he said flatly. Brandy's eyes flared with true anger, but he continued before she could respond. "I initially spoke to Chief Harkness about it. His response was… less than satisfactory, so I screened Lieutenant Tremaine to express my concerns. He seemed unimpressed. Which is why I'm contacting you directly."

"In what way was *Senior* Chief Petty Officer Harkness's response unsatisfactory?" Brandy asked coldly and watched the Marine's expression tighten at her pointed correction of Harkness's rank.

"He basically told me to wait my turn." Hendren's voice was equally cold. "I told him that was unsatisfactory, and he said that was too bad because there wasn't anything he could—or, apparently, *would* —do about it. Since he seemed intransigent, I asked to speak to Lieutenant Tremaine. He *is* the boat bay officer, I believe. But when I expressed my concerns to him, he told me he had no intention of overriding Harkness. I believe the term he actually used was 'second guessing.'"

"And did Senior Chief Petty Officer Harkness tell you what had occasioned the delay?"

"He said that my people 'broke the birds' by overstressing the impeller nodes in our last training exercise, and that he'd had no choice but to down-check both of them until he had time to run full diagnostics. Despite the fact that both of them showed green boards when we recovered to the bay after the exercise. "

"Senior Chief Harkness is one of the most experienced small craft flight engineers in the entire Navy," Brandy said. "He's certainly the most experienced one aboard *Prince Adrian*. If he down-checked your pinnaces because he's concerned about their nodes, I'm not at all surprised Lieutenant Tremaine declined to override him. I would have done the same."

Hendren's eyes narrowed.

"And would you have done that without even asking to see the evidence for his concern, Lieutenant?"

"When a petty officer with a quarter T-century's experience tells me he's 'concerned,' I tend to assume he has a reason." A small voice in the back of Brandy's brain told her she wasn't pouring any water on the fire, but at the moment she didn't much care.

"So, you wouldn't have?"

"I would have waited for his writeup of the problem. It may surprise you, Major, but *Navy* personnel can actually read and write."

Not good, Brandy, that little voice said more loudly. *Your mama taught you better than this!*

Which was true, she thought. Her *father*, on the other hand...

"I'm not surprised Navy personnel can read and write," Hendren said. His voice was still cold, but lava smoked in its depths. "I may, however, have some slight reservations about what some Navy personnel will *choose* to write."

"Which means what, precisely?"

"Which means, Lieutenant, that I've read Harkness's jacket. The man should be in the stockade, in my considered opinion. He's a walking discipline disaster, and he's never made any secret of his opinion of Her Majesty's Marines."

Brandy's eyes blazed, and her right hand clenched into a serviceable fist just outside her com's field of view.

"Are you implying that Senior Chief Harkness is fabricating his concern?"

"I'm *saying* that this petty officer has a problem with discipline, doesn't like Marines, and was rather vague in his explanation to me. And that his immediate superior—who, I see, has served aboard the same ship with him almost continuously for the last five T-years— didn't even call him in for a more comprehensive explanation. So, no, I'm not implying that he's 'fabricating his concern'; I'm simply observing that he hasn't given me any cause to believe he isn't."

"Let me explain some things to you, *Major*." Brandy's tone could have frozen helium, and the "courtesy" part of Hendren's courtesy promotion seemed sadly absent. "First, the operations of my department are my concern, not yours. Second, I have never known Senior Chief Harkness to be less than fully professional where his shipboard duties are concerned. Third, Lieutenant Tremaine is one of the most competent young officers I've ever had the pleasure of working with, and—as you've just pointed out, as a matter of fact— he's known Senior Chief Harkness far longer, and better, than you possibly could on the basis of less than one month aboard this ship. I am not prepared to entertain aspersions against either of them."

She held his angry gaze with one just as angry, then inhaled.

"And fourth," she said, her tone marginally less steely, "this ship has been on continuous operations for well over a T-year with no opportunity for comprehensive maintenance. For your information, we're eighteen T-months overdue for general overhaul, and one of our reactors and about a third of our gravitics were scheduled for replacement at that time. We are well past mandatory replacement times on both. My people, including Senior Chief Harkness and Lieutenant Tremaine, although the lieutenant isn't actually in my chain of command, are working double watches just to keep *Prince Adrian*'s systems online. And while you may find this difficult to believe, Major, little things like—oh, I don't know, Fusion Two and Life Support One, let's say—take precedence. Senior Chief Harkness is short of his assigned personnel by almost thirty percent. That means he —and I—have to prioritize his time."

Hendren's jaw clenched.

"I assure you that he will provide me with a full explanation of his concerns no later than end of watch," she continued. "I will review that explanation exactly as I review all reports from my people. And if, as I do not for one instant expect, I discover that he's allowed his... fractious past with the Royal Marine Corps to affect his thinking, I will deal with that. But that is my affair, not yours."

Hendren started to open his mouth, and Brandy raised one hand, index finger extended.

"I advise you to let go of this until and unless there's some evidence—beyond your obvious personal dislike for what you *think* you know about Senior Chief Harkness—that he has, in fact, allowed his own feelings to affect the performance of his duty. At this moment, there isn't any. You are, of course, free to take your concerns up the chain to the XO or Captain McKeon, if you wish. I think it would be... unwise of you to do anything of the sort, particularly in the captain's case, unless you have substantially more evidence of misconduct on his part than you have so far shared with me."

The captain clenched his jaw again. Then, finally, he nodded curtly.

"You're probably right," he said. "And you're certainly right that the operations of your department are your affair—and responsibility —not mine. So, I'll leave this with you." *At least for now*, his tone added. "Please inform me of when I can have my pinnaces back as soon as you have that information."

"Of course, Major."

"Hendren, clear," the Marine said, and her display blanked.

"THAT'S NOT EXACTLY WHAT I TOLD HIM, MA'AM," HORACE Harkness said.

"Well, it's obviously what he *heard*. So, what did you say to him?"

Brandy raised her eyebrows and SCPO Harkness scratched his chin thoughtfully.

"I did tell him his birds would have to wait for their place in the queue," he said. "He didn't seem real happy to hear that. In fact, he told me it was 'not acceptable.' So, I told him I was sorry if it made problems for his people, but that *my* people had way too much on their plates for me to make any promises about adjusting priorities without clearing it with Mr. Tremaine, at least. And probably with Lieutenant O'Brien or you. That's when he screened Mr. Tremaine, I think."

"So, you never told him it was 'too bad' he wanted them back?"

"No, Ma'am." Harkness shook his head, then grimaced. "Not too sure that wasn't the way he *took* it, though. I wasn't trying to pick any fights, but I kinda had the feeling he expected me to."

"No, really?" Brandy's eyes widened. "How do you suppose he could possibly have leapt to a conclusion like that?"

"Ma'am, for whatever it's worth, you know I've never taken shortcuts or rearranged schedules just to spite the jarheads. May have been *tempted* a time or two, but I'd never do that. If nothing else, it'd give them too big a club to beat me with." Something that was almost but not quite a smile flickered in his eyes. "Besides, I don't pick fights with officers. Not even *Marine* officers."

And that, Brandy reflected, was true. In fact, Horace Harkness never actually *picked* fights at all, because he didn't need to. Instead, he'd perfected what her father called the art of "interpersonal judo" designed to suck an intended victim into what might be called an exposed position. He had a pronounced talent for inveigling even veteran Marines into taking the first swing, and he'd used it well over the course of his career. After the last twenty-odd T-years, his role as the innocent victim of Marine combativeness might have worn a tad thin, but even granting that, he'd never, so far as Brandy knew, lipped off to a Marine officer or even offered one of them what the service still called "silent insubordination."

"It would appear Major Hendren is unaware of your sterling self-restraint in that regard," she said.

"Yes, Ma'am. I sorta noticed." Harkness grimaced again. "I really tried to avoid stepping on his toes, but I think he takes his people's readiness states seriously. I don't blame him for that, and he's right,

Ma'am. Till we get these birds back up, they can't do their jobs, either. Gunny Babcock and I have already had that discussion."

Brandy snorted. Gunny Babcock—more properly, Sergeant Major Iris Babcock—was *Prince Adrian*'s senior noncommissioned Marine, and a more redoubtable individual would have been difficult to imagine. She had no doubt at all that Babcock had "discussed" the state of the Marines' pinnaces with Harkness.

Loudly.

"All right, let's leave that for the moment," she said now. "He told me both pinnaces were showing green boards."

Harkness nodded. "Far as the birds' flight engineers' boards go, they were. But I'm looking at the boat bay diagnostics and service flags, and they're edging into amber on four of Marine One's nodes and two on Marine Two."

"Only 'edging,' though?" Brandy asked thoughtfully.

The flight engineer's station aboard the pinnaces monitored current hardware states and functionality. Each time the pinnace recovered to the boat bay, however, *Prince Adrian*'s computers used the umbilical connections to generate a significantly more sophisticated analysis than its onboard systems allowed. Those same monitoring shipboard computers maintained a detailed, continuously updated history of every system aboard the pinnace, plotting trendlines over time and checking all of them against the "Book"-specified parameters for mandatory service.

Of course, the Book parameters incorporated a hefty safety margin. A point, she suspected, of which Captain Hendren was aware.

"Yes, ma'am. Edging. Right this minute, the computer's showing us a range between ten and forty-three percent into the Book's Service Immediately margin on the nodes I'm worried about. And, yes, the major asked the same question. Wanted to know why I was pulling the birds off flight status when they haven't actually reached the mandatory service point."

"And you told him—?"

"I told him we're taking maintenance histories and warning lights real seriously right now, on account of how overdue at the yard we are.

For that matter, I told him we're having issues with spares. Ma'am, I'm showing warnings on six of his nodes, and we're down to *eleven* certified replacement nodes. That's it, for *all* our birds, not just the pinnaces, and we don't know when—or if—we're getting more of 'em. Some things we can print ourselves; all-up node modules, we can't." He shrugged. "To be honest, I think the major's probably right that the ones I'm worried about aren't going to blow tomorrow, and none of them look like they'd produce the kind of catastrophic failure that could take down one of the birds completely. But if one of 'em *does* blow, you know we'll have at least some collateral damage, plus we're gonna have to write that node completely off and slap in one of our eleven replacements."

"So, what you really want to do is a teardown inspection and service-as-needed? Not a complete replacement?"

Harkness looked a bit surprised. "Yes, Ma'am. Why would we do a replacement before we even looked?"

"The major said you told him his people 'broke the birds.' That suggests something a little more serious than 'edging into amber' on the diagnostics."

"Ma'am, what I said was the *flight crew* might've broken the birds. I specifically said 'might've,' and I never said the jarheads had broken anything."

Brandy frowned. *Prince Adrian*'s naval personnel provided the pilots and flight crew for all her small craft. That included the pinnaces, although the Marines regarded those pinnaces as their personal property. Not without reason, from an operational viewpoint. What the pinnaces actually did, how they operated and—specifically— how hard they maneuvered while they did it, was determined by the Marines, and Marines had a reputation for being rough on their toys because of their aggressive training. As a consequence, there was a certain traditional tension between the Marines and their Navy "chauffeurs." Had Hendren thought Harkness was trying to blame the maintenance down-check on systems abuse resulting from the Marines'—which, since he was the senior Marine, would mean *his*— unreasonable demands on the Navy flight crews?

"What's the bottom line here on downtime?" she asked.

"My people still have two node replacements on the Number Three shuttle, and we've got that inertial compensator problem on the Number Two bird."

"I know." Brandy grimaced.

As Harkness had just pointed out, spare parts had become a significant issue, which forced *Prince Adrian*'s engineering staff to rebuild and refurbish components that would normally have been pulled, returned to depot for repair or reclamation, whichever seemed the simplest, and replaced with depot-certified components from her onboard stores. That tied up both personnel, workspace, and printer capacity in the cruiser's machine shops, which further slowed both repairs and replacements. And, as Harkness had *also* just pointed out, Brandy's department was responsible for keeping *all* of *Prince Adrian*'s small craft up and running, not just the pinnaces, and with Shuttle Two and Three down, the cruiser only had a single shuttle currently available.

"We can probably put the Three bird back online by the end of the next watch. Two'll take longer than that. Problem's not all that bad, but we can't just fix it in place. We'll have to open her up to get at the compensator, and we don't have the working space to do that until we get Three out of the way."

"And if we pull people off either of those to concentrate on the pinnaces, both shuttles stay down longer than that."

"Yes, Ma'am."

"Much as I hate it, I think we're going to have to do that, anyway. Or some of it, at least." Brandy didn't much like that thought. Especially if Hendren was going to take it as some sort of capitulation on her part. But they really did need at least one of the pinnaces back as soon as they could get it.

"Some of it, Ma'am?" Harkness repeated. From his expression, he suspected what was coming, and wasn't especially eager to hear it.

"I agree we can't take avoidable chances on losing any more nodes than we have to, but the major's right that his people need their birds back. So, what we'll have to do, I think, is put Marine Two back on limited flight status. They can have her in the event of an emergency, but we'll restrict her power levels to minimize stress on those iffy nodes. Then we'll prioritize getting Shuttle Three back up but move the inspection of Marine One up in the queue, before the compensator teardown on Shuttle Two. As soon as we can clear Marine One's return to full flight status, we pull Two off and keep her there until we've had time to get Shuttle Two back up."

"We can do that, Ma'am. Switching teams back and forth is gonna slow us down, though."

"I know. It'll take longer for each bird, but not a lot, and this way the Marines at least get half their capability back. I doubt Major Hendren—or the captain, for that matter—will be happy about having *only* half their pinnaces available, but the best we can do is the best we can do. I'll screen Lieutenant O'Brien and Lieutenant Tremaine to make it official, but you can go ahead and give your people a heads up now."

∽

HMS *Prince Adrian*,
    January 11, 1907.

"Excuse me, Lieutenant. Do you have a minute?"

Brandy Bolgeo didn't reply, but she did pause, then turned to look up at Captain Hendren with an arched eyebrow. The Marine had quickened his pace to make it into the intra-ship lift car before the door closed, and his expression was... odd.

It was the first time they'd physically crossed paths since Hendren's complaint about Harkness and Tremaine, and she'd been just as happy about that, thank you very much. Unfortunately, Captain McKeon followed a tradition he'd apparently picked up from Captain Harrington and dined at least twice a week with his officers. His dining cabin was a little cramped, however. So, with too little space to seat all of them simultaneously, he issued his invitations on a rotating basis.

Normally, they were enjoyable social occasions which also helped foster close personal—and working—relationships. Tonight, however, would be the first time Brandy and Hendren had been invited at the same time.

She hadn't been looking forward to it.

Now the far taller Marine looked down at her as the lift car began to move, and she thought she saw his lips tighten a bit at her nonresponse to his conversational gambit.

That was nice.

"Look," he said, after a moment, "mostly I just want to apologize for having been a dick."

Brandy's eyes widened slightly, and her lips twitched.

"I... ah, don't think I would have applied exactly that term," she said.

"I actually cleaned it up a bit." Hendren shrugged. "I was pissed off, I was worried about readiness states, and I'm sort of the new kid on the block here in *Prince Adrian*. None of which is an excuse. An explanation, maybe, but not an excuse. I hadn't realized just how behind the ship is on her maintenance schedule, or how overworked your department was. Again, an explanation and not an excuse."

"Not to mention the fact that you were predisposed to think the worst about Senior Chief Harkness, too," Brandy suggested, and he grimaced.

"Yeah, I was," he admitted. "I admit I shouldn't have been without personal first-hand experience, but you have to admit he has a... checkered record, to say the least, where Marines are concerned."

"That's probably fair," she acknowledged. "I'd say most of that is because he just likes to fight and he figures it's better to pick fights with somebody from outside his own department. But even though he's traditionally been a bit of a discipline problem, he hasn't shown much evidence of that aboard his last few ships. And there's never been a more qualified or *professionally* disciplined spacer in the entire Navy."

"You may be interested to know that someone else told me basically the same thing about him."

"Really? Who?"

"Gunny Babcock." Hendren rolled his eyes slightly. "Sort of pinned my ears back with that infinite 'You really *are* dumb as a rock, aren't you, *Sir*' courtesy only senior NCOs have truly mastered."

Brandy surprised herself with a snort of laughter. Partly because she understood exactly what Hendren was talking about, but also because she could just picture Babcock doing exactly that. Not so much because the sergeant major loved Harkness, but because she'd been aboard *Prince Adrian* long enough to know how much the cruiser's senior Marine didn't want to get on the wrong side of the ship's company. And, despite what Hendren had correctly described as a "checkered" career, in more ways than one, Horace Harkness was immensely popular with his crewmates.

Well, maybe not so much with the ship's *Marine* detachment, but he couldn't have everything.

"Anyway," Hendren continued, "I wanted to apologize, and I also wanted to thank you for working with us to keep at least one pinnace available."

"And did you read Senior Chief Harkness's post-inspection report on Pinnace One's impeller nodes?" Brandy pushed with gentle malice.

"Yes," Hendren sighed. "And he was right. It's not really my area, but the gunny pointed out to me that we'd have lost two of those nodes, almost for sure, if we'd had to go to max acceleration for any sustained period."

"Well," Brandy's tone relented a bit, "I have to say I'm glad they didn't. We managed a rebuild on both of them, which was huge from our spares perspective." She shook her head. "We're babying so many systems that really need overhaul right now that it's not even funny."

"I know… now." Hendren nodded soberly. "I had no idea how bad things were getting out here before they rotated me out from Manticore, though."

"I understand why we're still pushing," Brandy said, watching the display as the lift car slowed to a halt. "I'm not in favor of giving the Peeps any more time to recover than we can help, either, and I know that means running maintenance margins thinner than the Book requires. For that matter, I think at least some of that's probably inevitable under wartime conditions, even without the ops tempo we're maintaining. But it really is starting to get out of hand."

"Well," Hendren said, nodding her through the opening lift doors before he followed, "I have a better feel for the situation now. And, in the interest of non-dick-like behavior, I promise I'll do my best not to make it any worse next time around."

"That strikes me as a very good idea," Brandy told him with a small smile.

~

HMS *PRINCE ADRIAN*,
   May 3, 1907.

THE OFFICERS SEATED AROUND THE BRIEFING ROOM TABLE CAME TO their feet as Captain Alistair McKeon strode through the hatch. He crossed briskly to his own place at the head of the table, then nodded a bit brusquely.

"Sit. Sit!" he said.

They settled back into their chairs, and he looked around the compartment.

"It's official," he said. "Admiral White Haven's sending a task group to Swanson. Rear Admiral Steigert will command it, and CruRon Thirty-three's drawn the short straw as BatDiv Three-Oh-Three's primary screening element. That means us."

"I thought they were finally going to cut us loose for overhaul, Skipper," Lev Carson, *Prince Adrian*'s executive officer said, and Brandy nodded mentally. Over four T-months had passed since the episode with Captain Hendren's pinnaces, and while her own relationship with the Marine had improved significantly, the cruiser's maintenance problems had only worsened… a lot. They *needed* that overhaul. In fact, CruRon 33 was well short of its assigned strength because serviceability states for three of its units—*Prince Charles*,

Princess Adele, and *Prince Karl*—had become so bad, Admiral White Haven had been forced to send them home for repairs.

And *Prince Adrian* wasn't in much better shape than *they'd* been in.

"I raised that point with Admiral Steigert," McKeon replied with an affable smile that was perhaps one micron thick. "Actually, I told her that despite our engineer's daily miracles"—he nodded down the table's length at Brandy—"we're way past any sane reliability margins. In fact, I told her we're starting to push basic ship safety into the red. Her exact response was 'There's a lot of that going around just now, Captain.'" His jaw tightened for a second, then he shrugged. "In fairness, I don't think she's any happier about it than we are. "

"She can't be any *un*happier, Sir."

"I agree." McKeon nodded. "Which is no slam on you, Brandy." He looked at his engineer again. "When I said 'daily miracles,' I meant it."

Brandy nodded back, grateful for the acknowledgment, and he returned his attention to the rest of his officers.

"Swanson's supposed to be only lightly picketed," he said. "There's nothing there except the gas refineries, and while the Peeps still have a lot more hulls than we do, they're still badly short of experienced officers. That situation's getting better from their perspective, unfortunately, but it'll be a while yet before it stops inhibiting their actions. Given those circumstances, Intelligence thinks they're unlikely to have diverted a lot of combat power to cover what's basically a useful but not vital support facility for Barnett. Sure, they'd prefer to hold onto the system and the refinery complex, but they can live without either of them if they have to, and they need everybody they have to cover Duquesne and the approaches to Trevor's Star. If they have to choose someplace to skimp, it does make sense to pick Swanson."

Brandy considered that. She was neither an astrogator nor a tac officer, but she knew the Peeps had established their base in the Swanson System ten or twelve T-years before the shooting started to take advantage of its three gas giants. Swanson's atmospheric extraction ships and refineries had been intended to provide a sizable percentage of the reactor mass and thruster fuel for the enormous forward base they'd built in the Barnett System expressly as a jumping off point and logistics support base for their long-planned attack on the Manticoran Alliance. Duquesne Base had lost much of its offensive value in the wake of the Peeps' initial disasters, but it had become the linchpin of the Trevor's Star defenses. And Captain McKeon was right. If she'd been the Peeps and she'd had to leave a star system uncovered, she'd pick one like Swanson rather than one like Barnett, too.

"Anyway," the captain continued, "they'll be sending us; BatDiv Three-Oh-Three, minus one ship; and a destroyer division or two. We'll take a look, and if Intelligence is wrong and they've got a picket too strong to take, we back off. But we'll also take along half a dozen tankers from the fleet train. If we can pull it off, Admiral Steigert figures there's no reason all that nice reactor mass the Peeps are busy refining couldn't fuel *our* ships instead."

He smiled with genuine humor for the first time, and two or three of the officers around the briefing room table chuckled. Then he shrugged.

"It's more likely they'll blow the tank farm as soon as they see us, but we might get lucky. And Intelligence wants the base's computers. They don't expect us to find anything earthshattering, but it's probably worth trying."

"It's always worth *trying*, Skipper," Carson agreed. "Of course, they're just as likely to scrub the files as blow the tank farm."

"I didn't say anyone really expects us to get our hands on their files, Lev. But, like you say, they'd like us to try. We'll see if we can hack our way in while we're there, and one of our mission objectives is to haul their servers home with us for the forensics people back in Manticore. That's going to be your people's job, Clint." He nodded at Hendren. "We'll be putting you aboard their main platform. I'm sending Brandy along as senior officer onboard and to keep the lights on and bird-dog the computers for Anderson."

He twitched his head at Lieutenant Anderson McCloskey, *Prince Adrian*'s com officer, then looked at Lieutenant Commander Brian

Chen, *Prince Adrian*'s tactical officer.

"In some ways, I'd prefer to send you, Brian," he said. "Truth be told, I think you're a naturally more devious and suspicious soul than young Anderson, better suited for dealing with the wicked Peeps if they try to hide stuff. But if anything hits the fan, I want you closer to home, just in case, running Tactical. And let's face it, Anderson's better with computers than you are. In fact, now that I think about it, just about *anybody's* better with computers than you are."

"I'm crushed, Skipper. *Crushed!*" Chen protested.

"And if you understood anything more subtle than a pointed rock when it comes to breaking into an enemy database, I might have let you go anyway," McKeon replied dryly. "I said you were more suspicious than Anderson. I didn't say you were *smarter.*"

McCloskey buffed his fingernails on his tunic, then blew on them complacently, and Chen grinned.

"Okay." McKeon let his chair come fully upright and plugged in a data chip, and a file header appeared in the briefing room holo display. "We need to go over the rough—at this point, *very* rough—ops plan, but I did manage to get one promise out of Admiral Steigert."

They all looked at him and he shrugged.

"We're not the only unit of the Swanson task group who's overdue for a date in the yards. In fact, everybody they've picked for this little shindig is almost as overdue as we are, people. Assuming we manage to steal the Peeps' reactor mass, we'll send the tankers back to the fleet with the destroyers. Then the rest of the task group—including *Prince Adrian*—will continue straight home to the Star Kingdom." Brandy's eyes brightened and McKeon smiled at her. "I understand the *Hephaestus* yard dogs can hardly wait to see us!"

∼

Sigismund Alpha,
    Swanson System,
    May 14, 1907 PD.

· · ·

"You're kidding."

"No, Citizen Commissioner. Citizen Captain Rummo just confirmed it."

"He's *positive* it's not Citizen Commodore Androcles?"

"That's what he says, Citizen Commissioner."

"Oh, shit."

People's Commissioner Danielle Barthet glared at Porthos Radeckis. She knew it wasn't his fault, but he was the only person available to glare at. Even he wasn't close enough for her to do it in person, and all he could see was her com's personal wallpaper, anyway, since he'd woken her up less than two hours after she'd gotten to bed. At the moment, he wore the crimson tunic and black trousers of the Office of State Security while she wore nothing at all.

Her current bed partner had started yanking on his trousers the moment the com jangled, and she sat up she sat up in bed. Now she jerked her head at the sleeping cabin hatch and he vanished through it, carrying his boots in one hand and the rest of his uniform in the other.

The hatch closed behind him and she ran her fingers through her short-cropped blond hair while she tried to kick her brain fully awake.

"How bad?" she asked after several seconds.

"Rummo doesn't have definite numbers or classes yet." Radeckis shrugged unhappily. "His people picked up their hyper footprint about fifteen minutes ago. He says they're sixteen light-minutes from the primary—about seven from us—which is why he's sure it's not Androcles. There's been plenty of time for an arrival ID from her to reach us. As far as numbers are concerned, we don't have first-line sensor capability." That, Barthet reflected bitterly, was a colossal understatement. "But he says his people have identified at least three dreadnoughts or superdreadnoughts, five cruisers, and nine destroyers or light cruisers. So far."

Barthet's jaw tightened.

So much for its being Androcles. She didn't know exactly how powerful the citizen commodore's task group was supposed to be, but she did know its heaviest unit was supposed to be a battleship.

Damn it. I told them we needed to reinforce the system pickets!

We're too exposed out here! But did anyone listen? Not until it was too frigging late!

"What does he mean 'so far'?" she demanded.

"He says they're picking up five impeller wedges that could be additional dreadnoughts." Barthet flinched, but Radeckis wasn't finished. "As I say, he said they *could* be dreadnoughts, but at the moment he's inclined to think they're tankers, instead, based on their formation."

Barthet puffed her lips, then nodded grudgingly. That actually made sense, even if it didn't make Swanson's situation any better. The entire existing "Swanson System Defense Force" consisted of exactly six destroyers, which might—*might*—have been capable of scratching a single ship-of-the-wall's paint.

On a good day.

"So, they figure they can steal our reactor mass, do they?" she growled.

"That's what it sounds like, Citizen Commissioner."

"Well, we'll see about that!"

Barthet glanced at the time display.

"How long for them to reach us?"

"They're still over a hundred and twenty million klicks from the platforms," Radeckis said, glancing down to consult his notes. "Current velocity is about thirteen hundred KPS and they're pulling two hundred fifty gravities. That puts them just under four hours—three hours and forty-seven minutes, to be exact—from a zero-zero with Sigismund."

"Wonderful." Barthet inhaled sharply. "All right. Go ahead and activate Omega. And tell Rummo I'll be speaking to him as soon as I get dressed."

"Of course, Citizen Commissioner," Radeckis replied, and Barthet killed the circuit with a furious finger stab.

Radeckis's response had been just a little too toneless for her taste, but that wasn't surprising, given how little Omega appealed to him. Fortunately, he also knew better than to argue.

Unlike Barthet, Citizen Captain Porthos Radeckis had a lengthy history in the People's Republic's security forces. In fact, he'd been an Internal Security sergeant before the Legislaturalist coup attempt. That, however, was scarcely a ringing endorsement in Barthet's opinion.

She had to admit that Oscar Saint-Just and his Office of Internal Security had been instrumental in defeating the coup attempt. Yet, even though InSec had responded quickly and effectively after the traitors' initial attack, the fact that no one had seen it coming *before* that, and that the Legislaturalist coup had come so close to success—it had, after all, killed Hereditary President Harris and virtually every other member of his cabinet—made it obvious a fundamental consolidation and reorganization of the People's Republic's entire security apparatus was necessary. Saint-Just's decisive response to the coup had made him the only real candidate to command the Committee of Public Safety's newly created Office of State Security, and Internal Security had been folded into StateSec, along with the Mental Hygiene Police and half a dozen other, smaller security services.

After their leadership positions had been purged of Legislaturalists, of course.

Radeckis had come over to StateSec from InSec. Barthet hadn't. She'd been a member of Cordelia Ransom's Citizens' Rights Union, the proscribed action arm of the Citizens' Rights Party. In fact, she'd been one of the CRU "terrorists" people like Saint-Just had hunted for decades, while Radeckis had been one of the InSec thugs who'd done the hunting. That created a certain... tension in their relationship. And, frankly, she distrusted his commitment to the new, revolutionary regime trying to clean up the Legislaturalists' mess. In particular, he was far too prone to defer to Citizen Captain Rummo.

Barthet's own relationship with Rummo was less than congenial. Two T-years ago, Citizen Captain Rummo had been *Lieutenant* Rummo of the Peoples Navy's old officer corps. He hadn't been a Legislaturalist himself, or he wouldn't still be in uniform, but anyone who'd been commissioned before the coup bore watching. That was Danielle Barthet's job as his people's commissioner. And part of that job was keeping him aware that he continued to serve only on her sufferance.

She stood and reached for her own uniform.

"With all due respect, I think that's a bad idea," Citizen Captain Abelin Rummo said.

"Does that mean you intend to protest the Citizen Commissioner's orders, Citizen Captain?" Porthos Radeckis asked him.

"It means I think those orders should be… carefully considered," Rummo replied. His tone was respectful but unflinching, and Radeckis gave him points for intestinal fortitude. Arguing with Danielle Barthet wasn't the best tactical decision a man could make, though. Radeckis knew he should shut down this entire conversation quickly, but—

"Why?" he asked.

"I don't have any objection to destroying the tank farms or the refining platforms to prevent them from falling into Manty hands, Citizen Captain," Rummo said. "If we're going to do that, though, we should do it immediately. Or at least as soon as they formally demand our surrender. What the Citizen Commissioner is proposing could very well be interpreted as a violation of the Deneb Accords."

"I understand your concerns," Radeckis said after a moment. In fact, Rummo's "concerns" were a close mirror of Radeckis's own reservations. "But as far as not immediately destroying the storage and refining facilities is concerned, the Citizen Commissioner is basically playing for time. Citizen Commodore Androcles was already supposed to be here, and it's going to take the Manties at least a couple of days if they really intend to transfer all that reactor mass to their tankers. If Androcles turns up in the next, say, twenty-four hours, she may be able to drive them off without what they came for."

Rummo's eyes rolled ever so slightly, but he kept his mouth shut. He and Radeckis both knew how unlikely it was that the Peoples Navy had scraped up a picket force for a hole-in-the-wall system like Swanson that would have a chance in hell to "drive off" three dreadnoughts. It *was* remotely possible. So was the possibility that the system primary would go nova in the next twenty minutes. In the real world, the People's Republic was going to lose the storage tanks *and* the refinery platforms, one way or the other. That being the case, Rummo was exactly right, in Radeckis's opinion. They ought to blow all of them immediately.

And they sure as hell *shouldn't* blow them with Manticoran tankers docked to them. If they did that, if they killed the crews of those ships, the Manties would be fully justified under interstellar law if they destroyed every habitat platform in the system... without evacuating the Havenite personnel. Radeckis had pointed that out to Barthet when the people's commissioner first hatched Omega, only to be told that she had no intention of waiting *that* long. *Obviously*, the tank farm would have to be destroyed before the Manties actually docked to it!

But Radeckis had enjoyed more access to InSec's pre-coup files on Barthet than the people's commissioner might realize, and based on her CRU cell's taste for spectacular, mass-casualty events, he didn't trust the ex-terrorist's assurance about exactly when she intended to blow up the Swanson storage facility any more than Rummo did. Nor did he care for Barthet's decision for the system's SS personnel to "go to ground." He didn't object in the least to her decision against trying to defend the platforms when the Manties arrived. It seemed unlikely the Royal Manticoran Marines aboard those incoming warships would find it difficult to deal with little more than three hundred StateSec troopers, after all. And he would have had no problem with just stripping off his uniform and disappearing into the two thousand-strong Swanson workforce. Unfortunately, that wasn't what Barthet had in mind.

"As I say, I appreciate the reason for your concerns," he said, "but we both have our orders, Citizen Captain. Don't we?"

He held Rummo's eyes with his very best bleak, InSec gaze, and the naval officer inhaled deeply. His wife, two kids, three brothers, and parents lived in Nouveau Paris. Which meant he wasn't about to do a single thing that could point StateSec at the people he loved.

"Yes, we do," he said, and Radeckis nodded.

"The Citizen Commissioner will join you in Command One shortly," he said.

∾

Swanson System,
May 14, 1907 PD.

"There they go, Skipper."

Lieutenant Commander Chen sounded a bit disgusted but not surprised, and Alistair McKeon grunted in acknowledgment. He didn't blame the Peep destroyers one bit. They would have been hopelessly outclassed just by TG 33's own destroyers. Against Steigert's dreadnoughts, they might have lasted five minutes. On a good day.

"Smartest thing they could've done," he said, gazing at the large-scale plot, where the icons of the destroyers' impeller wedges had just crossed the hyper-limit. Five of them had disappeared into hyper as soon as they could, but one had remained behind.

"There wasn't a damned thing they could have done to stop us," he continued. "So, they leave one tin can to keep an eye on us and the others haul ass to spread the word."

"Think they're likely to bring back friends, Sir?" Chen asked.

"I doubt it." McKeon shrugged. "It's unlikely they have anyone close enough to get back here before we finish up and head for home. And if they did, the smart move would've been to send a single courier to call them in while the rest of the picket hung around and kept an eye on us." He shook his head. "No, I'm not going to make any ironclad assumptions that there *isn't* somebody close enough, but this looks more like spreading the word as broadly as possible."

"At least that's how they'll write it up for their reports," Lev Carson observed dryly from McKeon's com. The XO was in AuxCon with the backup bridge group. "If ONI's right about the new management's 'collective responsibility' crap, *I'd* make damned sure I covered my ass against any hint of cowardice or 'defeatism.'"

"So would I," McKeon acknowledged. "But the truth is, it's the best thing they could do, anyway. And—"

"Excuse me, Skipper," Lieutenant McCloskey said.

"Yes?" McKeon looked at him.

"Admiral Steigert's on the com for you, Sir."

"Thank you."

McKeon touched the acceptance key and Rear Admiral Jožefa Steigert replaced Commander Carson on his display.

"Ma'am," he said.

"They've surrendered." Steigert snorted. "Surprise, surprise!"

"Actually, I *am* a little surprised they haven't already blown up the tank farm, Ma'am."

"So am I," Steigert acknowledged. "Especially given how fond of shooting people the new Peep management seems to be. Of course, that could cut both ways. If you don't blow the tanks to keep them from falling into the hands of those nasty Manties, you're likely to get hammered—or shot—for lack of revolutionary zeal. But if you blow them in time to prevent that, you're probably just as likely to get hammered—or shot—for defeatism."

"I can see that, Ma'am. But if it was me, I'd have pushed the button."

"Well, Citizen Captain Rummo apparently doesn't see it that way."

"Citizen Captain?" McKeon repeated. "Not 'People's Commissioner'?"

"Regular Navy officer." Steigert shrugged. "Maybe they just haven't gotten around to assigning a 'commissioner' way out here yet."

"Maybe." McKeon nodded, but he also frowned. Admittedly, the Swanson System was scarcely a critically important installation, but the Committee of Public Safety had made a point of assigning their 'people's commissioners' to every single hyper-capable unit of the Peoples Navy. It seemed unlikely they wouldn't have made at least as strong a push to assign StateSec watchdogs to every system commander, as well.

"It seems odd to me, too," Steigert said. "And just between you and me, Alister, I'm not a big fan of 'odd.' Tell your people to watch their asses when they go aboard the main platform."

"Oh, I will, Ma'am. I will."

~

"Marine One is docking now, Ma'am. We're number two, behind Major Hendren."

"Thank you, Scotty," Brandy said. Lieutenant Tremaine was technically too senior for a mere shuttle pilot, but she wasn't surprised to find him when she boarded the shuttle. Tremaine loved small craft, and as *Prince Adrian*'s flight operations officer, *he* got to make the cockpit assignments.

That, no doubt, also explained why SCPO Harkness was Shuttle One's current flight engineer.

She smiled at the thought and leaned forward in her seat, craning her neck to watch Marine One settle into the orbital platform's boat bay buffers.

Like most industrial platforms, *Sigismund Alpha*'s design was bare-bones, practical, and as devoid of aesthetic value as it was possible to be. The main platform was an untidy aggregation of habitat modules, hydroponics sections, and cargo platforms, gleaming in the reflected light of Sigismund, otherwise known as Swanson III.

Swanson was unusual for an F8 star in its possession of three exceptionally massive gas giants. Sigismund, the largest of the trio, and the only one which had actually been named, was about ten times as massive as the Sol System's Jupiter, just short of "brown dwarf" territory. It wasn't significantly larger than Jupiter, only denser and more massive, but it supported two separate refinery platforms—Sigismund Beta and Gama—and a bountiful flotilla of atmospheric mining ships.

The refineries and storage tanks were well separated from Sigismund Alpha, probably as a safety precaution in case of industrial accidents. They were actually a bit larger than Brandy had anticipated, too. It looked like at least two or three times the storage capacity she'd expected. If those tanks were full, TG 33 should have brought more tankers.

Her lips twitched at the thought as she watched the boarding tube run out to Marine One and pictured Hendren and his Marines swinging through it to the Sigismund Alpha Boat Bay gallery. Over the last few months, she and Hendren had gotten past their rocky start... mostly. His apology had obviously been sincere, he'd done his best to avoid stepping on her toes again, and they'd even gotten as far as using one another's first names, occasionally. It was clear he still cherished a few reservations about SCPO Harkness, but given Harkness's record, she couldn't fault that. If she'd been a Marine, *she* would have had reservations about him! And whatever the Marine's other faults might be, at least he had a lively sense of humor. Brandy could forgive a lot in someone who knew how to laugh at himself.

His obvious competence was another mark in his favor. One reason he'd been so frustrated by Harkness's decision to ground both pinnaces was the way it had interfered with his training schedule. In Brandy's experience, Marines in general had something of a fetish about training, but Clint Hendren took it to an even higher level than most. His people spent a *lot* of time in small craft and EVA exercises. *And* in fully geared-up shipboard exercises, tasked both to defend and to seize the ship. In fact, the time they spent practicing boarding and SAR exercises put enough wear on "his" pinnaces to eat up a disproportionate amount of Brandy's severely overtaxed service and maintenance time. On the other hand, he'd become aware—one might have said *painfully* aware, given their initial contact—of how overworked her people were, and he'd assigned six of his Marines to help with the load. It wasn't the same as having additional trained Navy ratings would have been, but all six of them had extensive experience with engineering as damage control team leaders, and they'd proven extremely useful.

But she wasn't about to let him completely off the hook for how firmly he'd put his foot into his mouth that first time. Or, at least, she wasn't about to admit it to him. But he'd made some long strides toward rehabilitating himself in her eyes, and he—and the rest of his Marines, of course—were a very reassuring presence when she found herself going aboard a platform inhabited by the next best thing to two thousand Peeps.

"Bay secure, Ma'am," Tremaine announced, and the shuttle quivered as its thrusters engaged. "Initiating docking sequence now."

BRANDY BOLGEO FOLLOWED CAPTAIN HENDREN DOWN THE FINAL passage to Sigismund Alpha's command deck. As the senior officer present, she was technically in command, and where engineering issues and her party of ratings was concerned, she was just fine with that. But she didn't know a damned thing about boarding a hostile orbital platform, and she was delighted to leave the details of securing that platform up to the Marine.

Like the rest of her Navy personnel, she wore a standard issue skinsuit, but Hendren's Marines—aside from his single platoon in battle armor—wore Marine-issue armored skinnies. At the moment, the captain was watching the system schematic displayed on his helmet's HUD as he and Brandy moved at the center of a five-Marine diamond formation, and all of the Marines in question carried unslung M32 pulse rifles. At least no one in her immediate vicinity had unlimbered a tribarrel or a plasma rifle, she thought dryly.

Oh, stop that! she told herself. *They're doing their jobs, and they're doing them damned well, and you know it.*

She did. In fact, what she felt most of the moment was impressed... and reassured. She was an engineer, not a tac officer, and sure as hell not a *Marine*! She carried the mandatory sidearm, and she'd qualified with it, as required. She was fairly certain she could at least not shoot her own foot off. Anything more was... problematical. So, it was a good thing people who understood such things were along to keep her out of trouble.

And the fact that this is so far outside your comfort zone is one reason you're feeling nervous enough to make snitty remarks, if only to yourself, she thought. *And I hadn't realized how damned big this place was, either!*

In fact, compared to something like *Hephaestus* or *Vulcan* back home, Sigismund Alpha was tiny. Compared to *Prince Adrian,* it was huge, as was probably only to be expected of an orbital platform which housed a workforce closing in on three thousand. In addition to the environmental sections, there were engineering and maintenance spaces, docking racks for workboats and remote repair and maintenance drones, and God only knew what else, all located with the sprawling contempt for concentration microgravity made possible.

In addition to the boat bay—designed to allow the transfer of personnel in a shirtsleeve environment—which was located in its own module and covered now by one squad of Lieutenant Jeremiah Dimitrieas's First Platoon, there were five docking platforms arranged to service Sigismund Alpha's extensive cargo modules.

First was the only battle-armored platoon of the short company of *Prince Adrian*'s Marine detachment. It's second squad was distributed covering those cargo docks. The modules they served were *much* larger than Brandy had anticipated, but their size made sense when she discovered that all the system's spare parts and support equipment were warehoused aboard Sigismund Alpha, rather than distributed among the refineries and tank farm. In addition, the Peeps had been building a second refinery—and additional tank farms—in orbit around Swanson IV. Most of the materials support for *that* were passing through Sigismund Alpha, as well, and its cargo space had been expanded accordingly. All those docking platforms had to be covered, though, which had sucked away more of Hendren's battle armor than Brandy might have preferred. On the other hand, battle armor was bulky, and most of Sigismund Alpha's internal passages were too narrow for it to pass through readily.

Dimitrieas's third and final squad had been broken up into four two-person fire teams, rather than the standard three-person sections, and detailed to cover the platform's central lift shafts. The shaft access compartments were much wider than the connecting passages, which made them a more comfortable fit for battle-armored Marines. And a Marine in battle armor was a very un-tempting target if anyone felt fractious. If Hendren had to hang somebody out on his or her own— and he did, given the number of points that had to be covered—it made sense to use his best protected, best armed personnel.

Lieutenant Isaiah Gillespie's Second Platoon had been tasked for *internal* security. He and his First Squad had headed for Power One, located in Sigismund Alpha's central engineering section, along with Oliver O'Brien, Brandy's assistant engineer, to secure the platform's reactors. His Second Squad had already accompanied Scotty Tremaine and Horace Harkness to secure Life Support Central, and Third Squad was on its way to the command deck along with Hendren, Anderson McCloskey, and, of course, Brandy herself.

Lieutenant Bethany Clark and Third Platoon were still aboard *Prince Adrian*, skinsuited and ready to go in the second pinnace in case they were needed.

"Marine One, Marine Two-One," Gillespie's voice came over Brandy's earbug.

"One," Hendren acknowledged. "Go, Two."

"We're in Power Central, sir," Gillespie reported. "The Peep power crew chief is walking Lieutenant O'Brien through the control panels now. From the lieutenant's expression, I think he's getting the straight skinny."

"Copy your arrival," Hendren said. "Any sign of security types?"

"No, sir." Gillespie didn't sound entirely happy about that, Brandy noticed. "Haven't seen hide nor hair of them."

"Understood. Stay on your toes, Isaiah."

"Wilco that, sir! Two-One, clear."

Brandy couldn't see the captain's expression, but from the set of his shoulders, she was willing to bet he was frowning. She picked up her own pace until she was walking beside him, and he glanced down at her.

He *was* frowning, she saw. It wasn't all that *much* of a frown, but still…

"Yes?" he cocked his helmeted head.

"I hadn't really thought about the fact that we haven't seen any of their security personnel," she said quietly. "That seems… a little strange to me."

"Only a little?" Hendren snorted. "Everything we've seen about the Peeps since the Harris assassination says they've been beefing up their security forces, not just aboard warships but for every other imaginable base and outpost. Given this place's size, they ought to have at least a couple of platoons of their new StateSec goons to help their 'People's Commissioner' ride herd on everybody's political reliability."

"Apparently, Rummo doesn't have one," Brandy said.

"They don't?" The Marine sounded surprised.

"Nope. Surprised me, too, Clint. I would have expected their 'commissioner' to be hovering in the background when Citizen Captain Rummo surrendered, but there was no sign of one."

"There wasn't?" Hendren frowned. "I didn't see any of the com traffic," he added. "I should have figured something was odd when Captain McKeon told me Rummo would be the one surrendering the platform to us." His frown deepened.

"Do you think they're planning something?" Brandy was pleased her voice sounded so level, but she felt her eyes flit around the passage, and their escort no longer seemed quite so ostentatious.

"I think they'd be incredibly stupid if they were," Hendren replied grimly. "Unfortunately, nobody issues any guarantees that the people on the other side *won't* be incredibly stupid. So far, the platform maps they've provided seem to be a hundred percent accurate, and his boat bay people and now Engineering seem to be cooperating exactly the way he promised they would. So, he sure looks like someone who's minding his manners, but I don't know…" He shook his head. "It's just like I've got this itch I can't scratch."

"Lieutenant Bolgeo?" another voice said in her earbug, and she raised one hand at Hendren, index finger extended in a "hold that thought" gesture.

"Yes, Scotty?"

"The senior chief and I are in Life Support Central, Ma'am."

"Any problems?"

"No, Ma'am, but it's a little weird. Life Support was unmanned when we got here. Not a soul in sight."

"Really?" She glanced back up at Hendren. "Scotty says Life Support was unmanned when he got there."

The Marine nodded.

"We're a little concerned over the fact that we haven't seen any of the base's security personnel yet," she told Tremaine. "May be nothing but keep your eyes open."

"Gunny Babcock's already watching our backs, Ma'am. But we'll keep our eyes open, too."

"Good. Back to you later."

"How unusual would it be for that station to be unmanned?" Hendren asked after a brief, thoughtful pause.

"That's hard to say. It would depend on a lot of factors, including how sophisticated the control links from Command Central are and how short on personnel they are." Brandy shrugged. "On a Manticoran platform this size, everything—Power, Environmental, all of it—would be controlled from the command deck, so there wouldn't *have* to be any operators physically on station. Not for routine ops, at least. But we'd have at least someone physically monitoring on site, just in case. Even today, the human eye and brain are still about the best safety and servicing system around. And the Peeps tend to be more manpower intensive than we are because their system reliability's lower."

"So, there ought to have been someone on Life Support?"

"I'd say yes. Probably." She grimaced. "I have no idea how their purges have affected personnel somewhere like here in Swanson, though. Like I say, their serviceability's poorer, so I'd expect an experienced command crew to have duty watches on all the critical stations, if only for redundancy."

"An *experienced* command crew," Hendren repeated.

"Yes. But whatever they may have done to their officer corps, they have to have hung onto the bulk of their long-term noncommissioned," she said. "As I understand it, their career noncoms are the real backbone of their maintenance and operational personnel. They've got senior chiefs doing chores we'd hand off to a spacer-first, because their conscripts haven't got the training or the experience. So, I'm pretty sure if it was left up to *them*, they'd have had a Life Support duty watch up and running. If they don't, then presumably it's because their officers told them not to."

"Which indicates either sloppiness… or maybe that that itch of mine has a certain justification."

"I'd prefer sloppiness," Brandy said.

"So would I, Brandy."

They turned the final corner and found themselves outside the open hatch of Command Central. The first Peep Marine they'd seen was standing outside the hatch. His sleeve bore the chevrons of a sergeant, and the pistol holster at his hip was conspicuously empty.

He came to attention as they saw him, although he didn't salute.

"Sergeant—I mean, Citizen Sergeant Lloyd Bigby," he said.

Hendren looked him over.

"First one of those uniforms I've seen since we came aboard, Citizen Sergeant," he said, after a moment.

"Aren't many of them around, Major. I've only got twenty-seven people, all told." Bigby shook his head. "We're basically just traffic cops."

"And there's none of those—what? State Security types—around?"

"You see any?" Bigby shook his head again.

Hendren frowned, but then he shrugged and stepped past the citizen sergeant onto the spacious command deck.

A tall, brown haired officer in PRN uniform awaited them.

"Citizen Captain Rummo?" Hendren asked.

"I am."

"Major Clint Hendren, Royal Marines. And this"—he indicated Brandy—"is Lieutenant Bolgeo. She's now in command of Sigismund Able."

"I understand." Rummo gestured around the command deck. Only a third or so of its stations were manned by the obviously skeleton bridge watch. "My people will show your people anything you need them to, Lieutenant."

"I appreciate that, Citizen Captain," Brandy replied.

"Before you do that, Citizen Captain," Hendren said, "I'm a little puzzled. You seem pretty lightly staffed, and we're getting similar reports from Life Support and Fusion One."

"And you're surprised?" Rummo shook his head. "Major,

everybody aboard this platform—hell, everybody in Havenite uniform —is doing his damnedest to keep his head down. And to be brutally honest, no one wants to be accused of collaborating with your people after you finish your business here and withdraw."

"Including you, Citizen Captain?"

"*Especially* me, Major. Unfortunately, this comes with my job description, under the circumstances. Although"—he showed his teeth in something that certainly wasn't a smile—"you can bet I'm not going to 'collaborate' with you one damned bit more than I have to. My people will show you the basic hardware, but that's it. All you get." He looked Hendren in the eye. "I have family back in Nouveau Paris. Almost all of us do."

"Understood." Hendren nodded, then stepped back, positioning himself at Brandy's shoulder. She nodded to Rummo.

"And now, Citizen Captain," she said, "please be good enough to walk me and my people through your command-and-control systems."

"Of course, Lieutenant."

"I don't think Hendren's a happy camper right now, Skipper," Lev Carson said.

"And I don't think I blame him." Alistair McKeon's tone was a bit absent, but his eyes were sharp as he gazed into the main navigation display. "He's right that they seem awful light on security personnel over there. Twenty-eight Marines? None of them State Security, and the senior's a *sergeant*? With the next best thing to three thousand people to ride herd on?"

He shook his head.

"Should we put some more people onto the platform to back him up?"

"Who?" McKeon snorted and waved at the display. "All we've got is Clark's platoon, and nobody else is close enough to peel off any more Marines." He shook his head again, and Carson nodded.

The Swanson System housed a significantly larger Havenite

presence than ONI had allowed for. The People's Republic had obviously started ramping up for its attack on the Manticoran Alliance well before Hancock Station or Third Grayson, and it looked like Swanson's expansion had been part of that ramping up process.

The system's current refining capacity was at least three times the intelligence types' projection. Sigismund Alpha was twenty percent bigger than their prewar data had suggested, and in addition to the two refineries riding Sigismund's orbit with it, an entire secondary complex —including two more dedicated refinery platforms and their own fuel-holding tanks—had been built in Swanson IV's orbit, eight and a half light-minutes farther from the primary. It wasn't complete yet—it seemed likely the intent had been to build a complete clone of Sigismund Alpha—but the first few modules of an additional personnel habitat had been parked around Swanson IV. For the moment, only construction workers and a skeleton force, barely large enough to operate the refineries, actually lived aboard them, and the bare-bones habitat was obviously regarded as a hardship post. The prewar planners had clearly concentrated on increasing the system's refinery capacity first, with comfortable housing for its increased workforce second on their priorities list. Or even third.

Given all of that, the refinery workers cycled between Swanson IV and Sigismund on a monthly basis. The construction workers didn't have the same opportunity, but they at least got to visit Sigismund Alpha's "bright lights" occasionally.

The system's increased infrastructure made StateSec's curious absence even more puzzling, since it was clear Swanson had been more important to the Peoples Navy than ONI had assumed. It also meant Rear Admiral Steigert's task group had a broader volume to cover.

At the moment, Swanson IV lay almost sixteen light-minutes from Sigismund. Unlike Sigismund, it was also outside the system primary's hyper-limit, but both superjovians were large enough to generate hyper-limits of their own that were nearly five light-minutes deep. Steigert had opted to move her abbreviated wall of battle—all three dreadnoughts of it—to a solar orbit just outside the stellar hyper-limit and about midway between Sigismund and Swanson IV. From that position, she could move to either of them in the unlikely event that the Peoples Navy put in an appearance. Her destroyers were deployed to scouting positions, scattered around the system periphery, and she'd retained CruDiv 33.2, HMS *Magician* and HMS *Gladiator*, with her dreadnoughts. HMS *Princess Stephanie*, *Prince Adrian*'s sister ship and partner in CruDiv 33.1, had been assigned to ride herd on the Swanson IV facilities.

That left *Prince Adrian* all alone, keeping an eye on Sigismund Alpha. And that, in turn, meant that only Captain Hendren's Marine detachment was available. Two of his three platoons were already deployed aboard the platform. Lieutenant Clark's forty-four Marines were the only reserve Hendren—and McKeon—had.

"I'd feel better if Brandy had all of Clint's people over there," the captain said, looking back down into the display again. "But Lieutenant Clark's our only mobile response force. I can't afford to send her over there and get her tied down. Besides, all we have right now is Clint's 'itchiness.'" He chuckled harshly. "Not the most detailed threat assessment we've ever had, is it?"

"No, it isn't," Carson said after a moment, and grimaced. "The thing is, he's not the only one feeling a bit itchy just now, is he, Skip?"

"No. No, Lev, he's not. Not at all."

DANIELLE BARTHET SWORE SOFTLY, BUT WITH FEELING, AS SHE watched her displays.

She knew Citizen Captain Radeckis had thought she was paranoid, at best, when she insisted on fitting up their current hideaway in Cargo Seven. Actually, he'd probably thought it was her "terrorist" instincts coming to the fore, not that she'd cared about that.

She didn't trust the regular armed forces. For that matter, she didn't trust Citizen Sergeant Bigby and his Marines' loyalty to the Committee. She didn't really expect any recidivists to try something, but she'd also had no intention of being caught napping if that happened anyway. So, she'd created her hidey hole, with discreet taps into Sigismund Alpha's internal com and surveillance systems. One of her own techs had established standalone links to the system's surveillance platforms and communications buoys, as well, without mentioning it to Citizen Captain Rummo or his personnel, and all of them were tied into the three enormous crates in Cargo Seven's lowest tier of containers which had been fitted up as an emergency barracks and armory.

Her foresight had served her well when it came time to disappear, but at the moment "disappearing" was all she'd been able to do.

"Two of their tankers are heading for the farm, Citizen Commissioner."

"I see it!" she snapped at the hapless citizen corporal manning the link to the survey platforms. She tightened her jaw for a moment, then turned her glare on Radeckis.

"I should wait till they connect to the tanks, then below the entire fucking farm!" she snarled.

"Ma'am," Radeckis began in a careful tone, using the "recidivist" title to which only a people's commissioner was entitled, "if you do that when they're moored to the tanks, it'll be—"

"A violation of the Deneb Accords. I know that." Barthet's hands fisted at her sides. "It's all a pile of steaming shit."

"I agree," Radeckis said, with less than complete honesty. "But that's the standard the Manties will be operating under."

"Oh, yeah? They're going to blow Sigismund Alpha out of space with their own frigging Marines onboard?"

"I don't know, ma'am. All I know is that if they did, they'd claim they were justified under interstellar law." *And we'd all still be dead,* he very carefully did not say aloud.

"I know. I know!"

Barthet took a quick, angry turn around her cramped command center.

Half the troopers of Radeckis's StateSec company were concentrated here in Cargo Seven. The other two platoons were distributed between two additional hiding spots. Their concealment wasn't as good, but she'd managed to edit the schematics in Sigismund Alpha's computers to delete the compartments in which they were stationed, so the Manties' electronic maps didn't show them. The bad news was that if something started the Manties seriously looking for them, they'd be far easier to find than her command center.

The good news was that she had the Manties vastly outnumbered. There were less than a hundred of them onboard, and they were scattered out in vulnerable packets. She was confident she could take them all, especially with the advantage of surprise, but what then?

She growled deep in her throat and her pacing redoubled.

Porthos Radeckis watched Barthet striding around the compartment, and his eyes were unhappy. He had no choice about taking her orders, since his only alternative would have been a pulser dart, either from her or from a StateSec firing squad when her report reached Nouveau Paris. And, like everyone else in Swanson, he had "hostages to fortune" back home. He might've taken a chance for himself, but…

All you can do is say 'Yes, Ma'am, yes, Ma'am, three bags full, Ma'am' and try your damnedest to keep her from doing something outstandingly stupid, he told himself, and knew it was true.

But he would have been far happier if she hadn't been one of the CRU's terrorists. The kind of terrorist who thought in terms of hostage taking and "bargaining from a position of strength." He strongly suspected she'd already have tried something very like that if not for those Manty warships out there. In fact, it was probably what she'd had in mind from the beginning. But at least even she wasn't stupid enough to think she could face down ships-of-the-wall with pulsers and plasma rifles.

So far, at least.

"HYPER FOOTPRINT!"

Alistair McKeon wheeled toward Tactical.

"Multiple footprints," the sensor tech continued. "Range five-point-five-six light-minutes."

Brian Chen stood at the petty officer's shoulder, leaning forward to look at her display, and his eyes narrowed. He watched for another moment, then turned to McKeon.

"Hard to be certain from here, Skip, but it looks like a half dozen battleships, with escorts."

"I see." McKeon folded his hands behind his back and turned to the master display as CIC updated it. Hyper footprints were FTL. Both they and the gravitic signature of an impeller wedge could be tracked in real time, but more detailed information depended on light-speed sensors, and the data codes beside the blood red icons strobed to indicate uncertainty about their classes and tonnages. He waited as patiently as possible.

Some of them began to steady as CIC's confidence in its FTL data extrapolation solidified, but it took over five minutes before *all* of them steadied. They burned in the plot, and his lips tightened as he looked at the junior-grade lieutenant sitting in for Anderson McCloskey at Communications.

"Get me Lieutenant Bolgeo and Major Hendren, Lieutenant Horne."

"IT'LL BE A FEW MINUTES YET BEFORE ADMIRAL STEIGERT CAN confirm our numbers, given the com lag, but CIC's confidence is high," Captain McKeon's voice said in Brandy's earbug. She looked across at Clint Hendren as he listened to the same transmission. "We're looking at six battleships, five cruisers, and six destroyers. They were headed in-system, but they've cut their acceleration, at the moment. I suppose"—his tone turned very dry—"they may have spotted Admiral Steigert's dreadnoughts."

Brandy snorted. Her pulse might be beating just a tad faster and she felt an odd emptiness in her midsection, but she understood why the Peeps might feel a tad cautious. The Royal Manticoran Navy no longer had battleships, because they simply weren't fit to lie in the wall of battle with a modern dreadnought or superdreadnought. Actually, even dreadnought's place in the wall was becoming suspect. But each of Steigert's *Bellerophon*-class battleships massed just under seven million tons, whereas a Peep *Triumphant*-class battleship massed only about 4.5 million. That gave the newcomers a six million-ton advantage over Steigert, but each of their ships was more lightly armed, more lightly armored, with weaker sidewalls, fewer counter missiles, less point defense, and weaker electronic countermeasures.

And no missile pods.

Brandy might not bet a tactical officer, but even she knew battleships had no business going toe-to-toe with dreadnoughts even on a level technological field. Given the current imbalance...

"If they have any sense, they'll admit they got here too late and write the trip off as a bad idea," Captain McKeon continued. "Unfortunately, we can't guarantee that's going to happen. So, for right now, you need to sit tight while we find out what they're going to do. For now, I'm moving *Prince Adrian* a little farther away from the platform. I don't expect them to start chucking missiles in this direction, especially from a range like that, but they might, and I don't have the liveliest possible faith in their missiles' onboard tracking."

"Understood, Sir." Brandy was pleased her voice sounded steadier than it felt.

"IT'S *GOT* TO BE ANDROCLES!" PEOPLE'S COMMISSIONER BARTHET hissed triumphantly, eyes burning as she stared at the repeater display. It was too small to show a great deal of detail, but Radeckis felt unhappily certain she was right.

"Probably, Ma'am," he said, and she darted a withering look over her shoulder before she returned her attention to the display.

"Plug me into the com buoy," she said.

~

"IT'S A PITY WE WERE TOO LATE, CITIZEN COMMISSIONER," INGUNN Androcles said as CIC updated her flagship's tactical plot.

PNS *Splendor* and the other five battleships of Androcles' understrength Battle Squadron 217 coasted ballistically toward the system primary at a mere 1,410 KPS. That was the velocity they'd attained before her light-speed sensors detected the Manticoran dreadnoughts and their escorts at a three-light-minute-range, just outside the Swanson hyper-limit and almost directly between them and the primary. Manty stealth systems were far better than the PN's, and they'd hidden the dreadnoughts low powered impeller wedges. Fortunately, Androcles had known about their systems superiority, which was why she'd sent a trio of recon drones ahead of her. One of them had spotted the Manties optically and pointed them out to her more powerful shipboard sensors.

It had taken a little longer to detect the pair of heavy cruisers deployed to cover Sigismund and Swanson IV, but she'd known they—or *some* Manty ships, at least—had to be there.

"What do you mean, 'too late,' Citizen Commodore?" People's Commissioner Andre Simpson's voice was frosty.

Androcles's lips tightened. She made herself study the display for another handful of seconds—until she was certain she had her expression under control—and then turned attentively to her political watchdog.

"Citizen Commissioner," she said in a calm, respectful tone, "I'm afraid it's obvious that the Manties have already secured control of both Sigismund Alpha and Swanson IV."

"And?" Simpson frowned at her. "Your ships have more Marines than they could possibly have landed from a pair of cruisers. They'll have no choice but to surrender when you threaten to board."

"That would be true, sir, if we could take control of the planetary orbital space." She chose not to mention that Manty dreadnoughts carried *far* larger Marine detachments than their cruisers did. It would have been less than tactful and *might* have sounded "defeatist." It also didn't matter, however. "Unfortunately, we can't do that with three ships-of-the-wall hovering in the background."

"Then engage them," Simpson said coldly. "You have twice that many battleships!"

"Each of which has perhaps a third of the combat value of one of their dreadnoughts, Sir." Androcles folded her hands tightly together behind her back. "They have heavier broadsides, more active defenses, and much thicker armor than we do, Citizen Commissioner."

"Those are *Bellerophon*-class, correct?"

"That's CIC's identification, yes, Sir." Androcles kept her voice level, but her heart sank as she saw the triumphant glitter in Simpson's eyes.

"Well, I took the time to find them in the Intelligence database," the People's Commissioner said, tapping his uni-link. "According to that, each of them mounts a broadside of thirty-three missiles. So, they have a total of ninety-three in a single salvo, whereas your six battleships, with thirty launchers per broadside, has a salvo strength of a *hundred and eighty*. That gives us an edge of seventy-five missiles, Citizen Commodore—an advantage in 'throw weight' of over eighty percent!"

Androcles bit her tongue, but it was hard.

Two T-years ago, Citizen Commodore Ingunn Androcles had been *Commander* Ingunn Androcles, who'd never commanded anything bigger than a destroyer. But that had been before Hereditary President Harris's assassination.

It was amazing how much difference two years could make.

Personally, she'd never bought the evidence that Admiral Parnell had had a single thing to do with the coup attempt. Of course, she'd also known that saying anything of the sort would have bought her a one-way ticket to a prison camp... or a firing squad. Unfortunately, she was also the daughter of Dolists and a prewar member of the Citizens Rights Party. That had made her one of the handful of "reliable" officers in the Committee of Public Safety's eyes following the "Parnell Coup."

At first, the prospect of accelerated promotion had been seductive. But that had been before she found herself pushed up, first to battleship command and then to command of an entire battleship division. No one in the entire galaxy could be more aware than she of how completely unqualified she was to command a single capital ship, even one as small as a battleship, but saying "no" to promotion just wasn't possible in the current People's Republic. Things hadn't gotten any better when they assigned Simpson as her people's commissioner. His fervor for the Committee of Public Safety was matched only by his utter and complete lack of naval experience. He was probably the only person in BatRon 217's senior command even less qualified than she was, but he didn't seem to realize that. As far as she could tell, he honestly believed that looking up ship data in an electronic file qualified him to make tactical decisions. That was bad enough. The fact that his position as her official keeper put him in a position to *dictate* tactical decisions was far, far worse.

And then she'd found herself senior officer in command—under Simpson's beady, distrustful eye, of course—of a barely understrength battleship *squadron*... and escorts. But at least they'd only ordered her to picket a backwater star system, guarding a strictly secondary base.

And now this.

"It's true we have a large numerical advantage, Sir. In shipboard launchers, at least," she made herself acknowledge. "They also have fifty percent more—and substantially more *powerful*—energy weapons than *Splendor*."

Simpson's eyes narrowed, but she continued in the same measured, reasonable tone.

"Admittedly, the difference in energy armament wouldn't be a factor in a missile engagement, and we'd have the maneuver advantage. We wouldn't have to enter energy range, unless we chose to. But their missiles are also larger than ours, with more powerful laserheads. That means each hit will do more damage, which offsets some of our numerical advantage in launchers. If you'll recall, NavInt also estimates that their missiles are more accurate than ours, which means they'll score a higher percentage of hits, as well." She kept her expression gravely respectful. "The fact that their armored protection is substantially superior to ours, and that they have much stronger active defenses, further degrades our numerical advantage. And I must also point out that we don't know if they've deployed missile pods."

She watched his eyes, saw them flicker ever so slightly, and allowed herself a cautious glimmer of hope. The Manties' reintroduction of the missile pod was one of the reasons—indeed, the *primary* reason, she thought—the Peoples Navy's initial offensive had failed so catastrophically. And it had cost the Navy dear in multiple engagements since then.

"Pods are good for only a single salvo, Citizen Commissioner," she said, "but each of them mounts ten box launchers. That means three of them would equal a *Triumphant*'s entire broadside. And the missiles they fire are even heavier and more powerful than the Manties' standard capital ship missiles."

Simpson looked unhappy, but he also nodded slowly, and she let that glimmer burn a little brighter.

"Those are, unfortunately, reasonable points, Citizen Commodore," he said. "I still think that we should—"

"Excuse me, Citizen Commissioner. Citizen Commodore."

Androcles turned her head and raised one eyebrow at Citizen Lieutenant Hatcher, her communications officer.

"Yes, Ed?"

"I apologize for interrupting, but we've just received a transmission. It's a burst transmission from Citizen Commissioner Barthet."

~

"The Peeps are actually maneuvering to engage, Skipper," Lieutenant Commander Chen said.

"You're kidding." Alistair McKeon held up one hand, pausing his com conversation with Commander Carson.

"No, Sir. They've just started accelerating toward Admiral Steigert. Five-three-zero gravities."

McKeon looked at the master plot, and his frown deepened as he realized Chen was right. The Havenite battleships were accelerating toward Battle Division 303. That was either remarkably gutsy or remarkably stupid.

Or both.

At the moment, they were still three light-minutes from Rear Admiral Steigert. Effective missile range against a maneuvering target was only about 6.8 million kilometers, so they'd have to close the gap by at least two light-minutes before they could engage, which would take thirty-four minutes at their current acceleration.

The question was why they were doing something so... unwise.

There was a reason very few naval engagements occurred outside a hyper-limit. Assuming that its hyper generator was online, ready to engage, a *Triumphant*-class battleship could translate into hyper in less than three minutes. A *Bellerophon*-class dreadnought would require just over four and a half. That meant neither side could be compelled to stand and fight.

Of course, if the Peeps could close to missile range and launch at half-power settings, they'd be inside Steigert's reaction cycle when they did. Flight time would be only three minutes, a minute and a half less than her minimum time to hyper out. But only their first salvo could reach Steigert's ships before they vanished into hyper, and initial salvos were notoriously less accurate than follow up launches. So, unless she chose to stand and fight, they were unlikely to inflict any significant damage. And if she *did* choose to stand and fight, a missile duel between six battleships and three dreadnoughts, each with eight missile pods on tow would be a very unpleasant experience for the Peeps. Unless...

"You know," he said slowly, "there may just be a method to their madness. They may hope that if they close to the very edge of the missile envelope, they'll get inside the admiral's hyper cycle. They might be figuring on launching and then immediately translating out themselves, on the theory that even blind fire would score *some* damage. And if they could entice her into flushing the pods *before* they hypered out..."

"Not going to happen, Skip," Chen objected. "The admiral's too smart for that."

"Yeah." McKeon nodded. "But they can't know that unless they try, now can they? And if she doesn't bite, all they really lose is a little time and, maybe, the missiles they fling at her hoping to draw a response." He shrugged. "Makes sense to at least see if they can convince her to do something dumb, doesn't it?"

"WE SURE ABOUT THIS, CITIZEN LIEUTENANT?"

Citizen Sergeant Jean-Luc Demaret's voice was very, very quiet, almost inaudible in Citizen Lieutenant Désiré Fresnel's ear. He and the citizen lieutenant crouched side by side, just inside the innocuous panel that concealed access to what had once been a storage compartment for maintenance spares.

"I thought the citizen captain was pretty clear, Citizen Sergeant," Fresnel replied in an equally low voice, turning her head to look at him. "Was there some part of it you didn't understand?"

Demaret looked back at her levelly, and her nostrils flared.

They wore armored skin suits, like everyone else in the compartment, but their helmet visors were raised so they could speak to each other without using their coms. There were several reasons for that, including the fact that they'd been ordered to keep transmissions to a minimum as a security measure. The chance of the Manties detecting those transmissions was astronomically low, but it did exist, which was why Citizen Commissioner Barthet had decided her Omega contingency posts had to be linked for wired communications. Demaret thought that was a bit excessive, but neither he nor his citizen lieutenant had objected to avoiding their coms, just in case. Especially since all com traffic was automatically recorded. It would be unwise to say anything for the record that might suggest a lack of fervor, especially in the face of imminent combat operations.

And neither of them wanted to involve the platoon's forty other troopers in the conversation.

"I'm just thinking it might be better to wait a little longer, Citizen

Lieutenant," the citizen sergeant said after a moment. "Once we pop the hatch, it's gonna be kinda hard to disappear again, if we need to."

"I understand that." Fresnel's voice was still low, but her *tone* was much sharper. "But if we're going to be in position when the ball drops, we need to start moving before it does."

"That's assuming the ball *does* drop, Citizen Lieutenant. If it doesn't, then—"

Demaret shrugged and Fresnel half-glared at him. Mostly, he suspected, because she agreed with what he was saying.

Unfortunately, their hide was inconveniently placed relative to their assigned objective. They knew where the Manties were; the problem was that they had to cover over thirty meters just to reach the lift shaft, which they would then have to take one deck down to reach their target. And when they got there, the Manties would have a clear field of fire down an arrow-straight twenty-five-meter approach corridor. Trying to cover that distance against the fire of modern weapons in the hands of Royal Manticoran Marines would be a losing proposition.

Conversely, they could head forty meters in the opposite direction, crack the hatch on a service access shaft, and come directly at Life Support Central through the shaft. The problem there was the shaft's dimensions. They'd have to stack on the ladder between decks, and they'd only be able to come at the Manties one at a time through the hatch at its other end.

Neither proposition was attractive, but Demaret understood Fresnel's thinking. If the order to execute the attack came through— and Citizen Captain Radeckis had made it pretty clear Citizen Commissioner Barthet was *going* to give it—the less distance they had to cover before the Manties could react, the better. Especially since they would be only one of multiple attacks, any one of which could jump the gun and alert the Manties before the other attacks rolled in.

But, of course, the same thing could happen if one of the attack forces—like, say, their own—was spotted moving into position early.

The whole plan was way too complex, Demaret thought in disgust. Especially for something that was basically an improvisation. And even more especially given the presence of Manty ships-of-the-wall.

Citizen Captain Radeckis had been just a little vague on exactly how those capital ships would be neutralized.

"Look, Jean-Luc," Fresnel said, "I don't think this is a great idea, either. I think it's just the best of the crappy ones available to us. And because you're the citizen sergeant and I'm the citizen *lieutenant*, I'm the one who has to make the call on how we do it."

"Yes, Citizen Lieutenant." Demaret nodded. One thing about Fresnel, she never waffled. That made up for a lot.

"MARINE FOUR, MARINE TWO-ONE. COMS CHECK."

"Marine Two-One, Marine Four," Iris Babcock replied. "Read you five-by-five, Lieutenant Gillespie."

"Good to know, Gunny," Isaiah Gillespie said dryly. "Your voice is always such a comfort to me."

"What I'm here for, LT," Sergeant Major Babcock replied with a grin. Gillespie was one of her favorite junior officers, although she would never have admitted it, even under torture.

"Marine Four, Marine One-One," another voice said in her earbug as Jeremiah Dimitrieas checked in. "Coms check."

"One-One, Marine Four reads five-by-five."

"Five-by-five this end, too, Gunny. One-One, clear."

"Still good, Gunny?"

Babcock looked over her shoulder and smiled at Lieutenant Tremaine. He, too, was one of her favorite junior officers, even if he was Navy, and despite the fact that he had come equipped with Horace Harkness. That had definitely not been an entry in the plus column the first time they met, although that had been quite some time ago.

"Yes, Sir." She shrugged slightly. "Everything on the green, as far as I can tell. What about the Navy's end?"

"Well, that's an interesting question," Tremaine said. He and Horace Harkness sat in comfortable chairs at Life Support Central's primary board, watching the displays, but the lieutenant had plugged a smaller display into the station-to-ship net *Prince Adrian* had established so he could watch a tiny version of the cruiser's main plot. "Off the top of my head, though, this looks like a losing proposition for the Peeps."

The Peep battleships had been accelerating for just under an hour. They'd traveled almost 3.85 million kilometers, and their velocity relative to Battle Division 303 was up to 5,329 KPS. That was still less than halfway to any possible launch point, but they certainly looked like they meant business.

"I'm just fine with idiots running the show on the other side, Sir," Babcock said. She moved up to stand between him and Harkness, where she could see the same display. "Matter of fact, I prefer it."

"Me, too," Harkness said, but there was something a little odd about his tone, and she looked down at him with a raised eyebrow.

"I just don't want us getting so used to the Peeps screwing the pooch that we automatically assume they'll *always* screw it," the senior chief said. "Sooner or later, we're gonna run into somebody on the other side that doesn't. And that's really gonna suck if we walk in all fat, dumb, and happy."

"Point." Babcock nodded. "But you don't think that's what's happening here, right?"

"I dunno." Harkness grimaced. "Sure doesn't look like it, but I think that might be part of my problem. This is so goddamned dumb part of me keeps thinking there has to be a trick. Something we're just not seeing."

"Actually, it's not completely pointless," Tremaine said. "I've run the generator cycle times," Tremaine said. "If they start their translation clock and launch their first salvo the instant they enter powered missile range of the admiral, they can get off a total of nine broadsides—that'd be a total of two hundred and seventy birds per battleship, and she's got five of 'em, so call it thirteen hundred total. That's a lot of missiles."

"Yes, sir." Harkness nodded. "But in that same window, Admiral Steigert could get off *ten* salvos. That's three hundred per ship just from her internal launchers, so call it nine hundred there, plus whatever pods she's got deployed. And her point defense and ECM's a *hell* of a lot better than anything the Peeps have!"

"Yes, they are. But if the Peeps time it just right, they'll translate out about seventeen seconds before their fire reaches BatDiv Three-Oh-Three... or BatDiv 303's reaches *them*. And it'll take the *Bellerophons* a minute and a half longer to translate out." Tremaine shook his head. "Even if Admiral Steigert starts her translation clock the instant they enter range, she'll have to take four of her salvos and they won't have to take *any* of hers. They'll lose the control links to even the first salvo early, so their accuracy will suck vacuum, but even blind fire's likely to score *some* hits, and they wouldn't take any from us."

Harkness and Babcock looked at him.

"Gee, thanks, Lieutenant," the Marine said after a moment. "And here I thought this vacuum head"—she twitched a sideways nod at Harkness—"knew what he was talking about. For once."

"Yeah, thanks for making me look so bad in front of the Gunny, sir," Harkness added with a grin.

"Well," Tremaine said in a rallying tone, "all of that assumes the Peeps are as smart as me, and we all know how unlikely *that* is!" He smiled as both noncoms chuckled. "And it *also* assumes that Admiral Steigert wasn't smart enough to work out the same math *I* just did. And frankly," his smile turned into something much colder and harder, "that's a hell of a lot less likely."

CITIZEN COMMODORE ANDROCLES TIPPED BACK IN HER COMMAND chair, elbows on the armrests, her raised hands folded while she tapped her chin with her index fingers.

God, this is stupid, she thought. *Oh, I suppose it* might *work, if that Manty over there is as stupid as my own damned "people's commissioners." What are the odds of having three people* that *stupid in a single star system, though?*

She didn't know, but they had to be pretty low.

It wouldn't be the first time since the Parnell Coup that she'd seen lives thrown away by incompetent amateurs so utterly clueless they thought they were brilliant. It was just the first time she'd been cast for a starring role in the debacle.

At least the ops plan she'd sold to Simpson, coupled with her battleships' higher acceleration rate and lower generator cycle times, meant it wasn't outright suicidal on *her* part.

She just didn't like to think about how many people were likely to die aboard Sigismund Alpha in the next hour or so.

The tankers which had accompanied the Manty dreadnoughts had disappeared into hyper, which was wise of them. Manty fleet train units carried at least rudimentary point defense and ECM, but no one would ever mistake them for regular warships. They had no business anywhere missiles might be flying, and they could always come back once the dust settled.

She watched the plot while the kilometers fell astern and wondered what the Manty admiral thought she and her ships were doing.

She hid a frown of disgust behind a carefully attentive expression. The burst transmission from Barthet had come at the worst possible moment. She'd had Simpson *almost* convinced, and then Barthet had chimed in.

The entire idea was ludicrous. Even assuming Barthet's StateSec goons could take Sigismund Alpha away from what sounded like at least two complete platoons of Royal Manticoran Marines, it would accomplish exactly nothing unless Androcles's own command was able to defeat or at least drive off those Manty superdreadnoughts. First, there was no way in hell she would have backed StateSec against Manty Marines. StateSec was a bunch of head-bashing goons, and Manticoran Marines would eat them for breakfast. Second, there was equally no way in hell her battleships were going to defeat three *Bellerophon*-class dreadnoughts. She knew that, Citizen Captain Taylor, *Splendor*'s CO, knew that, and she was pretty sure that if Citizen Captain Rummo had known what was going on, *he* would have known that. Unfortunately, none of them could tell Barthet and Simpson to shove it up their asses.

They'd received three more burst transmissions from Barthet. Obviously, they couldn't reply without the Manties wondering just who her ships were talking to. That only made things worse, since she couldn't ask any questions, whose answers might have convinced Simpson Barthet was a frigging lunatic. She'd wanted to point out that there was no reason the Manty admiral couldn't simply blow away the system's infrastructure and leave, if Androcles made herself too annoying. It wouldn't take a lot of missiles, especially since the orbital platforms and tank farms couldn't dodge and had exactly zero in the way of point defense. The range wouldn't matter under those circumstances. Unfortunately, the other people's commissioner had actually convinced him her people could retake Sigismund Alpha, which would turn the Manty boarders into human shields—hostages— against that sort of parting shot. The three tankers currently moored to the tank farm would do the same thing for the refineries. The Manties couldn't take the platforms out with missiles without destroying their own ships… and if the tankers tried to disengage, *Barthet* would blow the tanks and destroy them before they could.

I wonder how much of it is that Simpson's *afraid of being made an example for "defeatism" if he doesn't go along with her*?

The thought made Androcles feel a trace—a very, very *tiny* trace— of sympathy for her StateSec keeper. Technically, he was senior to Danielle Barthet, but that wouldn't save him if somebody back in Nouveau Paris decided he'd shown too little élan in the People's service.

My God, she thought disgustedly. *We're hurting ourselves almost as badly as the Manties are, and nobody can do a damn thing about it because the people we're trying to save are liable to shoot us themselves if we try!*

～

CITIZEN CORPORAL GWEN LAWRENCE CAUTIOUSLY EASED HER WAY along the maintenance access trunk. It was a tight fit with the plasma carbine slung over her shoulder. She wished she'd been able to armor-up properly, but Havenite battle armor was bulky. In fact, it was slightly bulkier than the Manty equivalent, and there was no way she and the five troopers behind her could have squeezed their armor into a space this small. And those same constricted quarters were why she had a plasma carbine instead of a plasma *rifle*.

That made her just a bit nervous about what she was supposed to do when the balloon went up, because the Manty she was supposed to take out *was* in battle armor.

Won't matter if you surprise the bastard, she told herself firmly.

By this time, the Manties had to be convinced they had the situation firmly under control. If any of Sigismund Alpha's personnel had dared to cross the People's Commissioner, the Manties would have torn Sigismund Alpha apart until they found the State Security hideouts. So, unless something went wrong in a big way, she should have surprise on her side, and not even Manticoran battle armor could handle a direct hit from a plasma carbine.

Probably.

~

"Whoa," Corporal Montoya murmured. "What do we have here?"

"What'cha got, Timmy?" Corporal Handley, his teammate, asked over the com from her position on the far side of the central lift core.

"Don't know," Montoya replied. "Probably nothing, but the Gamma block motion sensors say there's movement."

"What kind of movement?" Handley's voice was sharper in Montoya's earbug.

"*Movement* movement," Montoya said. "That's all I've got so far. Hold one while I check."

"Roger."

~

Lawrence swore under her breath. She'd meant to ease the

access hatch no more than a centimeter or so, just enough to slip the camera snake out and take a look, but poor maintenance had caught up with her. Instead of swinging smoothly, one of the hinges had stuck and refused to move. She'd been forced to apply more muscle than she'd wanted to, and when the hinge finally gave, she'd lost her grip.

She'd just leaned out into the corridor, reaching to capture it and pull it shut, when something made her glance up.

She never had a chance to figure out what that "something" might have been.

~

"ALL MARINES THIS NET, MARINE ONE-DELTA-THREE. BANDIT. Repeat, Bandit!"

Clint Hendren twitched as Corporal Montoya's voice came over his earbug. A sudden strobing icon on his display showed him Montoya's position, three decks down from Command Central.

"One-Delta-Three has engaged," Montoya continued. "Bandit down. Repeat, one Bandit down. In armored skinny with plasma rifle. StateSec—I repeat, *State Security*—insignia!"

The high, shrill whine of a tribarrel on full auto came over the com. Montoya's visor had to be up for him to hear that, a corner of Hendren's brain thought.

"*Multiple* bandits!" Montoya said. "I have multiple bandits! Looks like they're using a service conduit!"

"All Marines this net, Marine One," Hendren cut in. "Case Hotel. Repeat, Hotel. The ball is in play!"

~

"OH, SHIT!" CITIZEN CAPTAIN RADECKIS SNARLED AS CITIZEN Corporal Lawrence's icon turned crimson on his master display. An instant later, three other icons from her six-trooper squad did the same thing.

That display showed the central portion of Sigismund Alpha, all its corridors and access routes, plus lift shafts, blast doors, and emergency airlocks. He didn't know what had gone wrong, but it was way too early.

"What is it? What happened?" Barthet demanded.

"I don't know. I just lost four of my people."

"To the Manties?"

"I don't know what else could've happened." Radeckis glared at the display. "But the bastards know we're here now!"

"Tell your people to attack!" Barthet snapped.

"They're not in position!" Radeckis protested, but it was pure reflex. At least two teams from Citizen Lieutenant Castaneda's platoon were already moving on their own. "Half my people just began moving two minutes ago," he said. "They're still at least ten minutes from their jump off points!"

"We don't *have* ten minutes! Tell them—*now*." Barthet glared at him, then turned to the com tech. "Burst transmission to Citizen Commodore Androcles and People's Commissioner Simpson!"

"Oh, shit, Ma'am—I mean, Citizen Lieutenant!" Citizen Sergeant Demaret looked up at Citizen Lieutenant Fresnel. "It's a go —*now!*"

"What?" Fresnel stared at him. "Why? What happened?"

"No idea." Demaret unslung his pulse rifle with one hand while he closed his visor with the other. "But whatever it is, it's not good."

Fresnel barked a harsh laugh of agreement and reached for her own rifle.

"All right, people! Let's hit these bastards!"

Demaret kicked the concealing panel aside. It clattered across the passage floor, and the citizen sergeant vaulted over it. The rest of Fresnel's platoon, minus the six troopers she'd sent into the access shaft, followed him, and boots pounded the deck as they charged for the lift shaft.

∿

"ALL MARINES THIS NET, MARINE ONE. CASE HOTEL. REPEAT, H—"

That was all Private Callie Owens, Manticoran Marine Corps, had time to hear before the plasma charge struck her squarely in the back. Not even her battle armor could take that kind of damage. She was dead before she hit the deck.

Corporal Trent Mehta was still turning in her direction when the trio of StateSec troopers—all of them in battle armor, in this case— came up the passage at him.

"Bandits! Marine One-Echo-Two! Engagi—"

His heavy tribarrel whined, and two of the Havenites went down.

The third StateSec trooper's plasma rifle blew straight through his breastplate.

∿

"CASE HOTEL!" SERGEANT MAJOR BABCOCK SNAPPED. "MEADORS, Brownback, Tremblay—on the door!"

She and Sergeant Quan had walked Quan's platoon through their contingency plans as soon and they arrived in Life Support Central, and First Section knew exactly what it was supposed to do. Private Liam Meadors tossed a pair of remote sensors into the passageway, rolling one of them each direction, then went prone at the base of the open hatch. Privates Brownback and Tremblay knelt on either side of him to cover the access passage in both directions. Lance Corporal Drinkman, First Section's grenadier, stood to Tremblay's left, his back against the wall, grenade launcher muzzle raised, waiting for one of the riflemen to call on his support, and Private Stuart, the section's plasma gunner, cradled his long, heavy weapon to Brownback's right.

The squad's second section spread out on either side of the door, ready to reinforce or replace casualties.

"Well, *this* ain't good," Horace Harkness muttered.

"Y'*think*?" Babcock snarled at him, and both of them looked at Tremaine.

"For now, we just hold what we've got," he told them.

TWO MORE OF JEREMIAH DIMITRIEAS'S TEAMS WENT OFF THE NET AS abruptly as Corporal Mehta's, and access to Sigismund Alpha's central lift shafts on Decks Five and Seven went with them. The two-Marine team on Deck Six tossed a grenade into the outboard shaft to disable it and settled into their preselected position to cover the *inboard* shaft. Nobody would be getting off on their floor, which meant no one could come at Power One that way.

The team watching Cargo Dock Two found itself under sudden attack by skinsuited StateSec plasma gunners who'd overridden the automatic alarms on two of the emergency airlocks to come at them from behind. One of the Manticorans died almost instantly. Her teammate bellied down behind a moored cargo sled and desperately returned fire.

The teams on the other cargo docks, alerted in time, were waiting when Citizen Captain Radeckis's troopers came at them.

As it happened, even Ingunn Androcles's more pessimistic assessment of the relative lethality of the Office of State Security and the Royal Manticoran Marine Corps had been wildly optimistic.

BRANDY WATCHED CLINT HENDREN RESPOND TO THE SUDDEN, unexpected onslaught. His voice was sharp, tense, but if there was anything remotely like panic in it, she couldn't hear it. And while she was the officer in command, she was far too smart to joggle his elbow at a moment like this. So, she stalked across the spacious compartment to Citizen Captain Rummo, instead.

The Havenite platform commander and the half dozen of his personnel present in Command Central knelt at one end of the compartment, now, hands clasped on their heads under the angry, watchful eyes of two Marines. She stopped in front of Rummo and glared down at him.

"No StateSec, was it?" She half-spat the words.

"I never said that," Rummo replied, meeting her furious gaze levelly. "And neither did Citizen Sergeant Bigby." He twitched his head at the Marine sergeant kneeling beside him. "We just never said there *were* any State Security people on the platform. And I told you when you came aboard that no one could afford to be accused of collaborating with you people." He shrugged. "I figure worst thing that happens here is you shoot me. If I'd told you there were StateSec troopers on this platform, they'd have shot my entire family. So, you tell me, Lieutenant. What would *you* have done?"

"How many of them are there?" Brandy demanded.

"You've got everything you're getting from me, Lieutenant." Rummo's eyes never wavered. "If that's not enough, you'd best go ahead and shoot me now."

She glared at him, sorely tempted to do just that, then made herself turn away. Hendren looked up as she stalked back across the deck to him like an angry treecat.

"Well, the good news is Jeremiah's got boat bay locked down and they aren't getting into it," the Marine said.

"And why do I think that if there's good news, there has to be *bad* news, too?" Brandy asked.

"Because he's not getting back aboard the platform anytime soon." Hendren grimaced. "They've got too much firepower in the access passages, and he's lost over half his dispersed teams. He's sending PO Brixton and the pinnace out to do what they can to support his people on the cargo docks, but he can't afford to send any of his own people along with them. So at least until Beth—Lieutenant Clark—can get here from the ship, they're on their own. Those I've got left."

Brandy heard the pain in his voice and laid a hand on his forearm.

"It looks like something went wrong with their timing, though," the Marine continued in a deliberately brisk tone. "They shouldn't have hit the boat bay in isolation that way. This whole thing is really, really stupid, but I'm guessing they thought they'd have the advantage of surprise going for them. Except that *this*"—he waved around the control room—"should have been their priority target, the very first thing they hit." He shook his head. "It looks to me like they were still getting to their jump off positions when Montoya spotted them, although I don't know what kind of tactical genius might've thought they could get into position *without* somebody being spotted. Or what they think Rear Admiral Steigert will do if they manage to pull this off, either. But"—he inhaled sharply—"that's not our problem. Kicking their asses is."

"I can get behind that," Brandy said, and he flashed her a tight smile.

"They haven't hit Life Support yet, and I don't think they can get to Power One past Jeremiah's people on Deck Six. Plus, O'Brien has Wright's squad for cover even if they get that far. But I imagine *we'll* be seeing them sometime soon."

He showed his teeth, then turned to Lance Corporal Fitzhugh and waved at Command Central's hatch.

"Go, Ezra," he said, and the lance corporal snatched up a heavy rucksack and headed for the access passage with Private Chornovil. Brandy raised an eyebrow, then stepped to the hatch and leaned out, watching as Fitzhugh dove into the rucksack and tossed Chornovil half a dozen fourteen-centimeter disks. They were about four centimeters thick.

"You've got inboard," he said.

"Gotcha," Chornovil said, and headed toward the central lift shafts.

Fitzhugh watched her go, then turned and trotted in the opposite direction.

~

"MOVEMENT ON SENSOR ONE!" SERGEANT MAJOR BABCOCK announced without looking up from the handheld display.

"Got it, Gunny," Colin Brownback replied, shouldering his pulse rifle as the lift shaft doors slid open. They were slower than usual, their motion uneven. "They're using the shaft but not the lift cars," he said. "Looks like they're opening the shaft doors by hand."

"*Some* brains on the other side, anyway. Damn it," Corporal Drinkman muttered.

The doors opened fully and something—*several* somethings, actually—sailed through them, obviously thrown by people still below deck level in the shaft.

"Grenades!" Brownback's voice was sharp, and the Marines pressed themselves more firmly against the bulkheads.

The grenades bounced down the passage. Some of them, at least, were flash-bangs and erupted in blinding bursts of light and concussive shock. The searing flash was disorienting—or would have been if anyone had been looking at them—but the thunderous concussions had little effect on Marines in armored skinsuits. Then aerosol grenades, and a blinding "smoke" designed to be opaque to thermal sensors and laser sights, filled the passage.

"*Go!*" Citizen Lieutenant Fresnel barked, and her First Squad flung themselves over the lip of the lift shaft door. They hit the deck prone and rolled toward the passage's bulkheads before they came up on one knee, rifles and flechette guns ready.

Fresnel hadn't liked using obscurants. She was supposed to be taking the Manties alive, and blind fire with automatic weapons wasn't conducive to accomplishing her mission objective. On the other hand, charging straight down that passage *without* covering smoke—and fire—would only get her people killed, which would also prevent her from accomplishing that. If that cost her a few dead Manties on the way in…

Citizen Commissioner Barthet would just have to settle for the best she could do.

"Position!" Citizen Corporal Danacek announced over the com.

"Second Squad!" Fresnel said.

Citizen Corporal Pasteur's squad rolled over the lift shaft lip, formed into an assault stick, and moved forward in a crouching run.

They were careful to stay in the exact center of the broad passage, tracking down the lane defined by the red lines projected onto their HUDs, while Danacek's riflemen sent pulser darts cracking past them to either side.

"Now!" Iris Babcock said, never looking up from the display.

The Peeps' covering smoke had blinded her Marines' thermal sights, but while the sensor remotes Brownback had deployed utilized the visual spectrum when they could, they were also equipped with sonar, though it wasn't as good as direct vision. The sound of the Peeps' boots generated a less than perfectly differentiated moving blob on her display which prevented her from picking out individual targets.

But she didn't really need to.

Meadors and Brownback swung into firing position while the supersonic darts of the Peeps' suppressive fire crackled past them. They sent their own darts howling back in reply, firing on full automatic and sweeping their muzzles across the passage. The suppressive fire ebbed abruptly, and Drinkman stepped out into the passage just long enough to send a three-round-burst of antipersonnel grenades into the Peeps' faces.

Three or four darts became screaming ricochets, bouncing from the grenadier's armored skinny, and he swore unhappily as he ducked back into cover.

"Fuckers winged me!"

There was more indignation than pain in his voice. He held up his right forearm and examined the ugly rip in the skinsuit's tough fabric. It had caught the outside of his arm on its way through and blood welled through the torn skinny. If it had struck him even half a centimeter to his left, he would probably have lost the arm.

"Well, next time don't stand in the middle of the fire zone unless the gunny or I damned well *tell* you to!" Platoon Sergeant Quan snarled as he grabbed the injured arm and sprayed a bandage over the wound. "Frigging *enthusiast*."

"Hey, Sarge, I was only—"

"Shut it, Drinkman!"

⌇

"Movement, Skipper," Private MacGregor announced. "Got movement on both sensors."

"Figures." Clint Hendren glanced at Brandy and shook his head, then returned his attention to the mini comp in his hands. "Told you we'd be high on the list."

"Wonderful." Brandy glanced down, checking the power and ammunition readings on her pulser... and visually confirming she'd remembered to switch off the safety. "Sometimes being popular really sucks."

"One way to look at it." The Marine actually chuckled. "Don't know how 'popular' we'll be in the next two minutes or so, though."

"Suits me just fine," Brandy said grimly.

"Just do me a favor and don't shoot any of *our* people," he replied, never looking away from the mini comp. "Wouldn't want to say anything unflattering about Navy marksmanship, but—"

She could actually *hear* the shrug in his voice.

"You are so going to pay for that one, *Major*," she promised.

"I can hardly wait."

He sounded a bit absent that time, like a man concentrating on something else.

⌇

Citizen Lieutenant Arsenault and Citizen Sergeant Brunel had worked carefully on their timing. The citizen lieutenant had gotten Fourth Platoon's troopers into position at both ends of the Command Central's access passageway by using the maintenance crawlways rather than the lift shafts, and he was confident—well, *pretty* confident—no one had seen them coming.

But spotted or not, he could be positive the Manties knew he was coming, damn it. When he found out who'd fucked up the timing on this, he'd—

Time enough, Jared. Time enough for that later. *For now, get your head in the damned game.*

They'd be waiting. That meant he was about to lose people. Probably a *lot* of them.

He knew that. He'd accepted it. But he was determined to lose as few of them as possible, and *that* meant getting in as quickly as he could.

Now his assault teams were racing down the passage, staying close to the sides, moving as fast as they could behind a rolling, bouncing barrage of smoke and flash-bangs.

~

"FIRE IN THE HOLE!" HENDREN ANNOUNCED AS THE THUNDER OF Arsenault's covering grenades vibrated the bulkheads.

His fingertip came down and four of the dozen directional mines Ezra Fitzhugh and Beth Chornovil had planted detonated. They'd been mag-locked to facing bulkheads in pairs, positioned to interlock their fire to maximum effect.

The lethal cyclones of antipersonnel flechettes sizzled across the passage in a dispersal pattern six meters wide, and the sensor remotes thoughtfully placed to cover the passage—coupled with Citizen Lieutenant Arsenault's meticulous coordination and planning—allowed Clint Hendren to time the detonations perfectly.

Twenty-three members of Fourth Platoon, Able Company, 43rd Battalion, Office of State Security, survived the explosions. Citizen Lieutenant Jared Arsenault and Citizen Sergeant Frederica Brunel were not among them.

~

CITIZEN CORPORAL HARRELSON SNARLED AS THE PLASMA BOLT HIT Citizen Private Jacobs and the citizen private's left arm disappeared, amputated by the incandescent fury. No one could hear someone scream through his battle armor's helmet… unless they happened to be on the com at the instant they were hit.

Like Jacobs.

Harrelson heard the citizen private's shriek of agony, and the bubbling wails that followed, only too well. In fact, he couldn't hear anything else and he wanted to scream at Jacobs to shut the hell up, or at least get off the tac frequencies.

He tried to see where the shot had come from without poking his own helmet up too high. They'd already lost three troopers—Jacobs made four—to the single Manty crouched behind the cargo sled. In fact, the single Manty left from *any* of the cargo docks guard posts.

There wasn't much left of that sled now, not after all the plasma fire and the grenades Harrelson's section had poured into it, but there was obviously still enough, and the Manty had taken down both of Harrelson's drones before they got a fix on him. Damn it, where *was* the sorry assed son-of-a-bitch? He had to be up there somewhere!

Jacobs' wailing sobs faded into silence and Harrelson tried not to feel grateful as the com net cleared.

"Tobias," he said into the silence, "flank left. Try to get around behind—"

HMS *Prince Adrian*'s Number One pinnace rose silently over Sigismund Alpha's curved flank.

Harrelson had a sliver of time to see it before its nose-mounted pulsers ripped him apart.

~

"They're what?" Citizen Commodore Androcles looked at Andre Simpson.

"They're attacking now," Simpson repeated. "Something gave them away. They had to go immediately—*now*!"

"No, Citizen Commissioner," Androcles said. "They aren't attacking *now*; they attacked eight and a half minutes ago."

Simpson's jaw tightened and Androcles managed to not roll her eyes. Even a people's commissioner should know enough to allow for transmission lag.

"Anything else from them yet?" the citizen commodore asked, turning to Citizen Lieutenant Hatcher.

"No, Citizen Commodore," the com officer replied, watching Simpson from the corner of one eye. "Not yet."

"Thank you."

Androcles looked at the plot. Her battleships were just under eighteen minutes short of her planned launch point. Closing velocity was up to 14,008 KPS and the range to the Manty wallers was down to 28,292,800 KM, but her powered missile range from that geometry was only 9,360,000.

The idiot people's commissioner—the idiot commissioner aboard Sigismund Alpha, that was, not the one aboard *Splendor*—was *supposed* to hold her attack until Androcles was in position because *both* idiot commissioners had expected the "simultaneous" attacks to break the Manties' morale when Barthet made her demands. The fact that the ships-of-the-wasll wouldn't know anything was happening aboard Sigismund Alpha until eight minutes after it did, had obviously escaped their attention.

But it doesn't really matter, she told herself. *Whatever Simpson and Barthet may have thought, nothing you do out here is going to affect what happens in Sigismund orbit. And you're not planning on hanging around long enough for anything that happens there to affect you, either.*

"*Shit!*"

Désiré Fresnel pressed closer to the lift shaft wall as the grenades bounced off the yawning void's rear bulkhead. They caromed back toward the front of the shaft, hit the wall less than a meter above the outthrust flange under which she sheltered, rebounded, and detonated. Lethal fragments erupted from the explosions, ricocheting from the bulkheads like deadly, screaming rain, and someone screamed over the com.

"Citizen Lieutenant—*Skipper*, we *have* to move!" Citizen Sergeant Demaret said, but she shook her head.

Inside, she knew Demaret was right. Her frontal attack, exactly the sort of frontal attack taught by the instructors responsible for training StateSec just as they had InSec, had been a disaster. She'd lost damned near half her platoon when she obligingly turned the passage into a kill zone.

And that's the difference between busting terrorists or "subversives" and going up against the fucking Manty Marines, she thought bitterly. *They weren't worried about what we were going to do to them; they were too focused on what* they *were going to do to* us. *Do to* my *people!*

The suppressive fire should have kept their heads down. The smoke and flash-bangs should have blinded and disoriented them. Even allowing for the protection of their skin suits, they should have at least flinched! But they hadn't, and they'd cut her first two squads to pieces. And now that frigging grenadier was dropping his grenades right into the lift shaft, and she couldn't get to the doors to close them.

The bastard was firing blind. Fresnel had personally caught—and destroyed—two of the remotes the Manties had tried to roll into the shaft with Four Platoon, and Citizen Private Garrett had batted a third back down the passage with the butt of his pulse rifle. But they couldn't keep that up forever, and when the bastards finally got one of the damned things past them—

"Not yet," she grated back, staring at the moving icons on her head visor's HUD. "Ten more seconds, Jean-Luc!"

Another three-round burst of grenades flew into the lift shaft and she pressed her helmet against the bulkhead as they plummeted past her people and exploded somewhere below.

∼

"I need a remote in that shaft, Meadors," Sergeant Major Babcock said pointedly, never looking away from her handheld.

"I'm working on it, Gunny," Liam Meadors replied. "I don't know how the bastards are spotting them. Should've brought some Mark Sevens!"

"I'll make a note of that." Babcock's tone was sour, and despite the moment's tension, Horace Harkness grinned at Lieutenant Tremaine and rolled his eyes.

Tremaine shook his head reprovingly, but not without a smile of his own. The Mark Seven was designed for battlefield deployment in both airfoil and counter-grav modes. It also had a deployed wingspan of over two meters, which made it... contraindicated for deployment in close quarters. What they really needed was something between that and the vastly smaller Mark Three remotes Private Meadors was trying to lob into the lift shaft. The Mark Three was actually designed for static deployment. It came without airfoils *or* counter-grav, and while it was very stealthy once it was deployed, it wasn't very hard to see if someone tried to toss one past you.

"We've only got five more, Gunny," Sergeant Quan pointed out. "At the rate Liam's using 'em up—"

"Hey!" Meadors protested.

"Just saying, Liam. Just saying."

Quan chuckled and moved closer to Babcock to look over her shoulder at the display.

"Point," Babcock agreed.

~

"Position!"

Citizen Corporal Dumont's voice sounded sharply in Citizen Lieutenant Fresnel's earbug.

"Go—go!" Fresnel barked back.

~

"Okay, Meadors," Babcock said. "You can try two more, then we keep the rest in reserve. She scowled. "Hell, we've got the passage covered and Drinkman may already have nailed 'em all and we just don't know it yet. But until I'm sure—"

"*Iris!*"

~

Simon Dumont pressed the button, the breaching charge blew, and he rolled through the new opening with his pulse rifle already in position.

He'd been nervous about drilling the tiny hole in the service crawlway's bulkhead, but the Manties hadn't noticed and he'd gotten the even tinier camera through it without being spotted. Despite his need for frantic haste, he'd spent several seconds studying the Manties, nailing down their positions in his mind and patching the same feed to the other five troopers of his section. They could only make entry one at a time and they damned well needed to know where the bad guys were before they did it.

The odds for the first man in the stick sucked. Dumont knew that, but he also knew he was the best man for the job. And the time he'd spent studying Manty rank insignia had paid off.

He knew exactly where the senior Marine was. If he could take the bastard out before they realized what was happening…"

~

Iris Babcock's head jerked up.

She was never certain later if it was the "CRACK!" of the breaching charge, the fist of overpressure, or the sound of her own name that did it. They all came so close together, in one shattering instant.

The handheld seemed to fall in slow motion as she dropped it, like an accident in microgravity. Her right hand found the pistol grip of her M32 with the clean precision of almost thirty T-years' experience, and she spun toward the explosion behind her, knees flexing into a firing crouch. But she was moving slowly—*so* slowly.

Too slow, something said in her brain. *To slow this time, Iris!*

And then a shoulder slammed into her, smashing her to the deck, and she realized whose voice had shouted her name.

∽

WHAT THE FU—?

It was a damned *Navy* puke. That was the last person Dumont had worried about!

The sheer surprise of it distracted him. Only for an instant, less than an eyeblink in the heart of eternity, but in that tiny sliver of time, the petty officer launched himself, slammed into Dumont's target, and knocked the Marine out of the line of fire even as Dumont squeezed the trigger.

The three-round-burst missed its intended mark. Dumont started to snarl as he brought the muzzle around, and that was when he discovered the other thing the Navy puke had accomplished.

∽

"No!"

Babcock heard herself scream as the darts meant for her ripped through Horace Harkness in a spray of blood.

The pulser in his right hand whined with lethal precision in the same heartbeat, and then he hit the deck with a horrible, limp looseness.

"No!" she cried again as she came up on one knee and her M32 rose. She had the opening now, and her fire ripped into it as the second StateSec trooper started through.

It was strange. A corner of her brain noticed, as she tracked onto the third Peep in the stick, there was something wrong with her eyes.

∽

"No good, Citizen Lieutenant."

The voice in Fresnel's earbug was faint and fading. She couldn't even identify it.

"Tried," it said. "Sorry… tried. But we're all… dea—"

It stopped, and she blinked burning eyes.

"Time to go, Jean-Luc," she heard herself say. "Pull 'em back. We're leaving."

"But, Citizen Lieutenant—"

"No more," she said harshly. "No fucking more of my people. Not today."

"Horace!" Sergeant Major Babcock ripped at Horace Harkness' skinsuit. "Don't you die! Don't you *die* on me, you miserable goddammed vacuum-sucker! Don't you *dare*, goddamn you!"

She could hardly see through her tears, but she recognized the second set of hands as Scotty Tremaine went to his knees on the other side of Harkness's motionless body.

Navy skin suits were designed to be removed in panels in the case of catastrophic wounds, and Tremaine peeled away the chest section while Babcock ripped open the torn and shredded upper arm. It wasn't a Marine skinny, with armor appliqués, but it was a combat skinsuit, and it had slowed the pulser darts.

Slowed, but not stopped, and Babcock's jaw tightened as she saw the wreckage in their wake.

The left arm was… gone. Just gone. Two of the darts had hit it, and the upper of the two, ten centimeters below the shoulder, had simply destroyed the humerus. Nothing remained but bloody rags of flesh, and only the automatic tourniquet the skinsuit had applied, just below the armpit, had kept him from bleeding out already.

But the other wound, the one in his chest—

"Missed the heart," she heard Tremaine say. "Hit the left lung, though."

His hands moved quickly, competently, spraying coagulant into the sucking wound, spraying a bandage to protect it, and his voice was calm. Impossibly calm. *Hatefully* calm, like an echo of her too many times before, kneeling over too many wounded, broken bodies. Keeping her head together. Doing her job. So why—

"I've got this, Gunny," the lieutenant said softly. She looked up, saw his eyes through his visor, realized she wasn't the only one crying.

"I've got this," he repeated. "See to your people."

~

"Breaching... *now*!" the voice in Clint Hendren's earbug said, and fresh icons blinked on his display as Bethany Clark's First Squad blew its way through the platform's skin and dropped in behind the StateSec troopers besieging the boat bay.

Third Platoon had been armed up and Marine Pinnace One had been spotted for launch, just in case, when all hell broke loose aboard Sigismund Alpha. Unfortunately, *Prince Adrian* had also been over a quarter million kilometers from the platform. Even at 4.4 KPS squared, the flight had eaten up eight minutes. But she was here now. Her Second and Third Squads had already made entry through the cargo docks, and Hendren smiled thinly.

"Marine Three, Marine One," he said now. "Secure boat bay, then take out the bastards on Deck Two. We're heading for the central lift shafts now. Meet us there."

"Marine One, Three copies. Secure the Bay, meet you at the lifts."

"And now," Captain Clint Hendren said coldly, "we have some StateSec ass to kick."

~

"It's over, Citizen Commissioner," Citizen Captain Radeckis said quietly.

He stood behind Danielle Barthet, watching the displays.

Fresnel's brutally truncated platoon had fallen back to its original hide with less than a third of its original personnel, but at least she was still alive. Fourth Platoon was still at almost half strength, but it had lost both its CO and its platoon sergeant. Its remnants had tried to hold the passage outside Command Central, but they were badly shaken and only too aware of how outclassed they were. When the Manties counterattacked out of the control room, a single squad had gone through Fourth like shit through a goose.

Second Platoon was down by a third and falling back from its abortive attempt to break through to Power One through the service access ways. Only Third Platoon, which had been tasked as Omega's reserve, remained intact, and it couldn't take the vengeful Manties long to track it down now that they knew it was here.

"No," Barthet said flatly.

"Citizen Commissioner, they *tried*," Radeckis said as gently as he could. "But—"

"It's not over!" Barthet shouted. She punched her com officer in the shoulder. "Tell Citizen Commodore Androcles we've failed to secure complete control of the platform, but that I remain confident of the final outcome."

The com officer hesitated for just a moment, and she punched him again—harder.

"Send it!" she snapped.

"Yes, Citizen Commissioner!" he said, and she turned back to Radeckis.

"The bastards haven't won yet," she said flatly. "We've still got the whip hand, as long as Androcles is out there!"

"Citizen Commissioner, she's got *battleships*, against dreadnoughts," Radeckis replied, trying to get through to her. "And for all we know, the Manties have deployed more of those damned *pods* of theirs. I'm afraid we can't count on her driving them off."

"No?"

Barthet's eyes glittered and she smiled. It was an odd, frightening, cold-eyed sort of smile, and something tightened inside Porthos Radeckis. She looked at him for a moment, then turned back to the com officer.

"Contact the Manties," she told him. "Tell them I demand the stand down of all their personnel aboard Sigismund Alpha. And arm the district circuit for Tank Farm Two. If they're not willing to see reason, we'll just blow one of their tankers to hell and see how they—"

Her head exploded, spraying blood, bone, and tissue across the control panel. The com officer lurched to his feet, retching, as the corpse hit the deck and the blood pooled.

"I don't think so, Citizen Commissioner," Radeckis said, and synthetics whispered as he holstered his pulser. He looked down at the sudden corpse for a moment, then back up at the gagging com officer.

"Stop puking, wipe that crap off the com, and contact the Manties. I'll be damned if I get any more of our people killed for that bitch."

~

"WELL, I'M AFRAID THAT'S PRETTY MUCH THAT, CITIZEN Commissioner," Ingunn Androcles said.

Her battle squadron was not quite seven minutes from her planned launch point as she looked across her flag bridge at Andre Simpson.

"Nonsense!" Simpson shot back. "Citizen Commissioner Barthet's first rush may have failed, but she hasn't given up yet!"

"With all due respect, Citizen Commissioner, it doesn't matter." Androcles shook her head. "The Manties have more than enough Marines to take Sigismund Alpha back. They'd have enough combat strength to do that even if she hadn't lost a single soul."

"But if she threatens to—"

"Citizen Commissioner, if the situation was reversed—if you were in the Manties' position—would *you* let a threat like that stop you from doing your duty?"

Androcles held the people's commissioner's eye until Simpson's gaze fell. He shook his head.

"Of course, you wouldn't," she said quietly. "And neither will the Manties. I just pray People's Commissioner Barthet's wise enough to not go through with destroying any of their ships. At this point, they'll probably be willing to let her people surrender. But if she kills more of them when it's obvious she can't win…"

"And if we succeed in defeating the Manty Navy?" Simpson asked.

"In that case, the position *would* be reversed, wouldn't it?" she said and looked past him to her ops officer.

~

"STILL COMING, MA'AM," COMMANDER POWELL SAID, AND JOŽEFA Steigert nodded.

"The question, of course, is how long they'll *continue* coming." Her tone was almost whimsical.

"I'm not worried," Powell replied, and she chuckled. A bottle of thirty-year Glenfiddich rested on the outcome of her bet with the chief of staff.

"A man of confidence, I see. You hang onto that, Adrian. I'm going to enjoy drinking your whiskey."

She watched the display for another two minutes, lips pursed, then looked at Commander Politidis.

"Send the launch code," she said.

~

CITIZEN COMMODORE ANDROCLES SETTLED DEEPER INTO HER command chair as the time display on PNS *Splendor*'s flag deck ticked downward.

It hadn't been easy to sell Simpson on the path of simple tactical sanity, but she'd managed it. Probably because he wasn't really suicidal.

"Launch point in fifteen seconds, Citizen Commodore," her tac officer announced.

"Astrogation, start the hyper clock in five seconds," she.

"Aye, aye, Citizen Commodore." Her staff astrogator acknowledged. "Five, four, three, two, one, Mark."

"Coming up on launch point," the tac officer said.

"Engage as specified," she said levelly.

AS IT HAPPENED, SCOTTY TREMAINE'S ANALYSIS OF CITIZEN Commodore Androcles's tactical options had been spot on. He'd deduced exactly what she intended to do, and Admiral Steigert and Commander Politidis had made the same calculation, which wouldn't have surprised Androcles. The options were simple enough, just as it was painfully obvious that five battleships didn't want to engage three dreadnoughts.

The fact that she'd accelerated straight at them for over an hour, building a vector from which it would have been impossible to avoid close action in n-space, was another giveaway that she had no intention of *remaining* in n-space. But it didn't really matter that they'd figured it out.

Except for one tiny detail of which she'd been unaware.

The first broadside erupted from her ships, streaming straight for the Manties. She'd have time for eight more launches, but even if the Manties launched right this instant, their birds would still be over a million kilometers short of *Splendor* when she and her consorts banished into hyper.

"Missile launch!" Tactical barked, and Androcles nodded to herself. Of course, they were launching. It was only to be—

"Missile launch at three-point-niner thousand klicks!"

Androcles jerked upright in her command chair. That had to be wrong!

"Confirm range!" she barked.

"Confirmed, Citizen Commodore," the tac officer replied. Then swallowed hard. "Second launch detected! Time-of-flight one-zero-two seconds!"

Androcles felt the blood drain out of her face.

"*Third* launch!"

"*What is it?*" People's Commissioner Simpson demanded. "What's happening, Citizen Commodore?!"

"The Manties have mousetrapped us," she said, almost absently, never looking away from the plot. Her own broadsides ripped out at twenty-second intervals, but the Manticoran salvos were launching every *ten* seconds.

"Mousetrapped?" Simpson repeated.

"Yes. I wondered why they didn't come out to meet us. I even considered that they might have more of those damned missile pods than they had tractors, so they couldn't tow them along. But"—she smiled with no humor at all—"it didn't occur to me that they might have already deployed them a half light-minute between them and the hyper-limit. Right where someone like us would sail straight into them."

"My God," Simpson whispered, his own face white as he stared at serried waves of crimson icons streaking across the plot. *"Do something, Citizen Commodore!"*

"There's nothing we *can* do," she said calmly as a fourth massive launch blossomed.

And this is how professionals *do it,* a corner of her mind thought as the uncaring computers updated the display.

There were a hundred and forty missiles in each of those waves. According to NavInt, the Manties' new pods had ten box launchers each. So that was fourteen pods per salvo. But if they'd had that many pods deployed, they could have fired even bigger broadsides. So why—?

Control links, she thought. *Thirty-three tubes in a* Bellerophon*'s broadside. And—what? Eight, in a* Prince Consort*'s. So, assume a twenty percent fire control redundancy and that would be about right. And ten-second intervals.*

Ten seconds. Just long enough for them to cut the control links to each salvo and update the targeting for the *next* one before it hit.

Four salvos, five targets. That's—what? Hundred and twelve per battleship? I wonder how they allocated them?

Thirty-three seconds later, she found out.

～

JULY 5, 1907 PD,
   HMS *Prince Adrian*,
   Manticore Binary System.

"WELL, FANCY MEETING YOU HERE, LIEUTENANT. I MEAN, LIEUTENANT *Commander*," Clint Hendren said as he stepped into the lift car. He checked the destination on the control panel, nodded, and stood back with his hands clasped behind him.

"Yes," Lieutenant Commander Brandy Bolgeo said brightly. "I am your superior officer now, aren't I?"

"No, you're *senior* to me," he replied. "I, after all, am a Marine… Ma'am."

Brandy laughed.

They'd come a long way from that first unpleasant encounter, she thought. A long way. And too many of his Marines hadn't completed the journey with them. But they'd done their jobs. By *God*, they'd done their jobs.

The laughter faded from her eyes as she thought about all the people they'd lost. Nineteen of *Prince Adrian*'s Marines had died, and three more had been wounded, two almost as seriously as Horace Harkness. That was a 16 percent casualty rate, but they'd have lost a hell of a lot more without Clint and Gunny Babcock.

"Actually," he said, leaning closer to her ear with a confidential tone, "a little birdie from BuPers just whispered in my ear, too."

"Oh? Really?" She looked at him.

"Yep. They're moving me when *Adrian* finally goes into the yard, of course."

"Of course."

She grimaced.

Rear Admiral Steigert's task group had arrived home two T-weeks ago, and they should all have been in yard hands by now, in Brandy's opinion. HMS *Memnon* and *Cyncnus* had both taken damage in what had been dubbed the Battle of Swanson, although their casualties had been thankfully light… unlike the Peeps. None of their battleships had lived to make it into hyper, and their personnel losses had been massive. Citizen Commodore Androcles had been among them, and Brandy had found herself wondering what the Peeps' final thoughts had been when she realized what she'd sailed straight into.

But the dreadnoughts' damages had required surveys, and that had backed up everything behind them, and somehow, *Prince Adrian* had lost her slot in the queue in the process. But BuShips had rescheduled her, in the end, and Captain McKeon would hand her over to the yard dogs—finally—in ten days. Brandy was glad. The ship needed it—she *deserved* it—and it was damned well time she got it. Yet even that had a downside. Given the current operational tempo, the one thing Alistair McKeon could completely count upon was that his tightknit, experienced ship's company was about to be mercilessly raided and broken up for other assignments.

Brandy herself already had orders to a brand-new *Star Knight*-class heavy cruiser. HMS *Conjurer* wouldn't commission for another five T-months, though, which would at least give her time to tuck *Prince Adrian* away in HMS *Hephaestus*'s capable hands and hand it off to her replacement.

And at least they'd gotten those three extra T-weeks first, she thought.

"And where are they moving you *to*?" she asked.

"Camp Edward," Clint said.

"Training duties?" Brandy stared at him, knowing how much he'd hate an assignment like that.

"Sort of." He smiled broadly. "Actually, I'll be standing up a new battalion. And the next time you see me, that 'major' won't be a courtesy promotion anymore."

"That's wonderful, Clint!" She reached out and squeezed his upper arm. "And you damned well deserve it!"

"We tried, anyway," he said softly, and she squeezed his arm again, then released it as the lift car came to a halt.

The doors slid open, and they walked down the short passage toward *Prince Adrian*'s sick bay.

"And I'm telling you, Doc," an exasperated voice said, "I've got better things to do than lie around here. And I sure don't need a transfer to Beresford!"

"Senior Chief—" Surgeon Lieutenant Ansari began.

"Will you please shut the hell up?" another voice demanded. "I swear to God. Even for a Navy puke! Do the words 'vaporized lung' mean *anything* to you? What the hell do you use for *brains*, Harkness?"

"Oh, that's rich, coming from a *Marine*." The first voice was a bit less forceful than its norm, but it rose gamely to the challenge. "On the other hand, guess it's not too surprising you don't know what *anybody* uses for brains. Not that many of them going around in Marine Country!"

"At least our senior NCOs don't have *negative* IQs. How the hell d'you find your way around that boat bay every day without cutting off your *other* arm?"

Brandy stifled a chuckle, her eyes laughing up at Clint as they entered the ward. Surgeon Lieutenant Evelyn Ansari stood to one side, arms folded and wearing a resigned expression. Horace Harkness—unshaven, one arm missing, his battered prizefighter's face still more than a little gaunt, but very much a going concern—was sitting up in one of the sick bay beds while Sergeant Major Babcock stood at that bed's foot, hands on hips, glaring at him.

"Unlike *some* people, *I* know how to do my job," he retorted.

"Oh, yeah? Then how come you're the one in the body shop?" Babcock demanded, but her voice had softened, and there was an odd light in the gray eyes which had smitten generations of Marines with terror.

"Oh, I dunno." Harkness's voice was softer, too, and the corners of his mouth twitched. "Just seemed like the thing to do. Probably because I've been hanging around with too many Marines. It's the sort of thing a jarhead would do, now that I think about it."

Brandy shook her head. For some reason, Iris Babcock had been spending a lot of time in sick bay on the trip back to Manticore. She'd checked in conscientiously on her three wounded Marines each time she visited, but somehow, inexplicably, she always ended up *here*, giving Harkness grief.

Harkness turned his head as they entered the ward.

"Oh. Good to see you, Ma'am—Major."

Babcock turned and came to attention.

"Sir. Ma'am," she said.

"Gunny," Clint answered for both of them, then looked at Harkness. "My God," he said. "If I'd realized what a useless, idle layabout you were that first day, I'd've really given you grief, Harkness!"

"Don't know if you want to admit that kinda prejudice with the lieutenant standing right there, and all, Sir." Harkness grinned, reached out with his remaining hand, and Clint shook it firmly.

"No lieutenants here, Senior Chief." He nodded at Brandy. "Just found out on the way down, somebody's a lieutenant *commander*."

"Outstanding!" Harkness held out his hand again and Brandy gripped it firmly.

"To what do I owe the pleasure?" the senior chief continued, looking between the visitors.

"Just thought I'd tell you that in addition to your wound stripe, you'll probably be picking up a Navy Star," Brandy said. "*I* told them you lacked the sterling character for that sort of recognition, but the major, here, and the gunny sort of insisted. So—"

She shrugged, and Harkness's eyes widened ever so briefly. Then they narrowed and darted to Babcock.

"You already know about this?" he demanded suspiciously.

"Who? Me? Recommend an award for somebody so stupid he couldn't even get out of the way of a batch of pulser darts?" Babcock shook her head, her eyes bright. "Must have me confused with somebody else, spacer."

"Yeah, sure I do." His voice softened and he smiled at Babcock.

"Well, anyway, just wanted to let you know," Brandy said. "And to mention that by the time you get done regenerating and finish PT, *Conjurer* will be in service. *Competent* boat bay chiefs seem scarce just now, but I suppose I could make do with you, instead. Somehow."

"I think I'd like that, Ma'am. Unless"—he looked at Babcock again —"something else comes up in the meantime."

"Just keep it in mind, Senior Chief." Brandy patted his good shoulder and looked at Clint. "Guess I'm about done here. How about you, Major?"

"Actually, I was just looking for the gunny," Clint replied.

"Yes, Sir?"

"When you're through here, Gunny, we've got some equipment inventories to beat into submission." He rolled his eyes. "I can hardly wait for BuSup to start going over the paperwork."

"Oh, wonderful... Sir." Babcock rolled her eyes. "I'll be along in... fifteen minutes sound about right, Sir?"

"That'll be fine, Gunny."

Clint nodded and waved for Brandy to precede him back toward the lift shafts. She gave Harkness another nod, then smiled at Babcock and led the way out of the ward.

"Couldn't get out of the way, huh?" they heard Harkness behind them. "Listen, at least I don't fall over my own two feet the way *some* people do. Not naming any names, but—"

The closing hatch cut off his voice, and Clint shook his head.

"I don't think the galaxy is ready for this," he said.

"Ready for what?" Brandy asked innocently.

"Babcock and Harkness." He shook his head again. "You know, Gunnery Sergeant Water and Senior Chief Oil? I mean, *listen* to them! There's not a single Marine anywhere in the Star Kingdom who'd believe what you and I just heard. Not *one*! Well, not outside *Prince Adrian*, anyway."

"You can't possibly be suggesting that there's anything going on between the two of them," Brandy said severely. "That would be a betrayal of... of *generations* of spacers and jarheads! The heart attacks would come fast and quick in the chiefs' messes. And I hate to think how your weaker, frailer Marines would handle such a seismic shock!"

"You're right. You're *right*!" Clint pursed his lips. "I don't know what I was thinking. Obviously, all nonsense. Besides, it'd never work. A Marine and a Navy puke? A travesty of nature!"

"Absolutely." Brandy nodded firmly as they stepped into the lift car. The door closed and she tucked one hand lightly into his elbow. "Unthinkable. A perversion of all that's right and good."

"Precisely what I was thinking."

He looked down at her and she smiled.

"Well, now that we've got that settled, Major… buy a girl a cup of coffee?"

ABOUT DAVID WEBER

David Weber was born in Cleveland a long, long time ago (1952 to be exact), and grew up in rural South Carolina. He was a bookworm from childhood, blessed with a father who collected autographed copies of every E. E. Smith hardcover and introduced him to Jack Williamson at the tender age of ten and a mother who ran her own ad agency and encouraged him to write. From that start, with a love of history from a very early age and as a practitioner of RPGs before the world had ever heard of something called *Dungeons & Dragons*, it was inevitable he would fall into evil company and become a writer of science fiction himself.

He sold his first novel to Jim Baen, his enabler at Baen Books, in 1989 (*Insurrection* with Steve White). Since that time, he has perpetrated over 80 solo and collaborative novels and an unconscionable number of anthologies upon an innocent and unsuspecting public. He is perhaps best known for his character Honor Harrington, whom he hopes never to meet in a dark alley, given all the bones she has to pick with him.

David currently lives in Greenville, SC with his wife Sharon, numerous cats, and a dog that used to think it was a goat. David's twin daughters are attending college and David's son is serving his country in the United States Marine Corps.

ABOUT THE EDITORS

CHRISTOPHER WOODS

Christopher Woods, writer of fiction, teller of tales, and professional liar was born way too long ago to be talking about and has spent most of his life with a book in hand. He is known for his popular Soulguard series and creating the Fallen World shared universe. He has also written several short stories and the Legend books in the Four Horsemen Universe as well as some works in the Salvage Title Universe. With books ranging from fantasy to post-apocalyptic science fiction and military science fiction. There should be something for everyone. He lives in Woodbury, TN with his wife, Wendy. As a former carpenter of 25 years, he spends his time between various building projects and writing new books. To contact him go to theprofessionalliar.com

T.K.F. WEISSKOPF

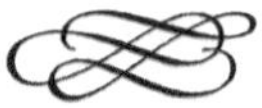

Toni Weisskopf, co-editor of this volume, succeeded Jim Baen as publisher of Baen Books, in 2006. She has worked with such nationally bestselling authors as David Weber, David Drake, Lois McMaster Bujold, Eric Flint, Wen Spencer, John Ringo, Mercedes Lackey, Larry Correia, Sharon Lee & Steve Miller, Charles E. Gannon, and many others. Baen is known for its innovative e-publishing program, which has expanded under Weisskopf's leadership to include titles from other publishers.

Weisskopf is a graduate of Oberlin College with a degree in anthropology. She is interested in space science and is on the Board of Advisors of the Interstellar Research Group. Weisskopf has been a guest speaker at many writers' workshops and science fiction conventions across the country, and is well known for her interactive, audience-participation discussion of Baen's books, covers, and artwork, ongoing and ever-changing since 1991. She considers LibertyCon her "hometown" convention.

www.ingramcontent.com/pod-product-compliance
Lightning Source LLC
Chambersburg PA
CBHW030703190726
48286CB00001B/138